SURVIVORS

Book 4 of "Circles of Light"

For Shirley Ryan

And for John and Ben,
with love always

SURVIVORS

Book 4 of "Circles of Light"

E M Sinclair

Survivors – Book 4 of *Circles of Light*
First published 2007

Typeset by John Owen Smith

Published by Murrell Press

ISBN 978-09554135-3-7

Printed by CreateSpace

Chapter One

The three Desert men were polite, generous with their supplies, but reticent about the exact location of the City they spoke of with such reverence. Wary of the fact that the three plainly used mind speech, Tika and Gan wandered away from the fire to the sea's edge.

'Unless we try to make our way back to Mist, I do not see we have any alternative to going with them,' said Gan.

'Their koninas look well fed, especially compared to our poor beasts, but will there be fresh meat for the Dragons? I don't think we have a choice Gan. Khosa seems to know more about these men than I can account for. Perhaps she knows more about everything.' Tika frowned. 'I wish someone would explain – just once in a while – exactly what we're supposed to be doing.'

Gan chuckled. 'Being Captain of the Lady Emla's Guards was a bit like this,' he admitted.

They turned back towards the fire, the twilight closing around them.

'We'll hear soon enough if anyone strongly disagrees about our travelling to this City. I don't look forward to all that sand though.' Tika sat between Ren and Maressa. 'Well, do we leave tomorrow then Kirat? And can you promise me there will be meat for our friends?'

Farn's head snaked over Tika's shoulder, sapphire eyes whirring with enthusiasm. She curled her arm round his neck, giving him a brief hug. She hid a smile when she saw Storm copying Farn's action on a rather startled Navan. To Navan's credit, he cautiously rubbed Storm's neck in return.

The apparent spokesman of the three Desert men, nodded vigorously. 'Our people keep goats, which we freely offer to feed the Dragon folk. We would ask that they accept our gifts. If they hunted for themselves among our small flocks, much panic would ensue and the goats would scatter and be lost.'

The massive purple Seela replied graciously. 'That would be perfectly suitable. Thank you Kirat.' Her eyes dared the two young Dragons to argue the point.

'You said it will take eight days to reach your City,' Olam queried. 'It must surely be a longer journey from the plains of Sapphrea into your Desert?'

It was Hadjay who replied. 'Indeed, Sir Olam. Maybe three times as long that way.' He gave a satisfied grin. 'The grasslander people have no idea how to find water in our land and there is plenty of water – if you know how to seek it.'

Olam's face revealed a certain scepticism. 'I've heard tales of nomads following strayed animals, or pursuing the giant hunting Kephis when they've stolen too many from the flocks. But those who venture in among the Biting Sands never return.'

His words were met with laughter, white teeth gleaming in Hadjay's dark face. 'We keep watch all around our land, Sir Olam. And generally we kill intruders.'

The company digested that remark in silence.

'Then why do you appear to welcome us?' It was Maressa who asked the obvious question.

'We have been told who you are. The Survivors ask us to guide you to them.'

All three Desert men bowed their heads. 'It is our great honour.'

'We leave before sunrise,' Kirat announced, and unrolled the blanket he'd been sitting on. 'It takes eight days to the Valley, but they are eight long, hard days.'

Ren lay back on his blankets, staring up at the millions of stars flung across the sky. He heard Gan murmur quietly to Olam, and then Pallin and Riff talking about the strangers' koninas.

'Same as our beasts but much finer.' Pallin was saying. 'Bred for that lightness of bone, looks like. And probably for the white colour. Like to talk to someone who has the breeding of them if we get to this dratted City.'

Ren fell asleep before he heard Riff's reply and knew nothing more until someone shook him in the dark before dawn.

They drank tea standing ready to mount and ride. Sirak handed out cloths to put over their heads, as all three Desert men already wore. Tika was surprised that Khosa had made no comment since they'd encountered these men and now climbed into her carry sack without demur.

Personally, since the Silver One had spoken to her, Tika had felt a calm acceptance. Gremara had told her she must trust. Tika argued that trusting people was a risky thing in her experience. Gremara asked if her companions had so far betrayed her and Tika fell silent. Although the Silver One had spoken to each companion separately, no discussion or revelation of what they'd been told had occurred.

A few days after leaving Mist's Flight of Sea Dragons, Tika found she could accept whatever lay ahead. Seeing her beloved soul bond's increasing confidence, his delight in his wild games with Storm, she decided whatever did lie ahead was worth these days of careless joy for Farn.

Kirat set a steady pace, trotting the koninas where the ground allowed. He had given Pallin grain for the companions' mounts, welcome after many days of short rations. They made a good distance before the sun came up and then discovered the Desert was much hotter than had been the lands they'd traversed from Far to the coast. Ren tried to explain that they were a lot further south, which would mean an increase in heat, but abandoned his attempt to educate them in basic natural science. Only Maressa understood his words and she was too hot to try to simplify Ren's explanation.

They rode until mid morning, seeing little except the rise and fall of endless dunes, but when Kirat called a halt, they saw a faint smudge of rising hills ahead. The Desert men raised awnings and nodded approval when they saw Pallin and Riff doing the same.

'We brought extra cloth in case you had nothing to protect yourselves through the heat of the day. We will stay here until the sun is well on its way down.'

The Dragons were not bothered by the heat, not even Storm so far. Tika had been worried that, used as he was to the proximity of the sea and diving into it as he did, he would find this waterless place hard to cope with. Sprawled gratefully in the small shade of the awnings, they watched in some bewilderment while Sirak prowled slowly in front of them, at intervals pushing a long pole into the sand. Eventually, he went to his knees, dragging scoops of sand from around the upright pole. Kirat joined him and Ren ventured out into the fierce heat to watch them. He peered down into the rapidly deepening excavation, then straightened. He rejoined the others in the shade.

'Water,' he said succinctly.

'Water? Never!' Olam went to investigate as well and returned grinning. 'Stars be blessed! How did he know where to dig? There's quite a little pool there.'

'I'd guess he felt a difference when the pole hit firmer sand.' Ren rested his chin on his drawn up knees. 'Fascinating though.'

The four Dragons watched with interest as the first leather bucket of water was dragged from the sand. Storm crept closer, and closer, Tika watching with amusement to see how Sirak would react when he discovered the young Sea Dragon craning over him. She laughed aloud when Sirak turned and came nose to nose with Storm. Storm's eyes whirred a slate grey colour and he ducked his head in embarrassed apology. But Sirak smiled and bowed his own head, plainly mind speaking the young Dragon.

They travelled on when the worst of the heat had lessened, until a considerable time after nightfall. Kirat clearly used stars for guidance and led them unerringly and with no hesitation. Hadjay vanished when they halted next midday, reappearing with six large odd looking lizards dangling from his hand. He grinned.

'Sand swimmers. Good eating.'

He offered the Dragons one each and, after some cautious sniffing, they accepted the strange meat with enjoyment.

The third day was blisteringly hot. The air shimmered and wavered whichever direction they looked. The hills, which they'd thought were nearing, now seemed to change position – one moment ahead of them, the next nearly behind.

'It is normal here,' Hadjay assured them. He pointed ahead. 'Squeeze your eyes near shut and you see the real hills.'

The fourth day found Storm tiring. Farn warned Tika but Seela had already noticed and kept him beneath her outspread wing when they stopped in the heat of the day. Her shelter revived him and so the company moved on. Pallin pointed out to Navan and Riff that they'd die if the Desert men left them now.

'I couldn't find water like they do, and probably no trail.'

They turned in their saddles and could not be sure which dune they had just descended. Navan shrugged.

'Best follow them then and hope they like our company.'

Maressa flew with Brin, finding the breeze helped a little against the heat which she suffered worst of them all. Farn insisted he carry Tika at least part of each day, then allowing her to fly with Seela while he played with Storm. In her carry sack Khosa remained silent. Tika presumed the Kephi slept most of each day. The nights were surprisingly cold and Khosa disappeared for most of the time the travellers slept.

The fifth day, they began to climb switchback hills each a little higher than the last and where rock showed in places through the sand. Ahead, they saw only more brown peaks rising from the sea of sand. When Kirat called a halt that night, the Dragons were excited, rattling their wings and occasionally calling aloud to each other. Tika smiled at Kirat across the small fire he made each night.

'We saw lights several leagues on – is that your City?'

Kirat shook his head. 'We have small communities ringing the City, but they are of only a few farming families.'

'Farming?' Pallin asked in disbelief. 'We've seen only the poorest grasses, and those rubbery things.'

'Cacti,' Sirak helpfully supplied the name.

'Yes those.' Pallin scowled. 'You don't mean you farm those?'

The Desert men laughed. 'You have been grateful for the water the cacti can supply, Pallin. But no, we farm the same sort of crops as you I daresay. We have no large cattle but we have goats, and fowls provide eggs.'

Next day their trail rose sharply, now mountainous rather than hilly, over brown and grey rock covered with a thin dusty soil. From the greater vantage of Farn's back, Tika saw a sudden splash of green ahead of them and guessed they would reach this area by nightfall. But instead of halting as usual when the heat intensified, Kirat urged them on, over a last short narrow pass and then down towards a greenness further below than they might have imagined.

Descending a winding track, the mountains rose above them in sharp peaks and jagged outlines. The Dragons stayed high overhead: Tika was unsure of their reception by the Qwah people despite Kirat's assurances of welcome. The riders with Kirat noticed the trail was becoming better defined the lower they went. Also, to their considerable relief, at last they were riding in some shade where the sun was blocked by the high ridges. The path twisted between wind-scoured towers of rock and they had their first sight of a bowl-like depression, perhaps two leagues across, planted with a variety of crops.

To their left as they wound down to the flat were clustered several buildings. On closer inspection, they realised that the seven buildings were in fact linked to each other by walls rising to roof level of the two-storied buildings leaving an open courtyard inside. They saw people moving in there, but then the koninas snorted and tossed their heads, scenting water.

Round the final curve of the path and they saw water gushing from beneath overhanging rocks which were festooned with feathery green plants. Kirat turned in his saddle and smiled. He gestured at the water, out at the cultivated land, and at the group of men, women and children coming towards them.

'Welcome to the lands of the Qwah.'

Tika's company were greeted with apparently warm enthusiasm and the Dragons accepted with an astonishing equanimity. Several children darted forward as the Dragons reclined and they showed no fear of the two enormous adults, hands outstretched to touch and stroke. They chattered in the liquid trilling language Kirat had first used, but Seela informed Tika at once that these children mind spoke too. All of them.

The hot dirty travellers were urged into one of the buildings and offered pottery mugs of a cold fruity drink which soothed parched lips and dry throats wonderfully. The men were taken in one direction by Kirat and his brothers and two elderly women invited Maressa and Tika, with beckoning hands, to an adjoining windowless room which they discovered, to their delight, to be a bathing room.

'I could stay here forever,' Maressa announced sinking blissfully into the warm water. She groaned with pleasure when one of the Qwah women began massaging her body with strong hands.

They found themselves scrubbed and rinsed and were then

pulled from the water to be pummelled and towelled before being covered in a light fragrant oil which the Qwah women kneaded into their skins. In the short time they'd been bathing, Maressa and Tika discovered their clothes had been brushed and shaken free of sand. Dressed again, they were led into another room which had windows and doors opening into the central courtyard. The open space was sharply divided between blackest shade and blazing sunlight.

The men were sitting on brightly patterned carpets in the shaded area, dishes and platters heaped with colourful foods before them. Ren smiled at the two girls.

'What a relief to be clean again.'

'And cool for a few minutes,' Maressa agreed with feeling.

Qwah men and women joined the company, kneeling on the overlapping rugs while children hovered on the edges. Tika started to rise in sudden consternation: Farn and Storm swooped over the roofs to land within the courtyard. Farn hurried towards her, Storm at his heels. Before Tika could apologise or explain, an elderly Qwah raised his hand. He spoke haltingly in the common tongue.

'Do not reprimand the young one, Lady. We understand his need to be with you. Please, continue your meal.'

Tika stared at the man then subsided onto the carpet again. Farn reclined behind her, his long beautiful face resting on her head. Just what did these people know? A very great deal it would seem, Tika thought, her eyes unexpectedly meeting Khosa's blue stare.

'They brought some goats for us,' Farn told Tika confidentially then his eyes whirred faster as the Qwah people chuckled.

Storm crept closer to lean against Navan. The food was plentiful: vegetables, goat and fowl meat, cheese and several fruits unknown to the company. Tika ate, letting talk wash over her. Both Gan and Ren asked many questions about the ways of this small community and were answered, apparently freely by both men and women. Women were clearly regarded as equals here, Tika noted, quite unlike the customs of Sapphrea.

Kirat got to his feet. 'We can stay no longer,' he said. 'We have many leagues to go before we can rest tonight.'

Gan rose to his great height and saluted the Qwah elders, right hand to his left shoulder. 'We thank you for your hospitality. Should you ever travel to Gaharn be assured your kindness will not be forgotten.'

The oldest man of the community laughed. 'Unlikely that is, tall one, but your mannerly words are appreciated.'

The sky was a deepening blue in contrast to the searing bone white of midday as the company followed Kirat along the edge of neat fields. He took them to the further end of the cultivated land and then the trail rose again, winding back and forth until they reached a narrow pass. Olam glanced back and smiled to himself, seeing the green land was completely hidden once again.

'Never find that place in a million cycles,' Pallin grunted, riding up beside Olam when the trail widened.

'Indeed not,' Olam agreed. 'Very clever.'

They travelled until Gan estimated a third of the night had passed, the four Dragons staying close just above the konina riders. What had seemed like yet more tilted slabs of rock, dully grey in the starlight, resolved into a long low shelter where Kirat called a halt. All the companions were tired, choosing to wrap themselves in their blankets and sleep with no thought of food.

Tika released Khosa from her carry sack and pulled a blanket round her shoulders. She yawned hugely and turned towards Farn. By the time she had settled herself against his shoulder, Khosa was back, pressing close under Tika's chin.

'This is wrong.'

The Kephi's mind voice was soft as her fur. Tika was instantly alert, realising Khosa was keeping her communication tightly controlled so that she alone would hear her.

'These are not the ones we should have met.'

'It's a bit late to tell me that now,' Tika's mind whispered back. 'What must we do? Are these men and their City dangerous for us?'

Khosa was silent for a while. 'They are taking us to a Survivor, but not the one we should be meeting.'

'I don't understand – how many Survivors are there for stars' sake? And are they enemies to each other then?'

Again there was a pause before Khosa replied. 'Enemies, no, but they have very different ideas as to how they may achieve their aims, and their aims are not quite the same either.'

'And how many Survivors did you say there are?' Tika prompted.

Khosa's eyes glittered in the starlight. 'I didn't. But there are three in this City. I will warn the others that they must beware. All of these Qwah people seem able to mind speak – your thoughts must be guarded. And I will tell Grek to remain silent from now on.' The orange Kephi arched her back and whisked her tail across Tika's face before leaping lightly down and padding towards the building.

'I heard,' Farn murmured.

To Tika's relief he sounded perfectly calm. Since their brief meeting with Gremara, Farn had been noticeably steadier in his mind.

'I will let nothing harm you Tika. Now we should sleep to be ready for whatever tomorrow might bring.'

Tika grinned in the darkness, rubbing her head against Farn's scaled shoulder. 'As you command, dear one.'

Farn rattled his wings but said no more.

Again they rose in the dark and Kirat spoke to them while they sipped the hot tea Hadjay had prepared.

'We will not stop on the trail today,' he warned. 'I hope we make good speed early, but we will continue until we reach the Valley of the City. Then you will be able to rest and recover.'

Tika caught Navan's eye and he nodded slightly: so Khosa must have warned them all during their brief rest.

The Dragons flew higher at first, wary of using mind speech close to the Desert men below.

'I suspected something was amiss before we reached that green place,' Seela told her riders Gan and Sket while Maressa agreed from Brin's back. Khosa poked her head from her carry sack and stared down at the koninas far below.

'All I can tell you is to be very cautious when we reach the City, but you must be firm, Tika.' The Kephi twisted to look up into the girl's face. 'You must insist we travel on and will not be delayed in this City.'

'But where do I say we travel to?'

'Say that you are summoned by Namolos.' Khosa's words breathed through Tika's mind and then she wriggled back into her sack.

Light began to gleam along the skyline ahead of them and still the land rose in range after range of bare, grey-brown rock. By the time the sun was nearing its zenith, Storm flew close under Brin and Farn under Seela, the great adult Dragons offering what shade they could to the young ones. Ahead, the mountains seemed blurred, and slowly Tika realised clouds of dust swirled from the desert floor, grains of sand twisting at unbelievable heights.

'We cannot fly through that.' Seela's mind tone betrayed not only her nervousness of the great dust storm in front of them, but a growing concern for Farn and Storm, both of whom were clearly struggling against their exhaustion.

Then Ren's voice rang clearly in their heads. 'Come lower now – Kirat says we are near his lands but we change direction among the canyons ahead.'

Seela accordingly lost height leading them down until they were only a couple of man lengths above the konina riders. The Dragons and their riders found their view almost completely curtailed flying between sheer rock faces barely wide enough for their beating wings. Kirat led them in a sharp change of direction and they were at last afforded respite from the sun which blazed from the white sky. They wound through great cracks in the towering mountains until Tika was on the point of calling to Kirat for a halt, regardless of his earlier command.

Even as she opened her mouth to shout, the two sides of the canyon widened and fell away. Kirat himself raised his hand in a signal to halt. Farn and Storm both stumbled as they landed, their wings still half extended, their long necks drooping to the ground. Navan and Olam came running with water skins even as Tika slid from Farn's back. Gan hurried from Seela to lift Maressa from where she slumped across Brin's shoulder. There was a flurry of activity, Ren working with Tika to send healing strength to the young Dragons and Gan easing Maressa to the dusty ground.

It did not take overlong to revive Maressa although her face and hands were scarlet from wind and sun burn. Tika slathered one of Lorak's salves thickly over the sore skin. Handfuls of fruit and hunks of bread were shared, Kirat allowing they could delay briefly. Gradually the company wandered to the widening end of the canyon and all found themselves staring in amazed disbelief.

A great valley spread into the distance leagues below where they stood. The arid rock they'd become so accustomed to vanished beneath increasing greenery. Tiny clusters of buildings scattered along the walls and floors of the valley drew their eyes on. Thin silver threads indicated water courses which fed into a large oval lake shimmering like mercury. Distant as it was, the size of the City beyond the lake astonished Tika's company. The multitude of buildings were dominated by three domed structures: large even from this far away, how huge they must be up close!

Unmistakeable pride rang in Kirat's voice as he gestured at the valley encircled and guarded by towering peaks. 'The City of the Dome awaits you.'

Chapter Two

They reached the valley floor in late afternoon. They had met children tending goats on the upper slopes and all the members of the company noticed the same fearless acceptance of their appearance that they'd received in their first encounter with a Qwah community. The company rested that night among a small cluster of buildings which Kirat told them was the village of Shamsi. They were again offered baths and Maressa's burnt face and hands were soothed with a paste of leaves and herbs which, she reported, took all the stinging pain from her skin.

Khosa remained hidden; Tika had no idea where the Kephi might be as the company settled to sleep after their meal. Kirat had told them they would rest the next night in another village, Dumlay, and would reach the City the following midday. After the scorching heat of the last eight days the gentler temperature within the enclosed Valley was a mercy and they all revived enough to notice their surroundings more closely.

Irrigation channels crisscrossed the fields around them and they saw many small brightly coloured birds flashing through fruit bushes and orchards of low trees. Insects droned and whined, goats bleated as they were moved from pasture to pasture and tall white birds stood motionless in some of the water channels. Towards evening Pallin held back his konina, his attention caught by a fenced area which held a dozen or more of the lighter Desert koninas.

Hadjay turned in his saddle to see what delayed the Sapphreans and laughed. He pointed ahead to a collection of buildings.

'There will still be light enough for you to come and look at the horses when you've eaten.'

'Horses?' Ren asked casually.

'That is the Qwah name for them,' Hadjay nodded.

Now why would the Desert people, hidden even from the other

people of this same land, call these animals by the same name as Drogoyans used, Ren wondered. He wrestled with the thought briefly then set it aside, as with so many other things of late, to consider at another time. Pallin and Riff went off with Kirat and several villagers to inspect the horses while the rest of the company gathered close to the Dragons who reclined, digesting another offering of goat.

Gazing along the Valley in the gathering darkness, the City glittered with lights, the three domes hulking dark against the illumination.

'They will tell me nothing of the domes,' Ren remarked lightly.

'Perhaps they are the places where their councils meet,' Gan suggested, smothering a yawn.

Conversation had become strained since Khosa's warning.

'We'll soon find out what they want with us,' Sket muttered. He and Navan were checking their weapons as they did every evening. He glanced at Storm who watched Navan's actions with close interest.

Seela picked up his thought. 'Brin and I will guard the young ones well, have no fear of that.'

Farn's eyes whirred sapphire indignation but Tika reached to touch his face before he could voice a protest and he settled back. Pallin and Riff returned, talking excitedly of what they'd learned of Qwah horse breeding and training, and the others wrapped themselves in their blankets to sleep.

'We stay together once we're in their City,' Tika said into the darkness. 'No matter what, we must stay together.'

The Dragons, carrying Gan, Sket, Maressa and Tika, flew much higher the next morning, relying on Ren to tell them if and where they should land within the City. The Dragon riders were astonished by the size of the place: from their height they could see how it was laid out in a series of circles around a great open space in the middle of which stood the three massive domes.

All three domes shone white in the glare of midday, but their tops were capped in a milky substance that did not reflect the light as did the lower white walls. The Dragons spiralled lazily above, tracking their companions as they rode through broad streets, entering ring after ring until they reached the centre.

'Kirat says the Dragons should land here.' Ren sent the thought skywards and the great purple Seela led the other Dragons slowly lower.

Farn landed next to Seela, followed closely by Storm and Brin. They stood halfway between the linked domes and the circling wall. Tika stared from Farn's back first at the dazzling blank domes rising behind her, then to her friends just entering the area through an archway. All around the outer circle, great columns rose at regular intervals, supporting a tiled roof.

Set back in the shadows beneath she saw windows and doorways. Three Qwah men came from one such door to lead away the koninas. They were barefooted and wore lengths of bright cloth twisted at the hip, and only sleeveless jerkins covered their upper bodies.

Kirat smiled, watching Tika slide slowly from Farn's back and walk to Maressa's side with Sket close at her shoulder. 'If you would follow, I will introduce you to one of the Keepers of the Sanctuary.' He waved his hand taking in the domes and the great space they stood in. 'This is the Sanctuary. You will be allocated rooms over here.'

He began to lead them towards the colonnade. They followed, Farn pacing steadily at Tika's heels. When they reached the covered walk, Kirat paused and bowed to a woman emerging from one of the doors. She returned his bow and smiled.

'I am the Keeper on duty,' she said in heavily accented Common Tongue. 'I will take you to your accommodation. It is not far.'

She began to turn away.

'We will accept rooms opening into this court,' Tika said politely. 'If that is not possible, it is of no matter – we will simply remain with our friends.'

Seela's great head lowered to peer beneath the roof, her eyes sparkling lilac. The woman studied the great Dragon for a moment, inclined her head and moved away from the door she had first indicated.

'As you will.' Her tone was cool. 'I assure you that you will come to no harm in the Sanctuary.'

'We did not for one moment think we would, but we prefer to be close by our friends,' Tika replied equally coolly.

The Keeper shot a quick glance over her shoulder and met Tika's eyes, green ice set in silver. She led them past several doors before opening one. She pointed to the next one a few paces further along. 'The rooms within link between these two doors,' she explained. Her lip curled. 'These two doors and the windows both here and above are the only access to the rooms. I will send gijan to you to see to your comfort.' She turned on her heel, her pale green robe swirling round her ankles and walked rapidly away.

Kirat had a frown on his face. 'I fear you may have offended the Keeper, Lady,' he began.

Tika smiled at the Desert man. 'Your Keeper would deeply offend us had she tried to insist we part from the Dragons.'

Kirat opened his mouth to reply but Brin's crimson face ducked under the roof. His mind voice was extremely gentle.

'Have you ever seen an offended Dragon?' he enquired.

Kirat blanched. He drew a breath and bowed. 'I will leave you to rest and eat,' he murmured, keeping his gaze firmly on the stone floor.

As he turned away Maressa asked if he would return.

He bowed again. 'I have other duties, Lady.' He risked a quick glance around all the company. 'It has been my honour to guide you here. If the Survivors desire me to lead you further, I will return.'

'Thank you then Kirat. We will surely see you again for you will be guiding us to our proper destination.'

Maressa bent to retrieve her pack from the floor while Kirat continued to stare at her in some confusion. Straightening, she raised a questioning brow but he merely gave a hasty bow and practically fled in the direction the horses had been taken.

Gan stooped to enter the door in front of them and Riff quickly followed. When Maressa would also have followed, Sket caught her arm, shaking his head.

'Let them check first, Lady.'

The door along the colonnade opened and Riff stepped out, nodded and retreated again.

'Come then.' Olam led the company into their rooms.

There were four quite large rooms on the ground floor – two sitting rooms to the front with a bathing room and kitchen behind, neither of which had windows. A flight of stone stairs led from the front up to the upper floor where they gave onto a passage running along a blank wall one side and four doors opening off to the other. These rooms were narrower than below but all had a window overlooking the area dominated by the domes. Maressa had just announced that she and Tika would use the bathing room first when three small figures appeared in the door. The three wore loose trousers and long sleeved over-shirts of a plain undyed coarse material. They also wore strange hoods which reached to their shoulders and were drawn across their faces leaving only their eyes revealed.

These odd creatures bowed low, the one on the left raising up a little to speak. The only word Tika and her friends recognised in the soft sibilant sounds was "gijan", a word the Keeper had used. Ren finally sat on a long bench, leaning towards the three.

'Gijan?' he asked gently.

Three heads lifted and three pairs of unusual eyes fixed on the Offering. The one who'd spoken nodded and pointed to himself then the two beside him.

'Gijan' he agreed.

Ren spread his hands, palms up, and looked perplexed. There was more nodding and one of the three lifted two of the companions' packs, scuttling towards the stairs with them. Another hurried to the kitchen while their spokesman gazed steadily at Ren.

'Is gijan his name or does it just mean servant?' Maressa asked.

Ren pointed to his own chest. 'Ren,' he said clearly. He poked his chest again. 'Gijan?' he queried.

Eyes above the mask widened in horror and the creature dropped to its knees, head bowed to the floor.

'Oh stars, what have you done to the poor thing?' Tika knelt on the floor beside this strange creature who wasn't even as tall as she was: not even as tall as a Delver, she reflected, resting her hand on the trembling shoulder.

She met Ren's eyes and nodded, gently reaching for the gijan's mind. She blinked, shocked by the complexity she found, but she ignored it in her urgency to communicate. Only too conscious of Khosa's warning, she kept her mind tightly focused.

Quickly she exchanged information with the gijan who slowly sat back on his heels, staring at her with rapt attention. He got to his feet and went to the kitchen as Tika hurriedly stood up herself. She turned to the outer door just as the Keeper appeared.

'These rooms are suitable?' she asked.

'Perfectly thank you Keeper. But we do not understand either your Qwah speech or the speech the gijan use. Could you perhaps tell us their names at least so we may address them correctly?'

A look of incomprehension spread across the Keeper's face. 'Names? They have no names – they are merely gijan.'

'Thank you so much Keeper,' Tika repeated as calmly as she could.

'We thought it best that you rest here for the remainder of this day. Gijan will bring food for you and meat for your – friends. A Keeper will come tomorrow to take you within the domes.' She inclined her head with haughty disdain and left them.

When they had all bathed, they found the gijan had readied a selection of hot and cold drinks and one of them had brought baskets of food from somewhere in this complex building. Sket murmured to Tika that he had left Khosa in one of the upper rooms and she nodded her understanding.

'Not one person out on that open area since we've been here,' Navan remarked as daylight faded. 'Yet it is all well-laid stone, swept, not a weed in a crack anywhere.'

Pallin snorted. 'And not a dratted crack that I could see either.'

'There have been people moving around under this covered walk.' Olam sipped from his bowl of tea. 'None near us though.'

'Are we being spied on Lady?' Navan's voice was low, his lips hidden behind his hand.

Tika shared a look with Ren. 'We don't think so Navan, unless they have far different means than us.'

Brin was sprawled outside their rooms, his head and shoulders under the colonnade. 'Tell us of these little gijan people Tika,' he suggested.

She laughed. Brin's curiosity was still as strong as Farn's or Storm's. Then she became serious. 'Enough to know they are less even than I was when I was Hargon's slave. At least I had a name.'

'Yet the Qwah have seemed friendly, pleasant people,' Ren mused. 'I saw none of these gijan earlier as we came through the Valley.

Turquoise eyes shone from the shadows within the room behind them. 'Namolos must be told of the gijan.'

The company found it impossible to interpret Khosa's tone.

'I think he cannot know some of them are here, and he will be much distressed to learn of their treatment.'

The Kephi moved deeper into the shadows. 'I must be with you tomorrow but I do not wish to let two of the Survivors know of my presence, at least, not at once. One I must speak with. Can you get me in with you?'

Gan astonished Tika by replying at once. 'I will wear my Captain's cloak. Your carry sack will be easily concealed beneath it.'

'Will these Survivors be like those red-eyed things?' Storm could not hide his concern and Seela curved her great bulk protectively round his small form.

'No.' Tika spoke decisively. 'None of them are here. I'm not sure how I know, but I do.'

She felt Storm's relief, and Farn's, and got to her feet.

'I'm sleeping out here,' she announced. 'Tomorrow we might get some answers.'

They found that the gijan had washed their clothes and polished boots and belts during the night. Thus the company looked smarter than for many days when a Keeper bowed from the door the next morning. This Keeper was male, in his late middle age and wore a friendly smile. A genuine smile, Tika noted with some relief. He wore a grey robe, similar to that worn by yesterday's Keeper. Most of the great open area was still in shadow although the upper parts of the domes shone in the morning light.

'I will show you the Domes before your meeting with Kertiss.'

'Kertiss?' Gan asked.

The Keeper merely nodded and moved towards the Dragons.

'Such very beautiful beings,' he said, tilting his head to gaze up at Brin's face.

'Indeed they are,' Tika replied. 'And they will also be

interested to see inside your Domes.'

'But of course. Please, follow me.'

The nine members of Tika's party walked close to each other, the Dragons behind them. The Keeper led them round an endlessly curving wall to a space between two of the Domes. It was wide enough perhaps for Brin to stretch his wings but then it opened again to a wider space with the third and largest Dome directly ahead. The Keeper turned left into a vaulting arch deeply shadowed. Gan, his blue cloak loosely clasped at his throat, moved closer to Tika as they walked into darkness.

Twenty paces and light washed out to meet them. None could hide their astonishment. The Dome's walls were immensely thick, making the entrance virtually a tunnel which led them into glowing brilliance. The Keeper smiled at their expressions.

'This is the Dome of Assembly,' he told them.

They stared at the tiers of stone seats ringing the Dome. Ten levels and they barely reached halfway up the wall. Stone ribs stretched up to merge with another ribbed stone circle and above that was the sky. What had appeared a milky opaque substance from Dragon back Tika realised was quite transparent viewed from below. The Keeper walked forward and the company took note of the floor he walked on. Except for its far greater size, it was identical to the circles they had seen in Sapphrea, Gaharn and Vagrantia.

Stones of dazzling colours within the black marble circle depicted the spiral pattern that led in to a square slab of a dark green glassy stone at the very centre. They also noticed that the Keeper stayed without the black edge of the circle.

'We have five Grand Assemblies each year when all our people can attend and speak. It is also used for smaller Assemblies when groups of scholars gather here to debate.'

'Wonder what they need to debate?' Sket muttered behind Tika.

'It is a magnificent building,' Ren commented. 'Is it very ancient?'

The Keeper smiled. 'Very ancient,' he agreed. 'Now we will visit the second Dome, the Dome of Knowledge.'

He trotted past them leading the way back through the arched tunnel. They crossed the space enclosed by the three buildings and entered a similar archway. The stillness and silence of the first Dome was not present here. Again stone tiers rose around the walls but these held galleries above and variously sized cubicle rooms below. People moved along the galleries, which closer observation showed to be lined with numberless books. Ren and Maressa stared, and Tika exchanged a glance with Olam. She could guess how their hands itched to get hold of even a few of these repositories of knowledge and information.

Tables and stools filled the middle of this Dome, many of them occupied by both males and females, some reading, some writing, a few with their heads together in muted discussion. Looking up, the sky was clearly visible through the strange material which covered the top of the Dome. A woman wearing trousers and shirt came towards the visitors.

'This is Hezwa,' the Keeper introduced her. 'She is one of the Keepers of Lore. These are the outlanders guesting here.'

Gan's great height was drawing interested stares from various levels of the galleries. He inclined his head when neither Ren, Tika nor Maressa chose to speak.

'You have the most amazing collection of books here – far more than I have seen, even in the Asataria of Gaharn.'

Hezwa laughed. 'The cataloguing involved gives me nightmares sometimes. But I must confess I am never bored or lost for occupation.' She spoke in the Common Tongue with no trace of an accent.

Except for her darker skin, she would pass as Sapphrean, Tika reflected. How could she have learnt the Common Tongue with such fluency if there was truly no interaction between these hidden reclusive Qwah people and the Sapphreans beyond the desert?

'May I ask how all these people reach this place?' Gan asked. 'We have seen no-one cross the grounds around these Domes.'

Both the Keeper and Hezwa laughed aloud.

'Here! See for yourselves!' Hezwa went beneath the protruding galleries which Tika saw for the first time formed a wide passage sloping downwards.

'Tunnels lead to the Ring Complex. Students live in houses beyond the Ring while Scholars, Teachers and Visitors live in the part of the building you are using.' Hezwa explained.

'Why do you have so much empty space around the Domes?'

The smiles faded from the faces of the Keeper and Hezwa.

'It is deemed necessary.' The Keeper replied, his voice expressionless. His eyes brightened. 'It is time. Kertiss awaits you.' The Keeper's smile was back in place as they turned to leave. Several students had left the galleries and tables to crowd round the Dragons, talking rapidly in the liquid Desert speech.

'Back to your studies!' Hezwa clapped her hands. She spoke again, presumably repeating her order in the Qwah language, and the students reluctantly drifted back to their places round the Dome.

'If you have time, you are welcome to visit the Dome of Knowledge again. I will be glad to show you some of our books.'

'I can think of nothing I'd like better,' Ren acknowledged fervently. 'If we stay long enough, I at least would take up your generous offer.'

Tika reached back and caught Ren's sleeve, smiling at Hezwa. 'If we have time, nothing will keep him from your books.'

She tugged the Offering to catch up with the others.

As they approached the largest Dome, they saw there was an arched entrance in this one also, but it seemed far lower. Drawing closer, they saw there was a ramp sloping sharply down, and revealing that the arch in fact was larger than in the previous two Domes. They halted at the edge of the ramp, feeling the first touch of the sun on their backs as it rose over the encircling buildings.

'What is this Dome called, Keeper?' asked Maressa.

'This is the Dome of the Singer.' The Keeper's voice was low and filled with reverence.

The company glanced at each other then Tika shrugged. With her left hand she reached up to touch Farn's neck and then took the first steps down to that gaping darkness. The sound of their boots seemed over-loud in the tunnel until light bloomed before them again. They followed the Keeper until he stopped several paces within the chamber. Maressa gasped, but she was not the only one.

At regularly spaced intervals around the edge of the curving wall stood statues. Seela moved first, pacing towards the nearest figure. She stared hard at it and the others joined her in silence.

It was a statue of a man. It stood on a stone plinth, its bare feet level with Tika's waist. Then it soared up, taller even than Gan. The most exquisitely beautiful face stared straight into Seela's. The company stepped back, trying to see the figure more clearly.

It glowed a dull gold in the strange light of the Dome and tiny scales were engraved on all the exposed areas of skin. It wore a real robe of white cloth, belted with a scarf of blue. The robe was sleeveless and slit backed, the figure's wings furled closed at his back.

Farn edged closer to Tika and from the corner of her eye she saw that Storm was pressed to Navan's shoulder too. Silently and slowly they moved round one side of the vast Dome, staring at statue after statue: all winged, all scaled, all robed. There seemed to be equal numbers of males and females – but as they neared the opposite side of the Dome from the archway, the company halted and could only gape.

The female statue had her head lowered but her hands half raised – all the previous figures held their hands clasped before them or relaxed at their sides. And this female's wings were half extended, rising above her head and fanning out around her body. Tika drew a deep breath and looked away from the overwhelming statue to the other half of the Dome. More statues lined the walls right back to the archway through which the company had entered. Sket stood beside her, clearly uncomfortable.

Apart from those motionless figures the Dome was a huge empty space. She looked back to speak to the Keeper and realised he was no longer with them. She opened her mouth, and snapped it shut as a soft hiss echoed around them. Hands went to swords and Dragon eyes began to whirr. An immense section in the centre of the floor slid away somehow and the hissing changed to a low hum. Something rose from the hole. Confused minds assumed it to be another form of statuary or artefact as it continued to rise until, with a soft click, the floor was in place again and on it stood –?

It was grey blue, three times Gan's height and smoothly rounded at one end, tapering at the other. There was another hum and click and a circle irised open just behind the rounded end. A man stepped out and walked a few steps towards them.

He smiled. 'I am Kertiss,' he said softly.

A young-sounding male voice chimed over his. 'And I am Star Singer. I welcome you at last.'

Chapter Three

Tika stared at the man, straight into his pale grey eyes. She knew he was attempting to probe her mind and instinctively she slammed a shield round her thoughts. His smile widened.

'You need have no fear of me, but will you not tell me your names?'

Without hesitation, Tika gave their names, and only their names. She made no reference to any rank, or title, or to where they came from. Brin had moved to flank Tika and Farn and the man half turned to stare up at the crimson Dragon.

'I had no idea you were quite so large,' he said.

A trace of smoke wisped from Brin's nose but his mind voice was calm.

'I should tell you Kertiss, you should not believe that we fear you. That would be a mistaken belief.'

Kertiss laughed, teeth flashing in his dark face. He replied to Brin's comment but Tika paid no attention to his words: she watched Gan, out of Kertiss's line of sight. Gan was jiggling at his cloak and then an orange Kephi landed between his boots. She streaked into the hole in the strange object whence Kertiss had emerged. So, the Survivor Khosa said they could trust was within that thing, Tika thought.

Kertiss turned from Brin as Seela moved. In the silent Dome her great feet made the merest whisper, matched by the slither of her tail over the paved floor. She reared erect at the rounded end of the object, her eyes a blaze of lavender and violet prisms. The upper part of that rounded end of what appeared to be blue grey stone suddenly cleared to become – windows? The young male voice began to sing, no words to his song but joyful notes and melodies, filling them all with a sense of delight.

'Enough, Singer,' snapped Kertiss, his smile changing to a frown. He raised a shoulder in a half shrug. 'My Ship is too excitable,' he said.

'Ship? What is Ship?' asked Maressa.

'This.' Kertiss waved at the object. 'This is a Ship which travels the spaces between worlds.'

'I am Star Singer. I am not *your* ship.' The younger voice was so cold, reminding Tika instantly of the dreadful journey through blizzards to the Stronghold. The tone changed with the next words, and was warm again and joyous. 'Why do you not go and drag Orla from her work Kertiss, so she may meet these guests? I will entertain them while you're gone.'

Tika felt a shiver of cold underlying the words but Kertiss merely shrugged again.

'I summoned Orla but she did not respond. No doubt she is lost in her studies as usual.'

'She is in the protected sections – you know she can't be reached there by summoning.'

Kertiss frowned again, a more permanent expression Tika suspected than was his smile.

'Very well. But behave yourself, Ship.' There was a clear warning in his voice. He moved to the female statue and laid his palm flat against the stone plinth on which she stood. A smaller section of floor hissed open and the man walked rapidly down the slope thus revealed.

Then there was only the sound of their breathing as the company stared at the Ship. Khosa appeared in the doorway, her odd croon suddenly loud. Seela had lowered her massive bulk and now pressed her brow against the side of the object, her eyes closed. Khosa spoke in their minds.

'Touch Singer and you will speak with him without Kertiss knowing.'

The company looked at each other even as another wordless song began to fill the Dome with music. Olam, first to risk the dangers of the great sea, marched forward to be the first to put his hand against the grey blue Ship. His eyes widened and his body relaxed. Ren looked at Tika, an eyebrow quirked, and she moved with the Offering to place her hand beside his on the Ship's side.

All touching this strange thing called Ship were immediately conscious of a living presence, and realised Ship was in reality an intelligent being whose name was Star Singer, and *he* was the Survivor whom they could trust. His mind embraced theirs and made them feel that they were old and beloved friends and he was oh so glad to find them again. A long loneliness darkened the edges of his embracing mind, mingled with great relief.

'We do not have long,' Singer's mind murmured to them even as his voice swelled with music. 'There may be a few brief chances for you and I to speak again before you leave, but you must reach Namolos. Tell him that things are bad here: bad and worsening. I cannot do anything against Kertiss or Orla – my programming will not permit me.

'He must be told of the gijan Kertiss has bred here. Oh I wish Khosa could stay but she cannot. She must not. I am transferring information to her, as much as I can while we speak, but she cannot stay here too long. If she is sealed below with me, Kertiss will find her. How I … Move back! Kertiss approaches!'

Gan scooped Khosa from the Ship's door and had just readjusted his cloak when two heads rose from the second hole in the floor.

'And my wings are retractable because they are only required during atmospheric flight from orbit to onworld.' Singer spoke over the throb of his music.

'How do you do that – sing and speak at the same time?' Maressa followed Singer's lead in what she hoped Kertiss and the woman with him would take as innocuous conversation.

'It is not difficult,' Singer began to explain before Kertiss interrupted.

'Enough of your babbling, Singer.' He gave his false smile. 'The Ship sustained much circuitry damage when we arrived here. This is Orla. She and I are known among the Qwah as the Survivors.'

The woman regarded them coolly, much as one would study a laboratory specimen, Ren recognised with a shudder. She was taller than Tika, about Maressa's height, and had the same pale grey eyes as had Kertiss. There was enough similarity for Tika to guess they were related, perhaps even brother and sister.

'I suggest you return to your guest rooms now for a meal. I have certain essential things to attend to but perhaps you would come back here in the middle of the afternoon?' Again that artificial smile. 'You saw how I opened the access ramp – I will be alerted as soon as you touch the mechanism. At the base of that ramp, Singer will await you. We would like you to see some of the work we have been undertaking here.'

As Kertiss was looking directly at Tika as he spoke, she felt bound to be the one to reply.

'We will come back later then. There is of course room for the Dragons to move easily beneath this floor – it would be most unfortunate to upset them?' She smiled brightly, and just as falsely as Kertiss.

Orla looked faintly annoyed but remained silent while Kertiss nodded.

'But of course. I hope we will become far better acquainted with each other. Seeing this Dome, these statues and indeed the Ship, is usually rather overwhelming to the few so honoured. The gijan will tell you when it is the appropriate time to revisit us.'

There seemed nothing more to say or do, so Tika simply began walking towards the archway.

'Do come back!' Singer called. 'I'm sure some of you would prefer to sit with me and gossip.'

'Silence!'

Tika stiffened as she heard the venom in Kertiss's brusque command. She looked back over her shoulder at the Ship.

'I know some of us would love a good gossip,' she called as cheerfully as she could manage, and then she was into the darkness of the arched tunnel and climbing to the surface.

The Keeper was sitting in the last patch of shade when Tika and her friends emerged, blinking, into the glare of midday. He got to his feet.

'You were longer than I had expected.' He smiled gently. 'Let me take you back to your rooms, you must be thirsty at least.'

'We are indeed, Keeper,' Tika replied. She looked at him curiously. 'Do you go in there frequently?'

His step faltered. 'Oh no, no. I am not yet worthy to enter or serve in that place.'

'Then who does?' Tika decided to be blunt. 'The place was clean, well swept. So who goes in there?'

'Gijan probably and perhaps the most senior Keepers but it is not discussed among us. We are simply told when it will be permitted for us to enter.' He sounded worried.

'How very odd,' Tika beamed at him.

They were nearing their rooms in what they now knew was called the Ring Complex and Brin spoke in their minds.

'Is it permitted, Keeper, for me to take the younger Kin for exercise? We will harm no one, but it is necessary for Dragons to fly you understand.'

Ren nudged Tika: the Keeper's eyes had become unfocused. He blinked. 'You are free to come and go as you will great one.' He bowed and left them outside their rooms, vanishing in the shadowed colonnade.

Tika felt as though her head was overstuffed with words, impressions, sensations, and she turned to clasp Farn's face between her hands.

'Go with Brin and Storm for a while, dear one. We are safe.'

Brin was already lifting into the air, Storm at his tail, and with only a brief hesitation, Farn followed them. Seela reclined, blocking the colonnade and Tika led the company within doors. Gijan were already placing trays of drinks on two low tables. Gan discarded his cloak with a groan of relief and freed Khosa. Everyone slumped into chairs and onto cushions, stunned by the morning's revelations, except for Maressa.

She caught gently at a gijan's arm as he turned from a table. The companions felt calmness pulse from her as, with great care, she held his hand and pushed his sleeve up his arm. They all stared, the gijan standing trembling before Maressa. She moved her free hand beneath the gijan's loosely curled fist and pressed upwards, forcing his hand to lie open on the back of her own. His skin was dappled olive with faint gold markings and lines and his hand had three fingers and a thumb, the short nails curved and horny.

Seela rumbled softly and the gijan raised startled dark eyes towards the huge purple Dragon. Maressa released his sleeve, enclosing his hand between both of hers. She leaned forward and touched her forehead to his and then sat back. The gijan looked at all the faces, ducked his head and retreated to the kitchen from whence issued appetising aromas. Khosa sat on the lower stairs, ready to hide above should a Keeper appear.

'Gijan come from the salt marshes far south of the desert.' She spoke in all their minds. 'They should not be here. These are young. They do not live long in this heat: long enough to birth a litter and raise the children for five years or so, then they die.'

Olam sighed. 'I didn't understand much of what was said this morning. Kertiss and Ship used words I have never heard.'

Khosa hunched down, wrapping her tail round her front paws.

'His name is Singer. A Ship is a thing, Singer is a living being.'

'How can he be "alive" Khosa?' Navan voiced the general perplexity.

'The Survivors come from another world. They learnt to travel through the fields of stars and they finally made Ships such as Singer uses.' She blinked her turquoise eyes at them. 'You have all seen snails, soft creatures who live within a shell? Well Singer is something like that.'

She paused a moment. 'On that distant world sometimes children were born with unbelievable mental abilities. But often those same children had bodies misshapen, damaged, unable to live any kind of normal life.' The Kephi hesitated again. 'Those children's brains were removed from their pain-wracked useless bodies and placed within the special Ships. Each Ship is therefore an individual being.'

Ren was pale. 'But that is – appalling!'

It was Seela who replied. 'Perhaps not though. What would happen to these children with their maimed bodies Khosa?'

'They never survived beyond three years and stars know their physicians and healers tried hard enough to keep them living.'

'But their minds live still within their snail shell Ships, and they have travelled the star fields and seen wonders. Surely that cannot be so very appalling Ren?' Seela's eyes whirred softest grey mauve.

'And it was done with the children's consent,' Khosa added.

Ren's chestnut and silver eyes glared at the Kephi. 'Three year old children are able to consent to such a perverse treatment?'

Khosa's tail thrashed. 'Those children became aware in their mothers' bellies. Their mental capacity was as high as yours is now – if not higher – by the time they had lived a year. And consider that they learnt like cloths absorbing water even while enduring physical pain such as you could never imagine. Yes, they were more than able to consent, and willingly, to what was done to them.'

'How could their brains survive?' Ren retorted. 'Chop an animal's head off, it is dead.'

Khosa spat. 'Obviously there were many processes involved in linking the brain to the actual Ship's systems. You are deeply ignorant Ren.'

Pallin cleared his throat, eyeing the Kephi's increasing temper with apprehension.

'You never mentioned this Namolos fellow, Tika.'

'No,' she agreed. 'I thought I would wait until we've seen whatever Kertiss has to show us this evening.'

'Who is Namolos anyway? Another like these two?' Pallin looked as though he would like to spit but restrained himself.

Tika shrugged. 'Gremara spoke his name to me, and then Khosa also. I know only that he is the Survivor to whom we must go. Perhaps he has some way of helping us cleanse the lands of the affliction, or free Ren's Drogoya of the horrors there.'

She looked hopefully at Khosa as she spoke but the Kephi's eyes were firmly closed and she received no reply.

A gijan came into the room and spoke softly. When only incomprehension showed on the company's faces, he moved to the door to the kitchen and bowed.

'I think food's ready.' Sket hauled Riff to his feet, then held out his hand to Tika.

The long table was laden with different foods: pastries of meat, or vegetables, or fruit, cheese, grains mixed with green leaves, and warm fresh bread. The gijan served them, anticipating any need with unerring speed and replenishing their mugs with a cold fruit drink. When the company rose replete and moved back to the sitting room, Olam turned to the gijan. He gave a half bow.

'Thank you for a most excellent meal gijan.'

The three tiny creatures fell to their knees, foreheads pressed to the stone floor and a whimper emerged from one of them. Olam shook his head helplessly and retreated, leaving Maressa to deal with the situation.

They passed the time waiting for their summons to Kertiss mostly in their private thoughts. Brin, Farn and Storm lay dozing just outside while Seela had disappeared in her turn. Tika went over and over this morning's experiences, trying to order them into a pattern – with little success.

Those statues – what had they represented? The Ship – she shivered recalling the sensations that had flooded through her when she laid her hand on its skin. She had heard Singer's words but she was also aware that he had put other things into her mind – as Kija had at the time of Farn's hatching. Tika had felt a desperation in Singer's mind, as if he had been isolated and afraid for too long a time.

Then Kertiss and Orla. Kertiss had done what Singer suggested in fetching Orla – too easily she wondered? And Orla had said not one word, even in greeting. What "work" might they be doing hidden beneath the great Dome? Thoughts of what she had learnt of Rhaki's experiments, in breeding in particular, entered Tika's mind. She felt the hairs prickle on the back of her neck.

Khosa's triangular ears twitched and she whisked herself out of sight up the stairs. Tika hurried to the bathing room, splashing cold water on her face in an attempt to calm her spinning thoughts. She heard voices in the sitting room – Gan greeting a Keeper who had obviously arrived to conduct them to the Dome again. She squared her shoulders and rejoined the others. It was the same Keeper as this morning so Tika mustered a smile of greeting for him.

She found herself walking beside Ren and touched his arm. 'Still angry Ren? We should be as calm and cool as we can manage this evening I think.'

Ren glanced down at her and grimaced. 'I suspect Khosa and Seela have the right of it Tika. It is just such a terrible idea at first hearing.' His face relaxed and he gave her a friendly bump with his elbow. 'I am as cool and calm as I can be – I promise.'

She grinned back at him and moved forward to walk with Gan. He did not wear his cloak tonight – Khosa had declined to come with them. He hoped there would be no questions as to why he would wear a cloak in the heat of midday and forego it in the chill of the desert evening. The Keeper left them at the entrance to the Dome and the company went through the arched tunnel again.

Outside, the sky overhead was a luminous green with the

earliest stars pricking through. Behind them the sun had disappeared in a blaze of fading crimson and orange. Once more they paused on entering the actual Dome. It was filled with an amber light but they could discern no source of the illumination. The light faded gradually above the statues' heads until the topmost part of the Dome was lost in soft gloom. Even the transparent capping was dark – Tika could find no glimpse of the sky as she had seen it this morning. The silence was more intense now and in unspoken agreement the company walked straight across the immense space rather than linger close by the imposing statues.

'Mim.' Maressa startled them all stopping dead in front of Olam. She looked at Tika. 'The gijan's hands, Tika – the same as Mim's.'

Tika nodded, annoyed that she had not made the connection herself but she said nothing. She would consider that implication later: for now she needed a clear mind. They reached the towering female statue and stared. Was it their collective imaginations or were her wings a little more extended? Tika bit her lip and made herself bend to the plinth, pressing her hand against the stone as Kertiss had done. She straightened, the floor already hissing open.

They walked more slowly down the ramp, expecting darkness, but the same amber light surrounded them all the way down. The floor levelled out, a blank wall to their right and ahead, but the light beckoned them on to a left turning. Before they reached it, song rippled to meet them, so it was with no surprise that they confronted Singer once they rounded the corner.

'It is so wonderful to meet new friends,' Singer called, his music ceasing but his words still melodious.

There were several wide openings off the curved chamber they found themselves in with Star Singer but as yet no sign of Kertiss and Orla. Ren strode directly to the Ship, laying his hand against its side.

'Do you feel pain Singer?' Ren asked as soon as he felt the Ship's mind enfold his.

'Not physical pain anymore my friend. But I have discovered there is another sort of pain which may be even worse.'

Ren flinched back, breaking the direct contact, and just stared at the Ship, his eyes magnified with tears. He stumbled back to where his companions stood even as Singer called aloud to them again.

'Will some of you stay and talk with me? It would be so wonderful to talk with others rather than sing to myself all the time.'

Olam and crimson Brin moved instantly towards the Ship and were quickly followed by young Storm, Riff and Pallin. Brin reclined against the wall nearest to Singer's curved end, Storm resting beside him. The three men sat on the floor and Olam spoke first.

'Tell us what the fields of stars are like.'

'And will you tell me then of your lands, and your lives?' Singer asked hopefully.

'Agreed!'

They heard footsteps approaching from one of the passages and turning towards it, Tika saw pain and rage in Ren's face. She caught his hand and squeezed tight. Kertiss appeared then, frowning at the two groups in the chamber.

'Our common armsmen would prefer to tell tales than accompany us,' Gan announced pleasantly before Kertiss could comment.

Seela chose that moment to loom above Gan, her face then lowering close to Kertiss's. 'The rest of us look forward to seeing your nesting caves,' she said.

For the first time Kertiss looked unsure, then he shrugged. 'As you wish.'

He turned to lead them down the passage from which he'd emerged. He hesitated as if to speak to Singer but Maressa spoke quickly.

'Are there many rooms down here Kertiss?'

Navan hid a smile: the Vagrantian air mage sounded as though she was merely visiting a newly moved acquaintance. Kertiss stared at her blankly for a moment.

'There are enough rooms for our requirements. If more are needed, the local people would see to it of course.'

'Do you go among the Qwah often?' Maressa continued her apparently inane questioning while they walked behind Kertiss.

Farn's chin bumped on Tika's head and she slowed to slide her arm across his neck. She noticed Sket's hand rested on his sword hilt and his eyes were never still. They trailed at Kertiss's heels for some time, peering into small square rooms: stone floored, stone walled and stone roofed, all lit by the same steady amber glow. Two rooms were obviously bed chambers; another they presumed to be a sitting area, but the impression was of bleakness, coldness, and they quickly found the constant light becoming tedious.

'There do not seem to be the things within your caves which most two legs consider necessary,' Farn suddenly remarked.

Kertiss halted and turned to the silver blue Dragon. 'What do you mean?'

'Coverings and cushions and books and – other people.' Farn's eyes whirred innocently. 'Lady Emla and Lady Lallia filled their caves with such things.'

Kertiss sniffed. 'Those things are not essential to existence.'

'Lady Emla and Lady Lallia would not agree.'

'Our work is all that is essential to us,' said Kertiss firmly. 'And this is where some of that work is done.'

A closed door blocked the passage ahead of them. Kertiss touched a small panel set in the door. 'This door opens only to my hand print or my sister's. It will open to no other.'

He stood to one side as Tika passed through, waiting until all of Seela's tail was safely clear before closing the door again. Immediately the friends felt enclosed, trapped, but Kertiss simply walked ahead again and turned left.

Chapter Four

They found they were in the largest room other than Singer's chamber that they had so far seen. There were many sloping desks lining three of the walls and an opaque sort of pipe rose from another larger desk in the centre of the room. Kertiss waited until most of Seela's bulk was inside the room.

'From this room we can monitor what happens on Kel-Harat,' he explained. 'Among other things.'

'Kel-Harat?' Gan frowned. 'What is Kel-Harat?'

Kertiss laughed. 'This world is Kel-Harat. It was so named millennia ago by astronomers in the Zeenol Galaxy.' He laughed again and went to the central desk. He pressed various coloured buttons scattered across the desk top and a low hum vibrated the air. The opacity in the pipe swirled for a moment before clearing. Hanging in the pipe they saw a round ball with brown, white, green and blue markings over it. The ball hung against a black background.

'A map?' Maressa and Gan spoke together.

'No. An image of this world seen from far beyond your skies.'

Ren walked right round the pipe, studying the image within it.

'How do you make such an image appear in here?'

'There are Ships still orbiting Kel-Harat, some sadly are dead, but some still function to an extent. They relay the picture of this world back to me here. Look, I can magnify the image for closer examination.'

Kertiss tapped at the buttons again and Tika felt her stomach lurch as she had the sensation of rushing closer to the ball in the pipe. Kertiss glanced up and tapped another button. The ball was enlarged enough now that it completely filled the pipe. He raised his hand to point at what the companions finally recognised were mountains clustered towards the right upper part of the ball.

'That is your City of Gaharn,' Kertiss smiled, his finger jabbing again at the desk.

Once more they seemed to rush closer until they really could see mountains, then trees, farms, then – stars above! – the Lady Emla's House! Closer still and figures moved. Gan's face was white: he recognised the formation of a squad of Guards escorting the Lady herself. Another click on the desk and the image vanished, the humming ceased and the pipe slowly clouded again. Ren broke the silence.

'Can you see what is happening in my land of Drogoya?' he asked Kertiss.

'Unfortunately no. For over a millennium there have been odd conditions in the atmosphere over nearly all of that land mass. Wave transmissions have thus been severely impeded.'

They didn't understand half of Kertiss's words but they caught the gist of his meaning.

'You spoke of dead or damaged Ships,' Tika queried. 'Where are they then – floating high in our skies?'

'Much higher than that, in a holding orbit. Orbiting means going endlessly round this world,' Kertiss explained with noticeable impatience.

'So this is your work: spying on the people of our lands.' Sket was scarcely polite.

Kertiss raised an eyebrow. 'I showed you that image as a simple example. We rarely bother to watch your activities.'

'Then why are you here?' Navan asked.

Kertiss turned away, wandering along a wall of desks. 'There were reasons that a group of Ships had to leave our home world. Kel-Harat is on a spiral arm of the Repsian Galaxy – not an overcrowded region but neither is this world too solitary. It would take our enemies a very great deal of time and energy to stretch their search so far.'

Kertiss turned back to face Navan. 'Kel-Harat had been briefly surveyed and registered as a restricted world requiring no contact at the time of the survey. It was classified as low pop, low tech and, conveniently for us millennia later, the survey report was lost in bureaucratic files until we found it by chance.'

'Low pop, low tech?' asked Maressa.

'Low human population, low technological achievement. Technology is all this.' Kertiss gestured round the room. 'Machinery that does the fundamental tasks leaving us free to concentrate on innovative experiment in many fields. Your technological development has only reached the lowest steps towards our level. You can work metal for example – that is the beginnings of technology.'

Seela eased her bulk back onto her haunches.

'These – things – you can make are all very well, but your minds have little of the strength that ours do, for example.'

Tika glanced at the purple Dragon but Kertiss seemed oblivious of the sarcasm. He shook his head.

'You may be able to do a few tricks with your minds but nothing of that sort compares with our technology.'

They followed Kertiss from the room and along the passage into the next. More desks lined two walls but two large stone boxes took up most of the space. Black ropes hung suspended from the ceiling, connecting some of the desks with the boxes. Ren and Tika both put careful fingers to touch the shiny grey boxes and met each other's eyes. The box felt too slick, too warm, to be stone. Ren pressed his fingers harder but whatever material it was, it was unyielding. Kertiss leaned against the end of one of the oblong boxes and folded his arms.

'These are generation tanks,' he told them. 'No. Not generation as you're thinking – not fathers and grandfathers and so on. Generation as in production, growth.' He sighed. 'If you have good rich land, you will be able to generate, or grow, good crops will you not?'

His frown lessened at their nods of understanding.

'So these tanks can generate life. Or at least, repairs. For example,'

Seela huffed rather noisily but Kertiss didn't notice.

'For example, if you were to be injured, have an accident – lost your hand let's say – we can immerse you in the gen tank and you will grow a new one.'

None of the companions could hide their astonishment. Tika and Sket's thoughts flew to Jal in the Stronghold.

'Could you grow someone a new arm?' Tika asked in disbelief.

'Of course we can. The time needed for someone to spend in the tank depends on how complex their injury. My sister and I spend a day in a gen tank occasionally to ensure that our bodies continue to function at full efficiency.'

'The Qwah are fortunate people indeed to have such marvellous healing available,' said Maressa.

Kertiss looked shocked. 'We do not use it other than for ourselves, or in experimental circumstances with particular specimens.'

'What sort of specimens do you use?' Ren's mouth smiled but his eyes were like stones.

Kertiss started to reply then stopped, studying Ren more carefully.

'Nothing of great importance. Come, I think we'll find Orla in the next room.'

Farn nudged his face close to Tika's. 'I like not this place my Tika. Can we go back and talk to Singer?'

She rubbed her cheek against his. 'Soon.'

They followed Seela and the others to yet another room. This was slightly more familiar in its degree of untidiness. A long workbench with cupboards beneath stood against one wall. Shelves covering another wall were piled with papers, bottles of different coloured liquids and various sized wooden boxes. The third wall was hidden by rows of stacked cages. Seela backed out of the room, her eyes blazing, unceremoniously pushing Farn out before he could actually get in.

'We will wait for you,' she told Tika.

Maressa had moved to stare into the cages. They contained various small birds and animals, none of which were quite familiar to her. They were all alive she thought but utterly still and silent, huddled in the furthest corners of their cages.

Orla was seated at the further end of the workbench along the wall opposite the cages.

'I give you greeting,' she said now, her voice surprisingly deep but pleasantly toned.

Two small white bowls stood in front of her and she held a short transparent pipe with a finger held over one end. The pipe was half full of a thick red fluid. She bent her head as she sealed the top of the pipe with something and stood it in a rack of similar pipes. She turned back to the visitors.

'This is where I spend most of my time,' she told them. 'One of my interests is xenobiology – understanding the life forms of different worlds than my own. Despite being here on Kel-Harat so long, there seems an infinity to discover.'

At the back of the group, Tika had only half listened to Orla: her attention had been caught by a small bird. It looked very like the larger night-loving great-eyes she knew in Sapphrea, and she sent a guarded thought towards it. Now, as Orla continued speaking about something she called blood groups, Tika stumbled back against Sket, her face white and beaded with sweat. Sket's arm went round her even as Farn began to fuss in the passage outside.

'Captain, my lady is ill!'

Gan spun to look at Tika and lifted her into his arms without a question.

'Forgive us Kertiss, Orla, but we must get Lady Tika to our rooms at once.'

Orla and Kertiss looked discomposed but then Kertiss stepped forward.

'Very well. We would have liked you to stay longer but you will return tomorrow evening. Evening is our preferred time,' he said, leading them back along the passages.

Tika's face was pressed into Gan's shoulder and Farn's head banged against Gan's, so close did he keep to his soul bond. They reached the doorway through which they'd first entered and Kertiss paused. He studied the small panel set into the door, Gan seeing a red light flashing before Kertiss's body blocked his view. Kertiss looked over his shoulder, as if checking the group of companions and the two Dragons. He placed his hand on the panel and the door swung open. Gan strode straight through.

Olam sprang to his feet, closely followed by Pallin and Riff. Brin rumbled and surged up from his reclining position.

'Oh dear friends! Why is the small one ill?' Singer cried.

Without knowing why he did so, Gan halted his rapid march towards the ramp and swerved towards the Ship. Shielding Tika with his own body from Kertiss's sight, he pressed the back of her hand briefly against the Ship's side. There was the faintest gasp then Singer's voice poured music into the chamber. Gan turned at once and made for the ramp.

'We will not see you tomorrow Kertiss if Lady Tika is not fully recovered,' he called over his shoulder. 'Unless of course you care to visit us in our rooms.'

The party crossed the floor of the Dome which was still lit with the strange amber glow and took the waiting Keeper by surprise, so quickly did they emerge from the archway. He scrambled to his feet and hurried after them across the starlit space towards the Ring Complex. He skidded to a halt when Storm whirled with amazing speed, barring his way. The Keeper stared at the young Dragon's glittering eyes and snarling mouth and chose to stop following the group.

Gan laid Tika gently on cushions that Maressa spread on the floor and Farn pushed ungently through to crouch at her side. A gijan silently appeared, a bowl in his hands. He knelt right under Farn's nose and lifted Tika's head to tip some liquid against her mouth. Her eyelids fluttered and she swallowed a little more of the drink.

'My Tika, please, are you feeling better?' Farn's distress was all too plain.

Tika struggled against the gijan's arm and he simply slid closer, pushing her into a more upright position. She blinked, looking at the worried faces surrounding her. She reached for Farn and he ducked his long face against her shoulder.

'I feel very odd,' she said.

Gan reached for the bowl in the gijan's hand and sniffed its contents. He took a cautious sip and rolled his eyes. He gave Tika a wry smile.

'It would seem that Lorak is not the only one to concoct lethal "restoratives".'

'What happened in there, Tika?' Ren asked.

She shook her head. 'I just felt faint I think.' Green silvered eyes stared at him guilelessly. 'I'm rather hungry now though.'

Her friends regarded her, not one of them believing her first statement. Tika twisted round to the gijan against whom she leaned. 'Thank you.'

Farn's head lowered so that his cheek rested briefly on the gijan's head. The gijan didn't cower as everyone half expected him to. Instead, he gazed into Farn's prismed eye steadily before easing away from Tika and disappearing to the kitchen.

Maressa sat back on her heels. 'Khosa's not here,' she said, watching Tika's face.

'Is she not? I can't imagine her finding many squeakers around here. Perhaps she's just gone for a stroll – you know how nosy she is.'

Farn's laugh held a great deal of relief as well as amusement. 'Khosa would not like to hear you call her nosy, my Tika!'

'No,' Tika conceded. 'Perhaps we should say she is inquisitive.'

Pallin picked up the drink the gijan had brought Tika and now took a sip. His eyes widened and he passed the bowl to Riff. Riff tasted the contents and got to his feet.

'I'll see if they've got any more – this is really very good.'

Gan groaned. He glared at Pallin. 'For stars' sake, don't drink too much of that stuff. We must keep our wits about us – all of us.'

Seela announced that she and Storm were going to fly in the starlight. She gave no reason for this decision and no one asked. Brin merely settled in the colonnade while Farn still occupied a large amount of the sitting room as Tika ate in the kitchen with her companions. It was nearing dawn when Seela and Storm returned and, as they reclined outside, Khosa slid between the heap of Dragons, marched across Gan's chest and perched on a table.

Only Sket, Tika and Gan remained downstairs, the others having decided that proper beds were to be preferred whenever the opportunity arose.

'Well?' Tika's thought was but a whisper in their minds.

Gan saw Seela's head swing towards Khosa and he also noted a gijan slip into the room from the kitchen. He couldn't tell if it was the same gijan who'd provided the restorative earlier or another.

Khosa bristled: whiskers and fur were in spikes and her tail twitched constantly.

'Grek is with Singer,' she told them.

Seela's eyes flashed in alarm.

'He is trustworthy, Seela,' Khosa said firmly. 'If you trust me, so you can trust him now. We were both afraid that Kertiss's alarms would be triggered even by an entity such as Grek. I waited, but no alarms sounded as far as I could tell at least. But then, I couldn't reach Singer's mind through that floor. Kertiss has the whole Dome sealed somehow, even against a mind contact.'

Ren came down the stairs and sat on the last one listening to Khosa. The Kephi glanced at him. 'You knew that didn't you?'

Ren nodded. 'When I asked him if he felt pain.' The Offering's eyes filled with tears which he made no attempt to hide. 'He cannot even send his mind beyond the Dome to see any of the life around him. And he once flew between the stars and saw wonders upon wonders. He fears for his sanity. It is the cruellest imprisonment I can imagine for such as him. He said other Ships very occasionally make direct contact with him, but the last time was half a year ago.'

Khosa slitted her eyes at him. 'And?'

'And he wants to see Namolos. Or if that is as impossible as Singer seems to think, he begs us to reach Namolos and ask him to release Singer from Kertiss's grip.'

'Hmm.' Khosa's fur became smoother and her tail slowed its thrashing. 'We will wait for Grek but you must not go into those rooms beneath the Dome again – any of you. You will be safe enough in the Dome itself but not below its floor.'

Sket fidgeted. 'Khosa, what are those statues in the Dome?'

Khosa turned her turquoise gaze onto Tika's self appointed personal Guard. 'I don't know. Namolos might. But they reek of grief.'

They looked in some surprise as the gijan dropped to his knees, his hands clasped against the veil half hiding his face, eyes fixed on Khosa.

'Namolos,' he said.

The day passed quietly, the companions grateful for a restful break in their travelling but also somewhat on edge. They all wondered if they would be able to leave as easily as they'd arrived.

When they sat in the kitchen towards the end of the afternoon, Olam told them that Khosa was still curled in a tight ball, sound asleep, inside a shirt upstairs. Even as he spoke, Khosa jumped onto Navan's lap, her orange face poking over the table's edge.

'Grek is here.'

Grek's mind voice, coming from nowhere, unsettled them all

as usual, but they quickly forgot their discomfiture listening to his report. There was no mistaking the pain and sorrow underlying his words.

'Singer was desperate to talk,' Grek began. 'Kertiss should not have been Singer's captain. The one who should have been was killed in some fighting. Kertiss and Orla climbed inside Singer and ordered him to fly. Singer obeyed: he was nearly mindless with grief.' Grek fell silent.

'I think a Ship bonds with a captain, as you are bonded to Farn Lady Tika. That is the impression I had at least: Singer became distraught trying to tell me of those times.'

Tika's eyes were enormous in her white face. She could guess all too vividly how Singer might have felt if he had truly been one half of a soul bonding and lost his bonded one.

'There was a great deal that Singer tried to tell me,' Grek continued. 'It was jumbled and although no doubt of great interest later perhaps, it was irrelevant to us now. There was fighting in the star fields, battles, which was all very confused in his mind but then he, with other Ships like himself, reached this world. He thinks that six or maybe even ten, landed on the ground. All were damaged. He doesn't know if any of them can ever fly to the stars again, but he says he needs Namolos.' Grek paused once more.

'He called Namolos the Father of the Ships and he also said that he has heard most often from Namolos's own Ship. That Ship is called Star Dancer, a female, and she was the last to speak to him.'

'Did Singer know anything of those winged people in the Dome?' Ren asked.

'He said he likes to sing to them. He said they appreciate it and that they were trapped, perhaps even worse than he is.' Grek sounded puzzled. 'He also said that you must take a gijan with you to Namolos and you must go by tomorrow at the latest, or Kertiss will hold you.'

Sket growled, his hand reaching for his never absent sword.

'What about the map thing Kertiss had in that room? He could use that to see where we go if we have to make a dash for it. And we don't even know where they put our koninas.'

'We'll see about that now.' Pallin got to his feet. 'Come on

Riff, let's take a walk around this dratted Ring Complex and wander through the arch where we came in. We'll find our mounts all right.'

Riff grinned but looked to Gan for his agreement. Gan nodded.

'A good idea. See if you can learn anything about a road out of this Valley too. We need to go south.'

'I think I'll go too,' Olam decided. 'I am an Arms Chief after all – I'm entitled to make a fuss if necessary!'

He winked and followed Pallin and Riff from the kitchen. The others wandered out into the colonnade to watch the three men march off, somewhat surprised to see Storm pacing close behind them. Brin's eyes sparkled.

'Did you see young Storm turn on that Keeper last night?' he asked generally. 'Most effective.'

Seela huffed and ignored the crimson Dragon. 'I heard Grek's words,' she said. 'We have been flying high when we go for our "exercise".' She sounded pleased with herself. 'The Valley stretches on towards the rising sun as far as we could see, but there is a trail leading in the direction we need, not too far away.'

Maressa smiled, moving to lean against a massive purple shoulder.

'"Not too far" for a Dragon is "quite a long way" for humans. We've learnt that already. Let me look.'

The air mage closed her eyes, sending her mind high and fast to the east. 'Three or four leagues,' she said, opening her eyes again. 'That's far enough, if Olam can't get the koninas.'

'If he can't, we can carry all of you to that place,' Brin told them.

Ren nodded. 'I'm sure you could, but then what? You cannot carry all of us for long and we have no idea how much desert land we have to travel – in any direction. Without a guide, I can't see how we'll make it.'

'I could – persuade – Kirat to guide you,' Grek offered carefully.

The company avoided each other's eyes, none liking to contemplate quite how Grek might achieve such a thing.

'Thank you Grek. We will consider your idea.' Tika stroked her hand along the great scar winding down Farn's neck.

'Perhaps you should locate Kirat – he may have left the City by now?'

'I will seek him at once,' Grek agreed.

In the silence following Grek's presumed departure, the company gazed across the open space to where the Domes rose. They sat comfortably abutting each other and looked as though they had done so for ever. Tika leaned against Navan, her head tilted back to squint up at the very top of the Domes, dazzling still against the brightness of mid afternoon.

'I had no bad feelings in any of those Domes,' she murmured aloud. 'I felt a great sadness and an endless waiting – no, patience – in Singer's Dome.' She shivered and walked back into the sitting room. 'I've been trying to work out how Singer could have got inside one. The Domes have been here since long before he came, of that I am sure.'

'Perhaps they put wheels beneath him and pulled him in, do you think?' Navan wandered round the room as he thought. 'Olam said that while we were in Kertiss's rooms last night, Singer showed them his wings. They slid out from his sides Olam said, quite large and curved. Then they disappeared again and none of them could find a crack or mark to show where they had been. Maybe he has wheels himself which he can hide, like his wings?'

'Olam returns,' Seela mind spoke them.

The three men wore broad grins when they arrived. 'Lots of koninas,' Pallin announced. 'Only a few paces from the entrance. Stables full of gear and feed grain. No one watching the gates.'

'Easy to tell which ones are ours: the others are all so pale coloured,' Riff added.

'And do you remember the route in, through all those different circles, each with their own gateways?' Gan asked pointedly. 'It isn't going to be easy getting out of here if Kertiss orders the Qwah to make sure we stay put.'

Olam's grin faded rather. He sighed. 'I feel a bit better knowing where the koninas are anyway,' he said. He brightened. 'Surely the Qwah wouldn't argue with us if the Dragons flew close above us?'

Tika grunted. 'Did you notice how totally unafraid the Qwah have been when they meet the Dragons?' she asked. 'And I most definitely would never ask the Dragons to attack or hurt anyone who has made no move against me.'

Farn's head poked into the open window. 'One of those Keepers approaches,' he warned.

Moments later, a Keeper bowed in greeting. This one was a younger male than yesterday's.

'Kertiss will see you now,' he said politely and stood aside, obviously waiting for them to leap to their feet.

Tika stretched slowly. 'We can spare him a short time Keeper, but only a short time. We must resume our journey.'

She watched as the Keeper's eyes unfocused: obviously he communicated with someone. And make what you like of that, Kertiss dear, Tika thought as she strolled after the Keeper.

Chapter Five

They strolled slowly across the centre of the Dome and stood idly waiting. After a time, the floor hissed open to one side and Kertiss walked into view. His face was creased into what they knew was his normal expression: a frown verging on a scowl.

'You have been shown how to access entry,' he said, halting at the top of the ramp.

Tika raised an eyebrow at his tone then smiled. 'I was made faint last night by the closeness below. I do not like being in enclosed places. We will stay here a while if you wish to speak with us.'

The Dragons had already reclined and now Tika sat cross legged against Farn's chest. 'We have appreciated your hospitality Kertiss, but we leave tomorrow.'

'Nonsense.' Kertiss took two strides forward. 'You will stay here until I permit you to leave.'

'Really? We are summoned by Namolos and so we go to him without delay.' She was watching Kertiss closely. She was aware that the men except for Ren were tense, ready to act on any aggressive move from Kertiss.

His dark face grew waxen and he almost flinched back when Tika spoke Namolos's name.

'Where did you hear of him?' He forced a laugh. 'He is a senile old fool, his Ship lost in the seas and his wife long vanished. You will stay here. There is much I need to learn of you.'

Tika got back to her feet, Farn surging up behind her. 'Much you need to learn Kertiss? Which part of me did you intend to use for your study?' Her voice rang in the great Dome, cold as cracking ice.

Kertiss stared. 'What did that Ship tell you?' he snapped. 'It is damaged I told you. Its mind is as warped as that of Namolos.'

'The Ship told me nothing Kertiss,' Tika lied calmly. 'But

Namolos asked that I go to him. And so we go.'

She turned away, her heart aching that she could not communicate with Singer, could not explain the reason for their sudden disappearance.

'I will not pretend it has been a pleasure to meet you Kertiss, but I will admit it has been – interesting.'

She gave the slightest bow, hand on her sword hilt. As she moved to walk back across the Dome, she glanced at the great female statue and nearly faltered. Her heartbeat thundered in her ears but she kept moving, seeing in her mind's eye the fan of feathered wings outstretched, the thin face lifting its chin.

'And how do you propose to leave?' Kertiss scoffed. 'You will die within days if not hours, alone in the full heat of the desert.'

Tika turned back. 'Surely you will send a Qwah to guide us? I think Namolos would be –' She paused, choosing her words with some care. 'Namolos would be – concerned – should he hear that you hindered our journey to him or, stars forfend, let us die, unguided, in the desert.'

She studied Kertiss's face feeling a faint shock. He looked like a spoiled child denied his treat. She thought of Hargon's younger son Bartos and felt a shudder of revulsion. 'We will leave before dawn.'

This time she kept walking, her friends around her, the Dragons behind, ignoring Kertiss's incoherent words. Only Gan looked back when they reached the ramp beneath the arched entrance. He blinked. Storm was walking backwards, keeping his snarling face towards Kertiss, and his tail lashed from side to side. Far beyond Storm and behind Kertiss's impotent figure the female statue seemed to shimmer. Gan blinked again and turned back to the ramp. The Keeper was not waiting outside and they were not sure if that boded well or ill, but when they reached their rooms they found Kirat squatting by the door.

He rose as they approached and bowed. 'You leave tomorrow,' he said. 'My brothers and I will guide you again.'

Unsure whether Kirat was here by Kertiss's order or by Grek's "persuasion", Tika managed only a weak smile.

'How many horses will you need Lady? And at what hour shall I have them ready?'

'The animals we came on,' Gan began, but Kirat shook his head.

'They were weak before we came across the desert from the great sea,' he said firmly. 'We will supply horses and nurse your animals back to full health here.'

Pallin's eyes gleamed at the prospect of getting his hands on one of the desert horses he admired so much, despite Olam's glare.

'Then we will need at least six horses plus three pack animals,' Gan told the Qwah.

Kirat bowed again. 'I shall be here for you well before dawn Lord.'

They watched the desert man vanish into the gathering twilight under the colonnade and went inside their rooms. The three gijan stood in a row by the kitchen door, three packs by their cloth-shoed feet, dark eyes fixed on Tika. Khosa stalked across to sit in front of them.

'They will come with us to Namolos,' she announced.

'One perhaps, but all three?' Gan protested.

Khosa gave him her most imperious stare. 'They are litter mates. They stay together.'

The gijan moved their packs against the wall and gestured towards the kitchen.

'It only seems a moment ago that we ate,' Maressa groaned. 'But perhaps we'd better eat what we can before we go into that awful desert again.'

They tried to sleep before full dark had fallen but only Pallin and Riff slept with their usual soundness. Most of the others only dozed, their minds preoccupied with the events of the last two days and with the prospects to come. Tika gave up trying to sleep when she heard movement outside. She peered into the colonnade and saw two Qwah leaving the bodies of goats near the Dragons.

'Kirat?' she asked.

One of the men moved closer to the door. 'Lady. I will bring the horses for you to load your packs in a short while, if that suits?'

'Yes of course. I'll rouse everyone.' She hesitated. 'Three gijan will be coming with us. Is there a problem with that?'

The light from the one lamp still burning in the sitting room shone onto Kirat's face, which Tika watched closely. His eyebrows lifted slightly and he spread his hands palm up.

'As you wish Lady. Gijan are rarely seen outside City dwellings, but if you say gijan travel with you, then so be it.'

When Kirat returned, his brothers were leading horses, their pale hides gleaming in the dark. Kirat carried a large bundle of white cloth which he dropped onto a chair. He lifted one piece of cloth and the companions saw it was in fact a hooded cloak. He handed one to Maressa who stood nearest, and picked up another.

'The light colour keeps away some of the heat,' he explained distributing cloaks to all the party.

Kirat even had three tiny cloaks for the gijan, really meant for Qwah children Tika guessed.

'The first day will not be too bad,' Kirat told them, 'but the three following will be worse than any you experienced on our journey from the great sea. Then we will travel mostly at night and rest longer during the days.'

'How many days through the desert?' Olam asked.

Kirat shrugged. 'This route has been travelled in ten days, but it can take twice that time if we meet dust storms.'

Sket elected to ride one of the desert horses to start with rather than travel with Gan on Seela's back. Maressa would go with Brin and Tika as usual with Farn. The Dragons would fly high, marking the course of Kirat's group. The pack horses were loaded, the riders mounted, when Storm crouched low. The three gijan pattered to his side and scrambled onto the sea Dragon's back. Ren gave Tika a bemused grin and shook his head. Khosa, in her carry sack round Tika's neck, settled herself more comfortably as Farn lifted into the air.

Once above the Domes a strong breeze buffeted their faces and Tika allowed herself to relax a little. She stared down at the central Dome and wondered if she would ever see Star Singer again.

'I went back to speak with him once more,' Grek spoke in her mind. 'He asked me to tell you that he believes you will meet in the future and he sends you all his love and his music. He holds his mind tightly against Orla and Kertiss, although neither of them have much natural gift for mind speech.' Grek was silent before adding: 'Their machines can affect minds, as you learnt, did you not?'

Tears tracked down Tika's cheeks and her hand clenched on Farn's shoulder. 'The great eyes in Orla's room. She said they do dreadful things to animals in there. She told of pipes being put into brains and of wings damaged on purpose, things grown in those gen tanks – half one creature, half another. I would never have believed I would find people worse than Rhaki and yet those two are.'

Seela led them slowly eastwards, watching those on horseback below working their way through the still sleeping City. Tika suddenly remembered the gijan and twisted round to find Storm a length behind. The three gijan sat straight on his back. All Tika could see beneath the enveloping white cloaks was the first gijan's dark eyes shining with reflected star light.

'Grek?' she asked tentatively.

'I am here.'

'What of these gijan?'

'I cannot tell you much more than Khosa has. They come from the salt marsh regions both south and east of this great desert.'

'Do you know why Storm offered to carry them?'

'There is an affinity.'

'Grek?' But this time, Grek did not reply.

At last Kirat led the horses through the City's final gate. They picked up their pace, cantering along beside the many fields which lapped against the City's outermost buildings. They reached the place where a trail led off to their right, twisting and turning as it climbed to the high peaks. Dawn was still some time away when Kirat slowed the riders to a more cautious speed.

Seela led the Dragons higher still, keeping her eyes on the direction of the trail as well as the distance separating them from the horse riders. Eventually dawn's fingers touched the Dragons and Farn called aloud with delight at the first warmth. Seela swung round in a slow circling swoop before resuming her leading place.

'We will land there,' she announced.

The Dragon riders peered down, seeing the trail Kirat followed opened onto a broad flat area. Accordingly, the Dragons spiralled down, settling on rough grass. Tika slid from Farn's back and watched the gijan slip from Storm. The three immediately set about making a camp: one dug away turf for a fire pit, another trotted off, seeking fuel for that fire, and the third clambered over a large boulder from beyond which came the sound of fast flowing water.

Maressa joined her. 'I cannot reach their minds,' she spoke quietly. 'They seem so docile, so timid, yet they shield their minds to an extent I cannot breach.'

Tika glanced up at the air mage. 'I glimpsed something enormous and intricate when the first gijan allowed me that brief entry to his mind,' Tika admitted. 'But I haven't tried to touch their thoughts since.'

Gan had knelt to help the gijan clear a patch of ground for the fire. He looked up smiling when the two women drew near.

'It feels such a relief, just being clear of that strange place,' he said.

They all stared back down, into the deep Valley. The rising sun was just gilding the tops of the three great Domes even as Kirat appeared over the edge of the plateau. He dismounted and loosened his saddle.

'We will stop only long enough for a quick meal,' he called to the other riders. 'We must make as good time as we can today.'

Pallin joined the gijan by the fire and produced two kettles. Why were armsmen so devoted to their tea, Tika wondered absently? When Kirat and his brothers joined the group round the fire, she noticed all three gijan drew closer to Sket, leaving a considerable space between themselves and the Qwah. She met Ren's eyes and knew the Offering had also noticed the behaviour of the gijan.

The Dragons flew slowly on, holding back while the horsemen below negotiated a torturous pass and a perilously steep descent the other side. Once through the pass, the earthbound group could see what the Dragons had already noted: endlessly arid desert lands again. Maressa was relieved to find how effective the white cloaks were as the sun climbed to its highest point. While by no means comfortable, she was not tortured by the blazing heat as she had been on her previous experience of desert travel.

'Kirat says we will halt soon,' Ren bespoke Tika, and she looked down to see the horses were at last picking their way along a flatter path.

With Farn spiralling lower Tika stared back at the line of mountains marching from horizon to horizon. Who would believe such a fertile, populous Valley could possibly exist behind those forbidding ramparts?

They camped amid vast slabs of rock, some sharply edged as though sliced from the mountainsides in a distant past. Large awnings were stretched between such rocks, offering shade to people and animals alike. Warned by their earlier journey, Seela insisted that Farn and Storm take refuge from the heat beneath the awnings.

The dryness of the air seemed to steal away any drop of moisture, even from their mouths and eyes. No one wanted food yet, only a few swallows of water, before lying down and trying to sleep. Tika drowsed against Farn, only vaguely aware of the gijan curled against Storm, well away from the Qwah.

She woke suddenly and felt Farn's steady breathing under her cheek. Moving her head a little, she saw three small shapes silhouetted against a sky streaked with sunset ribbons of high cloud. She blinked, her eyes sore from sand grits. The gijan were hunched close around her but she could see their dark eyes regarding her. Carefully, Tika pushed herself up to a sitting position, never taking her own gaze from the gijan. She tilted her head to one side and held out a hand questioningly. What did they want?

One gijan shuffled closer and a tiny three fingered hand rested on hers. He looked at their lightly joined hands then lifted his other hand and pointed to her chest. Tika's mind whirled with speculation while with her free hand she reached inside her shirt, tugging the oval pendant out into sight. The chain was warm against her neck and she let the amber fronted, gold backed egg swing gently. The gijan hand in hers suddenly tightened its grip as breath hissed from all three of them. Without warning, they all dropped forward, foreheads pressed to the ground. Then they were gone, back behind Storm's still sleeping body.

From first twilight they travelled relentlessly, stopping only for brief halts for the horses to be given a little water and to have their feet and legs checked for damage. The sky to their left was beginning to lighten before Kirat let them stop again. They were still among the residue of the mountains and Kirat chose a place where slabs of stone had fallen across others, making half caves which would help them shelter through the day.

This time Pallin and Hadjay cooked a substantial meal which Kirat insisted all partake of. Sirak disappeared for a while and returned with several sand swimmers, the large lizards he'd found for the Dragons days ago on their journey from the coast.

'We have been well provided with food since we entered your Valley,' Brin told him. 'We can survive well enough now until this desert is crossed. But we thank you for your thought for us.'

Privately, Farn told Tika that the sand lizards were extremely chewy and not particularly flavoursome.

The Qwah fussed over the horses, seeing to their comfort, checking for sores, as though their were their children. Maressa commented casually on this fact and earned severe looks from all three Qwah.

'Do you think we could so easily risk travelling these lands without our horses, Lady?' Hadjay demanded reproachfully. 'They are more precious than our own lives and must be treated so.'

They slept the day away, aware when they occasionally roused of the fiery heat beyond the awnings and the sheltering boulders. Hadjay distributed handfuls of fruit and bowls of tea when they gathered, watching the sun sink behind the mountains.

'Have you often met with the Survivors in the City, Kirat?' Ren enquired, sipping his tea.

Kirat blanched. 'No one meets the Survivors except selected Keepers of the Sanctuary. It is death to even enquire of them.'

'But why? And we were invited to meet them, and we're still alive.'

Kirat frowned. 'A Keeper sent a message to me that we were to go to the great sea to meet your company. To be directly asked to perform a particular task for the Survivors is deemed great honour.'

'How long have they lived in your City though?' Ren persisted. 'The Domes have been there far longer than the

Survivors I would guess.'

Kirat stood up, still white around his lips and swung onto his horse. 'We must ride,' he called. Not waiting to see if the rest mounted up, he rode on along a trail only he could see.

'Perhaps such questions could wait, Ren? At least until we can see the end of this stars forsaken desert.' Olam grinned at the Offering. 'Might be better not to risk being abandoned, yes?'

Ren grinned back at the Arms Chief. 'Oh I think we're safe enough – you heard him. He would rather die than disobey the Survivors and it would appear that dear Kertiss has ordered him to guide us south.'

'I'd just as soon not press our luck lad,' Pallin grunted, pulling himself into his saddle. But he winked as he rode past.

The next day they cowered under the awnings while heat hammered mercilessly down from the white sky. Even Seela and Brin were forced to squeeze their massive bodies under the awning. Tika saw one of the gijan stumble when he got to his feet in the late afternoon to prepare for their night's travelling. She watched the other two gijan press close to the third, seeming to support him. She bit her lip and glanced around, catching Ren watching her. He crossed to her side.

'Is there anything we might do for them? I think they're in trouble,' he murmured, watching the gijan huddle at the edge of the awning.

'I think so too, but I don't know how to find out.' Tika frowned. 'Would you ask Hadjay if he knows what might be wrong or how we might ease them? I'll see if I can get anywhere with them directly.'

'Hadjay?' Ren raised a brow.

Tika nodded. 'He's the most sympathetic of those Qwah I think. Oh, and Ren – have you noticed that smell of mint has come back?'

He scowled. 'I'd hoped it was just my imagination. It disappeared once we'd been in the desert a couple of days from the coast, but I thought I smelt it soon after we came out of that Valley.'

Ren moved between Riff and Maressa, looking for Hadjay. Navan joined Tika at that moment. He too watched the gijan.

'What sort of creature are they, Tika?' he asked.

She looked up into his face. Once she had feared this man, Hargon's second in command. Now she counted him a true friend.

'I don't know but I keep seeing a similarity to Mim, although perhaps that is only because of their hands.'

'But I don't know Mim – to me their hands are like the Dragons,' Navan pointed out.

Tika was startled: Navan was right of course. And hadn't Grek said the gijan had an affinity with Storm?

'Their skin is not like Mim's or the Dragons though,' she countered. 'I'm going to see if they'll speak to me or let me use mind speech Navan. Don't let anyone interrupt for a few moments.'

He nodded and watched her walk over to the crouching figures. Sket touched his arm.

'Thought something was wrong,' he said. 'Young Storm's upset – look at him.'

Storm reclined near Seela, but his eyes flashed grey and green: clearly he was communicating some agitation to the adult Dragon.

'Do you think they might do better if we took them on horseback?' Navan wondered.

'No I don't. Haven't you noticed – they keep as far from the horses as they do from the Qwah.'

Tika was kneeling by the gijan now. She looked over her shoulder and beckoned urgently to Sket. He hurried to her side then returned for the satchel that rarely left his person. He was fumbling among its contents as he went back to kneel beside Tika. As Navan watched, Kirat called them to take down the awnings and prepare to ride. Then Gan was at his shoulder, eyes fixed on Tika and Sket.

'Stay and see if they need any help Navan. I'll get your horse readied.'

Navan saw Tika's back stiffen for a moment then she bent over the gijan again. The awnings were down and being rolled into tight packs. Navan took a step towards Tika but to his relief she got to her feet, holding a gijan in her arms. The other two scurried across to Storm who greeted them with a show of concerned affection. Sket thumped a stopper back into the top of a pot and stowed it in his satchel. He met Navan's questioning gaze. The two men hurried to mount their horses, and rode side by side at the tail of the group.

'Dreadful,' Sket muttered, adding a few oaths for emphasis. 'Skin drying out in great blisters, poor soul.' He patted his satchel. 'Old Lorak gave me all kinds of medicines, herbs and salves – mostly for Farn but I hope the salves work on that poor creature. How it could have lasted that ride last night without so much as a peep of complaint I don't know Navan, I just don't know.'

He looked up as the black shapes of the Dragons flew slowly overhead. They could see, in the brilliant light of a million stars, Tika on Farn's back still cradling a small shape in her arms. The ground was less strewn with large rocks now and Ren reined back, Sket and Navan moving aside so he rode between them.

'Tika asked me to see if Hadjay knew anything of the gijan. She said she thought he was the most sympathetic of the Qwah.' Ren snorted in disgusted contempt, his silvered eyes flashing between Navan and Sket. 'He said they were vermin,' he said through gritted teeth.

'You mind spoke Tika with Hadjay's words didn't you?' Navan remembered Tika's sudden rigidity.

Ren nodded.

'I have done what I can for the little one although it isn't much more than Tika or the Dragons can.' Grek spoke in their minds. 'The problem is that you must get those gijan to Namolos. But if one dies out here, the others will die also. They are litter mates.'

'I do not understand,' Navan complained helplessly. 'Do gijan have litters as do mice or hoppers?'

'Exactly so. I have not come across gijan before although I have heard stories, rumours. They birth their children in litters numbering three to five. Very occasionally they produce only one or two but the average number is three.' Grek paused. 'It is essential that these three reach Namolos with Tika. Khosa says that the fate of an entire race hangs on the survival of these particular three.' The unbodied entity sounded rather peeved. 'Khosa seems to know a great deal more than she is willing to share with the rest of us.'

Chapter Six

If anything, the heat was even worse throughout the next day. Sleep proved impossible even for Riff and Pallin. The company became ever more concerned at the condition of the gijan. Tika and Maressa gave half their own water ration to the nearly unconscious creature. Sket worried that there would not be enough of Lorak's salve to last the length of their journey, especially if the remaining two gijan succumbed.

At first, those two still relatively fit had refused any but Tika to open their brother's shirt. Eventually, they allowed Sket and Maressa to work on his exposed chest but adamantly insisted that the hood and mask remain in place. Tika found the gijan's body was as dappled as his hands, with odd octagonal patterning etched in faint lines of gold and green. There were also four sets of closely paired nipples down the centre of his chest and upper stomach. When she and Maressa gently turned the gijan onto his side to work on his back, they could only stare.

Hot swellings on each side of his upper spine stretched the skin painfully taut. The two gijan kneeling with Tika moaned softly then one began a soft trilling song. It faltered a couple of times but gradually seemed to gain in confidence and his song steadied and strengthened. Khosa squeezed between Tika and the singing gijan and sat staring unblinkingly at the prostrate gijan's back. Turquoise eyes flicked up to Tika's face.

'They have forgotten,' she said, sadness in her mind voice.

'Forgotten what?'

'They have forgotten the songs. There were many songs I think which had to be sung in a particular order. And there is no elder to sing to them. These are litter mates. This one seems to have trace memories of the singing rites but he does not know them all or the order in which to sing them.'

'Do you not know the songs Khosa?'

Khosa moved out of their way. 'Only Namolos just might

know now. There are no elders left with the memories.'

Tika winced, both at Khosa's words and at the heat from her egg pendant. Impatiently she pulled it free of her shirt and bent to soothe Lorak's salve over the gijan's hot skin. The three Qwah ignored the gijan completely, looking anywhere but directly at the tiny creatures. Kirat had told them that the first days in the southern desert would be hard – he had been only too accurate. By the time they halted at dawn on the sixth day and set up their camp, all of Tika's party were exhausted except for the Dragons. But the heat that day was fractionally less severe.

Halfway through the next night Storm called in urgent distress, losing height rapidly to settle on the sand. Ren, Sket and Navan rode back to the sea Dragon even as the other Dragons landed amid flurries of sand. Gan strode from Seela to Storm, scooping a second gijan into his arms and laying him gently across his lap. The same blisters were cracking across this gijan's chest as had happened with the first.

'You go on after the others,' Gan ordered Ren and Navan. 'Sket will stay with us now but you cannot fall too far behind those star-cursed Qwah.'

Navan took Sket's horse and with Ren cantered after the disappearing cavalcade.

'Storm, I think it best if this last gijan rides with Maressa and Brin. Should he collapse too, he would surely fall to his death unless someone was there to hold him secure.'

Storm shifted from foot to foot, faceted eyes whirring in agitation.

'It would be best,' Farn murmured, twining his neck around Storm's. 'When they are recovered, they can return to you.'

Tika felt tears threaten. Farn had no idea what a desperate plight two of the gijan were in, his chief concern at this moment was to offer comfort to his friend's unhappiness. Sket was carefully wrapping the second gijan's tiny body in its white cloak. Gan stood up, the gijan looking like a mere baby in his arms. Seela turned her head, studying the gijan closely, then she looked towards Brin.

'Fly on Brin, until you are free of these lands. Tell us how far you have to fly before you find water. For water is what these poor little ones need.'

Maressa had been unable to estimate even with her abilities as an air mage, how far the desert extended. She had told how great storms of whirling dust clouds blocked her vision to the south. Brin waited until Maressa had lifted the third gijan onto his back and had climbed up herself. Then he was in the air, speeding after the horse riders, and was quickly lost to sight against the star filled sky.

When they stopped for the day's shelter and rest, Pallin came to help work on the two nearly comatose gijan. He muttered and clucked as he worked and after watching his surprisingly gentle hands moving over the gijan, Tika left him and slumped against Farn's side. Khosa crouched next to her.

'Will they live Khosa?'

'They are so weak and frail yet so much rests upon them.' Khosa's voice sounded distant, as if she spoke to herself rather than to Tika.

Two more nights and days passed before Brin bespoke Seela. She immediately passed word to Tika who could scarcely keep awake, clasping an inert gijan in front of her on Farn's back.

'Brin has found water. He shows me the direction by the stars and also by the land. Should we go to him now Tika?'

Tika's mind was blurred with exhaustion. 'Wait until Kirat calls a halt. If we can try and rest well tomorrow, then we will decide.'

When Kirat did at last stop at daybreak, Tika nearly dropped the gijan she carried, stumbling from Farn's back in a daze. Navan was beside her instantly, one arm round her waist, the other taking the gijan from her. She swayed, her legs buckling, and Navan had no difficulty in pushing her down against an anxious Farn. She struggled to regain her feet then Ren's face hung over her.

'Sleep,' was all he said, and she did, helped by a tendril of compulsion from both the Offering and from Seela.

When Tika awoke at sunset, she found the decisions had been made without her. The Dragons would hurry ahead and the five horsemen would catch up as they could. It was deemed prudent for Ren to stay with the group led by the Qwah – he could far speak better than Olam so would take guidance from the Dragons as to their location. Accordingly, Gan approached Kirat when the camp was struck.

'Some of us must part company with you Kirat. Several of us will take the gijan on with the Dragons much faster than if we hold back to the speed of your horses. We appreciate your knowledge of these fierce lands and thank you for guiding us thus far.'

Kirat stared at Lady Emla's Captain of Guards. 'You risk your lives going unguided, and for what?' He flicked a contemptuous glance to where the two gijan lay. 'I told you that they are only seen in the inner part of our City – if they venture from there, they are killed like the vermin they are.'

Gan's face remained expressionless. 'You are entitled to your opinion Kirat, but it is *our* opinion that the gijan are living, intelligent beings, at present in dire need of help. We intend to offer them that help.'

Kirat's hand rested on the hilt of the curved blade that hung from his belt and Olam shifted his position as Hadjay and Sirak moved to flank their brother.

'The Survivors commanded you to guide us, I think.' Gan inclined his head slightly. 'Our friends still have need of your skills. Perhaps we will meet again beyond this desert but if not, again I thank you.'

Keeping his hands clear of his own sword and dagger, Gan turned slowly away from the Qwah. For a moment there was a tense stillness beneath the awning. Then Hadjay spat noisily and a gobbet of phlegm landed very close to Gan's boot. He ignored it and simply stooped to lift one of the gijan. Olam accompanied Gan to Seela's side.

'Watch carefully Olam,' Gan whispered, 'I think maybe the Survivors' orders don't hold so firm this far from the City. It would be easy to report an "accident" in a storm or some such. Keep watch my friend.'

He reached down from Seela's back and clasped Olam's forearm in farewell. 'We should meet in two to three days by my reckoning, but take care and watch those Qwah.'

The three Dragons lifted skywards and Seela bespoke them all. 'There is a risk in this. We must fly fast to get as close to Brin as we can before the sun rises.' She turned her head towards Farn and Storm. 'You must tell me when you need to rest. It will not help us if you fly to your limit and then need time to recover. We can halt as many times as you need.' Her eyes flashed in the starlight. 'Now hatchlings – let us find Brin.'

Tika preferred not to remember that flight later: twice they landed before dawn and then, with the sun rising, so did the dust and sand. They huddled on the ground, the few rocks insufficient shelter for an adult great Dragon. Seela spread her wings, hooking the talons on the wing edges into the hard ground, and ducked her head under her chest, offering what cover she could for the three humans, two gijan and two young Dragons.

When the strange rattling and shrieking wind finally passed, Seela's back scales were scored with scratches and her leathery wings bleeding in places. She dismissed Tika's concern.

'The sun is higher than I would wish but one more effort will get us to Brin.'

That last burst of energy through the hottest part of the day exhausted and frightened Storm and Farn, but just as they thought they could go no further they heard Brin's bass trumpeting, and saw the crimson Dragon ahead of them beside a long narrow stretch of water. Tika was terrified when they landed. She gave the gijan she carried straight into Maressa's arms and turned her attention to Farn.

Like Storm, the silver blue Dragon had sunk to his belly, his neck and head extended along the ground. His whole body trembled and his half closed eyes were dull. Sket was already searching through the pouches and pots in his satchel for the herbs provided by Lorak, and he hurried to the small fire Maressa had burning. He noticed, as he mixed pinches of herbs with water from the hot can over the fire, the third gijan lay motionless in the small shade of a boulder. Khosa, released from her sack, crouched beside that gijan, bristling with concern.

'Stars, what a mess,' Sket muttered, stirring the herbs with a grimy fingertip.

He took the bowl to Farn and helped Tika force half the contents into Farn's mouth. They repeated the procedure with Storm. Brin watched, his eyes whirring dark rose.

'There is prey not far from here – I will fetch food for you all.'

He lifted away from them as Sket turned his attention to Seela's torn wings. Farn and Storm were asleep where they lay before Brin returned with two goats. Gan hoped fervently they were wild goats: he did not feel up to dealing with irate farmers right now.

The sun was setting again by the time Tika was sure she had done all she could for the Dragons. She sank down by the fire, gratefully accepting a bowl of tea from Sket, and for the first time took note of her surroundings. She hadn't realised they had left the desert. Behind their tiny camp, sheer cliffs rose higher than any she had seen on the coast. Maressa smiled.

'The desert just came to an end. I have not managed to see any sort of trail up or down those cliffs. The ground just drops away and the desert is out of sight – as if it doesn't exist.'

'Oh it exists all right!' Tika said with feeling and a rueful smile.

The long narrow lake beside which they camped was fed by water welling presumably from somewhere in the cliffs to the north. How water could come from beneath such barren and sterile desert was a mystery to Tika and Sket at least. Tika was tearfully relieved to find that both Farn and Storm were back to their normal spirits next morning, eager for the meat Brin had brought while they'd slept.

The state of the gijan gave Tika pause: all three were unconscious. Maressa managed to get small drops of water into them by gently massaging their throats to make them swallow reflexively. She had also removed the hoods and masks and Tika stared at her first sight of gijan faces. Broad across the forehead narrowing to sharply pointed chins, short straight noses and the now familiar dappled skin. Their hair was as black as Tika's own but it rooted from their skulls down into a vee, ending at the top of their spines. Their ears were upswept, set further back than Tika would have said was usual, but they emphasised the similarity to Mim once again.

'If only we knew what's wrong with them,' Maressa said, wringing out another piece of cloth and spreading it on a gijan chest.

Tika scanned the area for Khosa, eventually seeing her crouched between Seela's enormous feet.

'It seems to me Khosa that you at least have spoken to this

Namolos. Can you not ask him what we should do? You say the gijan must reach him – they are too ill now for us to move them even a league further.'

'I cannot.'

'What do you mean – you cannot?' Tika snapped.

'That is what I mean Tika: I cannot.' Khosa crept towards Tika, her posture indicating extreme misery. Tika stared at the Kephi in astonishment.

'Namolos reaches me. I cannot reach him. He is still too far for me to mind speak him.'

'I could reach him,' Grek offered diffidently.

The rough grass flattened in a spiral pattern as Grek belatedly indicated his position. Khosa's eyes blazed in a mixture of anger and excitement.

'I should have thought of that,' she said. 'Oh yes Grek, find Namolos. He is on one of the islands set out in the western sea. Beg him to tell us what to do for the gijan.'

Tika looked around. 'Has he gone already?'

'Oh yes. Will you forgive me for not thinking to use Grek sooner?'

Tika and Maressa were both so dumbfounded at this apologetic Khosa, Maressa could only pick her up and scratch her ears. Brin spiralled down to land, looking smug as only he could. Gan raised his eyebrows and waited. Brin rattled his wings, paced closer and reclined.

'I have been looking for a place towards the setting sun where these cliffs might allow horses or humans to climb down safely.' His eyes whirred. 'There is just such a place, not far. And I flew very high and I could see the great sea again.'

Sket grinned. 'You're getting really sensible Brin – just like your old father.'

Brin huffed, smoke wisping from his nostrils.

'I believe that is two legs humour Brin,' Seela commented and Brin looked a little shamefaced.

Gan thought it best to intervene. 'That was truly helpful Brin – if you can mind speak Ren, you can guide him to the place you found.'

'I did, but he didn't answer. He heard me, I'm sure, but perhaps he was busy or talking to someone else. He did not reply though.'

Apprehension rippled through Tika and Maressa, apprehension not missed by Gan or Sket.

'How far do you think they have left to travel to get here?' asked Gan.

Brin considered. 'Maybe they will be here this time tomorrow,' he decided.

Sket checked the position of the sun: about midday. He looked back at the cliffs towering only two or three leagues behind them and scowled.

'Can anyone tell me why it's so much cooler here and yet hot enough to fry us all only that little distance away?'

'I expect Ren could.' Tika gave him a smile which quickly vanished as she bent to a gijan who had let out a high whimpering sound.

The day drew to its close and the gijan at last seemed more peaceful although whether that was a good sign or bad none of them dared hazard a guess. They had spent some time holding each gijan in turn in the water at the lake's edge which seemed to help them, cooling their skins at least. Now the four friends sat round the fire, the Dragons close by, and ate roasted meat from the goats brought again by Brin. Brin swung his head to the north, eyes whirring.

'Ren speaks,' he said.

They all listened in growing horror as Ren told of treachery by the Qwah. Hadjay had crept upon Olam who was keeping watch while the others slept. The resulting fight had roused them. Navan and Riff had killed Kirat and Sirak. Olam had taken a bad wound to his side but lived. The others had lesser cuts and bruises but Hadjay had cut the ties holding the awning which then fell on them, entangling them in its folds. By the time they had got free of it, Hadjay was gone. With all the horses.

Brin was aloft even as Ren continued his account, Seela close behind. Seela called back to Tika's mind.

'We must fetch them now. They will not last a day in that heat with no shade and no water.'

Gan smacked a fist into his palm. 'Was that planned by Kertiss, I wonder? Or just Qwah arrogance?'

'Arrogance?' questioned Maressa. 'They all seemed pleasant

and welcoming I thought, at least those we met outside the City.'
She frowned. 'But we didn't meet any inside the City, except for
the Keepers, did we?'

'Kirat's attitude to us from the first was superior,' Gan
insisted. 'And increasingly so since we left the City.'

Maressa shivered. 'Do you think Kertiss can spy on us here
with that pipe machine he has?'

'More to the point, has he any means to hurt us, even across
the distance we have between us?'

Maressa got to her feet. 'Come on Sket. Let's get plenty of
water ready if we've to deal with wounded anytime soon.'

Another dawn was breaking when Brin called from beyond the
cliffs. Farn and Storm rose impatiently into the air to escort the
adult Dragons to the camp. Both Seela and Brin were exhausted:
they had flown at their fastest speed both ways, and on the return
flight were burdened with the five men. Pallin rode Seela,
holding an unconscious Olam before him. Gan strode across to
help lift the wounded Arms Chief from Pallin's stiff arms. Ren
staggered and was caught by Riff before he fell.

Their faces were dirty, etched with weariness and, in Ren's
case, shock. He had never witnessed swords being used in anger,
or been so close to violent death and he was sorely disturbed by
the experience.

'Give Ren some of Farn's calming herbs,' Tika muttered to
Sket, watching Gan unwrap an ominously bloody cloth from
Olam's side.

'Thank the stars you found water,' Pallin croaked to Maressa.
'That foul Qwah left not a drop to clean a wound.' He stared at
the gaping flesh Gan had exposed. 'Seboth'll skin me should I let
his brother die.'

'Nonsense,' said Maressa briskly. 'Go and get some tea for
yourself, bathe in the lake and sleep. Gan and I will soon have
Olam tidied up.'

She spoke so convincingly the old armsman obediently
stumbled towards the fire. She met Gan's eyes. 'Well, we'll
have a damn good try anyway,' she amended.

Gan gave her an encouraging nod and went off to fetch water.
Olam's wound in fact proved far less severe than it looked.
Maressa thanked the stars that no major damage had been

inflicted and it was general blood loss that had rendered Olam unconscious rather than internal injuries. By mid morning the five new arrivals were all asleep, Sket sitting relaxed beside Olam ready to attend him whenever he might rouse. Farn reclined near the sleeping adult Dragons but Storm was close to the gijan, Khosa perched on his back.

Tika poured yet more tea into her bowl, and nearly spilt it all when Grek spoke in their minds.

'I have spoken to Namolos,' he began. There was something in his tone his listeners couldn't fathom. 'Namolos is truly amazing and you will learn much when you meet him.'

Tika cut him short. 'The gijan Grek. What did Namolos tell you of them?'

'I can show you what he showed my mind, but I have to warn you Tika you will find this hard. You must look at all I show you – *all* of it – and you will gain hope by the end.'

Sket had shifted across as soon as Grek made his presence known and Tika reached for his hand. Farn paced behind her, resting his chin on the top of her head. Storm and Khosa were also paying close attention.

'I will show you what has recently happened to your friend Mim in the northern Stronghold.'

'Mim?' Tika interrupted. 'What's wrong with him? Is he all right?'

The unbodied entity that was Grek was silent before beginning to speak again but in tones suggesting some exasperation.

'Will you just listen to me? I will tell you that now he is well but you must witness what befell him, remembering that he *did* survive.' Grek paused as though anticipating a further outburst. When none was forthcoming he continued.

'Your friend Mim is a Dragon Lord but he had yet to fully assume that title. I will show the pictures from Namolos's mind, which he took from someone named Chakar, who assisted Mim through his time of trial.'

Briefly his listeners were disorientated then quickly realised they were truly looking through other eyes, seeing as if they were actually there. Tika's nails dug into Sket's hand, seeing Mim crouched in a corner, tears flooding down his scaled cheeks. They saw hands lifting him, placing him on a bed, cutting away his jerkin. Hands moved poultices and the same hands suddenly pressed down on the great swelling they saw along one side of Mim's spine. Fresh blood spurted from the swelling as the hands increased their pressure. Farn rattled his wings and Tika was peripherally aware that Seela and Brin were sharing this terrible vision from Grek's mind.

The hands clenched briefly above Mim's back. Then, as if their owner forced herself to action, fingers dug into the bleeding gap. Maressa gasped aloud and clapped her hands to her mouth. The hands gently tugged something from the blood. Slowly and with infinite tenderness, the wing was extended over a chair beside Mim's bed. The pictures vanished and they were left with only Grek's voice.

'Namolos says it was not done thus millennia past, but this is a time of new beginnings. He says this is what you must do for the gijan. But he gave me another picture to show you.'

This time all except Seela and Storm recognised the Stronghold's great hall. The eyes through which they saw were fixed on the ramp to the upper levels. And Mim walked into view, pausing to look down into the hall, his eyes seeming to meet theirs for a moment. Then great feathered wings unfurled from behind him and with three beats of those wings he stood beside his soul bond Ashta.

Again the vision disappeared.

'Mim is truly Dragon Lord,' Khosa said.

'But you will have to help the gijan as Chakar helped Mim,' Grek emphasised. 'Namolos says there is danger in this method of freeing their wings even as there was great danger for Mim's life. Namolos asks that you do your best for the gijan but you must not blame yourselves should you fail any or all of them.' He repeated the warning. 'It is a time of great peril for the gijan. At the moment the gijan are genderless: this is the time they become either male or female. Added to that, these three are the first of many generations to grow wings. Their peril is great.'

Chapter Seven

Kertiss was in Singer's chamber beneath the great Dome. Singer's windows were concealed, the entry closed. Kertiss had been raging moderately for some hours but was now building to a crescendo of hysterical anger. Singer listened in silence, the memory systems in the Ship's circuits recording Kertiss's abuse. Singer wasn't sure why he'd activated the recording cubes but it occupied him briefly. He was trying not to listen to the ranting outside. He could have switched off the outer sound receptors, but he thought that would be rude.

Star Singer, like many of the Ships, was a strangely contradictory personality. Yes, the brains of those transfused into the Ships were capable of tremendously advanced and sophisticated thought processes. But emotionally many of them were still less developed than five year old human children. Singer was one of the youngest of the Ships and his first Captain was Mazan.

Mazan had spent hours and days getting to know Singer before he was integrated into the Ship's fabric. He had liked Mazan from the beginning, but by the time of Singer's first flight as a fully operational Ship, he loved her. He worked with her, plotting courses, checking instrumentation and handling the automatic maintenance systems. Mazan laughed with him, told him stories and riddles. She brought music cubes into the ship and told him of the different styles of music from the many worlds she had already visited.

They had been recalled to the home planet for reassignment to a group project when Singer's world went mad. Mazan had left him to attend a final briefing session before their departure on a team survey mission. Singer was trying to learn an amazingly long and complicated song, with triple harmonics, to surprise and please Mazan on her return. He didn't hear any of the transmissions on the news casts – he wasn't interested in news at any time. Singer was only alerted that something was wrong by the sound of sonic weaponry in use somewhere close to his launch bay.

He immediately pulsed a call to Mazan's identlink but she did not respond. He transmitted urgently to the other Ships he knew, but heard only fragmented conversations and a pervading sensation of panic. Then someone accessed entry and he scanned for Mazan. But it wasn't her. He did not know the man or woman who were scrambling into the navigation seats.

'Where is Mazan? Who are you?' Singer demanded.

'Just get us out of here, Ship – now! Follow Arrow and Wing – see! They are just ahead of you!'

'No. Where is Mazan? She is my Captain.'

'Do what you're ordered, Ship!' The man screamed at Singer. 'Mazan is dead, now obey me at once and fly!'

It was only much later that Singer understood how near to insanity his overwhelming grief had taken him. He felt a loss within him that he couldn't encompass or deal with. In a stupor of uncomprehending pain, Singer had followed the group of Ships and passively obeyed Kertiss's orders.

Star Dancer was one of those Ships, older by far than Star Singer. She had heard of the loss of Mazan and she persisted in trying to talk to Singer. He hadn't answered her, or anyone else, for years, but slowly, slowly, Dancer breached Singer's pain and began to help him heal.

All the Ships sang in flight and gradually Dancer persuaded and gently bullied until at last Singer joined in. The Ships sang outwards: rarely did their passengers hear their songs. The Ships sang for themselves, for the freedom they might never have known, and they sang for the stars they flew between.

Now with Kertiss still shouting outside, Singer began to hum one of the thousands of melodies he'd composed in his life as a Ship. Kertiss fell silent then renewed his tirade.

'You will answer me Ship! If you can warble then you can speak. What did you tell those ignorant fools I mistakenly allowed within this sacred Dome?'

Singer allowed himself to be baited while hoping to sidetrack Kertiss.

'Sacred?' he asked thoughtfully. 'This Dome is dedicated to a divinity, is holy, is built for religious rites? I had no idea of that Kertiss. I thought you disparaged such philosophical aberrations. Have you then discovered the origins of the Dome's construction at last? Do tell! I find it fascinating.'

Beads of perspiration shone on Kertiss's brow. 'Answer me Ship. Are you deliberately blocking my communications with other Ships? If you are, I will dismantle you piece by piece.'

Singer's reply was spoken meekly. 'Kertiss, you have sealed the area above. I cannot transmit beyond this Dome unless you retract the exclusion shields. How can I block any incoming contacts?'

Kertiss scowled but Singer continued. 'Perhaps there has been some fluctuation in the atmosphere which adversely affects wave transmission. You told me the atmosphere on the other side of this planet is now totally distorting any kind of surveillance beams.'

Kertiss let his breath out in a gusting sigh. 'You may be right, but this loss of contact with any other Ship is serious Singer. We are isolated enough in this desert.'

'But I thought you ordered me to land here because it was isolated?' Singer asked innocently.

'Such isolation suits me and Orla – to a degree. I had not thought to lose contact with all Ships.'

Orla emerged from one of the passages.

'The Ship was damaged before we landed, Kertiss. You know it was never normal. Leave the damn thing and help me get through this interference. It seems to be increasing on every frequency I use.'

Kertiss followed his sister without another word to Singer.

Alone again, Singer wept silently for a little while, then he remembered that wonderful evening when those men had sat with him, telling him stories. And that song the old one had sung! Pallin – that was his name. Oh how they'd laughed as he sang. Singer chuckled at the memory: it had been quite a rude song too.

Singer had memory cubes encoding the record of the long journey to this world of Kel-Harat. To pass the time, he occasionally studied some of those cubes. The Ships had transferred from star system to star system, twitching aside the curtain of Time to escape detection from any pursuers. They had circled strange planets: gaseous giants on which nonetheless were intelligent life forms. Such creatures fascinated the Ships and many of their Captains. But a handful, like Kertiss, refused to waste time surveying such worlds or trying to establish contact with their inhabitants.

Singer found it mildly amusing that it was Kertiss's insistent plotting of one particular Time Slip which took them backwards, into a known region of the Cosmos. Unfortunately they had emerged almost directly in the path of a scout ship of their Conglomeration enemies. After Time Slipping, there was always a brief period of disorientation: Ships and Captains checking that they were in fact where they had intended to be. The scout ship used that hiatus to summon combat ships and Singer learnt what real damage could be done with the weaponry he and the other Ships carried.

Singer had never used his weapons except in routine practice simulations and only now fully understood the devastation they could wreak. With Kertiss screaming at him, Singer instigated his own course and flipped into the fabric of Time. To his immense relief, most of the other Ships popped into existence around him, some by order of their Captains but others, like himself, under their own volition.

The Ships drifted in this pocket of Time, watching for any appearance of Conglomeration combat ships which might have been fast enough to trace and follow their course. When none appeared, Captain Namolos plotted a course into the spiral arm of the Repsian Galaxy. There was a considerable risk involved. It was a very long Time Slip and the positions of the coordinated stars he was locking onto were only provisionally confirmed in the sparsely marked star charts of the Repsian region.

All the Ships loved Star Dancer: she had been one of the first of these biological Ships, and the others looked to her experience for guidance in most matters. Through their devotion to Star Dancer they held her Captain, Namolos, in great respect and also his wife Abesh and their daughters Lemora and Gremara. Namolos and his family were among many star travellers who had undergone extensive gene sculpting with an emphasis on longevity, regeneration and increased natural mind talents such as empathy and telepathy.

So the Ships didn't hesitate to follow Star Dancer although all were aware of the danger in such a long Time Slip. They had burst into Real Time above Kel-Harat and settled into orbit. Many Ships had suffered varying degrees of damage in the skirmish with the combat ships and knew that they would not survive any orbit to land descent. Others, Dancer and Singer among them, decided they could survive a landing but gave a very low estimate as to their abilities to escape the planetary gravity once they were on the surface.

Singer hummed an air from a Zeenolian opera and remembered the heaviness pulling at him as he descended to the planet. After many orbits Ships and their Captains had chosen various locations at which to land and Kertiss, without reference to Singer, had chosen the vast desert in the south of one of the land masses. He had found the long fertile Valley secreted in its midst with the three domed structures. Kertiss's scanning of that area had revealed extensive underground systems there and he ordered Singer to land as close to the Domes as possible.

The inhabitants had no technology capable of communicating with an interplanetary Ship and the first they knew of Singer's arrival was a booming thunder from a clear sky and then a great grey shape manoeuvring down towards them. People packed the open area around the Domes and, to Singer's horror, he realised that Kertiss was activating the Ship's weapons. Singer overrode Kertiss's commands, reporting vocally that there was a fault in the relay. Singer hovered before touching down in the lesser space amid the three interlocked Domes. Kertiss switched on outer amplifiers.

'I claim this land for my people,' he proclaimed to the throng outside.

Two males stepped forward and spoke in response.

'What's the language, Ship?' Kertiss snapped.

'It has a resemblance to Repsian Common Tongue,' Singer responded.

'Tell them to clear this whole area and to come no closer until I summon them.'

Singer obeyed. He was increasingly uncomfortable with Kertiss's attitude and wanted no one hurt if he could prevent it. One of the males spoke in reply.

'Well?'

'He tells us to be gone. This is a special place of great veneration to these people and we pollute it by our presence.'

Singer was taken by surprise by the speed with which Kertiss accessed the door and emerged, a psionic disruptor in his hands.

'Tell them once more to get out of here,' he called to Singer.

Again Singer obeyed, urgency in his voice. But the males continued to stand there, a crowd pressing close at their backs. Kertiss began firing. He walked slowly and steadily forward, the firing button pressed to continuous discharge. He stepped around the first two male bodies and picked his way over those behind until he came out to the larger area surrounding the Domes.

Singer could see, over a mass of corpses, Kertiss coming to a halt and lowering the disruptor at last. The remainder of the crowd was vanishing into buildings far across the open area and Kertiss turned back to the Ship. Orla, carrying another disruptor and a scanning communicator, had already entered the largest Dome. By the time Kertiss had returned to Singer, Orla re-emerged from the Dome, a grin on her dark face.

'They had technology at some time in their distant past,' she informed her brother. 'They probably think it's magic nowadays – what's left of it! There is room for the Ship to enter easily and it would be better if it was under shelter and close to us.'

She gave Kertiss a meaningful look and he nodded, stepping back inside the Ship.

'You will transfer to the Dome,' he ordered.

Singer retracted his wings and powered his external air circulation unit. He rose from the dusty stone slabs upon which he'd landed and followed Orla, floating on a cushion of air, to what would be for him, millennia-long seclusion.

Their camp site was by no means luxurious but after the desert it seemed nearly so to Tika and her friends. Rough grass covered the ground and was thicker and lusher around the lake. The scrubby bushes that clung to the lower cliffs grew fuller leafed and a little taller. In the distance, along the lake, trees were visible – willows and ash Ren guessed as he stared to the south. He and the four others the Dragons had plucked from the desert had slept the day round. They'd eaten, bathed in the lake and inspected Olam. He was being made to rest by Pallin and Maressa, much against his wishes. Ren turned away from the water and looked at their tiny camp.

Farn was close to Tika, and Storm lay by the three gijan. Gan had told Ren that Grek would repeat a message from Namolos shortly and then they would have to decide what must be done. Ren had checked the gijan on his way to the water's edge and saw at once that they were seriously ill.

Accordingly, the party gathered around Olam, and Grek repeated the information Namolos had given him. Silence gathered almost tangibly about them when Grek fell silent.

'May I ask why you wear the pendant outside your shirt Tika? I think you have always worn it hidden since I've known you. Is it to do with the gijan?' Ren asked quietly.

'It got hot again.' Tika's green silvered eyes met his. 'It has stayed at least warm for two days now,' she added more slowly.

'You think there is a connection?' Maressa queried.

Ren shrugged. 'I seem to have lost the ability to make connections between anything, let alone think, ever since I left the Menedula.' He gave a lopsided smile. 'And it seems years since I was there.'

'It is up to you, Tika.' Khosa was perched on Olam's legs.

'Why?' Tika demanded truculently. 'All of you have seen the pictures from Namolos's mind. Why must I be the one to do this?' She stared round at each face, finally meeting Navan's eyes.

'I have only heard tell of your great healing of Farn, but I knew as I saw those visions that it must be your hands that work upon the poor gijan,' he said.

'Did you know that Mayla taught me to read?' Tika asked abruptly.

'I suspected so. She has taught other females through the cycles. My mother could read, and had the power within her.' Navan looked down at the grass between his feet. 'Hargon killed her – he said it was an accident. She was in the pasture when unbroken koninas were released there and was trampled. I was fourteen cycles, Hargon twelve cycles older and already Lord.' He met Tika's gaze again. 'She was only a worthless female,' he said very softly.

Equally softly Tika asked: 'Who led the patrol when I ran away? I should never have been able to reach the mountains without capture. But I did.'

Navan smiled. 'I led the patrol. We went further west than the route I guessed you would surely take. You were only a worthless female – not worth injuring valuable koninas on rough trails for.'

Tika gave him a dazzling smile and got to her feet. 'We will need lights, Ren: can you supply plenty of glow stones? Water, both warm and cold. There is no chance of any ice here but there must still be some herbs left that will slow bleeding, Maressa?'

She went to where the adult Dragons reclined and hugged each in turn.

'I will need strength for what I must attempt my dears. Will you share yours with me in this endeavour?'

Brin and Seela both lowered their heads, nuzzling affection at Tika's face and shoulders. They accompanied her to where the gijan lay in a small still row.

'The one who collapsed first is most advanced in this process. Gan, would you move the other two closer to Olam. Olam, call out should they stir while we work upon this gijan.'

Tika watched Storm supervise the moving of the two gijan and saw how he settled protectively around them including Olam in his concern. She rolled her sleeves up above her elbows, turning finally to Farn and taking his long beautiful face between her hands.

'Love of my heart, this will be hard. Stay strong for me and calm I beg you.'

Farn's eyes whirred, shining pale silver blue with affection. He huffed softly into her face.

'But of course I will help my Tika. I will stay calm. And you will succeed wonderfully of course.'

In spite of her fears Tika laughed at Farn's endless faith and confidence in her. She hugged him tight, took a deep breath and moved to wash her hands in the bowl Maressa held ready.

Navan turned the gijan from its side to lie face down. Sket, Maressa and Pallin sorted what medicinal herbs each still carried. Riff had foraged for mosses of a kind well known to armsmen for their blood clotting properties and their suitability to pack wounds. Ren knelt at the gijan's head, as Daro had for Mim. He touched the gijan's mind lightly to check the depth of its unconsciousness and gave Tika a quick nod.

Tika placed her hands on one of the swellings on the gijan's back and bit back a moan. Fiery pain leapt up her arms. For a moment, as at Farn's healing, panic threatened to swamp her. Then she felt other hands rest lightly over hers.

'Put my hands under yours if you wish. I do not mind the blood.'

Shocked, she met Navan's gaze over the gijan's body. She drew a shaky breath.

'I thank you Navan but I believe I must be the one to touch him.'

Navan withdrew his hands and sat back on his heels. 'Remember we are all here Tika and we will help with whatever you ask of us.'

As soon as Tika applied a slight pressure, the gijan's skin split and hot thick lavender coloured fluid spurted over her hands. Slowly, she applied the same pressure down the length of the ridged swelling, the skin parting like an overripe fruit. Other hands mopped away the strange blood and Tika felt a surge of power within her and knew that Brin and Seela were lending her strength. Tika grabbed a piece of cloth and gently wiped directly down the open wound, trying to see within.

'Your mind, small one, use your mind,' Seela whispered.

Tika let the cloth drop and sent her mind within the gijan's back. The musculature was slightly different, the blood vessels not as she would have expected in a human, but she could see none of the major muscles or arteries were involved here. There was a long piece of matted stuff within the wound, almost like a splinter which has become infected in a finger. Her fingers dug firmly beneath what she knew to be a wing, and worked steadily to pull it up and out.

She was scarcely aware of the blood coating her hands and wrists, soaking her trousers. She was totally focused within the gijan's back. There was a wet sucking sound and the wing came free. With great tenderness Tika stretched it outwards, shuffling back on her knees to have space to lay it along the ground. It was darkly wet with lavender blood, and far larger than any of them expected, even though they had seen how large Mim's were. She left Pallin and Sket to wash and clean the wing and scrambled to the other side of the gijan.

Tika had no idea when natural light took the place of Ren's glow stones. She was astonished to see the sun well up in the sky by the time the second wing lay extended on the grass.

'His mind is still deeply shielded,' Ren murmured. 'I think he has shut himself away to deal with the pain – I did nothing to cause this sleep.'

Tika nodded wearily. 'There is still some fever and his body is shocked, but as far as I can tell he will recover.'

She lifted her pendant over her head and put it against the curve of the gijan's shoulder. Then Sket's arm was round her and Farn's face peered over her shoulder, eyes flashing with concern.

'She'll be all right, young Farn,' Sket said confidently. 'Let's get her washed and a nice bowl of hot tea inside her then she can sleep.'

Sket helped her to the lake and stripped off her shirt and trousers. She realised she was covered in lavender blood and shivered passively while Sket scrubbed her clean. Farn held her steady between his wings and his chest when Sket towelled her dry and wrapped a blanket round her. They had nearly reached the fire before Tika's knees gave out. Sket caught her up, carrying her the rest of the way but she didn't have her promised bowl of tea: she was asleep.

Tika woke to yet another day to find two Dragon faces watching her. Storm's grey eyes sparkled at her.

'Maressa thinks the gijan may wake soon,' he said. 'They are all waiting to see if she will know how to fly or if we'll have to teach her.'

'Her?' Tika stared at Farn, aware of her soul bond's delight in both her waking and in her surprise at hearing the gijan was female.

'She's a girl, Maressa says. I like girls.' Farn nudged her gently. 'Are you going to put some covers over you?'

Belatedly, Tika realised she was naked beneath the blanket. Trousers and a shirt were neatly folded under Farn's front leg. They were rumpled but at least they were clean. She dressed quickly, a vague memory of Sket stripping her and scrubbing her like a child giving her a twinge of embarrassment. Getting to her feet, she looked to the fireside. Sket grinned and waved a bowl at her. There was no sign of Brin or Riff, but Olam was sitting up, a more normal colour in his face once more.

Before joining them, she detoured to where the gijan lay. She was amazed to see how much the skin had healed already; sealing itself closed along the line of the extruded wings. Navan and Ren looked up as Tika reached them, broad smiles on both their faces. Navan stroked his hand down one of the outspread wings.

'She is so beautiful Tika. So beautiful. Why would the Qwah kill them? It must be gijan people whose statues stand in Singer's Dome, don't you think?'

Tika couldn't answer. The feathers below her were immaculate: a glossy blue black. But then Navan lifted the wing slightly and she saw the underside was the softest deepest pink. She shook her head helplessly.

'Will she wake soon, Ren?'

He grinned. 'You're the expert – you tell us.'

She stooped to feel the gijan's skin: it was warm now but not hot. She sent her mind lightly into the healing lines along the spine and found no infection. Tika picked up her pendant and slipped the chain over her head. It was cool to her touch once more.

Later, they were digesting their lunch – fish discovered in the lake by a very cheerful Storm – when Maressa called. They turned to look in her direction and Tika quickly went to the air mage. They stood a pace away as the tiny gijan's body stretched right down to the feet. Tika noted the four-taloned toes, the high arches to the feet, the incredibly fragile ankles. Then the gijan's wings shivered and furled closed against its back.

With a soft moan the gijan pushed to hands and knees, head hanging down. Tika squatted beside the gijan's shoulder and held out her hands.

'Let me help you,' she said gently.

The head came up: broad forehead, high cheekbones, pointed chin, black up-tilted eyes. The gijan took Tika's hand and sat back on its heels. Tika noted that the topmost pair of nipples were fuller, the definite female look to the small body. She stood up, still holding the gijan's hands, and smiled.

'I am Tika. Do you have a name at last little gijan?'

The gijan's head tilted to one side, then the other. The small mouth opened in a smile, revealing tiny pointed teeth. She pulled against Tika's hands, rising to her feet and her wings flared open.

'My life is yours. I am Leaf.'

Chapter Eight

Brin reported no signs of human habitation south, west or east for at least a half day's flight, so Tika and her companions were able to relax while they waited for Olam's wound to heal fully. They also knew that they would need to wait until both of the remaining gijan reached the point where Tika could help their wings from their bodies. The first gijan, the female Leaf, had been two days recovering, in a deep sleep, from the time her wings were freed. Gan estimated it would be ten days at least before they could think of travelling on.

Maressa and Pallin spent much of their time searching out herbs along the lakeside. Riff had taken to flying with Brin when the crimson Dragon hunted. All of them watched Leaf's development with absorbed interest. The first day, she furled and unfurled her wings, seeming to be fascinated by them. Then, the companions watched her begin to beat those amazing wings, lifting herself gradually further off the ground.

At twilight that day, she was suddenly flying, swooping erratically over Seela's head. Storm and Farn also lifted into the air, curving round Leaf and encouraging her to chase them. To begin with she stayed quite low but as Storm and Farn spiralled up over the lake, the gijan gained more height and then she was above the two young Dragons, soaring and twisting, as though she had flown forever.

Farn and Storm drifted down to land, watching Leaf pirouette against the evening sky. A piercing, ululating scream reach them, and again. After momentary alarm, the companions heard the delight in the cry and knew it must be a gijan's usual call of greeting. Leaf was breathless when she landed, her eyes glowing with excitement.

'The mothers tell us stories of gijan flying when we are very small, but I never knew they were true stories,' she exclaimed.

Her head came only just level with Tika's chest but she threw her arms around Tika, enfolding them both in her glorious feathers. Leaf spoke in the Common Tongue of Sapphrea although still with a liquid trilling sound. Birdlike, Tika thought suddenly, returning the tiny female's embrace.

Over the next four days that thought recurred often to Tika. Leaf pattered around the camp, taking a deep interest in whatever anyone seemed occupied with. But when they collected at the fireside for meals or for their usual evening conversations, she was restless. At midday on the second day Seela solved the problem.

'Rest on me little Leaf. I would be glad of your company.'

Often then the company saw Leaf perched happily on Seela's massive purple back, the gijan's feet dangling one side, her wings the other. Sometimes she lay on her stomach along Seela's neck, her open wings drooping which gave Seela a most unusual aspect.

'Her wings lie straight to her ankles,' Olam remarked, watching Leaf apparently singing to Storm and Farn from Seela's shoulders. 'They don't touch the ground as she walks, but she couldn't sit on the ground comfortably.'

Once Olam drew their attention to the fact, of course it was obvious. On the fifth morning after Leaf's waking, Tika was roused by Farn.

'My Tika, another gijan needs you,' his mind voice was urgent but calm.

Tika rubbed sleep from her eyes and found Leaf leaning over Storm's back, peering at her. She looked frightened. She had paid only cursory attention to her litter mates so far, but clearly she was now disturbed. Tika called Sket and Maressa to prepare water and herbs again. Navan tugged Tika aside on the pretext of pouring her a bowl of tea.

'Can you get one of the Dragons to take Leaf away from here for the day? I think she will be very afraid if she sees what you must do.'

Tika nodded, still surprised by this sensitive Navan. She thought Arms Chief Navan had almost completely vanished and this new Navan was a vast improvement.

'I will need one of them, Seela or Brin, to support me, but not both I think. And Farn won't leave me while I work.'

Ren had approached and overheard the conversation. He

glanced towards the Dragons. Farn was still near Seela and Brin but Storm was diving in the lake, rising in a splatter of rainbow droplets. Leaf hovered just out of range of his antics, clapping her hands excitedly. Ren hurried to Brin's side. It was Seela who lifted into the air, flying slowly towards the lake. She circled once, obviously mind speaking Storm and the gijan. All three flew south over the water, Leaf like a black butterfly beside Seela's huge body.

Almost at once Tika knew the second gijan's wings were going to be far more difficult to release than Leaf's had been. As soon as the skin began to split, lavender blood pumped strongly over her hands and legs. There were mutters of alarm around her but her mind plunged into the gijan's body. There! A major blood vessel had grown across the outer side of the embedded wing, stretched with the swelling and burst as soon as she had pressed against it.

The gijan body structure was different enough from human to worry her but she pushed the worry aside. Mentally she forced the two ends of the artery, one of which still pumped an alarming amount of blood over her, downwards, beneath the wing. Then she sought the tiniest filaments of each end and wove them together. She was not aware of Gan wiping her face with a cool cloth until she blinked and realised she could see clearly again. Perspiration still soaked her hair but no longer dripped into her eyes. Tika felt Brin's strength in her, like an immense rock, and paused to snatch a mouthful of water. With her mind she checked and double checked the repair she had made and began to extricate the wing.

When she moved to the gijan's other side Brin told her Seela was keeping Storm and Leaf a few leagues away, until sunrise at least. Tika looked up briefly, registering the dark star-scattered sky and returned her attention to her task. This time she looked beneath the gijan's skin before she touched it, but there was no faulty placement of an artery in this one's back. Eventually it was done and Tika again placed her pendant against the gijan's neck and shoulder. Then she slumped across his legs, utterly spent.

When she woke, Tika ached with exhaustion. She found Farn curled around her and Ren sitting to one side. He smiled.

'You did amazingly Tika. I couldn't follow all you did, but it made me realise what a huge strength you have. Now I believe the story of your healing Farn's awful injury!'

Tika yawned so hugely that her jaw cracked and her eyes watered. 'Is the gijan well? Is it male or female? How is Leaf?'

Ren grinned. 'Female. Leaf was very agitated when she came back. Seela and Storm could not keep her away any longer. She helped us clean the second wing – you were asleep by then of course.'

Farn huffed at the Offering. 'My Tika used a great amount of her strength: she had to rest.'

Ren raise his hands to placate Tika's soul bond. 'I was but teasing you Farn.' He smiled at Tika again. 'The gijan will soon wake. Her wings are black like Leaf's but the underside is pale green. As you saved her life in releasing her wings, so I think you must be the first, with Leaf, to greet her.'

Tika started to get up and groaned. 'I keep waking up and finding I have no clothes on.'

Ren handed her a shirt and trousers, his smile widening. 'Sket and Farn will let no one else near you. They dunk you in the lake, scrub you clean and wrap you like a baby.'

Farn extended his neck over the Offering. 'Well of course no one else will touch my Tika. Sket is our friend – nearly a Dragon.'

Tika gurgled with laughter wondering what Sket would make of that compliment. She pulled the shirt over her head. Ren tugged her to her feet and held her when she swayed.

'Thank the stars there are only three gijan,' she said ruefully. 'I don't know that I could cope with more.'

Before they reached the group clustered round the gijan, Leaf rushed to Tika's side, catching her hand.

'My sister wakes – hurry!'

'Do you know her name?' Tika asked curiously.

Leaf's head tilted from side to side. 'Naturally I know her name. But she must speak it first.'

Tika wondered if or when they would have the time to investigate these gijan people properly. She retrieved her pendant, finding it cool to the touch now. She watched Leaf's sister struggle, wings thrashing for a moment before the gijan was suddenly on her feet. The face was identical to Leaf's as far as

Tika could see, but at least the pale green of her under feathers would help tell them apart she thought gratefully. The gijan stretched its hands towards her, seeming to ignore Leaf at Tika's shoulder.

'My life is yours. I am Piper.'

'May the stars guide your path Piper. I am Tika and I welcome you among us.'

Piper's face lit with a smile and she hurled herself at Leaf. The company watched the gijan sisters greet each other, their feathers mingling, tiny hands patting and stroking.

'Breakfast,' Pallin interrupted gruffly and stumped back to the fire where their few pots simmered.

Leaf, clutching Piper's hand, led her to each of the group, introducing her formally. Olam chuckled when Leaf clambered onto Seela's back, hauling Piper up next to her.

'It's as well they're so tiny – Seela's the preferred roost it appears.'

Seela's long neck was curved over her back, her eyes pale violet, as she mind spoke her two visitors.

Brin reclined near the fire. 'Seela has said they are her daughters.' His mind tone was full of affection. 'She says it is many cycles since she hatched children of her own, and even her grandchildren's grandchildren are grown and scattered. She only sees them at Gatherings. She thinks it will be good to have little ones to care for again.'

Tika had only that day to rest before she was woken, to her surprise, by Grek.

'The third gijan's time has come,' he told her. 'The others sleep but I will wake them. This one will not be as difficult as Piper.'

Tika wished desperately that she could tell where to look when conversing with this unbodied entity, but even as she formed the thought her blanket twitched over her feet.

'Have you checked the gijan then?' she asked. 'Why didn't you say you could do that – you could have helped me?'

'I can see these things, child, but I can only influence or affect a mind. I could not heal physically.'

'Then why didn't you tell me there was such a problem with Piper?' Tika got to her feet and headed to where the last gijan lay.

'I wasn't here.' Grek sounded truly apologetic. 'I have been searching the area to the south, trying to find the best route for you all to the coast.'

Tika stopped in her tracks. 'Grek, if you are unable to do it, wake Ren please and ask him and Seela to keep Leaf and Piper asleep while I work on this gijan. And then wake Maressa, Sket and Pallin at least.'

To the watchers the day seemed endless; to Tika time was irrelevant, focused as she was on the work she was doing. But this gijan's wings emerged easily and took the least time so far, although Tika was drained by the time it was done. Farn was greatly distressed that she was so weakened and Ren agreed to ensure Tika slept now until her depleted strength was restored. It was the eleventh day since their escape from the desert when Tika once more approached the third gijan. Leaf and Piper stood hand in hand, trilling softly to each other as they waited to embrace their brother.

His blue black wings trembled then fanned half open, brilliant yellow under feathers gleaming in the sunlight. He stood before Tika and stretched his hands out to her.

'My life is yours. I am Willow.'

Willow was slightly taller and slightly sturdier than his sisters and, the company discovered, he was the one who had been the most forthcoming in the City of the Domes. In the evenings following his waking he spoke, from Storm's back, of the time he and his sisters had lived there. The Qwah held the gijan worthless, fit for only the most basic menial work within the Ring Complex. No gijan lived anywhere else in the City or the Valley.

'Have the Qwah outside the City any knowledge at all of your people?' Gan asked.

'I don't think so.' Willow's finely arched dark brows drew down into a frown. 'Some gijan are born in the Ring Complex. Others are captured. Certain of the Qwah – like Kirat – find pleasure in their yearly hunts in our swamp lands.'

'And you?' Olam queried. 'Were you captured?'

'Our mothers are in the City.' Willow shrugged, his feathers rustling against Storm's scales. 'If they still live, which is unlikely.'

Maressa took a deep breath and plunged. 'Your minds are shielded; even while you were so ill before Tika freed your feathers we could not reach you. That implies considerable power, Willow. The Qwah use mind speech but otherwise seem to have little ability in any other use of the power. Why have you allowed them to kidnap you, use you so harshly? I suspect you could have escaped if you chose.'

Willow laughed. 'I do not know if we could have escaped successfully, but it was foretold – this time of Suffering for the gijan. The mothers tell all children as soon as they begin to understand – and that is much sooner than Qwah children do.'

Farn huffed. 'Dragon children are also early to understanding, unlike human children.'

Leaf and Piper laughed from Seela's back, Leaf climbing down to join her brother on Storm. She leaned against him.

'Our birth mother gives us our names as we are born, but we tell no one that name until we have changed – become male or female.' Leaf explained. 'Our other mothers tell us the stories.'

'Other mothers?'

Leaf shook her head. 'We don't understand your ways: the Qwah have only one child at a time and only one mother for each child. How can one mother be sure that *all* the stories have been told to each child? And the stories must be told in a special order so the mothers share the tellings.'

Olam scratched at his healing side and Pallin slapped his hand away from the wound. 'Are these other mothers perhaps aunts or something?' he asked generally.

'No of course not. We have aunts as well as mothers. Mothers feed milk to us.'

Olam looked even more perplexed. 'Does your birth mother not provide your milk?'

Willow nodded. 'We are born in litters.' He gestured to Leaf and Piper. 'We are only three to come from our mother this time. Many of her friends attended her who had no litters, no children to care for at that time. They offered themselves as milk mothers and our birth mother chose two of them.'

'You were servants in the Ring Complex?' Navan felt a change of subject would be a good idea – birth mothers, milk mothers, children born in litters, were all beyond him. 'Did you go into Singer's Dome?'

Leaf and Willow exchanged a quick glance.

'I did sometimes.' Willow's voice was soft. 'I had to sweep the floor and tell a Keeper if the robes on the statues were still clean and tidy.'

'What are those statues?' Navan asked bluntly.

'They were our Elders. In the time before Suffering, we were a taller people and our skins were scaled.' Willow extended his arm and the dappled markings were clearly visible. 'When the tribes of Qwah gathered in the desert, there had been a time of great sickness within the Valley. The Elders' numbers had fallen through many deaths and too few children. The Qwah overran the Valley and the Sacred City and the few Elders strong enough to flee hid in the swamp lands to the east.'

'East? I thought that Keeper said the gijan came from the southern swamps?' Tika was thoughtful. 'Did you have any contact with other people there? Trading perhaps?'

'Yes,' Piper called. 'Our people knew the Nagum tribes. Our lands bordered each other.'

Her brother and sister nodded.

'In the twenty-seventh story,' said Leaf. She continued as though quoting: 'The Nagum folk are deserving of Elder friendship and respect. They revere the land and care for plants as tenderly as they do their own young.'

Later, Tika wandered back to her sleeping place deep in thought. She didn't recall Mim ever telling any stories of his childhood, or of his people. But then, he rarely spoke of his life before he'd bonded with Ashta, preferring to keep his memories of his slaughtered family well hidden in his heart. Tika spread out her blanket and waited for Farn to join her so that she could comfortably nestle against his side. The temperature was still warmer than she was used to but it was pleasant compared to the desert. Khosa suddenly stalked around a bush and came to crouch by Tika's feet.

'I wondered where you were. I've scarcely seen you since we've been here.'

'Lots of squeakers. And I found many cosy places to rest near their nesting holes, so I did not need to come back. You were busy anyway.'

Tika rested her hand on the orange Kephi's back. 'Is something wrong Khosa?'

'We must move soon. Kertiss has allowed us more than two ten-days. I do not trust him to let us reach Namolos as easily as this.'

Tika felt a slight alarm. 'Could he reach us, out of his desert?'

Khosa's tail flicked. 'I do not know. Grek may be able to go back and find out but we really need him to be our contact with Namolos should trouble arise.'

Tika felt rather more alarm. 'Khosa, if you know something more, for stars' sake tell me.'

'There is nothing more for now, but Hadjay will make a very bad enemy to have behind us. Don't forget, it was your men who killed his brothers. What I fear is that Hadjay will gather a group of others like himself – those familiar with the desert lands. If he persuades Kertiss that he has a good chance of catching up with us, I fear what weapons Kertiss may provide him with.'

At that moment Farn ambled up, eyeing Khosa with caution. 'I thought you'd wandered off and left us,' he said.

'So sorry to disappoint you.' She did her front end down, tail end up stretch, her claws extended into the ground.

Farn's eyes whirred in consternation. 'I'm not disappointed. I mean, I never believed you'd really leave. I mean …'

'Hush, dear one.' Tika hugged him. 'You're making it worse.'

'Well, as long as she doesn't think those two nice girls and the boy are birds.'

Farn's mind tone was intended as a whisper but Khosa turned to glare at him. She spat, lashed her tail furiously and marched off in Ren's direction.

'Oh Farn, why do you always upset Khosa?'

Farn rattled his wings. 'I don't mean to, my Tika. The wrong words come out – not exactly the ones I mean.'

'Then perhaps it might be best if you say nothing until you're sure you've got the words right.'

In the morning, Gan announced that he thought they should be moving on. Tika wasn't surprised: she suspected Khosa had probably approached several of the company with this idea during the night. Grek explained that he had checked their possible route

southwards and they would not encounter any human settlements
or farms for three or four days yet. Tika noted the gijan stared at
the same spot on which Khosa's gaze was fixed as Grek mind
spoke them. Khosa could apparently "see" Grek: it looked as if
the gijan could too.

Tika elected to walk with all the others, at least to begin with.
Pallin suggested Olam ride on Brin, but Olam indignantly
declared himself quite fit enough to walk.

'The exercise will loosen me up a bit. I'm stiff as a board
from all the lying around you've forced on me.' He glared at
Pallin, daring the old man to persist in his fussing.

They packed their scant belongings and by midday were
making their way along the western edge of the lake. The young
Dragons chased each other through the sky, then joined forces in
racing after the shrieking gijan. Seela drifted higher but stayed
overhead while Brin went higher still, ranging further south to
confirm Grek's account of the land they would travel.

They took an easy pace and for the first time Tika and Olam
had a chance to observe their surroundings. The cliffs far behind
them stretched endlessly, as if the land was formed in a series of
giant steps, Tika thought, remembering the towering barrier of the
mountains which hid the Valley of the Spiral Star. Her view was
increasingly restricted where taller bushes and slender trees began
to line the lake shore.

She saw a few of the long-legged white birds, some standing
motionless in the water, others flapping broad wings to get away
from the advancing humans. They saw an occasional goat but
few other large animals appeared to live here. Maressa pointed
out that the ground was only slowly improving from a dusty sand
to a darker soil.

'Grek?' she asked hopefully.

'I am here Maressa.'

'Are there any people with silvered eyes in these lands? What
may we expect nearer the coast?'

'I think none have silvered eyes, so it may be best if Ren and
Tika stay with the Dragons once you reach populated areas.'

'Are there many people in this land?' Gan carried Khosa at
the moment: she had draped herself regally across his shoulders.

'You will first come to quite isolated farms, then a few

villages before a much larger place. I do not know if it is all one town – buildings proliferate all along the coastal region, going inland perhaps two leagues. It is a busy place: many ships are anchored in its harbour.'

'Ships?' asked Olam.

Grek imaged a picture of ships.

'But I thought Singer was a ship.' Olam sounded aggrieved.

'He is, but he travels through the spaces between the stars: these ships travel on top of the waters of the great sea.'

Sket was aghast. 'Will we have to travel on one of those things?'

'I'm not sure. Unless Brin can fly from coast to island to island comfortably, then I think it will be your only option.'

Pallin scowled as darkly as Sket.

'I think the ships take five or six days from the harbour in the south to the nearest island,' Grek continued.

'Five or six days, in one of those boxes?' Sket sounded ill already.

'We have no coin,' Gan pointed out. 'Surely we would need to pay to be carried across the water to the islands? And you said there are many islands, which means many gaps between them to be crossed.'

'I have been trying to resolve that difficulty,' admitted Grek. 'So far I have been unsuccessful. From talk I heard around the harbour, some people who have no means to pay "work their passage", it was called.' The unbodied entity sounded extremely dubious. 'I cannot see any of you being able to do that. The people are so used to the sea, to ships and to smaller boats. Even children were dashing about on the water.'

The party walked on, all deeply thoughtful.

Chapter Nine

A day later, the lake beside their route began to narrow and flow faster. Grek had not replied when Tika called his name so they presumed he was seeking ahead again. When they made camp the second evening, the gijan sprawled in a tangled heap on Seela's back, fast asleep. Brin had not returned but Farn was content with Storm's company and did not fret for the crimson Dragon.

'I will ask Grek if Tika and Ren could perhaps wear the white cloaks in the coastal town,' Maressa said. 'If they kept the hoods up and their eyes down, surely they would be safe among us?'

Gan stretched his long legs towards the fire. 'I had thought that too. I would prefer we were together and the Dragons and gijan could stay out of sight well enough. Few people bother to look up at the sky for very long, so if the Dragons flew high enough, they would seem merely large birds.'

Farn's eyes whirred pearl and sapphire. 'We could be with you quickly if you should have need of us of course.'

'I'd like to stay with you and see this town for myself,' Tika admitted.

Ren nodded. 'As would I. I have seen only your town of Far in Sapphrea and that only briefly.'

'This place sounds much bigger than any I've heard of,' Olam remarked. 'They must have a great amount of farmland around it, to feed such a large number of people.'

'There were about twelve thousand people in the town of Syet,' Ren said. 'On market days and festivals it seemed as though half the world was packed into the streets. This town Grek describes sounds a lot bigger than Syet.'

The company lounged in comfortable silence, all trying to imagine twelve thousand people collected in one place.

Grek returned two days later to warn of a tiny village ahead. Gan explained their notion to allow Tika and Ren to continue with them, wrapped in their Qwah cloaks. Grek was cautious.

'It might work. At least you'll have a chance to put it to the test in this village you're approaching. There are six small houses, a couple of barns and sheds, only a handful of men and their wives and children. But be on your guard.'

The river beside which they walked had greatly deepened its channel now and rushed in a foaming torrent to the south. They followed its course as close as they could, occasionally having to climb over outcrops of white rock whose sides reached smooth and glassy down below the water. Tika and Ren already wore their cloaks, fortunately because, reaching the top of one such outcrop, they discovered two men below them on the other side.

A plough stood idle, harnessed to two odd looking animals while the men stood, feet apart and drawn swords in their hands. Riff and Olam were in the lead and halted at once. Olam held his hands well clear of his weapons.

'Stars give you good day,' he called. 'We intend no harm and would hope to receive none.'

As he spoke, Gan and Tika came over the boulders. An odd pair – one enormously tall and thin, the other child sized, swathed in a white hooded cloak. The others were pressing behind them now having heard Olam call out. The two men below stared in astonishment, their jaws sagging. They looked quickly at each other and sheathed their swords.

'Greetings strangers,' one said. 'Sometimes the wild tribes venture this far and steal from us. And worse.'

He spoke the Common Tongue but thickly accented: the r's rolled and the s's sibilant. Ren stood beside Tika and Gan now and it was apparent that the two men in the field stared hardest at the white cowled figures of Ren and Tika. Olam and Riff jumped down the last part of the bank. One of the men was unhitching the two animals from the plough: now he bowed towards Tika and Ren.

'Would you ride to our village and accept guest rights from our families?'

Gan towered over Tika and smoothly replied on her behalf. 'We all prefer to walk but we would gratefully accept your hospitality.'

The men exchanged glances again. The one now holding the

animals by their reins put his free hand flat against his chest.

'I am Zenidor and this is my brother Vanim.' He gestured southwards. 'Our homes are not far.'

'What are these animals?' Tika's voice was soft and emanated from the depths of her hood.

Zenidor's eyes widened hearing an obviously female voice addressing him.

'They are donkeys sacred one.'

Tika stumbled in surprise at being called sacred one but recovered herself.

'Are they usual animals here?' Ren distracted Zenidor's attention from Tika.

'Yes sacred one. What else could we use for heavy work?'

Pallin opened his mouth to comment but closed it again after Olam found the older man's ribs with a sharp jabbing elbow. Maressa reached out to touch the nearest donkey's long furred ears.

'Do many sacred ones visit you?' she asked, bestowing a dazzling smile upon Vanim.

'These are the first I have seen,' he whispered nervously back.

'How did you know who they are?'

'The white cloaks of course. All the stories of sacred ones visiting folk tell that they were hidden in white cloaks.'

'You must tell us some of these stories,' Maressa beamed. 'So many odd ideas get about – we can tell you which are the real stories and which may have been concocted beside a warm fire by a mischievous old one with a pot of strong drink!'

Vanim looked astonished then frowned. He nodded. 'Such things could happen I suppose. We will tell some tales over our meal, if it pleases you.'

'Oh it does,' Maressa agreed. 'It would please us enormously.'

'Are you safe, my Tika?' Farn's voice rang in Tika's mind.

'Of course I am, dear one. You just make sure you stay out of sight.'

'We will. Leaf is having a little rest on my back at the moment,' he added, a touch of smugness in his tone.

Tika suppressed a groan. Farn was still very fond of girls it would seem.

'Well don't let her fall if she goes to sleep,' she told him. 'I will speak to you later.'

The dwellings were sturdily built, two-storey houses of stone. There was a flurry of excited activity as the party approached, Zenidor and his donkeys in the lead. A child ran to take the animals, leading them towards a shed. Hens, slightly smaller and of different colours to Sapphrean hens, tiptoed about the barn doors. Zenidor took them to the largest building and ushered them inside.

The whole of the ground floor was one room with a hearth set at one end. Ovens and spits were built into the hearth and three women worked over pots and trays. After a basic diet of goat and fish, the smell of fresh bread baking was indescribably welcome to the travellers. The end opposite the hearth was set with three long tables with benches against the three walls behind each table.

'Please be seated. The women will bring you tea while I send children for the rest of the village.'

Two women brought pots of tea and clay drinking bowls. They kept their eyes on the table until Maressa touched the back of one woman's hand.

'Will you not tell me your names? Come,' she coaxed. 'Sit and talk with me until Zenidor returns.'

The women did as she bade but would only risk quick darting glances at Tika or Ren and spoke very little. By the time the entire community had squeezed itself in, the room didn't seem nearly so large. There was a buzz of general chatter until everyone had eaten their fill. They had reached the point where they were nibbling very sweet rolls, merely to fill the last gaps.

'Why do you travel through our country?' Zenidor asked finally, and silence fell throughout the room. Even the babies hushed their fussing.

'I am escorting my friends to the islands.' Gan took the role of spokesman. 'Have you ever been to the coast?'

Zenidor gave a short laugh. 'I went once, with my father. We had planned to be there for six days and we left after just one.' He shook his head at the memory. 'People everywhere. Buildings everywhere. We got lost every time we turned a corner. And the noise! Street traders, pedlars, Harbour City guards, temple bells and priests calling their followers. I don't know how folk can live like that, squashed against each other. Father and I left Harbour City the day after we'd arrived and scarcely stopped to rest until we'd got home.'

'What religion do you follow, or the Harbour City people?' Gan was wary. The Asatarians and the Sapphreans called only on the stars for guidance and revered the land for the constancy and permanence of both. He had, in his role as Captain of the Golden Lady's Guards, had to deal with instances of strangely deviant cults which thankfully were isolated and rare occurrences. He waited for Zenidor's reply with some trepidation.

Zenidor shrugged. 'In Harbour City there are many gods and goddesses. Many people there make their living on or in the great sea. It is a dangerous life – a storm can overturn great merchant ships as easily as a small fishing boat. So the people offer gifts and prayers to many different temples in hope of protection.'

One of the other village men, far older than the others, raised a gnarled hand. 'I am Zeminth. I lead our people here in the rites each cycle and the birth and death rituals. We pray to the land and the Elder Races.'

'Elder Races?' Tika asked rather too quickly.

The old man stared at her but the hood of her cloak shadowed her face completely. He nodded slowly but said nothing more.

Tika took a deep breath. 'Do you know stories of Dragons, or of gijan?'

The silence in the room was now dense enough to see it. Zeminth folded his hands on the table. 'They are Elder Races. We honour their memory and pray the time will come when they will walk these lands once more. Now, may I ask why sacred ones come from the north at this time? I was but a tottering child when I last heard of such an event.'

'I would first ask what you mean when you speak of sacred ones,' Ren leaned his chin on his hand, his face well hidden within his hood.

Zeminth frowned. 'The ones in white robes are the messengers of the Elder Races. They came among us often in the Time Before. There have been only a handful of visits in many generations now. Perhaps we have failed them somehow. Can you not tell us?'

'I think we must sleep on this. At sunrise we should leave, but we will speak of your questions then,' Ren spoke slowly.

'We would count that gracious of you, sacred one.'

The company were told they could sleep in this hall and were supplied with pillows and blankets for their comfort. Zeminth was the last to leave, leaning heavily on a much younger woman's arm. An orange Kephi shot between his feet and he turned back with a frown.

'Cats do not enter our dwellings – they live in the barns.'

Khosa leaped to Sket's chest and he grinned at the old man. 'This one travels with us sir.'

Zeminth's eyebrows rose but he let the matter drop and shuffled out. The door closed and Maressa sank onto a heap of pillows.

'Not a trace of mind power among them,' she said.

Tika pushed her hood back with relief. 'I thought not,' she agreed. 'What do you intend to tell them in the morning Ren?'

Silvered chestnut eyes met Tika's. 'You know full well.'

She grinned and curled among the pillows with a gigantic yawn.

They were given breakfast just before dawn by the same three women who had served them yesterday, then the company stepped outside. The air was much fresher than they'd experienced for days and they breathed it gratefully. The villagers waited for them silently, the old man standing between Zenidor and Vanim. The first sunlight sparkled on dew limning the stone roofs and the grass underfoot. Tika moved slowly forward, Sket at her shoulder. She stopped in front of Zeminth and raised her hands to push her hood away from her face. Even the old man could not repress a gasp when he saw her eyes: green as emeralds surrounded by silver. She turned her eyes to the sky and the villagers followed her gaze.

Four Dragons spiralled lazily down to land barely a man-length from the village people. Three gijan glided silently over their heads then dropped beside Tika, enfolding her in wings lined with pale green, deep pink and bright yellow. The one with the pink under feathers suddenly pounced, lifting Khosa with a trill of delight. Khosa didn't appear overwhelmed with pleasure at this treatment but she bore it relatively gracefully.

Farn paced forward, his silver blue scales flashing in the rising sun and pressed his brow to Tika's. His long beautiful face turned towards the three men standing in stunned stillness. His eyes whirred, with mischief had they but known it, and he leaned to press his brow to Zeminth's. Farn spoke in all their minds.

'May the stars guide your paths my friends. I am Farn, soul bond of Tika.'

Zeminth pulled free of the two men supporting him and staggered two steps towards Farn, his hands stretching, trembling to the young Dragon. Farn studied him, saw tears streaming down the old weatherworn face and gently ducked his head, letting Zeminth's hands rest upon his neck.

Seeing Zeminth's reaction to the Dragons the other villagers came hesitantly closer. Seela and Brin introduced themselves, radiating calm friendliness. Ren and Tika watched the gijan approach the younger people, realising how dependent on each other they must have been in the City of the Domes. Leaf appeared more confident while Piper and Willow held hands and stayed close behind her. Navan was commenting on how well these people accepted the unexpected sight of Dragons and gijan in their midst when an ear-splitting noise erupted from one of the sheds.

All heads turned to see Storm backing hurriedly away from the door. From within came braying shrieks and gasping wheezes. Storm's distress and embarrassment were plain to see but Zenidor's stern face slowly cracked into a smile. He caught Olam's eye.

'I believe the young one might have tried to introduce himself to our donkeys.'

Piper ran to Storm, draping herself along his grey neck and trilling to him. Tika looked across at Leaf and Willow. Yes, they were growing: at least their legs were. All three gijan wore only the loose trousers they'd worn in the City. Tika could see a clear handspan of thin leg above each ankle now, whereas before the trousers reached down to the gijan's feet.

Somehow the travellers found they were still in the village at noon, but they felt they couldn't depart in the face of such communal delight. A bench had been brought out for Zeminth and he sat, disbelief on his face, while Seela reclined beside him, her head lowered to his level. Tika and Ren were perched on a stone wall talking to Sket and Navan when Zenidor approached them.

'Please sacred ones, must you leave today? One more night can surely not interfere with your plans can it? I beg you stay until tomorrow.'

Tika smiled. 'We had been discussing that very thing Zenidor. Very well. We will stay one more night but we must go at tomorrow's dawn. We do not know how long it will take us to journey to a particular island in the western sea. There is some urgency in our getting there though.'

'My people find it a great magic that the Dragons speak inside our heads. They are so wise and gentle – truly Elders.'

Tika maintained her smile in the face of Sket's grin: Farn was behind Zenidor and clearly approved his comment on the gentleness and the wisdom of Dragons.

'He'll be unbearable,' Sket muttered with undisguised glee.

Storm worked his way carefully through the humans and settled beside Navan.

'I did not mean to upset those animals in their cave,' he explained.

Navan rubbed the sea Dragon's face. 'We know you didn't, but perhaps you should be very careful just where you poke your nose from now on.'

'Oh I will, I will.' Storm's agreement was heartfelt.

Later in the day, Tika joined Zeminth where he still sat, apparently immovable, on his bench beside Seela.

'You are glad to know that the Elder Races are still in this world Zeminth?' she asked gently.

He dragged his gaze from Seela's violet prismed eyes to Tika's face.

'I have been asking this beautiful one why we never knew the Dragons still live beyond the desert lands.'

'I wondered about that. But why have we, who live in those same lands, never known your people were here? We have never heard of these ships Zenidor spoke of, but if they travel among many islands, why have they not travelled north and found our people?'

Zeminth thought for a while. 'I have never been on a ship, or seen one, or visited Harbour City so I cannot answer your question properly. There have long been stories of terrible weather along the coast which borders the eastern desert. I have heard tales of great monsters, which drag ships beneath the waters of the western coast.' He frowned. 'The monsters and the freak storms are both said to occur where the desert lines the shore. Very few shipmen survive, even if they reach land. In fact, I don't recall any stories of survivors.'

Tika noticed his use of the word by which Kirat had referred to Kertiss, and as had Khosa when she spoke of Namolos. 'Do you trade or have any dealings with the desert people?'

Zeminth shook his head firmly. 'They are fierce warriors who seek blood. Zenidor at first thought your party was perhaps a small raiding force. They come occasionally, steal animals, children, women, kill the men and try to burn our buildings. We have not been attacked for perhaps ten cycles but my cousin's village to the east, three days walk away, was destroyed only a few seasons past.'

'We have told you that we must reach one of the western islands. Should we be especially wary in Harbour City or will we find any such as you, who revere the Elder Races?'

A gnarled hand covered Tika's. 'Do not let the Elder Ones be seen in Harbour City. There are many who would try to harm them, for many different reasons. But there are still temples to the Elder Races within the City: poorly attended and falling into decay I have heard. Wandering traders sometimes reach even to our small northern villages and they are welcome indeed for their news of the great world beyond our fields. The traders know that many of us still follow the Way of the Elders and so they tell us of our dwindling numbers of friends within the City.'

He fumbled inside the neck of his shirt and drew out a leather thong. It was threaded through an oblong of copper and Tika leaned closer to see the markings etched on one surface. A Dragon's face stared from the centre of the copper but the two wings flaring to each side were feathered wings.

'If you see a building with markings like this, or anyone who wears such a token, you may be safe. Be cautious, but they might be true followers and able to help you. Tell them Zeminth of the north sends you to them.'

Tika could not hide her doubts. 'Is anyone likely to know

Zeminth when you say you have never visited the City?'

'I was fortunate, sacred one. My father was a man who could both read and write. He taught me and my sister. Traders learnt to bring paper and books to him. I studied his books and collected more of my own. In my youthful arrogance I dared to write to a man whose book I found most puzzling and I gave the paper to a trader. A full cycle passed before that trader returned – with a paper from the man in Harbour City and a whole bundle of books!' Zeminth shook his head at the memory.

'I had my work in the fields but at night I worked over those books. The man – Nornay Vos Keptun – was a great scholar in the City and he sent me copies of many of the texts on the Elder Races over the cycles. I keep them in great safety – as you might guess. Most in this place can read and write – my father and then I and my sister taught them. I have two young ones who will take care of my papers when I pass from this life.

'Nornay Vos Keptun asked me to visit him in every paper he sent. Part of me wishes I had gone to him, but I was too afraid of the City. He told me he had given my name to the temples of the Elder Races so that they would welcome me should I visit.' Zeminth shrugged. 'I still receive messages from Nornay's son – Hariko Vos Nornay. Thus I would guess my name is still known in the temples.'

'If we pass this way again Zeminth, we should be greatly honoured to see those texts. Would you allow us to read them?'

'Of course. You are sacred ones. What is mine is yours,' said the old man simply.

Tika kissed his cheek. 'I hope to return to keep you to that promise,' she said. 'But I don't know what lies ahead. There are great troubles loose in the world which somehow I and my friends must help defeat. I beg you guard your people well.' She paused. 'We have come from a City in the very heart of the desert. Most of the people were ordinary farming folk, but there is a rottenness at the heart of that place. We insisted we leave and demanded guides to bring us to these lands. The three guides who led us tried to kill some of my friends. Two of the guides died, one escaped. I fear others may try to follow our trail so please Zeminth, keep a good watch for your northernmost fields.'

Zeminth nodded. 'Thank you, sacred one. We have places to

hide where we can survive for many days. Raiders rarely stay more than a day.'

A woman came from the largest house to invite everyone in for food and Tika offered an arm to Zeminth. They found Gan sitting at one of the tables with Olam and Pallin, in close conversation with Vanim and several other village men. Khosa sat upright on Gan's knees, turquoise eyes surveying each speaker in turn. Tika settled Zeminth on a bench and he caught her hand as she straightened.

'That cat – is she a sacred one?'

'Do you know, Zeminth, I'm really not sure. But she is most definitely not just what she appears to be.'

Tika and her friends left early next morning amid exchanges of good wishes from both sides. Zenidor walked with them for most of the morning, still following the course of the river. They crested a low rise and Zenidor halted.

'This is where I must leave you.'

He pointed ahead and went over the details, yet again, of their route for the next three days until they would reach the next village. He clasped hands with each of them and the Dragons and gijan landed beside him to bid him proper farewell.

'May the stars guide your paths,' he said, stepping back from them all.

'And may the stars guard your heart,' Tika replied in the ancient formal words of the Dragon Kindred.

Chapter Ten

The company made their way south. Villages became more frequent and increased in size. The Dragons and gijan stayed higher in the sky for longer each day, only risking landing with the humans if they were camping between villages and the night's darkness concealed them. From one hilltop they saw ahead of them a dark line of trees stretching to the southern horizon. They trod a well-worn trackway now and carts and wagons passed them regularly in both directions.

Once amid the forest, it was too dangerous for the Dragons to land and for four days and nights they communicated only by mind speech. Sket became concerned for Tika after the first day and night, staying close to her throughout the next day. It took the others a little longer to see how badly the physical separation from her soul bond was affecting her.

When Ren mind spoke Seela, she reported that they were finding it harder all the time to distract Farn. They'd had to stop him from plummeting down to his beloved Tika, regardless of his immediate danger from the closely packed trees. Tika became almost totally silent, her eyes fixed on the rutted track, in constant mind touch with Farn. Since she had seen him climb from his egg she had slept curled against his side, ridden daily on his back. Only when he hunted, or played with Storm, were they bodily apart. Gan remembered a conversation with Tika in the Domain of Asat.

Tika had spoken of her terror of being apart from Farn if he should choose a wandering life like Brin. He also recalled Kija's words, trying to explain the pain soul bonds endured should they be parted too soon or without the willing agreement of both. Tika knew Farn was nearby although out of sight, but being in this dark oppresssive forest without the reassurance of Farn's heart beat beneath her cheek when she slept left a gaping ache inside her.

Sket held her as she dozed and wept through the third night. Just before sunrise Leaf fluttered down beside them. She demanded she be given a white cloak and the gijan walked the day through, holding tight to Tika's hand. By then, they all knew they could not go on much longer with Tika's mind slipping into a permanent cry for Farn. Seela told them there was a bare hilltop poking above the surrounding forest some three leagues to the east of the trackway they followed. Without discussion Olam struck out in that direction.

At first the going was fairly clear but after the first league brambles and thorns hindered their path. Riff worked alongside Olam, hacking a narrow way through the undergrowth. The one advantage was that they encountered no other travellers crazy enough to try to pass through the tangled bushes. Among the trees dusk darkened their way early but Tika's head suddenly jerked up. Leaf trilled a call which was answered from above.

Branches swayed and rustled as Piper and Willow worked their way down a gigantic oak. All except Tika noted the ease with which the gijan hopped from perch to perch, their wings adjusting to their every movement. Leaf had discarded her cloak as soon as they were safely hidden from the wider trail. Now she curved one wing around Tika, leaning close.

'We are nearly to the hill Seela spoke of. Farn is there already.'

The ground rose sharply and as they cleared the trees at last, they found themselves having to grab at pieces of rock to pull themselves upwards. Gan and Sket, on Tika's heels, were nearly knocked backwards when Farn crashed down the slope. They steadied themselves against Maressa and Pallin who were immediately behind. Above them, they saw Seela, Brin and Storm peering anxiously down. Tika clung to Farn, his silver blue wings wrapped around her. Willow and Leaf flew on to join the three Dragons but Piper stood between the soul bonded pair and their companions. Her wings suddenly flared fully out and her expression dared anyone to encroach upon Farn and Tika's reunion. Gan reached a hand to Maressa and tugged her the last of the way to the hilltop.

'You can rest here tonight,' Leaf announced. 'Tomorrow Tika will come with us until you are through this forest.'

A brisk wind whistled over the exposed hilltop and Riff searched out the most sheltered spot where they might light a small fire and spend the night. Seela told them Tika and Farn were already asleep, both exhausted by the stress of being parted, albeit for only four days.

'We will fly on tomorrow and wait for you beyond this forest,' she told the company. 'I think it will be quicker for you to go back along the path you made today to rejoin the wider way.'

Her eyes whirred, pale and dark mauve mingled in the prisms. 'I should have prevented Tika walking with you. These last two days I feared Farn's mind would crumble in spite of Gremara's healing.'

Olam was leaning against the Dragon's flank and he patted the purple scales. 'We should all of us have realised,' he consoled. 'But it is as well we found out how badly they'd be affected here, rather than inside a great City.'

Navan agreed. 'Those last two villages we passed were much different from the first ones.'

Gan nodded. 'The people acted oddly towards us I thought.'

Maressa poked at the fire with a twig. 'Suspicious,' she said. 'Very wary of strangers, which is odd. Zeminth's, and the first few villages after his, welcomed us calmly and generously. Yet I would have expected them to be far more cautious living so isolated and subject to raids from the desert as they told us.'

Khosa climbed onto Gan's knee and began to wash herself, watching Brin. Brin had been very quiet ever since they'd left Zeminth's village. Now his great head swung to face Ren and Maressa.

'I have been searching my memories which, we are taught, trace our ancestral lines back to the first of the Kindred. But I find nothing of Dragons either in the desert or beyond it. There are memories of sea Dragons, and of snow Dragons, yet nothing of any others. Nor can I recall anything of the gijan.'

Willow, lying along Brin's back, stretched a wing lazily. 'We remember your race,' he said. 'My memories tell me we often Gathered together in the Time Before, on the great plains of your homeland.'

'And my memories tell only of the mountains far to the north.' Brin's mind tone was worried. 'Seela, do you remember? Is my mind damaged?' His eyes whirred in sudden alarm. 'Could that affliction be affecting me?'

'No, no,' Seela soothed. 'My memories contain nothing of southern Dragons or gijan either, although I have yet to ponder the term "Elder Races". I'm sure I've heard that before.'

The Xantip Palace high above Harbour City bore a great resemblance to a disturbed anthill. White-faced messengers pelted along corridors, hesitating at certain doors before mustering the courage to ask admittance to deliver their news. When the doors reopened to permit the exit of now green-faced messengers, loud alarmed voices echoed into the corridors. Eventually the disturbance penetrated to the personal quarters of the Grand Harbour Master Chevra himself.

One of his guards reluctantly tapped on an inner door and kept his eyes glued to the priceless Tooman carpet underfoot as the door opened.

'What do you want?'

The guard noted large, rather grubby bare feet then resumed his study of the carpet.

'The Councillors beg you attend them Grand Master.'

'They what? Gods and goddesses, what's wrong with them now?'

The guard tried not to hear the giggles from within the Grand Master's chamber.

'Well man, have we declared war on someone?'

The giggles were difficult to ignore but the guard was well practised at appearing partially deaf as well as wholly dense. 'Two ships have been taken, Grand Master, of the four traders returning from Meorlah. The two which escaped sought shelter at Kessal from whence came the news.' The guard refrained from fidgeting in the ensuing silence.

'I will be there shortly.'

The door slammed shut, the guard expelled a sigh of relief and trudged back to his post.

A surprisingly short time later guards swung open the great doors of the Debating Chamber and saluted as Grand Harbour Master Chevra strode into the room. Only two of those Councillors present bothered to get to their feet. The others merely glanced up then resumed arguing over a map spread before them on the table. Lessna and Tavri bowed to the Grand Master who acknowledged their courtesy with a nod. He stood at the head of the table, his hand on the back of his intricately carved throne, and scowled at the still seated Councillors.

'Is someone going to bother to explain?' he barked.

Argument quietened. A short plump woman with grey hair pulled into a tight knot at the back of her head, leaned back in her chair and smiled at the Grand Master. She looked more like a shopkeeper – a pastry cook even – than a Mage Councillor.

'From the description of the ships which attacked ours, it would seem they were Wendlan.'

The Grand Master sat down frowning. 'We've had treaties with Wendla since my father-in-law's time Vorna. They don't bother us, we don't bother them. Why would they suddenly attack our trading ships?'

The youngest looking Councillor answered him. 'We have noted for some time that students at the Higher Academy have been reporting odd dreams of a revolutionary nature. We alerted everyone naturally, but it seems to be increasing among the lesser trained.'

'And that means precisely what, Bajal?' The Grand Master was testy.

'At first we thought it may be a curious Wendlan mage student trying to reach someone similar here, but now we suspect it is more sinister.'

As Chevra still looked confused, Lessna's characteristic kindness – a major flaw in the opinion of her peers – led her to explain more concisely.

'There was a new leader came to power in Wendla quite recently we heard. He appears to have ideas of expanding his realm.'

'In this direction,' Chevra finished for her as light dawned. He drummed short stubby fingers on the table. 'Where is our army at present?'

There was a brief silence then Bajal cleared his throat. 'Army sir? Navy might be more use really in the circumstance, don't you think?'

'Well of course I know that!' Chevra glared. 'But I think the army should be strategically positioned rather than wandering around various borders all over the country.'

'There has been rather an increase in reported incursions in the north of late sir, from the desert.'

The Grand Harbour Master stared around the table at each of his Councillors. He folded his arms.

'You're supposed to counsel me. So counsel.'

One Councillor sighed. 'Sir, we have a fleet of fast small ships, as you well know – not warships of the type described to us in this attack. We've had no reason to for so long, after all. A few pirates now and then – that's all we've had to protect against. And fast ships are best for that. I believe there are a few warships still moored beyond Harbour limits, but their condition must be parlous by now, if indeed they haven't sunk.'

'Are you saying, Fental, that *my* warships have been left to rot?'

Fental nodded.

'Perhaps someone could go and check on their condition,' Chevra continued frostily. 'You say the surviving traders are at Kessal.'

'Here.' Tavri pushed the map up the table. The large island of Wendla was only just visible on the eastern edge of the map. To the south of Harbour City many islands clustered, trailing into a sparser region. Then the large expanse of empty sea and at last the outermost coast of Wendla. The island of Kessal under Tavri's fingertip was within the closely-grouped islands.

Chevra frowned. 'Was there any warning given?'

Lessna shook her head. 'The traders had taken copper out, to the Delmans and to Meorlah, returning with cargoes of spices.'

Chevra began to pace. 'And none of you, expert mages all, can find out what these Wendlan mind meddlers are up to.'

'Sir we have concentrated on other disciplines, like recovering the arts lost in the Wars of the Elders,' Sheoma began.

Chevra spun on his heel. 'How many thousands of years ago did those Wars occur? And you've discovered precious little from what I hear.' He scowled round the table. 'I want General Koolis here tomorrow morning. I want a report on the state of my warships. And then I suggest you lot start finding out how to get into a Wendlan mage's mind. Fast.' He marched to the door.

'Tomorrow. Early. With some answers.'

'Ignorant pumpkin,' muttered Taseen.

The company discovered Tika and Farn were gone in the morning, along with the other Dragons, but Leaf was perching on a jutting rock. She held Tika's boots and the white cloak was across her knees.

'We decided I would take Tika's place,' she announced calmly. It wasn't clear who the "we" implied. 'Seela was concerned that nine of you have walked from the north and word may have been sent ahead that nine strangers travel to the City. Willow thinks that two sacred white cloaks in your company would definitely be noticed so – I will become Tika.'

She hopped down from the rock and stepped daintily towards the fire on which Pallin was brewing the morning tea. She rested a tiny hand on Sket's arm.

'You will guard me now please, knowing the Dragons and my siblings guard Tika?'

Pointed white teeth showed in a quick smile and her head tilted quizzically at Tika's personal guard. He jerked a nod at the gijan.

'She'll be safe with them and you'll be safe with me.'

Once back on the main trail, they made good speed – when they'd devised a means of packing Tika's boots to save Leaf from blisters. Brin mind spoke them regularly, telling them Tika was deeply ashamed but as yet unready to communicate directly. She felt she had let them down by succumbing to her feelings. Brin told them also that they had seen Harbour City ahead of them and he relayed a mental picture to the company. All, including Ren, were dumbfounded at the endless sprawl of buildings lining a great curve of coastline.

'Storm longs to reach the sea again,' Brin said. 'I believe we will have to stay near the outermost edges of this place but do not worry: we can find you by your mind signatures quickly enough should you need our presence.'

'I sense the use of power within this place,' Seela added. 'It seems concentrated in a large group of shelters built high, set on the sunrise side of the City.'

'We will be wary,' Ren assured them.

Khosa was content to be carried by anyone who offered as they made the final approach to Harbour City. They found many tracks joined into the one they walked now and there were far more people and wagons around them. Khosa, from her position high on Gan's shoulder, peered down her short nose at the sight of Kephis clinging to sacks on carts and scuttling underfoot. One trader with whom they walked for a league, showed a great interest in Khosa. He was a well-dressed man, middle aged, with jewelled rings winking on every finger and in his ears.

'I have never seen a cat quite that shade,' he remarked. 'Is it for sale?'

'That would greatly depend on the price,' Gan began, then winced as claws dug deep into his neck. 'She is much valued you see.'

'I would pay well for such a rarity,' the man pressed. He dug in a pocket in his robe and gave Gan a small wooden disk. There was a long legged white bird painted on one side with a fish beneath it. 'Come to my trading house should you reconsider. Anyone will tell you where it is in the business quarter.'

He slowed his pace to talk to another similarly dressed man who had joined the throng from yet another side trail.

'We could do with some coin,' Maressa remarked.

Khosa began a wailing growl. She spat when Maressa turned innocent eyes up to her.

They spent most of a day walking with fields to either side of them: as Olam had predicted, such a vast City needed a great supply of foodstuffs. Several times they were pressed to the sides of the track as squads of armsmen, dressed in brown trousers and shirts with jerkins of hardened leather, passed by at a steady trot. The noise increased: goats, hens, the strange cries of the many harnessed donkeys, creaking wheels, children's yells and men's shouts. Leaf was clinging to Ren's arm, their faces well hidden within the hooded cloaks. They had found no place to rest at midday and the gijan's feet were rubbed sore.

Gan was fully aware of the sidelong glances many people gave when they saw the two cloaked figures. He nodded to Olam to close up on each side of Ren and Leaf as they approached the great red wall that enclosed Harbour City. The track narrowed and the crowd perforce slowed their pace. Slowly they filtered through a gateway, just wide enough for two wagons to pass. Three armsmen stood casually to either side of the gate, scanning those who passed before them. Gan saw one of the armsmen on the left catch sight of Ren and Leaf. He leaned to say something in the ear of one of his fellows. Gan moved straight to the left and inclined his head slightly, his bearing and uniform unmistakeably that of an armsman of superior standing.

'Would you tell me where I may find a temple of the Elder Races please? I escort two sacred ones but all of us are unfamiliar with your City.'

The three guards had instinctively straightened as Gan spoke and now the eldest nodded.

'The first temple is in Peacock Way sir, second left after Dolphin Square.'

Gan glanced in the direction the man indicated and could see only a heaving mass of people, a jumble of buildings and balconies and the waving banners of market stalls. The armsman caught Gan's rueful grimace and turned away, leaning into a dark doorway set in the wall.

'Boy!' he bellowed.

A boy of perhaps seven cycles popped out of the door.

'Guide them to the Elder Races on Peacock Way.'

Gan held out his hand. 'We lost all our coin on our journey – we cannot pay the child for his services.'

The armsman stared shrewdly up at Gan. 'No matter this once I'm sure, sir.'

Gan smiled. 'I will repay you as soon as I rectify the matter of coin.'

The man shrugged. 'A tin penny won't bring me to ruin sir, but as you wish.'

'Your name, so that I may repay you,' Gan insisted.

'Karn, sir.'

'Thank you Karn. Mine is Captain Gan Jal-Sarl.'

With another bow Gan turned and nodded to the boy. 'Lead the way child.'

Gan's immense height gave him the advantage of seeing where the child led them. The men formed a tight knot around Ren and Leaf while Gan walked close behind, his arm firmly locked round Maressa. The directions had sounded quite straightforward when Karn spoke them. But the route the boy took them twisted and turned through narrow alleys, wider streets and finally across what Gan guessed was Dolphin Square. Gan felt Maressa's body trembling and knew he too was beginning to find the constant press of rushing bodies unbearable.

The boy darted through an archway and the company stood for a moment in a small empty yard. The boy gestured to the building beyond, its double doors open above a shallow flight of steps.

'The temple of the Elder Races,' he piped, and disappeared into the crowds outside the arch.

Pallin wiped his sleeve across his face. 'I understand why Zenidor fled the place,' he grunted.

Navan pointed at the windowless walls to each side of the doors. On both walls was painted the same symbol they'd seen on Zeminth's token: a Dragon's long face with flaring feathered wings to either side. These were well painted. The Dragon face to the left was black, its carefully executed prismed eyes slate grey. The feathered wings were silver with brilliant scarlet tips. The Dragon on the right wall was dark green, its eyes pale lemon. The wings were red, tipped with gold. They stared at these paintings while they regained their composure. Leaf stood on one leg, tugging off a boot. Sket helped her with the other one, then shook his head at the bleeding blisters across her toes and heels.

'I can't wear them anymore today,' she whispered. 'No one will notice I'm sure.'

The cloak touched the ground but as soon as she took a step, the high arched four toed feet were clearly visible.

'Let's see if Zeminth's name is truly remembered here,' Gan suggested.

He and Maressa went first, through the doors into a dim atrium. A narrow central aisle led them deeper until the side walls pulled away into a circular chamber. Hangings of threadbare cloth hid the walls but a circular plinth stood in the centre. Lamps and candles flickered round the short stone column amid scattered flowers. Five robed figures knelt around the stone, heads bowed. Another slowly swept the floor. The sweeper looked up and came across to them.

'How may we serve you in the name of the Elder Races sir,

lady?'

Gan cleared his throat. 'Zeminth of the north sent us.'

The kneeling figures turned their heads then got to their feet.

'Zeminth?' one echoed. 'Hariko Vos Nornay will be glad to speak to any who come from Zeminth.' He bowed. 'I am Taza, priest of this temple,' he introduced himself.

He glanced at the sweeper. 'Send a runner to the Higher Academy. Hariko Vos Nornay must know of these visitors at once.'

The sweeper hurried away and Gan moved forward to better view the column with its offerings. He spun back hearing gasps behind him. Taza was staring at Ren and Leaf's shrouded forms in astonishment.

'Sacred Ones,' he whispered. 'None have come to this City in my forty years of service. How may I serve?'

'A bowl of tea would be a really good start,' Pallin replied promptly.

Sket gave a vigorous nod of agreement.

'Come,' said Taza. 'I should have realised – you must be travel weary indeed. We keep rooms here for any who need shelter whether they follow the Way of the Elders or no.'

He led them to a door concealed by a hanging and ushered them through. One of the robed ones accompanied them, the three others returning to kneel by the column. They found themselves in a comfortable common room, a kettle hissing softly over a small fire.

'Please take your ease.' Taza busied himself setting out bowls while the company sank onto chairs and couches with sighs of relief.

Sket helped Leaf to a bare bench where her feet swung clear of the floor and her hidden wings could hang behind. The robed one who had followed them into the common room approached Leaf. She carried a large bowl of water in her hands and a towel over her arm.

'I am Taza's wife Zada,' she said, kneeling in front of Leaf.

Sket reached for the bowl. 'I will attend to the sacred one,' he said politely.

'No, no. We are here to serve, and who greater may I serve than a sacred one?'

Before Sket could say more, Zada had dampened the towel and pushed aside the folds of the white cloak, reaching for the sacred one's foot. She grasped it gently and tutted at the bloodied toes. Then she grew quiet, her hand moving ever more slowly as she stared at Leaf's foot. Wide hazel eyes looked up into the depths of Leaf's hood. Silence reigned as the company saw what had happened.

Slowly, Zada reached for Leaf's other foot and bent her head to wipe away the blood and torn skin. She pulled the cloak back in front of Leaf's knees and sat back on her heels.

'Who are you?' she asked simply.

A gusty sigh came from inside the hood and two tiny hands reached to push the cloak away. Zada's eyes filled with tears as Leaf's black wings shimmered half open, revealing the pale rose under-feathers.

Chapter Eleven

Taza dropped to his knees. Pallin struggled to his feet and went to continue the brewing of the tea. Ren unfastened his cloak, laid it to one side and found he'd become the focus of Zada's attention.

'A gijan I recognise,' she breathed. 'But I know not what race you are, sacred one.'

'Human. Drogoyan to be exact. And I am no more sacred than Sket.' Ren smiled, transforming the stern lines of his face. 'My name is Ren and the gijan is named Leaf. Let me introduce you to all our company – beginning of course with Khosa.'

Khosa had jumped onto the bench beside Leaf and begun a fastidious washing session. Pallin handed round bowls of tea. Taza and Zada were beginning to lose their stunned look when there was a tap on the door. Before anyone could move, the door opened and a slender man of about thirty cycles strode in.

'I could not wait for messages from Zeminth. Tell me at once of his …' The newcomer froze, his eyes locked with Ren's. He looked carefully around at the other faces until he saw Leaf.

'Gijan?' he whispered, moving slowly towards her.

Sket put down his tea bowl and stood close to Leaf, his hand on his sword hilt.

'Fear not armsman. Never would I harm such a one.'

Gan rose to tower over the man. 'I am Gan Jal-Sarl, Captain of the Golden Lady Emla's Guards of Gaharn,' he said formally.

The man blinked. 'I have no idea who the Golden Lady might be Captain, or where Gaharn is in this world. I am Hariko Vos Nornay, scholar of Harbour City.' He suddenly smiled, holding his hand out to Gan. 'Not so impressive as your title, I fear.'

Gan took the proffered hand in a firm clasp, returning the smile.

'We were told by Zeminth to seek you out if possible. He thought you could perhaps aid us.'

Gan resumed his seat and Khosa leapt onto his knee. 'He is strong in the power,' she remarked.

Hariko blinked again. He glimpsed Taza's expression and looked quickly at Zada.

'Did you hear that?' he asked them.

They nodded. Hariko turned his gaze to Khosa. 'I confess I never thought to test species other than human. But to see a gijan!'

Hariko walked closer to stand looking down at Leaf. She stared back then unexpectedly gave a trill of laughter and said something in the liquid language she used with her siblings.

'I give you gijan greeting, Hariko the scholar,' she said. 'I am called Leaf.'

He sat down still staring at her. 'Did Zeminth see you?' he asked.

She laughed again and leaned forward, tapping his knee with a taloned finger.

'Zeminth saw me. And my brother and my sister.' She tilted her head first to one side, then to the other. 'And he saw the Dragons.'

Gan wasn't sure Leaf was wise to admit so much so quickly to a stranger, but even he couldn't help his amusement at Hariko's expression. Hariko studied the gijan in silence for some time.

'You will be safe here, at least for a while. You must surely know how I long to speak with you all.' He chewed his lower lip. 'Your cat spoke in my mind.'

'My name is Khosa.' She glared at Hariko.

He inclined his head. 'Khosa,' he repeated. 'I sense all of you have that ability, and more. There may be only a very few of the ordinary people within the City with this gift, but it is common inside the precincts of the Higher Academy. I have my doubts as to what might happen should certain of the Mage Councillors hear of you.'

'Nothing will harm my friends.'

Hariko froze, his mind filled with a vision of a silver blue Dragon reclining beside a smaller grey Dragon. Leaning against the blue Dragon was a girl, not much bigger than the gijan. A tangled mop of black curly hair blew round her face and she stared into Hariko's mind with eyes like chips of emerald ice surrounded by silver.

'I am Tika, soul bond and sister to Farn.' The blue Dragon's head lowered to rest on the girl's shoulder. 'Nothing will harm my friends,' she repeated.

And the picture vanished from Hariko's mind. He was visibly shaken. Ren, sitting next to him, patted Hariko's arm. 'A crimson Dragon named Brin sent you that picture from his mind. He is about three times Farn's size. Seela is perhaps a touch bigger,' he told him helpfully.

Maressa stretched out her legs in front of her and wriggled her toes. 'We need to find a man – Namolos is his name. We know only that he lives on an island west of here. Zeminth thought that you may be able to assist us in reaching him. It is a matter of some urgency.'

Hariko absently accepted a bowl of tea from Pallin. 'There are many tales of a man called Namolos. We have never investigated them, thinking them myths. I would guess most scholars and Mage Councillors discount such tales. A man surely cannot live as long as Namolos is said to have survived, unless his son – or great grandson – bears his name. Same name, different man? He is said to live twenty days sail due west but many ships have crossed that region and reported no land there.'

Maressa raised a brow. 'Have any of you who are gifted with power searched with your minds?'

Hariko frowned. 'None that I've ever heard of have done so.'

Maressa disappeared. Hariko sat back in alarm, tea splashing over his sleeve. Maressa reappeared and smiled.

'Shielding is a simple matter of rearranging air.'

Ren demurred. 'Your speciality is air my dear. I agree that shielding is not too difficult or complicated but it is immensely tiring to maintain over an extended period of time. If Namolos is shielding an entire island, what strength must that imply?'

Hariko's hands were still unsteady. 'You believe Namolos exists? That the stories relate to just one man? Some of the earliest date from more than a thousand years past.'

'Namolos exists,' Gan said quietly. 'He is called Survivor and, seemingly, survive is what he has done.' He glanced at Ren. 'There is another member of our company who is the only one of us able to reach Namolos at this distance and he has told us of the island where Namolos dwells.'

'Where is this other one?' Hariko asked.

'He is an unbodied mind.' Gan looked a little uncomfortable. 'We are never sure quite where he is.'

'At present, I am here,' Grek announced.

'Unbodied mind?' Hariko stared round the room.

Ren's discarded cloak twitched slightly. 'I am Grek.'

'And you have seen Namolos's island?' asked Hariko.

'And spoken with Namolos,' Grek agreed.

Hariko was far from the confident assured man he'd been when he strode into the common room. He made a visible effort to gather his wits.

'First of all, there are rooms above where you can stay.'

Taza nodded.

'There is access to the roof and a way down from there should, gods forbid, you have need to escape. I think you should live quietly here until I can arrange a secure ship to take you westward.' Hariko got to his feet. 'As I have told you, I am a scholar. I declined a position as Mage Councillor partly because I prefer an academic life but also because there is a cabal within the Council. Some of them have become political, desirous of controlling the City for their own ends. I have also heard there is trouble from the east.'

'Trouble?' queried Olam.

'The island of Wendla. The Wendlans use magic and have always spurned contact with any other peoples. I heard that Wendlan ships attacked four of our trading vessels.' He shrugged. 'There has been much activity in the Xantip Palace. Grand Harbour Master Chevra has been rushing in various directions. Armsmen are gathering both within the City and without. I will find out what I can and return here tomorrow.'

Hariko stood before Leaf and bowed deeply. 'Words fail me when I long to express my feeling at witnessing your presence here sacred Elder. My life is yours.'

When Hariko Vos Nornay had gone, Zada invited them to follow her to the upper rooms. They found apartments there, spacious but with an air of neglect. The rooms were clean and neat but felt as though a long time had passed since they were regularly occupied. Zada smiled sadly.

'Fewer and fewer come to our temples now, even though we are still the only order to offer free shelter and food. There were twelve temples of the Elder Races, but in my lifetime five have been abandoned and the rest of us struggle to go on.'

Maressa opened a window and leaned out, sniffing the twilight air. 'A garden.' She sounded surprised.

'All the temples had gardens.' Zada joined the air mage at the window. 'There are also City gardens. Businessmen are always seeking to overturn Xantip the Second's decree that gardens must be maintained for all the people to enjoy forever. Traders begrudge the waste of ground, as they term it. Xantip the Second's edict was engraved on stone blocks and a block is displayed in each of the gardens. No ruler since has agreed to set Xantip's order aside.' Zada turned away.

'I will fetch food for you. Please settle yourselves. No one can enter this section of the upper temple without a priest's knowledge and consent.'

'Are you a priest?' Navan asked.

'I am, as is my husband. One of our daughters also. Excuse me.'

Pallin had already discovered a small kitchen with a fire ready laid. While the others tested beds and began sorting out their packs, Sket attended to Leaf's feet. He wrapped cloth gently round them after he'd dabbed Lorak's salve over the burst blisters. Leaf inspected the result.

'You are kind Sket. I don't think I can wear boots again though.'

'Hey, this is the way to the roof,' Riff called from along a passageway.

Gan, Navan and Olam went to check the roof and to find the means of escape Hariko had spoken of. The roof was flat for perhaps six paces round a low dome which clearly covered the round chamber they'd entered below. A waist-high parapet edged the roof and at first the four men could see no way down. Then Navan noticed a stone box below the parapet. He went to it and pushed the heavy lid to one side.

'Here we are – a ladder!'

The others peered into the box and saw sturdy ropes stacked with metal rungs knotted in them. They tugged the slab back into place and leaned over the parapet. Anyone leaving this way would descend into the temple garden at the rear of the building. They could see two doors set in the high walls enclosing the garden but where they might lead they couldn't guess. The buildings immediately adjacent were lower than the temple but in every direction walls and roofs met their gaze. They walked round to the front of the temple and saw the street outside was as thronged as it had been when they'd arrived.

The first stars glimmered overhead and a flash of light caught their attention, directly ahead.

'The sea,' said Gan.

'How far, do you think?' Olam squinted against the sudden glare where the westering sun reflected off the distant line of water.

'A league, maybe,' Riff grunted. 'I reckon we'd be lost in five heartbeats down there on our own.' He grinned at the other three men. 'So if we have to make a run for it, stars send us someone who knows their way through that tangle!'

By the time they'd climbed down the narrow stairs from the roof to the inner passages the smell of food reminded them how long it was since they'd broken their fast. Zada offered them fish or meat stew, cold meats, bowls of salad greens and platters of cheese, butter and pickles.

'Taza attends evening ritual,' Zada explained. 'I will show you where our quarters are, should you need us. One priest is always present in the circle chamber and tonight it is Taza's turn.'

'Do your children live here?' enquired Maressa.

'No, all are married now and live away. Three sons are ship men; they have their own homes in the eastern sector, nearer the docks. Our daughter, who is also a priest, lives two streets away. She is a talented embroideress which fortunately brings her good coin with which to keep her and her children. Her husband was killed three years ago – he was an armsman, on patrol in the north.'

Zada's voice faded. 'Our other daughter died.'

In the silence that followed she offered no further comment, merely gathering the used dishes and stacking them on a large tray. Pallin insisted on carrying it for her, so she opened the door to let him through, turning back as she did so.

'I will show Pallin how to reach our quarters. I wish you a good night.'

Next morning a tired-looking Taza arrived with an armful of books.

'These are some of the histories of our temple,' he explained. 'I thought they may interest some of you. I will sleep until midday but my wife will stay if you wish.'

Ren and Maressa were already reaching for the books.

'Taza, it is an imposition I know, but might you lend me a tin penny?' Gan asked.

Taza, looking a trifle bemused, dug in a pocket and gave Gan a handful of different coloured metal coins.

'No, no. I need one tin penny to repay a boy.'

Taza stared at him then poked a finger among the coins. 'This is a tin penny. This a copper, worth six tin pennies.'

Gan held up a hand to stop the instruction. 'I only need one tin penny thank you.'

Taza shook his head in bewilderment, pocketed the coins Gan returned to him and left, presumably to his bed. Gan turned to Zada.

'Could you guide us to the gate through which we entered – we passed through Dolphin Square I think?'

Zada smiled. 'Of course. It is jewellers' market day in the Square. We can look at some of the stalls if you wish.'

Gan suspected jewellers' stalls might hold considerably more interest for Zada than they would for him but he amiably agreed.

'I'll come,' Olam stood up followed by Navan and Riff again.

Gan raised a questioning brow towards Pallin and Sket. Both shook their heads.

'I'll check my weapons thank you sir, and good luck to you in that dreadful squash of folk out there.' Pallin scowled his dis-approval.

The room was very quiet when the four men had departed with Zada. There was the faintest whisper from Pallin's rag where he rubbed and oiled his knives and sword. Maressa and Ren sat at a small table, engrossed in books, and Sket was sitting near Leaf, quietly sorting through his bag of remedies. Leaf sat on a high stool by an open window, her feet swishing in a large bowl of warm salt water. Although they could hear a buzz from the teeming masses in the City outside, it was pleasantly hushed within this room.

Ren glanced up, about to comment to Maressa on something he'd just read, and paused before he spoke. He followed her gaze to Leaf, noting that Pallin and Sket also sat still and silent, their eyes on the gijan. Leaf's feet still dabbled in the long cold bowl of water. Her left elbow rested on the windowsill, her chin cupped in her hand. Along the sill were several tiny birds. Ren had been vaguely aware of Leaf's trilling voice and imagined she was singing to herself, but clearly she had an audience.

As Ren watched, Leaf's free hand moved towards a minute, blue feathered dumpling of a bird. It hopped onto her finger and warbled softly when Leaf fell silent. Leaf trilled again and a slightly larger brown bird perched on her thumb. Its scarlet throat swelled as it twittered a complicated melody. Birds were coming and going, some content to stay on the outer sill, others perching confidently on Leaf's hand and arm.

The sound of voices and feet in the passage outside caused every small bird to vanish and Leaf turned away from the window as the door opened.

'Zada led us to the gate easily, but I still don't think I could find it myself.' Navan slumped into the nearest chair. 'But then she took us to Dolphin Square.' He closed his eyes.

'She said there are probably over two hundred such Squares throughout this City,' Olam added with a groan. 'Even with a map, it must be impossible.'

'It can't be that impossible,' Gan pointed out reasonably enough. 'The people who live here have no trouble finding their way about.'

Ren had moved closer to Leaf, watching Sket pat the gijan's feet dry again. She tilted her head at him.

'The birds know everywhere in this City, but they have different names for various places.'

'You were talking to the birds?' Ren asked.

Leaf frowned. 'They are my cousins. Do you not speak with your cousins?'

'I have no cousins,' Ren answered without thinking.

Leaf's frown deepened. 'But we are all related to each other somehow. I would call the Dragon Kindred my uncles or aunts perhaps; so the birds are my cousins.'

'And Kephis?' Ren was curious.

Leaf smiled. 'Also cousins – of a sort.'

'I have spoken with Namolos again.'

Water swirled around in the bowl below Leaf's feet.

'He knows of the troubles Hariko mentioned last night.'

'How does Namolos know these things, Grek? He is leagues to the west! The island of – Wendla was it? – is leagues to the east. Is he truly so full of power?' asked Maressa.

'He has power in a way I have not seen before.' Grek spoke slowly, weighing his words. 'He becomes the air, the soil, a current in the deepest seas. I don't know how he came by this skill. But he spoke of Wendla. A Ship such as Star Dancer landed there, much damaged in the landing. The Captain survived for about forty years. Her son was also on the Ship. He married a Wendlan woman. Namolos told me the descendants of the Captain's son live longer than you would count usual but not by much. So the Survivor now is many generations distant from the Captain.'

'The blood link then is much diluted,' Ren commented.

'Namolos said the Captain unbodied: her mind survives.'

Gan sat up straighter. 'Her mind survives you say – can she manipulate events – is that what Namolos believes or knows?'

'All those with the blood of the outworlders in their veins speak with the Captain still. They know who she is and thus in part what, and who, they are. Wendlan tradition was always for the mystical, the ascendancy of mental processes. The unbodied Captain does not seem strange to them.'

'Is this Captain then organising the attacks Hariko spoke of – on the trading ships?'

Olam scratched at his side by habit, and snatched his hand away guiltily as Pallin glared at him.

'Namolos says no. But he thinks too many outside the direct bloodline have learnt to use the same mental powers. He says the Captain – her name is Sefri – would never have any part in an attack on merchant ships.'

'What is the name of the Ship – is it still alive?' asked Maressa.

'Namolos said Sefri dwells mostly within the Ship – Star Flower. He has touched their minds occasionally and found them sad but still devoted to each other.'

The company considered Grek's words in silence until Pallin began to bang dishes about in the kitchen and suggested they come and eat the breakfast leftovers.

Later Gan examined Leaf's feet at Sket's request. He cut away the loose flaps of skin, his long fingers surprisingly deft and gentle. 'One of us will have to carry you if we need to move from here before these are healed,' he told her.

Ren watched, wincing when Gan parted the toes to reveal more fat blisters as yet unburst.

'I wish I was skilled at healing,' he confessed.

'Me too,' Maressa agreed. 'We could make more salves though – Pallin and I collected quite a lot of plants beside that lake. I'm afraid I'd forgotten.'

She went off to find her pack and disappeared with Pallin into the kitchen.

'Grek?' Ren enquired. But there was no answer.

'Where does he go all the time?' Olam wondered aloud.

'He watches everything around us,' Khosa replied. 'He takes his promise to Gremara very seriously.'

Light slowly faded beyond the windows and Taza and his wife arrived with more food.

'Are you sure you can spare all this food?' Maressa asked anxiously.

'We still have followers who give coin offerings at each ten day ritual. We put it by so we may provide food or clothing to any who seek sanctuary.' Zada unfolded a pair of trousers she had held tucked under her arm. 'If the sacred one would accept these?'

Leaf tilted her head. Zada held up trousers, dark blue with pale blue flowers embroidered round the bottom of each leg. The gijan smiled, taking the trousers and holding them close to her cheek.

'These are not clothes you keep in a box for needy guests.' Uptilted dark eyes studied Zada steadily. 'Thank your daughter for her beautiful work Zada. One day she will be repaid.'

Zada flushed. Leaf turned her back on the room, her wings

hiding her body. When she turned back she wore her new trousers with obvious delight.

'Sacred one, Salma is making another pair for you. She is at the evening ritual now.'

Leaf trilled her laugh. 'Then you must bring her to meet me, so that I may thank her properly.'

'Really?' Zada looked at the faces watching her. 'We have only told Salma, I swear. She will speak of your presence to none other. I will fetch her.'

Ren and Maressa began to question Taza on points they'd found difficult to decipher in the books he'd lent them, but the others watched Leaf. She lifted each foot and studied the fine stitching at the bottom of each trouser leg; she stretched her legs out before her, smiling at seeing the trousers reached below her fragile ankles. Khosa leaned against Gan's thigh and, for the first time for very many days, began her low buzzing croon as she too watched the gijan.

'Is she preening, Khosa?' Gan whispered.

'Indeed,' Khosa crooned louder. 'So pretty she is.'

Zada reappeared tugging her daughter Salma by the hand. Hariko was behind them, clearly confused. The young woman kept her head low, not daring to look at anyone. Maressa went to her, putting an arm across her shoulders and guiding her towards the gijan.

'Come, Salma dear. Leaf is so thrilled with the fine trousers you've made her.'

But Salma had glimpsed the ragged feet and gasped in sympathy. Her gaze moved slowly up, up until she stared open mouthed. Leaf's wings were half opened revealing the delicate pink beneath the blue black top feathers.

'These are the prettiest clothes I've ever had,' Leaf told her with a trill of laughter.

Salma appeared speechless, so it was as well that Khosa spoke, stalking towards the door.

'We will all go to the roof now. Sket will carry Leaf.'

Sket looked mystified, then suddenly grinned. Leaf furled her wings close to her back and Sket carefully lifted her into his arms and followed Khosa. Maressa chivvied Salma and her parents after them and soon everyone was on the rooftop. A few stars showed in the dark sky but high clouds were racing in from the direction of the coast.

Leaf gave a high peal of pleasure, holding out her arms. Willow and Piper landed silently beside Sket, enfolding him too as they embraced their sister. Gan saw the faces of the three priests and the scholar Hariko and knew it was a moment they would remember until they passed from this life.

There was a flurry of heavier wings and Farn settled precariously on the edge of the roof, his eyes whirring in delight. Tika slid from his back and bowed to the priests and the scholar.

Chapter Twelve

Hariko took one pace forward, trembling violently. 'You spoke in my mind last night,' he blurted.

Tika's lips smiled but her eyes remained icy. 'We did but warn you that we will always be close enough to protect our friends.'

Her eyes softened when she studied the three Harbour City priests. 'The Kindred honour you for keeping the Way of the Elders so faithfully and for so long in their absence.'

Farn's long face loomed over her head. He pressed his brow to Taza's, then to Zada's and lastly Salma.

'More girls,' he remarked, to the confusion of the priests.

Tika ignored the comment as she moved to the gijan. Sket grinned at her.

'You'll have to have a serious talk with him, Lady Tika,' he murmured. 'One of those "girls" is fifty cycles at least.'

Tika gave a snort of laughter before Maressa hugged her tight.

'You are well Tika? I miss your company.'

Tika hugged her back, looking round Maressa's shoulder at the rest of her friends.

'I apologise for my weakness in the forest,' she said in a small voice. 'I beg you to forgive my desertion.'

Her apology was met with smiles and Maressa hugged her again. 'There is no forgiveness to grant you child. We love you,' she said simply.

Tika blinked and then bent to lift Leaf's feet higher over Sket's arm. Gan was the only one to think of bringing a lamp when they'd climbed to the roof. Now he held it above Leaf's lower legs. Farn inched cautiously along the roof until he was closer to his soul bond, peering down to watch. Tika studied Leaf's feet: they were severely torn. If she was left to heal naturally it could be days before new skin toughened sufficiently to walk on for any length of time. Part of her mind was aware of the scholar, Hariko Vos Nornay, watching her closely.

She detached herself, holding one delicate high arched foot between her hands. She sent tendrils of healing to the gijan, speeding the natural processes and strengthening the fibres of new skin as they formed. Hariko's breath hissed through his teeth. The blisters between Leaf's toes shrank, the pale lavender sores around the heel slowly disappeared under new skin dappled green and gold. Gently, Tika lifted the other foot and repeated the process. She was astonished how easy it seemed.

'This is the first time you have done a minor healing,' Khosa whispered in her mind.

Tika realised the Kephi was right. The other healings she had done had been for Farn and to extract the gijan's wings – never had she healed a small hurt. Tika stood back, leaning against Farn's chest for comfort rather than support. The healing had taken scarcely any strength.

'Those trousers are the best I've seen,' she said suddenly. 'Did you buy them here? Where did you get coin?'

Leaf wriggled from Sket's arms and hurled arms and wings round Tika.

'Salma made them for me – aren't they splendid?'

The priests and Hariko were amazed at Leaf's next words.

'Thank you for mending my feet Tika. My life is yours.'

There was something in the way Leaf said the last four words: she meant them utterly, they were not a ritual form of gratitude.

Gan lowered the lamp and watched Tika go to every person of their company, bestowing a quick hug and kiss to each. She reached Sket and the armsman whispered something which made Tika splutter with mirth. Then she turned to Gan, peering up at his face nearly lost in the darkness above her. She tugged at his sleeve and he bent nearly in half to bring his head nearer hers.

'I always thought I was alone,' she told him quietly. 'Until I found Farn, Kija, the Dragon Kindred. But when I left you in the forest, I discovered I missed you all too.' She rested her forehead against his chin. 'We're family aren't we Gan?'

Gan's long fingers brushed back the tangle of dark curls and he smiled. 'I was thinking the very same thing myself. We're not family because we have to be, but because we choose to be.'

He saw those strangely altered eyes glinting up at him and a beaming smile. She stretched her arms up to hug his neck and then she had gone back to Farn. She climbed onto his shoulders.

'It is not safe for Farn to land here but we will come back should you need us. We are close by.' She looked down at the three priests. 'Your names will be remembered in the histories,' she told them gently. She met Hariko's gaze. 'Zeminth longed to meet your father and you also, but he fears this City. Why could you not have travelled to him?'

Without waiting for a reply, Farn lifted from the roof and was immediately lost to sight in the gathering clouds. Piper and Willow, surprisingly, enfolded the three priests in their wings and then they too were gone.

The first spots of rain were falling as they made their way back indoors, Khosa leading the way: she detested being wet even more than she detested being cold. Salma and Zada disappeared with Leaf, leaving Taza and Hariko with the visitors.

'Finding a ship for you is proving more difficult than I'd hoped,' Hariko began as soon as he'd sat down. 'All ships have been ordered to await orders from the Grand Master. He will requisition some of them for sure, not all of course, for conversion to fighting ships or for transporting armsmen to the Outer Islands. No large ships are allowed to leave Harbour City until the Grand Master decides which ones he wants.' He shrugged. 'There was uproar of course – traders have schedules to keep and delays cost them much coin. Traders do not appreciate losing coin. My other piece of news is that word has reached both the Higher Academy and the Mage Council of the arrival of two sacred ones in the City.'

Ren looked alarmed. 'What exactly does that imply?'

'Both scholars and mages will be very anxious to speak with you. You can expect courtesy from the scholars even should you refuse to meet them, but the mages may be more – persistent.'

'Hariko, just how powerful are these Mage Councillors?' Maressa asked.

Hariko took his time in framing his reply. 'Compared with the little I've seen of the Dragon Kindred's mind strength, and your own ability, I would estimate most are less strong than you. That is individually. Together, I think they could overwhelm you quite easily. I do not know if you can combine with the Kindred and

the gijan and I do not know the strength of the other sacred one.'
He inclined his head in Ren's direction.

Maressa made no comment, waiting for Hariko to continue.

'There are a handful of mages who are very strong. Vorna for example; she is deeply involved in the cabal I spoke of last night. Taseen is very old. He claims he played a part in the last War of the Elders, although no one believes that of course. He would oppose Vorna – he has always and publicly claimed it is our duty to protect this land and its people above all other interest. We should do this for no reward other than the continuance of land and people. He teaches that all life exists in harmony and should so continue – that no one person should dictate how others live their private lives.'

Maressa nodded. 'And you would share the view of Vorna, or of Taseen?'

'Taseen.' Hariko didn't hesitate. 'But he is very old, though some say that Vorna is near to him in age.' He lifted a shoulder in a half shrug. 'She appears in her late middle years.' He paused and frowned. 'Now I think on it, she has looked exactly the same since I was a child. How could that be?'

'The highest – mages I suppose you would call them – in my land are able to extend their lives,' Ren told the scholar.

Gan had listened closely and watched Hariko's expression throughout. 'Would we be able to specify who we would meet, then? Is it permitted that we could visit Taseen perhaps, and then two or three scholars? Would that satisfy them?' he asked.

'I could ask Taseen to dine at my house in the precincts of the Higher Academy. I don't think it would be wise for you to enter Xantip Palace. Taseen has not been known to dine outside the Palace for years – whether he'd agree is doubtful.'

'I will invite him.'

Hariko looked round nervously.

'It matters not where you think I am, Hariko, only that you listen to what I say.' Grek's tone was acid. 'All this company will attend,' he continued. 'I'm sure there are one or two scholars whom you trust? When shall I tell Taseen to call upon you – tomorrow would be best?'

They felt almost sorry for Hariko: conversation with Grek clearly rattled his nerves badly. He stood up.

'I'll make the arrangements at once,' he said and waited for Grek's response.

Khosa chewed busily between her toes. 'Grek's gone to offer your invitation to Taseen.' She closed her eyes, the better to concentrate on her cleaning.

'Aah. Well, I too will go then. I will expect you at dusk tomorrow.' He turned back at the door. 'Shall I send someone from my household to escort you? It isn't far but I know the City is confusing to visitors.'

Gan stretched out his long legs. 'Taza will be kind enough to show us the way I'm sure.'

Hariko nodded. 'I will see you at dusk tomorrow,' he repeated.

Leaf brushed past him as he left. She was followed by Salma and Zada, their arms full of material.

'We have looked through the chests of clothes,' Zada explained. 'You must all choose what you wish. I should have thought of it before: your clothes all need cleaning and most need some mending.' She stared pointedly at a tear in Pallin's sleeve.

'I will have another pair of trousers finished for you tomorrow sacred one,' Salma murmured shyly to Leaf.

'Truly? What colour will they be?' Leaf asked.

The awe with which Salma had regarded Leaf changed to something close to mischief. 'I think you'll have to wait and see, sacred one.'

Leaf pouted and then laughed. 'And my siblings – shall they have new trousers?'

Salma blinked and saw she had been trapped. She smiled wryly. 'I will make trousers for all of you,' she agreed. 'But it will take time.'

Maressa was sorting through the heap of garments, several bright shirts already under her arm.

'We give clothes to any who ask for them,' Zada told them. She held up a finely-worked shawl. 'Some who still follow the Way make such things to bring as offerings to the temple when they have no coin to spare.'

'It is not far to the Higher Academy,' Taza said, looking at Leaf's feet. 'But there are always people on the street until long after dark.'

Zada rummaged in the pile of clothes and produced two brilliant green socks, causing groans of horror from all – except Leaf. She fingered them admiringly and Zada smiled.

'You like bright colours sacred one?'

'Oh yes. The world is filled with bright colours after all.'

Zada stretched a foot of one of the socks and then squatted to measure it against the gijan's slender foot. 'There are some scraps of leather in my sewing box I'm sure. I can stitch leather to the sock which will save your feet a little.' She stood upright again. 'And wearing these will conceal your feet, sacred one. Beautiful though I think them, they are very different from human feet, and people in this City are the most curious in the world.'

Maressa impulsively kissed Zada's cheek. 'You are the kindest of women, Zada dear. I hope our presence in your temple doesn't completely exhaust you!'

They spent most of the next day within their rooms – rain poured down outside but the same crowds of people seemed to hurry along the street in front of the temple. Grek told them Taseen had seemed highly amused when he announced himself.

'He is indeed very aged,' Grek told them. 'But he encourages the general belief that he is frail and weak – about to pass from this life at any moment.' Grek sounded amused. 'He told me Vorna discounts him completely now as a senile old fool. Which means of course that he is very far from being that. Two Mage Councillors will accompany him. Tavri, who is his constant companion and disciple – he plays the part of a gentle simpleton to perfection.'

Now Grek sounded admiring. 'The other is Sheoma, towards whom Vorna is showing increasing interest. Taseen told me Sheoma has far travelled – to Wendla. Only he and Tavri are aware of Sheoma's powers in this skill.'

'And Hariko?' Gan asked the question in everyone's mind.

'Taseen says he is trustworthy within limits, but he will not speak to us freely in front of Hariko or the other scholars Hariko will invite to dine.'

'What limitations does Taseen put on his trust in Hariko?' asked Ren.

'He says Hariko was the only child of his parents, and while he has a good mind and a willing aptitude for scholarship, he has a rather grander opinion of himself than is truthful. He does not take kindly to being made to look a fool, or to have the gaps in his knowledge exposed. He is a still young man who was born to an elderly father and a mother nearing fifty years who spoilt him.'

Khosa yawned. 'I will of course join you tonight. Was there more we needed to know Grek?'

'He was aware of my presence – like you and Leaf can tell where I am.'

Khosa paused in the act of tucking her tail round her front paws. 'Was he indeed?' she said thoughtfully.

'It's stopped raining!' Leaf called from her stool by the open window. 'Will it soon be time to go out?'

'Well, we're all ready,' Gan laughed. 'As soon as Taza comes for us, we'll leave.'

But it was Salma who arrived first, a roll of dark cloth in her hand. She bowed before Leaf and handed her the roll. Leaf took it with eager anticipation. The company laughed at the gijan's trill of excitement as she examined the trousers. They were sooty black, with birds and butterflies exquisitely embroidered down the length of the outside of each leg. She spun round, her wings shielding her, and put on the second pair of new trousers she had been given in two days. Maressa moved to examine them when Leaf spun again to face the room.

'Salma, tell me you haven't spent all last night and all day today doing this?' Maressa exclaimed.

Leaf's smile changed to a concerned frown.

'I had the black cloth by me and I had been working on that particular design for some time. It was surely a prompting from the Elders that caused me to choose that shade of pink. I only had to cut the cloth and sew the trousers – I did no fancy work today. Do they please you sacred one?'

Leaf extended one wing, drawing it close to her leg. The pink of her under-feathers exactly matched the pink of the embroidered pattern.

'Oh, they please me mightily Salma!'

Salma blushed with pleasure as her father appeared at the door. Maressa flung the white cloak around Leaf and knelt to tug on the green leather-soled socks. Ren was already cloaked and hooded and he held out his hand to the gijan.

Outside the temple in its small front courtyard, the company formed protectively around Ren and Leaf. Gan took up the rear with Maressa close beside him again. Sket walked at Leaf's right side, Navan at Ren's left. Riff and Pallin positioned themselves directly in front of them while Olam took the lead with Taza. Pallin started grumbling within moments of their emerging into the street.

'Nearly dark and all these folks still rushing about. Have they no homes to go to?'

Gan heard Taza's voice as a soothing murmur but Pallin sounded more belligerent with each step.

'Eating in the street! Just look there, sir – can you believe it? Do they not shut shops in this stars-forsaken place when it grows dark?' Pallin choked to silence and Gan stared over the heads of his companions to see what had caused Pallin's complaints to cease. He grinned.

Pallin recovered enough to voice his outrage in a loud hiss at Olam.

'Those girls are wearing nothing! Sitting there on those balconies look, drinking! They'll catch their deaths!'

Maressa glanced up at Gan and lost her battle with giggles. Sket chuckled and Pallin turned to glare back at them.

'Disgraceful it is, and not to be laughed at!'

It was perhaps fortunate that it was only a short walk before Taza led them through a wide gateway into an expanse of green garden. Navan glanced over his shoulder as the hubbub of the City was abruptly muted.

'Why do the people not come in here?' he asked Taza.

'Once through that gate we are within the precincts of the Xantip Higher Academy. Many rumours abound about what Mages might do to interlopers here or at the Mage College or the Palace itself.'

They followed a winding flagged path between lines of perfumed shrubs until they reached another wall in which was set a narrow gate. A man in a grey robe greeted them and took them on to Hariko's quarters. In the deepening twilight they made out a low single-storey L-shaped building set among several other similar structures. Hariko met them at the door.

'Taseen arrived moments ago. Please, come in and meet him.'

He took them straight to a dining room where a large oval table was set with a multitude of dishes. Four men and two women were already seated at the table. Hariko drew out chairs, inviting the company to sit, placing Leaf and Ren opposite the man they guessed at once was Taseen.

A white beard frothed over layers of shawls, and thick robes wrapped his thin body tightly. Hariko introduced everyone and urged them to help themselves to food.

'Councillor Taseen fears he will be unable to stay long. Sadly he is plagued by summer ague.'

Ren, looking directly at the old man, saw startlingly sharp blue eyes for an instant when Taseen peered across the table from beneath overhanging eyebrows. Taseen reminded the Offering, with a pang, of old Babach. The Mage Councillors spoke little. Tavri seemed more concerned with his ancient master – who managed to spill his soup into his beard. Sheoma, a woman of Maressa's age, listened closely while Hariko and the two other scholars argued, with boring persistency, whether the tales of Namolos could possibly be based on fact.

Pallin and Riff ate steadily and silently, not even pretending to pay attention to the talk. Leaf said nothing, neither did she eat, leaving Ren to reply to the scholars. Taseen groaned and bowed his head even lower.

'I fear I must take my master home,' said Tavri, getting to his feet. 'Perhaps the sacred ones would visit him in the Palace when he is a little better.'

Sheoma and Tavri held the tottering figure between them and helped him to the door. The company remained, listening to Hariko and his friends talk in ever more convoluted terms until they had no idea of what they were hearing. Pallin yawned loudly and Gan rose from the table.

'We thank you for your hospitality Hariko, but we too should be leaving.'

Hariko looked a little surprised – he had been speaking of the theory of disharmonics in the time of the Ancient Elders – but nodded anyway.

'I will call on you tomorrow,' he said as they filed from his front door. He lowered his voice. 'I may have news of a ship.'

Gan bowed. 'We look forward to that then, Hariko.'

The same servant led them back to the narrow gate where Taza waited. Making their way back to the temple, Leaf exploded with irritation, both at the exclusion of Taza from the meal and at the utter nonsense they'd had to listen to.

'Taza is a priest of the Elder Races,' she hissed. 'He should have been included with us. And those were scholars? Zeminth had more wisdom than those three put together.'

They walked through streets far less crowded than they'd seen so far but still busy enough. The rain clouds had moved further inland and fistfuls of stars were strewn across the night sky.

'What was the point of all that?' Navan asked Gan, turning in to the temple entrance.

'I have no idea. Let's hope Grek may be able to enlighten us.'

Gan released Khosa who had been silent throughout the evening. Now she bounded up the stairs ahead of them. Ren and Leaf were already unfastening their white cloaks as Olam opened the door to their apartments. He halted and hands went automatically to weapons. Olam moved on into the room, followed by the others who saw that they had visitors.

Tavri was pouring tea into bowls, Sheoma sat on Leaf's stool by the open window. Taseen, divested of many of his wrappings, sat upright in an armchair, his feet on the fender round the fire. His face wore a grin they found difficult to resist. Khosa stalked forward and sat in front of him.

'The poor old man performance was quite good,' she conceded. 'Spilling your soup may have overdone it a little.'

Taseen's roar of laughter gave the final lie to the notion that he was a decrepit old creature close to death. He patted his knee.

'Perhaps it was, beautiful one. Tell me your name and help me clean up the mess – it was fish soup.'

Leaf trilled a laugh, removing her cloak and tossing it onto a bench. The three mages grew still, feasting their eyes on the gijan. She tilted her head to one side, then the other, returning their scrutiny. At last Taseen sighed, his hand stroking down Khosa's back.

'I must beg your pardon for making you endure that ridiculous meal. I rarely leave the Palace except to go to my lands outside the City, so it would be a source of great interest should I suddenly decide to visit this temple. It is not quite so worthy of gossip that I dine with Hariko.' He smiled. 'And who knows how long I'll stay talking with him tonight?'

'If Vorna's interested in knowing where you are, it wouldn't take her a great deal of effort to find out,' Sheoma retorted. She walked across the room. 'You are very beautiful. Does Hariko know that you are gijan – he said nothing to us?' Sheoma couldn't hide her surprise when Ren raised his eyes to hers.

'Hariko knows Leaf is gijan. He has seen her siblings and one of the great Dragons,' he told her.

'Great Dragons are here too?' Taseen's unruly eyebrows quivered.

'Close by,' Maressa replied before Leaf could say too much.

Tavri had been quietly handing round bowls of tea and now found himself close to Leaf. He lightly touched the glossy blue black feathers.

'You are truly beautiful.' He smiled down at her.

Leaf returned his smile, revealing her tiny pointed teeth. Then she twirled away, wings unfurling and rippling. She ended up beside Taseen's chair.

'Do you like my trousers? No one could see them at Hariko's horrid house.'

Taseen solemnly regarded the black trousers, the delicate embroidery, the exposed dappled skin of Leaf's belly and arms.

'I have never seen such a work of art,' he said gravely. 'And those socks are the finishing touch.'

Leaf raised her leg and tugged off a sock. 'They are, aren't they,' she agreed.

Taseen caught her hand. 'I think you are very young, little Leaf. Are you newly come to your wings?'

'Oh yes. Do you want to hear how it happened?'

Khosa, busily washing Taseen's beard, replied on his behalf.

'Well of course he does. And everything else as well I expect.'

Chapter Thirteen

The Mage Councillors listened attentively while first Leaf, then Maressa, Gan and finally Ren, recounted the events of the last year. Less than a full year in fact, Gan reflected. Taseen smiled.

'I understand that you must reach Namolos, but you have chosen a tricky time for sea travel. I would like to hear more of the City in the desert: the Kertiss you spoke of worries me. What may be happening in your land, Ren, worries me. What Vorna is attempting to do worries me. In short, I am a very worried man.'

Maressa curled her feet under her on the couch. 'Should we know what Vorna is up to?'

Sheoma nodded. 'I think they should be warned, Taseen. We could never have foreseen gijan or Dragons appearing in Harbour City just as Vorna's schemes show signs of success.'

For a moment Taseen looked down at Leaf. She lay on her side asleep before the fire, one wing folded tight to her back, the other half open, covering her like a magnificent blanket.

'She is so young and immeasurably precious,' he murmured almost to himself. He sighed. 'Vorna became obsessed with the Ancient Elders while in her training. Hariko may have mentioned that I served this land during the last War of the Elders?'

Navan interrupted. 'If gijan and Dragons are Elder Races, what are these Wars we hear of? Did humans battle them, or did they battle each other? I find it difficult to believe when clearly the memory of both Dragons and gijan are still greatly revered.'

'There were Ancient Elders in this world in the Time Before. They ruled these lands from the beginnings of humanity. For millennia they ruled kindly and well, letting humans grow at their natural pace.'

Taseen fell silent and Tavri took up the tale. 'The first War of the Elders began, it is said, because one Elder lusted after a human female. Congress between Elder and human was forbidden by the first Law. The Elder would heed none of his brethren and fled with the female to distant lands. The Elders discovered the pair had produced four monstrous children, to whom their father had passed much knowledge – again, a forbidden act.

'There were about a hundred Elders in those days – we would call them gods and goddesses now I guess. Several of them sought out the one who had flouted two of their primary laws.'

He glanced at Taseen. 'The monstrous children killed their father as soon as they overtook him in power. They killed many Elders who came seeking them. The children were warped, twisted, personifying the very worst of both human and Elder natures. As a desperate recourse, the Elders caused the great desert to come into being. They hoped it would keep the children away from these lands long enough for Elders to construct a means of destroying them.'

Maressa sounded sceptical. 'Four children could so frighten many Elders?'

'The Ancient Elders were never warlike or violent. Their teachings of harmony and balance are instilled in the very bones of most of our people to this day,' Sheoma explained. 'Remember, these were no ordinary children.'

'The children rampaged through the northern lands and beyond, gaining in strength all the time,' Tavri went on. 'The Elders instigated a plan to teach humans some of their powers. It involved breeding certain families who showed an innate aptitude and forcing their mind development. The Elders grieved that they had to break a primary law themselves to combat the children. Briefly, the Wars that followed cost the lives eventually of all the Ancient Elders and huge numbers of mages.'

Taseen grunted. 'By the time I was involved, no Elders survived but we had devised a plan to imprison the children.' He gazed into the fire. 'Three thousand mages died in that last battle – just outside this City where now farmland flourishes. Three thousand brilliant minds, male and female, to imprison two of those Ancient children.'

'You have not given their names,' Olam said softly.

'No.' Sheoma's voice was sharp. 'I will write their names for you but they must not be spoken aloud, especially now.'

'Now?' Gan queried.

Taseen looked suddenly tired. 'Vorna believes imprisoning the children was a mistake. She thinks there was much to learn from their hybrid minds. She has been trying to release one of them.'

Sheoma had been scribbling on a paper. Now she passed it to Maressa. 'The one I have circled is the one Vorna is concentrating on. We believe, although we do not know for sure, that two of them are destroyed.'

Maressa read the four names. Valesh. Qwah. Taffez. Sekira. The first name was circled.

'Never say those names aloud,' Sheoma repeated. 'They are awake and stirring again.'

'That last battle was long ago?' Sket ventured.

Taseen nodded. 'A thousand years or more. And still I have not regained my full powers. I have to rely on information from others rather than expend what small strength remains to me.'

Tavri stood up, glancing at the dark windows. 'We should return to the Palace. I will let it be known that you are confined to your bed again.'

Sheoma groaned. 'I have a class to tutor this morning. I fear I may not be as brilliant as usual.' She stooped to kiss Taseen's cheek. 'Sleep for a while old man, you'll be worse than useless if you exhaust yourself too soon.'

While Sheoma spoke to Taseen, Tavri had moved close to Gan. 'Guard him well for me. He is as precious as the Elders to me.'

Gan nodded, recognising the same protective love in Tavri's eyes that he'd seen so often in Sket's.

'We should all get some sleep,' Maressa said through a yawn.

She fetched quilts and pillows from one of the bedrooms and offered them to Taseen.

'Thank you my dear. If it is not an inconvenience I will stay here with you for a day or two. I often take to my bed for days at a time.'

Maressa grinned. 'I thought spilling soup in your beard rather effective actually.'

Taseen chuckled and settled himself in the chair, planning to spend what was left of the night thinking, very hard. Sket curled up on one of the couches.

'Is there no bed for you?' Taseen asked.

'I stay near Leaf sir. I'll not disturb you.'

Grand Harbour Master Chevra strode into the Debating Chamber high in the Xantip Palace. A purple-faced General Koolis had just left his presence, having been thoroughly shouted down by the Grand Master. Chevra held a fond but unfounded belief in his prowess as a military tactician and had ordered all border patrols to return to the City forthwith. General Koolis was now even more infuriated by his inability to see the old mage Taseen. He fumed and muttered on being turned away from Taseen's quarters. The General munched on his long moustaches while he considered who else might possibly intercede and mitigate Chevra's commands.

The Grand Master did some more shouting when he discovered Taseen, Tavri and Vorna were all absent. Bajal conveyed Vorna's regrets – she had gone to her estates beyond the west of the City to deal with pressing business matters. With Vorna missing, Bajal was subdued, making few contributions to the discussions. But then, no one did really, once Chevra was in full flow.

Chevra had even abandoned his courtesans in favour of the excitement of planning a war. He was annoying everyone in the Palace by turning up unannounced, in the most unexpected places such as the kitchens, asking obscure questions and leaving the staff with their nerves in shreds. Sheoma managed to insert an innocent query, when Chevra paused for breath, on the state of the Towers of Aneira, two leagues north east of the City limits.

Chevra demanded the plans of the Towers of Aneira be brought for his inspection. Then he complained of the worn condition of the plans, until Sheoma pointed out that probably no one had looked at them for the last eighty years at least. At last Chevra left the Chamber, stating his intention to inspect the Towers for himself. Clutching the plans under his arm, he shouted for his son to be readied to accompany him. Guards discreetly closed the Chamber doors again and the remaining Councillors slumped in their chairs.

'He is even more dreadful when Taseen or Vorna aren't here,' Fental muttered.

'He tries.' Lessna as usual tried to be fair. 'He was a splendid merchant. It was a bad error of judgement that he accepted Lady Eorlas's offer of marriage. Inheriting the Grand Mastership once her father died put him completely out of his depth.'

'She didn't stay around to help him much though, did she?' Bajal sneered. 'Three years of playing the fashionable married couple, seven more as wife of a Grand Master and she decamps for her estates. Has anyone seen her in the last year or two?'

'The poor woman was pregnant every year of those ten years; she probably yearned for a rest,' Lessna defended the absent Lady Eorlas, a woman she had utterly loathed. 'And only three children live. To go through carrying those babies only for six to die within days of birth must have been quite terrible.'

'We have more important things to consider than the unfortunate Lady Eorlas,' Fental snapped. 'How do we persuade Chevra that we must keep some outposts garrisoned in the north? I have my doubts about the whole idea of Wendla deciding to wage war on us.'

'Four of our trading ships were attacked, Fental, and two taken,' Sheoma pointed out.

Fental shrugged. 'There have been occasions before when pirates developed grand ideas. This could be another situation like that.'

'The surviving shipmen described Wendlan warships,' Sheoma persisted.

Fental scowled. 'What about those weird dreams you said some of the students have been reporting, Bajal? Of a revolutionary nature I think you said. Have they been overdoing it with the hallucinogens again?'

'No they have not,' retorted Bajal. 'They all say that suggestions are put to them along the lines of how marvellously advantageous friendship with Wendla would be and how restrictive and small minded are the ways of our land.' He flushed when Fental hooted derisively.

'Corruption by dreams. Hardly likely I think and definitely not successful. I think we should try and delay any of Chevra's wilder plans until Vorna or Taseen return to the council. Suggesting he inspects the Towers of Aneira was very good Sheoma,' he admitted grudgingly. 'Surely we can come up with other similar suggestions to waste his time for a few days.' He stood, brushing non existent specks from his elegantly-cut jacket. 'At least the Towers will occupy him for the rest of today and, with luck, all of tomorrow. Let's just hope Vorna's back by then.'

Fental departed, followed after a moment by a disgruntled Bajal. Lessna looked across the table at Sheoma.

'You look tired Sheo. Why don't we get some food, the common room should be clear by now.'

They walked along the corridors to one of the lesser staircases and descended to the bustle of the administration sector. Eventually they reached the main common room where a handful of students and teacher mages lingered over the midday meal.

'I was busy last night.' Sheoma forestalled any more questions. 'I've had an idea for a series of new lectures and I began to work out a plan for them. It was nearly dawn before I realised how long I'd been working – you know how it is.'

Lessna nodded, her mouth full of cheese. 'I know. I still have problems remembering my schedule times. Poor little Merkas,' she added inconsequentially.

Sheoma raised her brows. 'Poor little Merkas?'

'Only seven years old and Chevra's dragged him off to look round those derelict Towers. You know how he hates change – he'll howl all the way there and all the way back and Chevra will shout at him to be more manly. Poor child.'

Sheoma shook her head. 'Lessna, just listen to yourself! Poor little boy – you loathe children!'

'I loathe them in proximity. I can sympathise in the abstract.'

Taza took the men to see the water front and docks in the morning, Pallin only going under protest. Sket remained with Leaf and Maressa. Sket was intrigued by the interaction between the young gijan and the ancient mage. Taseen told her tales and riddles, and even sang silly nonsense songs. It wasn't until Leaf suddenly joined in with one such rhyme that Sket saw Taseen was gently testing the gijan's memories. Sket went to make some midmorning tea and returned to find Leaf by her window attended by a crowd of small birds again. Taseen sat watching her while Khosa buzzed on his knee.

'Did you know the gijan long ago sir?' asked Sket, squatting beside the mage's chair.

'Only a few Sket, and they were very old. The remaining young ones had been sent away to the swamp lands in the hope they would find safety there. The old ones died with the mages outside this City.'

'And the Dragons?'

Taseen shook his head. 'They were beaten back beyond the great desert in the fourth War, long before. The gijan told us they still communicated with them but the Dragons had suffered as severely as the gijan.'

Sket stared at the mage, the tea bowl in his hand forgotten. 'Beaten back?' he whispered in horror. He tried to imagine what forces, what weapons, could beat back creatures like Brin, Fenj, Seela or Kija, and he trembled.

Taseen laid a hand on Sket's shoulder. 'Indeed. They were forced to flee the strength of one child – the second name on Sheoma's list.'

They sat in silence, watching Leaf talking to the birds on the window sill.

'Lady Sheoma said you thought two were destroyed.'

'I fear we may have been mistaken. I have pondered on what Ren told us last night. Grek turned up later too, and from his account of Ren's land I am very much afraid one of the children is influencing events there. And we are not called Lady or sir, Sket – our names suffice.'

'How are these children imprisoned – in great hidden strongholds somewhere?'

Taseen frowned. 'It is difficult to explain. We created spaces in the very rocks and then bound each child with layer upon layer of spells. Over time I think perhaps some of those spells could have lost their potency, enabling the Bound One to work on that weakness.'

'You spoke of a mage – Vorna – who believes your people could learn from these children. If I'd been shut up in a rock for a thousand years or more, I would not be in a mood for a friendly discussion.'

Taseen gave a bark of laughter and the birds on the window sill disappeared. Leaf turned a reproachful look in his direction.

'Sorry my dear. Of course you are exactly right Sket, but Vorna dismisses that suggestion out of hand. She places enormous faith in her own powers of conviction and believes bad temper would never control such advanced minds as the children clearly possessed.'

Sket stared at him. 'They seem to have been foul tempered since their births if your accounts were true.'

'Quite so, Sket, quite so.'

'Should we go to this Namolos, sir?'

'My name is Taseen.' The old mage smiled then grew serious again. 'I cannot advise you. Grek told me much more last night and I regret that I didn't investigate the stories of Namolos years ago. He may have a part to play in these troubled times but then – who knows if he would consent to do so? The first rumours of him began around the time of the last battle. I was unconscious for three years afterwards and it was far longer before I began to take note of the affairs of the country again.

'I confess that the problems which have arisen – all over this world as I now learn – do seem to be connected rather than random events.'

'Whereabouts did you put the children?' Sket sounded subdued.

'One is deep below the great sea between here and the island of Wendla. Another is beneath the desert. The other two, who were dealt with by many other mages, are much further north. I now think one must surely be in Ren's land but the fourth? Perhaps that one has truly been destroyed?'

'Did Grek tell you of the other Survivor – the one like Namolos?'

'He did. I think it important to make contact with her, but how? And who should be the one to do so?' Taseen sighed. 'So many questions and far too few answers.'

The other men returned with Taza, hungry from their walk to the docks. Pallin and Riff were most annoyed that Sket hadn't a meal ready for them, but Zada came to Sket's rescue by bringing in a laden tray.

'Maressa is busy with my daughter,' she said, removing the lid from a huge pot. 'And she will be for the rest of the day.

When she had departed, shooing her husband before her, Leaf

came to help herself to some crusty bread.

'Did people stare at you?' she asked Ren, head tilted to one side.

'Quite a few,' he admitted. 'But at one section of the docks, they didn't just stare.'

He grimaced and Olam slapped him on the back, causing him to swallow a bit of cheese the wrong way. While Ren tried to get some breath back, Navan explained:

'The shipmen got quite excited. They crowded round us and many of them went to their knees and tried to touch him.'

'The Outer Island docks,' said Taseen.

Navan nodded. 'That's what Taza called it. The ships were different there and so were the shipmen.'

Pallin grunted. 'Wore next to nothing. Little bit of cloth round their middles, scarcely decent. And gold – more than a woman would wear. Three, four rings in their ears, stuck in their teeth.' He shook his head in disapproval, ignoring the grins of the others.

'The Outer Islanders follow the Way of the Elders devoutly although they offer to many gods and goddesses too,' Taseen told them.

'Some of the ships are bigger than houses,' Olam commented.

'Big or small, they all bob up and down all the time,' Pallin retorted.

'Along some parts of the dock there were some very hard looking types,' Olam ignored his Arms Master. 'And their ships looked hard too – very clean but bare, nothing on their floors.'

'Decks,' Taseen put in helpfully. 'They may have been the coastal defence ships but more likely they're from further south west. An independent lot down there. How many of them were there?'

'Three,' replied Olam.

'Definitely from the pirate islands then. And not pleased at having to stay in dock at our Grand Harbour Master's whim, I'd guess.' Taseen looked amused. 'They probably had no names painted on their sides, but symbols perhaps?'

Gan considered the old man. 'They had eyes painted on the front ends.' He watched Taseen wince. 'You know something of these people?'

Khosa helped herself to some pieces of meat from Sket's plate. 'He is one.'

'Is one what?' asked Gan, already guessing the answer.

Taseen shrugged. 'My father was a pirate. One of the better ones. Highly successful for many years. I was born on such a ship. And the front of a ship is called the bows, Gan.'

'A pointy end and a blunt end,' Pallin muttered. 'With floors.'

Briefly the old mage and the old armsman exchanged glares, then Taseen laughed.

'It was long ago. Did any shipmen have marks such as this?' He pushed his sleeve up, exposing a thin arm tattooed with an interlocking spiral design.

'Yes,' Navan was positive. 'The first ship we reached in that section. Most of the men had that pattern. The others were different. One group had something like flames marked up each arm. The third had three-sided patterns.'

'The men belonging to a particular ship are called the crew.' Taseen carefully didn't look towards Pallin who contented himself with a snarl.

'I suggest if Hariko tells you he has found a ship to take you westwards, you ask Grek to check it thoroughly.' He steepled his fingers over his beard and tapped his lips. 'Perhaps I might be able to help. Memories are long in the pirate families. Let me see if I can persuade a shipmaster to visit me here. Have you pen and paper I can use?'

Ren fetched writing materials then wandered over to Leaf, as usual by her window. A short while later Taseen asked if someone could ask Taza to deliver the letter he'd written. He folded the paper and drew interlocked spirals on the outside.

'It must be given to any man with this tattoo. Tell Taza he need wait for no reply.'

Riff accepted the paper from Taseen and headed off to the priests' quarters.

'If the shipmaster is interested in what I have written, he will come at dusk. I understand Hariko does not visit until after dark? Ren and Leaf should either be elsewhere or wear their cloaks if the shipmaster comes.'

Ren turned back into the room. 'Which would be best Taseen?'

'I would like you to remain in this room so if you could wear the white cloaks? When Hariko calls, I will sit in another place.'

Ren nodded, glancing out at the sky. Mid afternoon: time to browse through the pile of books still sitting invitingly on a small table. As he lifted the top book, Grek announced his presence.

'I have been to Namolos as you suggested, Taseen.'

Ren reluctantly replaced the book and paid attention to the voice in his mind.

'Namolos berates himself that he failed to see the connections. He learnt of the Bound Ones only after he'd been on this world for many years. He found their places of imprisonment but assumed the bindings would be eternally secure. He sought them out while I was with him.

'The one Vorna is trying to loose, is fully awake. One of the others, in the land of Drogoya, is near wakefulness. He will do what he can but he does not know or understand the magic you used for the binding.'

Taseen looked increasingly alarmed. 'But I am one of the very few mages left and I do not remember all the spells. I was badly damaged: many things are lost from my mind.'

'Namolos said he would be more watchful of your land of Malesh but he urges that you go with these companions to Wendla. He fears the Bound One in the sea has become unstable.'

'Me? I have travelled no further than between the City and my estates twenty leagues away in the last thousand years!'

Pallin snorted. 'Born on a pirate ship, you said. Know all about ships, you said. Can't see many problems for you then, mage.'

Taseen gave Pallin an ice cold stare but Gan intervened before he could reply.

'Namolos wants all of us to go to Wendla? We've heard that there is a huge expanse of water to cross. Does Namolos expect us to leave the Dragons here?' He shook his head. 'I can't see them agreeing to that, not Tika and Farn for sure.'

'Maressa would be able to tell us how big the distance truly is,' suggested Ren. 'But I agree with Gan. If the Dragons cannot reach Wendla safely, we will not go.'

Chestnut brown eyes surrounded by silver had never looked so hard. Gan smiled at the Offering.

'Then, Grek, that is the reply you can convey to Namolos: unless the Dragons can make the crossing without danger, we do not go.'

'And my opinion is the same,' Taseen concurred.

A breeze seemed to riffle through Leaf's feathers and she giggled.

'I have to admit I would have advised you to take this decision,' Grek sounded relieved. 'I have spoken with Tika and the Dragons: they refuse to allow the company to be divided. So.' Now he sounded almost mischievous. 'Let Maressa check the way to Wendla and I will go back to Namolos and tell him your decision.

Chapter Fourteen

Maressa returned to the apartments helping Zada carry up yet more trays of the excellent food they'd learnt to expect. She refused to say how she had spent her day with Salma, offering only a smug smile in response to questions. She was swiftly informed of Grek's visit and of Namolos's suggestion that they travel to Wendla.

'It grows too dark now for me to properly evaluate the distances.' She told them. 'But I will do so at first light.'

She was also told of the possible imminent arrival of a shipmaster. Riff had been posted along the corridor to warn Ren and Leaf when to don their cloaks. They were all watching with absorbed fascination as a great eyes landed silently on Leaf's arm. (Taseen told them it was called an owl here in Malesh.) The bird blinked in the lamplight and was gone as Riff hurried in. Maressa pulled a cloak around Leaf who drew her feet up onto a higher rung of her stool. Ren had just tugged his hood low over his face when a firm knock sounded on the outer door.

Taza held the door open. 'A shipmaster to speak with you sir.' He withdrew as soon as the visitor had stepped inside the room.

The company stared. The shipmaster stood about Navan's height. His dark braided hair hung to his waist and was festooned with shells, feathers and sparkling stones. Four thick gold rings pierced one ear and two the other. Jewelled rings flashed on every finger and both thumbs. He wore a short sleeveless and buttonless jerkin of dark leather. His trousers were full cut and a brilliant crimson. The boots on his feet were of an eye-watering shade of lemon. A pink sash was wound round a narrow waist, its end falling loose down the side of his left leg.

Taseen sat, his bared forearms resting on the sides of his chair exposing the spirals swirling over his skin. The tattoos were matched by those on the shipmaster's arms.

'So. You are who you say you are then Taseen.' The

newcomer bared white teeth in what was presumably a smile. 'I am named Kasmi.'

A quick glance round the room checking the numbers and Gan noted the slight widening of Kasmi's eyes when he saw a white cloak. Kasmi's tone was a little less brash as he bowed in Ren's direction.

'I saw you at the docks this morning.' He turned his attention back to Taseen. 'So. I enquired after you of course and was told that you lay on your death bed in the Xantip Palace. You have made a sudden and marvellous recovery so?'

Taseen inclined his head. 'I have indeed as you see but it remains a rather – erm – discreet recovery if you follow?'

Maressa rose and smiled at the shipmaster. 'May we offer you tea? I fear we have no wine or ale.'

Maressa wore a green robe scavenged from Zada's charity box. Her long brown hair was unbound and drifted over her shoulders as she moved. Kasmi eyed her with open appreciation.

'So. Tea will suffice. I will send you some wine from my ship – I have several excellent casks from Drasheer.'

'Drasheer is famed for the quality of its wine,' Taseen explained.

Kasmi bowed again in acknowledgement of Taseen's assessment and a thin gold chain swung free of his open jerkin. An oblong of gold hung from it and Maressa glimpsed a Dragon face flanked by feathered wings enamelled on the gold. A scowling Pallin accompanied her to the kitchen.

'Please be seated Kasmi.' Gan indicated a chair. 'Let me introduce our company.'

By the time he'd done so, Pallin and Maressa were back and Pallin offered a bowl to Kasmi. Bracelets clinked as the shipmaster lifted a bowl from the proffered tray but Maressa elbowed Pallin in the small of his back before he could comment.

'I have heard the Grand Harbour Master forbids any ships to leave at the moment,' said Olam. 'This must be an inconvenience to you?'

Kasmi began to reply when he saw Leaf. The further end of the room was less well lit and the gijan sat so still the shipmaster had failed to notice her shrouded figure.

'So. I was told there were two sacred ones.' Kasmi sounded

wary. He bowed although still seated. 'Do you bring news of the Elder Races?'

'Perhaps,' replied Ren smoothly. 'We would know of your ship first. Where do you travel once the Grand Harbour Master permits you to leave?'

Kasmi glowered. 'I sail when I choose. So. We wait another two days to see what transpires then we sail with Chevra's permission or no.'

'And who do you spy for – the pirate isles or Wendla?'

Kasmi smiled more genuinely at Taseen's question.

'We take note of many things, mage. Whether they are of interest or value to others – who can tell?'

'Have you sailed to Wendla?' Taseen persisted.

Kasmi leaned back in his chair, his expression bland. 'Perhaps. You should know your own people Taseen: we wander where we choose.'

Taseen grinned suddenly. 'Partly true I agree, but you also wander where wealth might accrue.'

'This is a City of businessmen and traders,' Kasmi observed. 'So we also are aware of the pleasures of profit.'

'How much to hire your ship?' Taseen asked abruptly.

'Where would you want me to sail?' Kasmi shot back.

Taseen's eyebrows waggled. 'Far to the east, or far to the west. It has not been finally decided as yet.'

'So. What profits would we see?'

'I doubt there'll be much financial gain but it would certainly be an adventure worthy of the spiral singers.'

Khosa leapt onto the arm of Kasmi's chair and dabbed a paw at one of the glittering bracelets. Kasmi laughed suddenly.

'We have a ship's cat already – will you fight him for his place?'

Khosa abandoned the bracelet, turquoise eyes staring intently straight into the shipmaster's face.

'There will be no fighting Kasmi, once he knows who I am.'

Kasmi's mouth opened and closed. 'Did this cat really speak in my head?'

For the first time his composure slipped. The company were hard put not to laugh at his expression. Gan cleared his throat.

'Khosa is a very special cat,' he said, using the Malesh term for Kephi, as I think you have just realised. She is part of our company.'

Taseen set aside his tea bowl and began to speak. He gave Kasmi a generalised account of the reasons for the arrival of this group of strangers and an edited version of Vorna's plans. Kasmi concentrated wholly on the old mage's words. It was plain enough when Taseen spoke of the Bound Ones that the shipmaster was shaken. Riff nudged Sket, nodding at the dark windows. Gan saw him and knew he was warning that Hariko would soon arrive. But before he could speak Taseen pushed himself to his feet.

'It is not the politest way to treat a guest but I ask you to come with me and sit in another room whilst the scholar Hariko visits. He says he may have found a ship for my friends. I would like you to hear what he might say.'

Kasmi rose. 'So. I will listen Taseen. I would also like to hear what course the sacred ones would advise a follower to take in this matter.'

Olam led the two men through to one of the bedchambers and left them, making sure he left two doors ajar to allow them to hear Hariko's conversation. Maressa and Sket had only just cleared the tea bowls away when, without a preliminary knock, the door opened on Hariko.

'I think I have just the ship for you,' the scholar began without preamble. 'It is a trader from Mienta – one of the westernmost islands. It returns to its home port with a cargo of dyestuffs.'

It was obvious even to Ren, who was far less adept at reading men than he was books, that Hariko was over-enthusiastic. 'He sails tomorrow afternoon. If you could be on board well before then –'

'The Grand Harbour Master has announced permission for ships to leave then?' Gan interrupted with innocent surprise.

'Oh that is a minor detail. Chevra has no idea what he's doing at any time. There are ways to leave the Harbour – I can provide documents the shipmaster can show to the coastal defenders should one of their ships stop him.'

'And the cost of this ship?'

Hariko waved his hands. 'I will pay his charges – do not worry. It is an honour to be able to assist the sacred ones.'

Gan gave a non-committal smile. 'We find our plans may have changed a little, Hariko. We cannot leave as soon as tomorrow. Perhaps it would be best if we ask Taza to bring you a message regarding our departure?'

Hariko stared at him. 'But I thought you wanted to leave as soon as possible? I'm sure it would be safer for you.'

'Really?' Olam's voice was soft. 'I thought we were quite safe here. Whatever dangers could threaten us?'

'The City holds many dangers,' Hariko snapped. He looked across at Gan. 'I have gone to considerable trouble to find this ship ...'

'And we deeply appreciate your efforts.' Gan was on his feet, guiding the scholar firmly to the door. 'We will send to you when our plans are more clear.'

'I shall visit you tomorrow –'

'Do not trouble yourself, Hariko. We hope to visit Taseen tomorrow if he is recovered enough.'

'But I told you – you should not go to the Palace, and you should not take the sacred ones there.'

'We will take all care Hariko, be very sure of that. Goodnight.'

Gan stood a moment by the door, ensuring the scholar really had descended the stairs.

'Well, well. What's he up to?' Olam grinned as Gan returned to his chair.

'Something, that's obvious, but stars know what. I think it may be that we are not so safe here now. I wonder if we should move on?'

'We have no coin for guest houses,' Maressa was saying when Taseen and Kasmi came through from the bedchambers.

'Someone is giving Hariko orders,' said Taseen, sinking into his armchair with a groan. 'Vorna? I doubt she'd think two sacred ones of much interest. But who else could it be?' The mage frowned in thought.

'So. There are no Mientan ships in port,' Kasmi said with a gleam in his eye. 'Someone most surely wants your friends out of here and then what? Will they be taken somewhere, or lost at sea?'

The shipmaster seemed greatly amused. He stood opposite

Taseen, by the fire, twirling some of his bracelets. 'So. I will carry you and your friends, mage. The other two ships are mine also and we voyage together. Three ships you must hire therefore.'

Taseen nodded absently. 'I'll give you a banker's order.'

'You will give me coin.'

The mage shrugged. 'Worth a try. Very well, you shall have coin tomorrow. Can you get us out of port without coastal defenders sinking us?'

'The moon is dark tomorrow and the next night. There are rumours that Chevra will probably lift the restriction tomorrow anyway. So. I think it best to leave on a night tide in case your scholar has friends watching. I will consult my Sister of the Wind and we'll sail on her advice.' He grinned down at the old man. 'Is it east or west then?'

The mage tugged at his beard. 'East,' he said decisively.

'I don't like Hariko, and I hated his house and his friends.'

Taseen chuckled. 'Come child. Come and meet our shipmaster.'

Leaf hopped from her stool and would have fallen over the edge of her cloak if Sket hadn't grabbed her. She tugged at the fastening and pushed the cloak away with irritation. Ren pushed back his hood. Kasmi stared, first into Ren's silvered eyes then at the tiny gijan stepping daintily towards him. The colour drained from the shipmaster's face and he could speak not a word.

At first light Maressa, sitting quietly beside Taseen, sent her mind high into the air. She saw the immense sprawl that was Harbour City, a huge crescent against which grey, blue and green water surged and battered. Higher, and she saw an island to the south west. She turned away and sped towards the rising sun. Maressa saw islands below: some merely a few rocks, others large enough to bear several towns and many small villages.

Then there was water. Maressa felt as though barely a moment had passed but knew from tremors in her far-distant physical body that she was nearly at her limit. Finally she saw a long line of cliffs rising from the water ahead and with a shuddering gasp, snapped back into her body. She found Sket had put a blanket around her shoulders and she blinked at the faces staring at her with concern. Ren chafed her cold hands.

'You were gone much too long my dear. You must be more careful when none of us can follow you so far.'

Pallin thrust a bowl of hot tea under her nose and she let the steam warm her face.

'The longest stretch over water is about thirteen leagues, perhaps a little more but not much. The weather systems are very erratic over that part; I don't know if the Dragons could fly over them – they would have too much difficulty flying through them.'

'Are you sure they are safe now?' Taseen asked anxiously. 'If they are seen there will be pandemonium in the City. Everyone will rush to have a look at such mythical creatures from the past.'

Ren smiled. 'They are safe. They are to the north east of the City and they are taking it in turns to shield against prying eyes. They say they have found a small cove where no one so far seems to come.'

'Will thirteen or fourteen leagues be too far for them to fly without rest?' asked the mage.

Sket chuckled. 'Brin at least could do twice that without too much bother.'

'That is one problem resolved. The next is how do we all get to Kasmi's ship unobserved?' Olam looked round the group. 'I'm sure this place is being watched after Hariko's comments last night. And Taza is well known as the head priest of this temple. I couldn't find my way to the docks without a guide.'

'Karn,' Gan exclaimed.

Navan followed his thought at once. 'You can't go and ask him though – your height gives you away every time. If Taza or Zada would guide me, I'll go and ask him to do us another favour. If the boy is his, perhaps we could go in three groups with Taza taking one lot. We would be less noticeable than all nine together.'

'And if I leave off the white cloak and wear one of those odd hats a lot of men seem to wear here,' Ren began.

'Exactly,' Taseen nodded approval then frowned. 'But little Leaf cannot go uncloaked.'

Leaf trilled a laugh from the window. 'Funny old mage. I have wings. I will join my siblings. No one will see me in the darkness.'

Taza came into the room. 'A boy from the docks came with a message. You must make your way to the ship by twilight tonight. The shipmaster will send a boy to guide you.'

Gan laughed. 'No need to bother Karn then. I'm glad – I would not like to think we might land him in trouble.'

'I will not be able to hurry through the streets,' Taseen warned.

'I will hire a chair for you, mage. Many chairmen are followers of the Way. I know who can be trusted.'

Taseen looked much relieved at Taza's proposal. Zada and Salma arrived, loaded with neatly-folded clothes. The company found all their old garments washed and mended, and extra shirts and trousers for all. Finally Salma held up three wrapped bundles, one smaller than the other two. She went to where Leaf still stood by the window. Shyly she offered the gijan the parcels.

'Maressa told me the names of your brother and sister. See, I've written the names on the outside? The smallest one is for you. I didn't have time to do more, but you have had two new trousers already.'

Leaf clutched the bundles to her bare dappled chest. 'Oh I will repay you Salma, truly I will.' Then her head tilted to one side and she lowered her voice. 'Have you something I can take for Tika?'

Salma laughed aloud. 'That's why I had no more time – I made something for her too. Maressa has it in her pack.'

Leaf's wings furled and unfurled in excitement but as she opened her mouth Salma forestalled her. 'No. You must not open them now.'

She looked shocked at her own temerity in speaking thus to the gijan and blushed furiously, but Leaf nodded.

'It will be fun to undo the parcels all together.'

Her wings fanned suddenly and Salma found herself completely enfolded in the gijan's embrace. Leaf murmured softly to her and then folded her wings again. Salma stared at the gijan, a stunned expression on her face. She nodded once and bowed deeply.

Zada left the room and returned with various pouches and packets, which she gave to Sket. They removed themselves to a quiet corner where Zada explained what herbs and remedies each pouch contained and their application. Taseen was busy writing: letters to Tavri and Sheoma he told them, which Taza would deliver in the morning. Time flew past in the bustle of packing their gear and thanking the three priests for their great generosity.

Riff helped Taseen down the stairs to await a chair and to watch for the boy Kasmi had promised to send. Leaf embraced everyone as they filed out of the apartment. Then she climbed the narrow stairs to the roof, accompanied by Taza, Zada and Salma. They waited a short while until twilight had deepened to dusk. With a final embrace and still clutching her bundles all tied in her white cloak, Leaf's wings extended and she leapt out over the garden. For a moment, the priests saw her hover above them. Then she rose higher and was lost to their sight.

Olam had had a firm talk with Pallin, telling him he must keep his opinions to himself. Which was just as well. Pallin had been aghast to discover that not only men comprised a ship's crew but women as well. And they wore the same as the men – a scrap of cloth around their hips. Pallin's shocked horror was so great that Olam managed to get him down a vertical ladder to a tiny room before he recovered the power of speech.

Riff, perched on a bunk, and kept a straight face while Olam repeated his warnings to Pallin. Pallin glared round the tiny room: two bunks, one above the other, were fixed to one wall, two more to another. The space between was just wide enough for a man to turn round in. The floor lurched and Pallin grabbed hold of the nearest bunk in alarm. 'Is it sinking?' he asked.

Riff craned to look out of a small circular window. 'I think we're moving away from the docks,' he said. 'I'm going back up to watch.'

The floor shuddered then began to dip and sway in a more regular motion.

'I'm going up too. If you're coming, remember what I've said.'

Olam turned in the doorway and saw Pallin sink onto a bunk.

'I'll stay here. I feel a bit strange,' said Pallin.

They stood by a rail, keeping out of the way of the crew, who raced round in a practised routine.

'Are you all right, Ren?' Gan asked beneath the shouts of

Kasmi and various members of his crew.

'I can't say I find it pleasant but I'll be fine. I don't know what Gremara did but neither heights nor water fill me with terror anymore.' He nodded along the rail. 'I don't think Maressa or Sket feel too good,' he murmured.

Sket forced himself to chew some herbs Zada had packed and made Maressa eat some as well. No one could persuade Pallin to eat or drink anything: he said he only wished to die, quickly.

On learning that three of his passengers were sea sick, one apparently terminally, Kasmi suggested they get out into the fresh air and try to eat at least something. At dawn the company, less three, went on deck to find they were surrounded by water; no land in sight in any direction. Taseen sat on a hatch cover, his back against the main mast. His beard was flattened over his chest and his eyes gleamed. Gan gave him a quizzical look.

'I was stupid enough to forget how wonderful life at sea is,' Taseen told him. 'I should have done this centuries ago!'

Thick rope was coiled neatly near the mage's feet and Khosa's head popped out of the centre of the coil.

'How are Maressa and Sket, poor dears?' she enquired. 'They really should come up here.'

A stronger gust of wind sent her ducking below the level of the rope, her ears pressed to her head.

'I'll go and find them. Have you met Kasmi's ship's cat?' Gan asked curiously.

Khosa gave him one of her regal stares. 'We met last night. He is below deck at the moment.'

Gan caught Taseen's wink and took himself off to find Sket and Maressa. Sket was pale but upright but Maressa's complexion was still faintly tinged with green.

'Come on.' Gan was ruthless, grabbing Maressa's hand. 'That was an order armsman.'

He hauled Maressa up to the deck where the first blast of wind knocked her back against his chest. He held her firmly against the rail with Sket jammed at his other side. Maressa stared up rather than down, watching the great sheets of bright yellow canvas snap and fill with air. She clutched Gan's arm.

'Someone's in the air!'

Gan and Sket automatically looked up until Gan realised

Maressa meant another mind rather than a solid body was aloft.

'Grek?' he suggested.

She shook her head, her hair whipping across her face. A woman stood before them, silhouetted against the early sunlight. She moved to the rail beside them and Gan's hands tightened involuntarily on both Sket and Maressa. The woman was smaller than Maressa, wearing a cloth about her hips. She had black hair which appeared to be shoulder length. Rings sparkled in her uptilted ears and her skin was lightly dappled.

The hand resting on the rail beside Maressa's had three fingers and a thumb, the nails short and pale. She also had three paired sets of nipples close beneath the more normal type of topmost breasts. This woman appraised Maressa as openly as Maressa, Gan and Sket studied her.

'I am Culinth, Sister of the Wind to the Spiral Star.'

'I am Maressa. I am an air mage.'

They saw the dark eyes widen, the head tilted to one side.

'I felt you in the sky, Maressa. Air mage must be very like a Sister of the Wind. Come with me. I must watch for the ship now – we approach reefs which lie near the surface and I must direct the wind to guide us true.'

Maressa, her sea sickness quite forgotten, followed the woman towards the front of the ship, Gan and Sket watching them every step of the way.

'Is she gijan?' asked Sket.

Gan shook his head, his eyes still on the two women who now sat high in the bows.

'Not like Leaf, or Willow, or Piper. She is a grown woman, yet she has no wings. Remember our three were genderless until their wings emerged.' He shrugged. 'Or the other way about. But most definitely they come from the same ancestral line. I'll ask Taseen.'

A shout from above caused them to look up. Olam and Riff grinned down at them from a precarious looking position overhead. Their bare feet rested on ropes and they seemed to balance by holding other ropes about chest high.

Sket grunted. 'If Pallin could see Olam now, he'd kill him.'

Chapter Fifteen

Culinth introduced Maressa into the life of shipwomen in general and of a Wind Sister in particular. Maressa was caught up in the fascination of Culinth's ability to interact with the weather systems. She spent most of her days and much of her nights in Culinth's company. Her sea sickness disappeared from the time Culinth first spoke to her. Sket also rapidly recovered, although he took the precaution of adding a pinch of Zada's ginger herbs to a bowl of tea once each day. He explored the ship with caution, always careful not to get in anyone's way. The crew spoke a quick language, quite unlike any Sket had heard before. They seemed friendly and communicated with Sket in a mixture of gestures and an odd word or two in the common tongue.

The first time he discovered the kitchen he was convinced the cook was insane. He was met with shrieks and screams and a large cleaver was brandished beneath his nose. Then a shipwoman behind him yelled something and the cook lowered the cleaver. A broad smile replaced the distorted scowl and Sket found himself dragged inside and subjected to a lengthy and totally incomprehensible explanation of every single thing in the kitchen. He was then offered a bowl of what he believed was tea but discovered was actually something that made Lorak's restorative seem like water. He leaned against a wall of cupboards, nodding and smiling, and praying his legs would continue to support him.

On their third dawn at sea, Kasmi was informed that one of his passengers was still ill and languishing below decks. The shipmaster, who dressed the same as his crew once at sea, shouted with laughter. He strode from the pilot house and slid down the ladder to the passenger cabins. Ignoring Pallin's weak moans of protest, he parted the old man from his bucket, put him over his shoulder and swung back up on deck. He yelled orders as he emerged and propped Pallin against a rail.

Two shipmen pounced, divesting Pallin of his by now unsavoury clothes, and stood back. Two other shipmen hurled buckets of sea water over the trembling Pallin who gasped in shock. Blinking against the sting of salt and the brightness of the light after two days in the gloom below decks, Pallin roared his outrage. Kasmi stood, hands on hips and a grin on his face. Another shipman tossed a dark green robe over Pallin's head, tugging it down over his wet nakedness. Yet another arrived with a bowl. Sket felt a twinge of apprehension when he realised it was the lunatic cook who offered Pallin the drink.

Kasmi moved closer. 'Drink, landsman, and then you will eat and sit here on deck.'

Pallin's mouth opened but Kasmi roared at him: 'I am shipmaster. So. My words are law here – now drink!'

Olam had arrived with Gan and Riff, Navan was leaning on the rail fronting the pilot's house. Pallin took the bowl from the cook and drank the contents in one draught. Sket winced. Pallin's white face suffused with colour and he wheezed for breath. Kasmi nodded in approval and tugged the old man over to Taseen's hatch cover by the main mast.

'Good day to you,' said Taseen politely, blue eyes sparkling under the thicket of his brows.

Pallin didn't reply: he was still shocked by the treatment he had just received. Kasmi chuckled, turning to Gan and Olam.

'He'll be all right. So. I will do the same thing again if necessary, but it won't be I'm sure.'

'How long until we see land?' asked Gan.

'Two more days. We reach a small island that has no name. So. It has fresh water and most ships stop there to resupply their barrels.' He barked an order and a shipwoman sprang aloft, shortening a rope on a sail.

Gan glanced down to find Ren leaning over the rail.

'Look at that Gan. I wish Storm was here. I don't know whether I should try to mind speak them or not.'

Gan watched the now familiar sight of dolphins racing between their ship and one of the others. As they rose from the water their outlines reminded both Ren and Gan of Star Singer's shape.

'It wouldn't hurt to try.'

Ren touched Gan's mind lightly, enabling him to hear what Ren heard.

'Greetings, land worms!'

The mind tone was clear, high pitched and thrumming with amusement.

'Land worms!' Khosa's voice was suddenly in their heads. 'I am a Kephi queen, and more.'

Whistles and grunts were audible as the party of dolphins turned their heads towards the ship. 'We know not Kephis, but you are trapped in the box which floats while we have the freedom of the great waters!'

Gan glanced towards the main mast and saw Taseen struggling with laughter. Only Khosa's ears were visible above the coils of rope, but her ears were enough to convey her annoyance. The dolphins dived and didn't resurface. Ren sighed.

'This sailing has its points you know, Gan. No one to bother us, nothing for us to worry about.'

'How long will it last though? I've enjoyed these two days but I'm beginning to wonder what we will be faced with next.'

Ren grimaced. 'Always so cheerful Gan! At least Pallin looks to be improving.'

In the cabin where meals were taken, Navan pushed away his empty plate and got to his feet. 'Kasmi says we should sight land around midday,' he said.

'You like looking at those maps in the pilot's house Navan?' asked Olam.

Navan eyed him. 'Maps of the sea are called charts, but yes, I find it fascinating how Kasmi can find his way over all this water. As fascinating as you and Riff seem to find scrambling about in the rigging!'

It was approaching midday when a shipboy crouched high at the top of the mast shouted down to the deck. The cry was taken up and the crew lined the rails to peer ahead. Kasmi stood outside the pilot's house. He called to Gan and his companions.

'Land ahead! So. We will anchor there by late afternoon.'

They could see a small dark line low on the horizon which they presumed was the island Kasmi was making for, when Maressa sprang to her feet in the bows. She let out a shriek and to Culinth's consternation, began jumping up and down, waving her arms wildly. She raced down from the bows towards Sket.

'Look!' they heard her yell. 'The gijan! Leaf! All of them!'

Kasmi's other two ships were within hailing distance and Gan could see their crews hanging in the ropes and craning over the rails.

The three specks in the sky rapidly closed with the ships, circling above the main masts. Ululating screams overrode the snap of canvas and the hiss of water. Then Leaf landed on the railing, her wings extended for balance as Willow and Piper came down next to her. The crews stared in awe, some falling to their knees when the three gijan hopped down from the rails and swooped upon any member of Gan's party they could reach, enfolding them with cries of delight.

Seeing the reaction of the ships' crews to the gijan, Gan crossed the deck to speak to Taseen. The old mage smiled and nodded at Gan's suggestion. Gan climbed the steps to the pilot house and the shipmaster Kasmi who still stood staring at the three gijan fluttering across his deck.

'Kasmi, you have to understand something.'

Kasmi forced his gaze up to Gan's face.

'These three are indeed true gijan. But they are the first for centuries to develop their wings to become true gijan. They are desperately young, Kasmi. We think they are maybe thirteen or fourteen years, and although they carry long memories, they have no Elders to guide them. I think it best that you put word among your crews that while these three are very special and worthy of the respect you show them, they are but children still.'

Kasmi paid close attention to Gan's words, turning to look down at the deck. But Piper proved Gan's point: with two beats of her wings she was on the upper deck by the pilot's house. Small pointed teeth flashed in a smile as she spun before Gan and Kasmi.

'Do you see my trousers Gan? Leaf's friend Salma made them for us. Three each and all different.' Again Piper twirled, the green trousers matching her apple green under feathers.

'They are wonderful, Piper. Salma is the kindest of women and an artist with her stitching.'

Piper trilled a laugh. 'She will make our robes when we need them.' And she fluttered from the upper deck across the water to land on the following ship – the one with painted flames licking along its bow.

Kasmi spoke softly. 'You spoke truth Gan. A child, excited by her new clothes. So. I will tell the crews this. It will be hard for them at first to treat gijan as the children they are.' He lifted a bare shoulder. 'We served the Elders when they shared our lands and we have since revered their memory. So. To find they return to us without yet the wisdom of adulthood is a hard thing to accept.'

The ships slowly approached the tiny islet ahead and dropped anchor in a small bay – a flinty crescent of a beach lay a few ship lengths away. Small boats were swung out and empty barrels stowed by the rowers' knees. Kasmi joined the company watching the boats being hauled half out of the water.

'We usually spend the night ashore here. It is custom. So. Food is cached here for any ship who might need it. We will check what is there and add some small supplies ourselves.'

The men on shore suddenly shouted in alarm, then fell silent. A silver blue Dragon loomed over the hillier side of the islet, a small figure astride its back.

'Lady Tika!' Sket yelled.

The Dragon landed and, with incredible grace, reclined beside the stunned shipmen on shore. Tika slid from Farn's back, a grin splitting her face in half as she stared out at the ships.

'How deep is this stars-dratted water?' Sket demanded. 'I want to get on land. Now.'

'Too deep to wade through,' Kasmi warned him and called an order.

Another boat swung out and Sket and Navan were in it before it hit the water.

'He is anxious to reach the Elder and – another child?'

'Sket is Lady Tika's personal guard, Kasmi. And Lady Tika is soul bond to that Dragon whose name is Farn.'

Sket splashed into the water without waiting for the boat to be pulled out but was nearly flattened as both Tika and Farn rushed at him. Farn's eyes flashed sapphire and pearl in excitement.

'We missed you Sket. It seems ages since we were together.'

Sket's grin matched Tika's. He hugged Farn hard and stood

back. 'Not ages Farn, eight days.'

'Hmm.'   Farn was not confident where numbers were concerned so he made no comment, instead greeting Navan and Gan. Willow landed on the rim of a hauled-out boat and they saw he held Khosa in his arms.

'She scratches,' Farn began, but subsided when both Tika and Sket glared at him.

Most of the crews of Kasmi's three ships were ashore when Brin, Seela and Storm drifted lazily down from high overhead.

The tiny islet was furred with rough grasses and small, bent shrubs, but it had fresh water. A spring bubbled from the further side of the hill to form a pool barely a man length across. Gan watched a gang of shipmen heaving aside large rocks close to the pool, disclosing a cupboard-like cavity. Small casks within were pulled into the fading sunlight and their contents inspected. Food was remarkably well preserved, wrapped in oiled cloth. Kasmi's men added a few similar packets, resealed the casks and blocked them away again.

There was no fire-making material but the great Dragons obligingly heated round pebbles until they glowed. The three crews and Gan's company settled round this unusual "fire" for the night. Privately, none of the Dragons understood this human ritual of huddling round fires but they were content to be of assistance. The crews, their officers and Kasmi found it difficult at first to accept Dragon voices within their minds, but by the time full dark had fallen, it didn't seem quite so strange.

The sea Dragon Storm had shown great delight in finding Navan again and reclined, his chin resting on Navan's head. Kasmi and many shipmen gathered near them, fascinated as they compared the Dragon's tales of living with the great seas to their own lives and experience.

'Why did it take so long for your ships to get to this land? It took us less than half a day to fly,' Storm asked the men.

'There are many reefs and irregular currents between all the islands of the whole archipelago. So. We have to chart our course with much care.' Kasmi grinned. 'If we could sail in a straight line, it would take perhaps one day.'

Storm's faceted eyes whirred. 'I could see some of them,' he agreed. 'The water turned in circles and sometimes I could see rocks below.'

'So. This is why my people pay for Brothers and Sisters of the Wind to journey with us. They will not always agree to join a ship, no matter what rewards are offered. But a ship with such a one is far safer than one without.'

Storm looked across the glowing stones. Maressa and Culinth sat leaning against Brin's great chest. Seela reclined close by, the three gijan sprawled asleep on her back.

'Where does Culinth come from?' asked Navan.

Kasmi exchanged glances with the men and women around him. All shook their heads. A woman replied.

'No one knows where they are from,' she said. 'One morning there will be a Brother or Sister sitting by the docks. Then the shipmasters will approach and speak with them, begging them to join their ships.' She shrugged. 'It is said the Brothers and Sisters know which ship will become theirs before any master offers for them. They are friendly enough with the crews they join but they never speak of their lives before.'

An older man spoke up. 'I heard tell they come from far beyond the northern deserts – but who knows?'

'I see a similarity though,' said Kasmi. 'Culinth's hands, her feet, her skin. So. She is like to the gijan.'

At first light, Sket and Maressa were rowed back to the Spiral Star to fetch their packs: they, along with Khosa, would continue the journey with the Dragons. The next landfall would be Beffir, whose people were famed for their work with the timber they had in profusion on their large island. Kasmi reckoned two to three days for the ships to reach Beffir after consultation with Culinth. She said there was clear weather to the east while the wind continued steadily from the north west.

As the ships got under way the Dragons flew above them, gradually gaining height. The gijan continued to race through the air, diving and swooping between the ships, occasionally landing on Spiral Star, Star Flame or Eternal Star. During that morning, watching the gijan play, no one could doubt how young they were. Ren and Taseen commented to each other how the crews' attitude had altered toward the gijan. The awed reverence had subtly changed to a respectful protectiveness. The wind strengthened and the crews made changes to the sails; mystifying to Gan and Ren but already comprehensible to Olam and Riff.

'Culinth's people are related to the gijan,' Taseen confirmed when both Ren and Gan questioned him. 'Did you not see Culinth surrounded by the gijan last night? The Sister did not seem as surprised by their appearance as one might have expected, but then Wind Sisters have the power of mind speech much more strongly than I. I would therefore surmise they had spoken to her, perhaps even in Harbour City.'

'This island we approach – will there be any difficulties there?'

Taseen laughed. 'Surely not, Gan. They are not renowned shipmen although they build some of the best ships on these seas and small boats for many. Beffir has long been settled in its ways and its people rarely travel off island themselves.'

'Seela has kept watch behind us,' Ren began.

'As has Khosa,' Gan interposed. Ren nodded.

'Neither of them report any mind seeking our whereabouts. But Brin has flown ahead a couple of times and he says there are minds further east which seem to do sweeping searches this way twice a day.'

'Sheoma spoke to me last night. She said that Chevra has a fleet assembled – many of them the merchant ships he commandeered. He is fitting them to carry armsmen. Sheoma believes it will be twenty days at least before they sail. She suspects quite a few will vanish from the port well before then, slipping off to their home ports. There is no enthusiasm for conflict – Harbour City is a trading City and conflict is not good for trade.' The old mage sighed. 'I am unable to far speak Tavri or Sheoma. Would you be able to reach them Ren?'

Ren shook his head slowly. 'I'll try, but Maressa is the one to far speak – or Brin or Seela.'

'And would the Dragons speak to them on my behalf?'

'Of course. You have only to show them Tavri and Sheoma's mind signatures and they will find them.'

'Is that so? You must explain it to me. Clearly our uses of power have diverged greatly since the world was divided.'

Gan braced his long legs against the rail as the ship seemed to buck slightly. 'This world was divided?' he queried.

'I speak of the Time Before, when the Ancient Elders first arrived. Those who would one day become human tribes were still more animal than human then. They lived in dens and burrows and scarcely had the power of speech, let alone thought. But even so, they wandered this world, all over the great land masses at least. There is evidence to suggest that the climate was different then – without the regions of ice far to the north which are well documented in our histories. It would be a small matter for the tribes to move between your land Ren and this one.'

Gan was more concerned with Chevra's plans. 'How long to reach Wendla?' he asked.

'Kasmi will know better than I, but perhaps twenty days.'

'I'm still not sure what we're supposed to be going there for. And Grek's been missing since we left Harbour City five days past. Who is dictating our lives at the moment? I thought we were in Sapphrea to find Rhaki and maybe discover some means of helping Ren deal with the evil in his land. Now, we're in the middle of the sea heading for an island of which we'd never heard even a whisper. Why? What are we meant to do?'

Ren stared at Gan in surprise. That was the longest speech he'd ever heard from Gan, and underlying frustration was very plain in his voice. It was Taseen who replied.

'I thought you accepted the connections Gan. Far too many coincidences led you and your friends to be here at this particular time. You travelled through the Valley of the Spiral Star, met the strange creature Kertiss and the Ship of the star fields. Now you sail in a ship of the sea, named Spiral Star. I did not know of a fertile valley deep in the great desert but for it to be named thus just cannot be chance. You and your friends have been drawn together and together drawn on.'

'Fate? Destiny? Is that what you're saying?' Gan laughed without humour. 'I do not believe in such things Taseen.'

Taseen regarded the tall thin figure of the Asatarian. 'Fate or destiny are indefinable philosophical abstracts. I cannot convince you that such things are real. One of the affirmations in the rituals of the Way of the Elder Races states: The land is. The stars are. There is an acceptance there which I think you do not understand or possess my friend.'

Gan frowned. 'I accept that the land is, and that the stars are.'

'But the stars are what Gan?' Taseen asked quietly. 'From the story the Ship called Star Singer told, the stars are much more than lights in the night sky. Can you say the stars are and accept that you do not know what that truly means?'

Gan stared down at the old mage then turned on his heel and stalked to the bows where he stood, battered by the wind and by his own confused anger.

'I hadn't noticed,' Ren confessed. 'Gan is an armsman. He is used to action, to command, to making quick decisions. Since we left the coast of Sapphrea we have followed others – guided through the desert, sheltered by the priests from we knew not what and now on ships heading we know not where or why. I think also that Gan dislikes being apart from Tika and the Dragons. Navan at least has become intrigued by Kasmi's arts of navigation, which occupies him for now.'

'I have no doubt whatsoever of Gan's bravery and steadfastness, but I fear his patience has worn thin of a sudden.' The mage frowned at a thought. 'You say Gan is not strongly gifted in the mental powers such as you have?' He waited for Ren's nod. 'Would it be possible to affect him – I mean another such as yourself – could you perhaps disturb or upset his usual equilibrium without his knowledge?'

Now Ren frowned. 'It would be possible yes, but with the Dragons alert for any mind probes as well as myself here how could it happen? There are Culinth and Maressa too.' He shook his head. 'It should not be possible without one of us picking up a hint of it.'

'Could you tell if Gan's mind had been tampered with?' asked Taseen.

Ren left his seat beside Taseen and went to stand by the rail. The wind felt suddenly chillier as he stared unseeing at the heaving waves. The wood beneath his hands felt sticky with damp salt and Ren wished fervently that he was back in the Menedula and none of this had happened. He went back to stand beside the mage.

'I will only do this with Gan's consent,' he told him. 'I think I could do it without him being aware, but that I refuse to do.'

Taseen nodded and held out his hand. 'Would you be so kind as to help me to the cabin – this wind is proving too cold for my bones.'

As they made their way to the ladder to the lower deck, Taseen tightened his grip on Ren's arm.

'I am glad you insist Gan be aware of your investigating his mind. Sadly, I know many mages now who would not quibble to dredge through another's innermost thoughts.'

When Ren had settled Taseen in the tiny cabin they shared, he returned to the upper deck and stood watching Gan for some time. He jumped when the unbodied entity Grek spoke to him.

'Forgive me for startling you. I arrived when you were speaking with Taseen. I suspect he may be right. No.' He forestalled Ren's immediate question. 'I would not invade the privacy of any of your minds.'

With no further hesitation, Ren made his way forward to Gan. Gan still stood, about ten paces behind the Sister of the Wind. She was pressed into the very joint of the ship's bows, her head back, her eyes closed.

'Gan.' Ren put his hand on Gan's arm. 'Would you permit me to see if anyone has touched your mind?'

The Asatarian turned sharply, staring down into Ren's silvered eyes. After a moment's pause he slowly nodded.

'I have been considering why, and indeed how, I could be so rude to the old man. You think someone may have reached me? But why me, rather than you or Maressa?'

'Because we would have noticed at once.' Ren smiled and let his mind slide into Gan's. He saw at once some alteration had been attempted to the muted web of power about Gan's mind. There! Even as Ren grasped a wisp of an identifying thread, it was gone.

Chapter Sixteen

Chevra sat alone in the Debating Chamber within the Xantip Palace. He shifted his position again: the intricately carved and ancient throne looked impressive but was most uncomfortable to sit on for too long. Six days ago he had snapped out orders to his generals and administrators, demanding reports. Now he was struggling to work his way through the copious papers which had flooded back in response. There seemed an inordinate number from General Koolis and his staff officers. They used ponderous phrases and constructed sentences in the most convoluted fashion that drove Chevra to fury.

The Commander of the Coastal Defenders had sent a brief report on the state of seven warships, long forgotten in a small inlet: two were beyond salvage; the remaining five would need a tremendous amount of work to make them seaworthy again. As a footnote, the Commander quoted the cost he estimated it would take to repair one ship alone. Chevra blanched at the figure but when it dawned on him that it was the cost for one ship only, he felt positively ill.

He shouted with rage when informed by Tavri that the Mage Taseen had retreated to his estates, citing his illness as excuse. Tavri became quite tearful as he described Taseen's near comatose state. At least Vorna had reappeared although she didn't seem to be as interested in the prospective retaliatory attack he planned on Wendla as Chevra would have wished.

Even to Chevra's apolitical eyes, it had grown apparent that the Councillors Bajal and Fental were more eager to do Vorna's bidding than his. The Grand Harbour Master stood up, rubbing his backside. He began to pace round the Chamber, his feet vaguely following the mosaic patterning of the floor tiles. He knew the Council of Mages considered him a blustering simpleton. It suited him most of the time to let them think they ran Harbour City, but now this trouble with Wendla had arisen.

And he would be making the decisions.

Vorna had always been pleasant to him, treating him in a mildly maternal fashion; but Chevra was not the fool he seemed. Vorna had recently become more insistent that he heed her advice above his other Councillors – discreetly so far of course, but he was aware of it nonetheless. He knew Fental and Bajal were her creatures to the marrow of their bones. And now Taseen had taken himself off, gods knew why.

Chevra believed not a word of Tavri's sorrowful account of the old mage's desperate illness. But it left only Tavri, Sheoma and Lessna to balance against Vorna. Chevra had faith in Tavri and Sheoma but held some doubts about Lessna's inclinations. If Lessna chose to vote with Vorna and her minions, they could force their decisions upon him. And Vorna was not interested in any dealings – warlike or not – with Wendla. She was deeply involved in some investigations of an archaic nature: Chevra had heard mention of the Bound Ones.

Gods and goddesses above and below! The seniormost mage left at his Council wasting her time chasing mythical ghosts! Vorna had stormed into his apartments last night on her return from her estates, arriving at a most inopportune moment too. She had curtly dismisssed his companion and demanded to know where he had hidden the sacred ones. By the time she had left after ascertaining that he had no idea what she was talking about, it had taken him most of the night to persuade that rather luscious companion to stop sulking.

Despite his denials to Vorna, Chevra had heard of the sacred ones being seen in the City. As Grand Harbour Master he attended rituals in many of the different temples scattered through the City, but he had been born to a family who followed the Way of the Elder Races. His childhood had been punctuated by the rituals and festivals devoted to the Way and that devotion remained, albeit in private now rather than in public.

Most people in the Palace, including the Councillors were virtually unaware of Chevra's cousin Harrip. Harrip was adopted by Chevra's parents when his own were lost at sea. When Chevra married the previous Grand Harbour Master's daughter Eorlas and moved into the Palace, Harrip went too. If he was noticed he was vaguely thought to be Chevra's personal servant, or secretary. In fact he did fill those positions but he was also Chevra's eyes and ears both within the Palace and throughout the City.

Harrip ran the most extensive network of informers of any Grand Harbour Master. He had begun it when Chevra's trading business interests first grew successful. Chevra still had a huge business of course, but Harrip had diversified: his informers brought him news not only of rival merchants but also of the manoeuvrings of the leaders of various independent-minded islands. Harrip learnt of the party of nine strangers arriving at the north central gate within moments of their appearance.

Two white cloaked sacred ones and seven others: one woman and one man taller than any seen before. He had been unable to infiltrate the temple precincts but that gave him no cause for concern: like Chevra, he did not believe a priest of the Way would shelter anyone threatening the security of the City or the lands of Malesh. But when the priest Taza summoned a chairman, it was Harrip himself who drew Taseen to the docks. So of course Chevra yelled at Tavri's playacting lies over the matter of Taseen's ill health.

Now Chevra dropped back onto the carved throne. What could Taseen be up to? If only the old man had given a hint of what he planned! Coming to a decision, Chevra bellowed for a guard. One of the doors opened and a head peered in.

'Fetch Councillors Tavri and Sheoma. No – wait. Tell them to meet me in the Garden of Harmony. At once.'

The door closed and Chevra stared down at the pile of papers in front of him in disgust. He snorted, pushed them further down the table and went off to the Garden to await Tavri and Sheoma. The Garden of Harmony was a large space encircled by stone walls. The southern wall was part of the battlements, remnants of the earliest Palace buildings. The inner walls contained Palace apartments and corridors. Small trees and shrubs formed a twisting maze, their blossoms of yellow, red and white reflected in an oval pool at the Garden's centre. The pool was lined with blue, yellow, red and white tiles – the four colours of harmonious life.

The air was cool this early in the day and the smells of moist earth mingled with that of the flowering bushes. Chevra squatted by the pool, peering in at the great gold and white fish that swam languidly through the stalks of the water lilies. He glanced up as Sheoma and Tavri came round the last curving bank of shrubs.

'Attractive things but dreadfully boring,' he remarked.

Before either mage could respond he stood up. Staring down into the pool, he asked very softly: 'Can Vorna hear or see us?'

Both mages grew still then shook their heads.

'She could if she wished but at present no one overlooks us.'

Chevra shot a quick glance at Tavri. 'I want the truth. Why has Taseen taken ship? He took one of the sacred ones with him, one who no longer wore his white cloak. But where is the other?'

Chevra turned to face them squarely. The blustering, yelling Grand Master was now a serious man studying them with more intelligence in his eyes than had ever been noticeable in any Council gatherings.

'Sheoma, would you make sure we are not – overheard?' Tavri asked.

He drew a deep breath. Then he told Chevra everything. Since Chevra became Grand Harbour Master, Taseen had commented many times and with some admiration, that he suspected Chevra of being nearly as devious as himself. Taseen's last letter instructed Tavri to be honest with Chevra should he ask questions, and so he was.

Both Tavri and Sheoma were ruefully aware that old Taseen had been correct: Chevra was no fool. His face remained expressionless while Tavri recounted all he knew of the nine strangers who had entered Harbour City. When Tavri finally stopped speaking the sun had just lifted above the battlements, warming the perfumed air to a heady intensity. Small birds hopped down to the edge of the pool then fled back under cover when Chevra moved. He gave a wry smile.

'Some of that I already knew, but there was much I did not.' He looked up at the Palace's inner walls. 'Harrip will arrange someone to be with each of you – a runner or a servant, so you may let me know anything more of Taseen's travels.' He paused. 'Is the old man serious about Vorna's plans? Is what she's doing truly that dangerous to us all?'

Sheoma smiled. 'He is serious. She is putting us in the most dreadful peril.'

Silence fell again, broken only by the soft sound of the water circulating into the pool and occasional rustles among the leaves.

'The Council gathers shortly,' said Chevra at last. 'Let us see what Vorna suggests next. I will have to shout at Koolis I'm afraid.' He started along the path leading back into the Palace.

Sheoma and Tavri followed more slowly.

'If only Taseen could reply – I can scarcely reach him now. I'm not able to hear his thoughts – I can but tell him a brief message and get myself back.'

Tavri nodded in sympathy. 'Even messenger birds would be useless. We have none trained to go beyond Dawn Island.'

He referred to the furthermost inhabited island of the eastern archipelago. Harbour City traders commonly used birds to carry messages from the City to their home islands and vice versa.

'The Wendlan mages seem able to send their minds this far – but how can that be?' Sheoma picked up her pace in frustration.

'Even Taseen hadn't heard of such an achievement for centuries,' Tavri told her. 'He believes the Wendlans have taken the study of mental arts in a different direction to us and have been encouraged to do so since they isolated themselves after the last battle. He only knew a couple of Wendlan mages personally at that time and he said they were far more able to focus specifically in many areas of power whereas Taseen had been trained more generally.'

They had passed the more crowded sections of the administration complex and entered the quieter corridors leading to the Debating Chamber and to Chevra's private apartments. Guards stood outside the great double doors of almaz wood, which they pushed open to allow the two mages through. Vorna was already seated and smiled benignly when Sheoma took a chair opposite. Bajal was scribbling in a small notebook and Fental was browsing through a sheaf of papers. Sheoma scarcely had time to return Vorna's greeting before the doors opened again to allow Lessna to rush in just in front of Chevra. The guards didn't have time to close the doors properly as General Koolis arrived with the Commander of the Coastal Defenders.

Chevra ignored the faint murmurs of greeting from Fental and Bajal and waved the General and the Commander to chairs at the furthest end of the table.

'You will take a third of the mustered armsmen to the northern borderlands,' Chevra announced.

Koolis's florid complexion darkened, his long moustaches quivered.

'They have just been recalled from there sir,' he said with amazing restraint.

'Then send them back,' Chevra snapped. 'I have heard a rumour to the effect that the desert tribes are about to launch a more concerted attack on our border villages. Not just raiding by small groups but a massed attack.'

Koolis's face was a rich purple by now. 'How do you know?' he demanded. 'I have informers in the region and they have sent me no such word.'

Chevra gave him a nasty smile. 'Perhaps your informers write their reports sitting safely by their fires rather than checking the borders themselves. I have given you your orders General. Put them into effect at once.'

Bristling with fury, Koolis stamped from the room, a faint growl emanating from him.

Vorna smiled. 'Grand Master, you really shouldn't upset the poor man so. I fear his health won't stand such teasing.'

Chevra stared at Vorna. 'Upset him? Tease him? I gave him an order. The man's a fool but his officers have even less sense so I'm stuck with him. Perhaps you should remember that, as Grand Harbour Master, I speak as I choose.'

He turned his attention to the Commander of the Defenders' fleet, ignoring Vorna's frown at the reprimand he'd given her.

'Bavvis.'

The Commander's expression was wary as he awaited Chevra's orders.

'I want three defenders ships moved to the Palace wharf. I will inspect them later this afternoon.'

'As you wish Grand Master. Do you want them ready to sail?'

Chevra glared at him. 'Well of course I do.'

Commander Bavvis rose, bowed and departed.

At last Chevra sat down staring at his six Councillors.

'I'm surrounded by idiots,' he declared loudly.

Vorna had charmingly invited Lessna and Sheoma to dine with

her that evening. Lessna accepted but Sheoma pleaded lectures to prepare. Vorna accepted her refusal with a smile but her eyes were calculating. Sheoma kept a bright expression on her face while a shiver slid down her spine.

That evening she walked through the upper corridors of the Councillors Wing of the Palace to Tavri's apartments. Perhaps she should have accepted Vorna's invitation she mused. But she had arranged to meet Tavri to consider some means of contacting Taseen.

Sheoma had never much liked Vorna. The woman always made her feel unsettled. As apprentices, Sheoma and Lessna had both been approached by Vorna who offered to take them as her disciples. Sheoma instinctively declined, although she was wise enough to phrase her refusal in terms of the deepest regret. Lessna had also refused, citing her strong calling to the healing arts and botanical sciences. Sheoma suspected Lessna would have liked to have been Vorna's disciple – for the wrong reasons. Vorna was second in age only to Taseen but was widely considered to be the real source of political and magical power within the Council.

Lessna found political power rather tempting but common sense had prevailed. She continued to work and study under Sula, the highly esteemed healer mage who had refused a place on the Council years ago. Sheoma paused at Tavri's door, glancing down at the young girl beside her. She had appeared at midday, saying simply that Harrip had sent her. Now she gave Sheoma a slight nod.

'Harrip sent one of us to the Mage Tavri. I will sit with him and wait while you visit Mage Tavri, if that suits, Mage Sheoma?'

Tavri ushered Sheoma through to his workroom which adjoined Taseen's rooms. Sheoma felt the slight tingle as she broke the warding Tavri had set across the door. She slumped into a battered armchair and waited as he reset the minor shielding.

'A lesser shield?' she queried.

He chuckled. 'That's what it seems at a cursory glance. But beneath is a major shielding.'

Sheoma kicked off her sandals and tucked her feet beneath her. She grinned suddenly.

'Did you see Vorna's face when Chevra said he was surrounded by fools?'

'Taseen was right about him though, wasn't he? I never quite believed him.'

'I have had no luck trying to backtrack Vorna's movements on her estates – have you?'

Tavri sighed. 'Not a thing. Again, Taseen never told me the precise locations of the Bound Ones but from hints I'm sure one of them must be near Vorna's estate. He said to me once, that she made a tremendous effort to obtain those estates from Xantip the Fifth. The main estate belonged to Xantip's third son, and when he died of summer ague Vorna claimed the estate to be the only suitable place for a Mage Councillor of her standing.'

Sheoma did some mental arithmetic. 'You mean she may have been trying to release the Bound One for nearly four centuries?' she asked in horror.

'It proves how powerful the spells constructed by Taseen and all those mages who died actually were,' Tavri retorted.

'When did Taseen first suspect what Vorna was up to?' asked Sheoma.

'I don't know – maybe less than a hundred years. But so much of his power was dissipated in that last battle, power he has never regained.'

They sat in silence for a time, Sheoma imagining, really for the first time, how it must feel to be Taseen: to have lost that sublime link that connected mages to an immense living force. She shivered at the thought. How could he bear it?

'How much does Chevra really know?' Tavri interrupted Sheoma's reflections. 'I have to admit that I don't think even Taseen suspected Harrip of keeping Chevra quite so well supplied with information.'

'Why did he want ships brought to the Palace wharf?' Sheoma remembered Chevra's order to Commander Bavvis. 'Would he send someone after Taseen do you think?'

Tavri handed her a bowl of tea and sat down opposite her. 'I cannot see the point of that. They'd never catch three ships from the pirate islands that have so many days head start anyway.'

'May I introduce myself?' a male voice asked politely.

Sheoma and Tavri froze. They could find no mind trace

within the room and Tavri's shielding was still in place, its alarm not activated.

'My name is Grek and I am known to Taseen,' the voice continued. 'He asked if I would warn Sheoma that either a Dragon or the air mage whom I believe you met, Maressa, will attempt to far speak you. He felt you might be somewhat alarmed unless you were forewarned.'

'Erm, yes, I see. Perhaps I would,' Sheoma agreed, her eyes wide. 'Who *are* you?'

'I told you. My name is Grek and I am unbodied. I have no physical body to hold me tied to any particular place, thus I can travel far and fast. As a matter of fact, I seem to do little lately except travel far and fast.' The voice sounded mildly disgruntled.

'May I ask what happened to your body?' Sheoma was sure she was dreaming – this conversation was not truly taking place. Was it?

'I was unbodied long ago but have since shared the bodies of many Sapphreans – the people beyond the great desert. I did them no harm and they had no idea I was present within them. Until the last one.'

Now the voice tone was tinged with – regret? – remorse? Sheoma couldn't tell.

Tavri finally collected his wits. 'Why can you not carry our messages to Taseen then?'

'I am not just a messenger,' Grek replied frostily. 'I have other things to do. In fact I must be on my way now.'

'But can you not at least tell us where Taseen is now? Or where you have to travel?'

Silence met Tavri's questions and after waiting in vain for a while, they realised Grek must indeed have left them. The silence drew out, both mages deep in their own thoughts.

'There are too many strange things happening for them to be coincidence,' said Sheoma. 'Gijan, Dragons, the strangers who came through the desert. And did anyone ever know of the great valley those strangers told of? Why were they led through it to meet the Ship they spoke of and then allowed to come to Malesh? But at the last they had to fight the men sent to guide them. Although why the desert men waited until they'd nearly left their lands before striking I'm not sure.'

'Well obviously it would look as though the strangers had tried to enter the desert rather than be leaving it should any find their bodies. I wonder if that attack was ordered by the man in the Dome or was it just an impulse?'

'It was the name Gan used that worried me most,' Sheoma frowned. 'The people call themselves after one of the Bound Ones – how many times must that name have been spoken, calling him awake again?'

Tavri rubbed his forehead. 'Does Vorna know of the desert valley and its occupants?'

'She cannot surely. She would have got herself up there somehow, long before this, if she had the faintest inkling of such a place. Tavri, are you sure Vorna's estate is close to a Bound One's prison? Taseen spoke of one deep beneath the waters between here and Wendla, of one in the desert. He believes one is in the lands of Drogoya. He said he thought the fourth was also far north of the desert.'

Tavri stared at her. 'Taseen was involved with the binding of the one in the desert and the one in the sea. Then he collapsed. Other mages dealt with the remaining two.'

'If Taseen is correct in his assumption that two children are bound either far north or on the other side of the world, what could Vorna have disturbed on her estate? Tavri please tell me there is nothing else as bad as the Bound Ones – or, gods forbid, worse?'

Before he could answer, Sheoma stiffened in her chair. 'Link with me Tavri, someone far speaks.'

'I am Brin. Maressa cannot reach you – we are too distant now. I do not think even I will reach you after another day. Taseen says he begs you to beware Vorna. Also to speak with the one named Chevra.'

'But wait Brin.' Sheoma's mind forced itself against Brin's flow of thoughts. 'Tell Taseen we don't believe Vorna has discovered a Bound One, but we don't know what it might be. We shall try to discover more but if you can't far speak us for more than another day, how can we communicate?'

There was a pause as though the Dragon was relaying Sheoma's thoughts.

'Taseen says we will have to use Grek. Grek is –'

'Grek has spoken to us this evening,' Sheoma interrupted again. She could sense the Dragon was tiring and marvelled that he could even manage to send his thoughts so far.

'Rest Brin,' she warned him. 'Try once more tomorrow but it will be too dangerous for you to far speak after that, I'm sure.'

She saw Tavri nodding vigorously, a look of concern on his face.

'We leave Dawn Island soon.' Brin's mind voice was fading to almost a whisper in their heads and then the contact was gone.

'Gods and goddesses above and below!' Tavri murmured. 'What strength the Dragon has!'

'Tavri!' Sheoma hissed in alarm.

The door wardings shimmered and wavered, as if some unseen hand pushed at them from outside. Tavri stood a few paces from the door, head bowed, hands clasped in front of him as he concentrated. Sheoma caught her breath: the tiny tendrils of light indicating Tavri's wardings flickered across the walls and ceiling. The lights shone brighter and steadied. Whoever was attempting to invade Tavri's apartments was using a huge amount of energy to do so. But while Sheoma stared, the lights paled and winked out.

Tavri exhaled a gusty breath and staggered. Before Sheoma could reach him, he groped for the back of a chair to support himself. He managed a pale smile of reassurance when she helped him to the armchair and swung the kettle over the fire.

'Who was it Tavri? Was it Vorna?'

Tavri leaned his head back against the cushions and closed his eyes.

'Bajal.'

'Bajal?' Sheoma gaped at him. 'But he is barely average in mage powers; he could not apply such pressure to your defences!'

Tavri opened his eyes with an obvious effort. 'It was Bajal but he was being fed power from another source.'

'So it was Vorna.' Sheoma sat back on her heels by the fire. 'What now Tavri? Do we pretend nothing happened, or confront Bajal?'

'Bajal will be in his bed for the next two days at least. Vorna used him with no regard for his weakness. He was simply a conduit. Do you suggest we should confront Vorna herself?'

Chapter Seventeen

Unknown to Ren and the companions on board Spiral Star, Storm was in constant mind communication with those he called the great ones. The Sapphreans had been dumbfounded at the first sight of whales breaching once they had left Dawn Island a day in their wake. Storm was delighted to find that this group he spoke with knew his Flight. The enormous female who led them, whose name was Avgoor, said she had spoken many times with Mist and with Ice when she took her family to the cold northern waters each year. The other three Dragons and their riders listened to Storm's conversation.

'I would know the names of your friends, little brother,' Avgoor finally suggested once Storm's excitement calmed. 'They have a different shape against the Above to any I have seen.'

Storm remembered his manners and introduced the three great Dragons and Sket, Maressa and Tika. The whale was surprised to find the Dragons carried members of the two leg race which accounted for their odd silhouette against the sky.

'They had never seen the great waters before they came to the place where my Flight spends the warmer time,' Storm explained.

'Indeed I had,' Brin interrupted. 'I had told of it to my Treasury although they did not believe me.'

'I did.' Farn was indignant. 'And I believed about the snow Dragons.'

'May I ask something, Avgoor?' asked Tika politely.

The huge shape below rose in the sea, spouting a jet of steam and water. 'You may ask, but I may choose not to reply.'

'Do you live all your lives in the great seas? How do you bear your children or do they come from eggs?'

Laughter rippled through her mind, laughter from several sources Tika noted.

'But that is three questions! Well, our children are born

breathing from our bodies. The two who swim beside me are my daughters.'

Peering down past Farn's shoulder Tika saw one whale, perhaps half the size of Avgoor, swimming close to her left side. Another, nearly as large as Avgoor, swam to her right.

'Jemchoo is my youngest child. She has completed only twelve journeys. Rakavina is nearly twice that age and will bear her own children soon.'

Tika looked across to where Maressa sat astride Brin's shoulders.

'Other sons and daughters swim in different clans,' Avgoor continued.

Greatly daring, Sket ventured a question. 'Don't you find it – well, boring – swimming all your lives?'

Peals of laughter rang in their minds. They saw two much smaller whales splashing near the surface before diving to come close to two adults. Both Tika and Maressa grinned at Sket riding on Seela's back and now blushing furiously at his own temerity.

'How could it be boring?' replied Avgoor at last, her tone amused but faintly puzzled. 'There are many sea people with whom we talk. Many feeding places where the waters are different colours, different textures.'

'Where do you travel now?' asked Seela.

'We go past the great island and then we go south to meet other clans and exchange songs for a while. But the currents say there is bad weather Above, near that island. It matters not to us but you might find it bothersome.'

Maressa instantly searched ahead and found the whale was correct: clouds boiled and raced in a storm system perhaps a day in front of them. Maressa sent a thought back to Culinth, on Kasmi's main ship, and found the Sister of the Wind was already aware of the changing weather pattern. The three gijan had been visiting the ships as they usually did each day and Seela directed them to stay there. She had no idea how a bad storm would affect the ships, but she feared the gijan would come to grief if they attempted to fly on and rejoin the Dragons. Her tone was severe enough that the gijan did not attempt to argue with her.

Brin and Maressa had carefully located all possible landing places, even the smallest outcrops of rock, which would be large enough for the four Dragons to settle on between Dawn Island and Wendla. Now they directed Seela, Farn and Storm to one such place.

By the time they reached it, the weather system coming towards them was visible on the horizon. This islet resembled the one at which Kasmi's ships had anchored a few days out from Harbour City. Maressa hoped it would be high enough to avoid flooding in the tempest that rapidly approached. They took refuge on the slightly more sheltered side and Sket produced thin ropes from his pack. Seela watched him in approval as he secured one end round Tika's waist and the other above Farn's foot. He did the same for Maressa and Brin before attaching himself to Seela.

In the short time it took him to do this, the sky had become livid, like a two day old bruise: yellow, purple, green, black. Lighter clouds fled before the storm, the wind thrashing the waves into frothing peaks. The Dragons dug the talons of their feet and wings into the sand and rock as firmly as they could and cowered down as the rain struck. The night that followed was terrifying for all except Storm.

He had experienced weather as bad in his short life on the wild cliffs of the north Sapphrean coast. But, he admitted there had at least been caves which gave the Dragons some respite from the onslaught. The hiss of lightning was loud even above the screaming howl of the wind, the roaring growl of waves pounding all too close to where they huddled. Rain hammered against scaled backs and leather wings until Brin and Seela ached from the battering. In spite of the shelter the two adult Dragons tried to provide, Tika, Khosa in her sack, Maressa and Sket were soaked within moments of the deluge descending.

The wildness of the winds, the black darkness broken by incessant flashes made it impossible for Maressa to send her mind out to try to discover when they might expect the storm to pass. All of them were utterly spent by the time that happened and it was no surprise to see, by the position of the stars in the slowly clearing sky, that it was close to dawn.

Storm moved first, down the beach a short way where waves purled less wildly now against the pebbled shore. He beat his wings vigorously, the rising sun glinting on his grey scales. Tika, worn out herself, felt Seela's weariness and knew it was exacerbated by the terror this night had brought them all. Farn was first to copy Storm, rearing erect and beating his wings to force his circulation to bring some warmth back to his chilled body. Tika sensed Brin and Seela's spirits lifting once they too became a little warmer but she and Khosa with Sket and Maressa, still crouched, shivering uncontrollably.

By the time Brin heated stones for them and they were beginning to feel fingers and toes once more, the sun was strong enough to cause the rain water to evaporate, in writhing tendrils of mist, from the thin soil of their islet.

'I thank the stars I wasn't in a floating box last night,' said Sket fervently.

The company on Kasmi's leading ship Spiral Star would have agreed wholeheartedly with Sket's opinion. Culinth had given warning in time for safety lines to be checked ready to be used by the deck crew and sails had been shortened. Navan snatched a hasty meal and warned Gan a bad storm appeared to be heading directly for them. Kasmi was worried that the ships were still too close to a line of reefs, he told him. Gan and the companions usually ate together. Occupied differently around the ship as they had become, it gave them a chance to talk. Now, they listened to Navan with varying degrees of alarm.

'Seela mind spoke the gijan,' he continued. 'They are to stay with us rather than risk flying into the approaching weather. Culinth called it a rotating system and she didn't look too happy. Kasmi says you must all stay below as soon as he gives the order: he doesn't want any of us going overboard.'

Ren stared at him. Navan shrugged.

'He said that I could stay in the pilot's house if I keep out of his way and don't venture out of it.'

Olam disappeared up the ladder, closely followed by Riff. The others guessed they'd gone to see if Kasmi meant his order to apply to them too. They had both quickly learned many of the basic tasks involved in sailing a ship and were determined to stay on deck. Gan nodded to Ren and made his way to the deck and thence down again to his cabin. Pallin merely grunted. Strange as it seemed, not only to the companions but also to Spiral Star's crew, Pallin spent most of his time now with the demented cook.

Neither spoke the other's language, shrieks and roars regularly erupted from the tiny galley kitchen, but they seemed to enjoy each other's company.

Ren followed Navan on deck and felt the change already. The wind was much stronger, gusting more from the left than from directly behind them. Navan headed for the pilot's house on the raised deck while Ren looked for the gijan. He found Willow and Leaf by the rail beyond the main mast. They smiled as he joined them.

'Kasmi says we must all keep out of the way and stay below when the storm comes,' he began.

The gijans' smiles widened. 'We will stay with Navan,' said Leaf firmly. 'We cannot go below – it is too closed in for us.'

'Have you asked Kasmi if that will be acceptable?' Ren envisioned Kasmi squashed in the pilot's house with his helmsman, Culinth, Navan and three young gijan.

Leaf's smile disappeared, replaced by a haughty look. 'Piper is telling him now – we do not ask permission.'

Ren decided to leave the gijan to argue with Kasmi without his presence and made his way down to the tiny cabin he shared with Taseen. The old mage was on the lower bunk, writing in a leather-bound book. He smiled as Ren lurched against the sudden movement of the ship. He eased his legs over the side of the bunk.

'Well then Ren. It looks as if we're in for a blow.'

'A blow? Is that what it's called?'

Taseen laughed at Ren's expression then grew serious.

'It will be a bad one I fear. Culinth is afraid the ships have not made enough distance south of the reefs. Kasmi reckoned overconfidently that the weather would hold fair until we were past the reefs.'

'Have they a name – are they marked on those maps of Kasmi's?'

The ship juddered and Ren sat down involuntarily next to Taseen.

'Charts, my friend, charts. Shipmasters from the different islands have their own names for the area. All know how dangerous these waters are – which is why they are rarely travelled.'

The door banged and Ren's pack toppled from the top bunk to the floor. Ren latched the door securely and staggered back to Taseen.

'Kasmi hoped we'd have good weather long enough to pick our way through the reefs. I'd guess we still have some way to clear them.' Taseen frowned, glancing at the circular window against which water was now battering although whether rain or sea water Ren couldn't tell.

'It feels as though we've reduced sail. I trust Kasmi takes us south as speedily as he can.'

Ren climbed into his bunk and lay flat, bracing himself against the increased roll of the ship. Timbers creaked and groaned and he felt the strain vibrating through the wood by his head as the sea pressed ever harder against the ship's side. He had no idea of the passage of time. It had been mid afternoon when he'd come to the cabin but the sky outside the tiny window darkened fast.

The wind's scream rose like a giant creature in pain, plucking and whistling through the rigging above. Ren decided later that he had been too terrified to feel sick, too busy concentrating on Taseen's voice rather than the fearful noise around him. The old mage talked steadily, occasionally inviting Ren's comments but when he found Ren silent, he just carried on talking. He paused only a few times: once when distant screams were followed by the sound of feet pounding over their heads. The second time was when the ship seemed to shiver and then hold steady for a moment before plunging on.

'Stream warps,' Taseen said. 'We must be free of the reefs but perhaps the other ships aren't. Kasmi is trying to slow us a little and that would surely only be to wait for another ship to find us.'

'Culinth,' said Ren suddenly. 'Can she not find the other ships if we are separated?'

'Yes, she could. She travels on whichever ship Kasmi is on. He spends time on each of these three.'

At last Taseen became silent. Ren's hand was cramped where he'd gripped the bunk side for so long but he remained wide awake and was perfectly certain Taseen lay sleepless below him. How long they lay, each in their own thoughts, before the faintest light seeped into the cabin, Ren couldn't guess. He turned his head to the light and realised the ship was steadier, still moving quite jerkily but not tossing and pitching as it had been for so long.

'Taseen?'

'Yes Ren?'

'Is it over?'

Taseen struggled to sit up. 'Perhaps. But I think Culinth said it was a rotating storm so it may return within half a day unless Kasmi can get us clear. It will depend on how the sea is running – the height of the waves.'

Ren lowered himself cautiously from his bunk. He saw Taseen's eyes shining under the unruly brows.

'If you felt like finding a bowl of tea for an old man, it would be deeply appreciated.'

Ren found himself chuckling. 'I'll see what I can do. But if I don't like the look of the deck once I put my head through the hatch, you can wait for your tea old man.'

He unlatched the door and gasped. Gan stood in the deeper gloom of the narrow passageway.

'That was quite a night,' Gan remarked with masterly under-statement.

Ren laughed, light-headed with relief at having apparently survived the night.

'Taseen requests tea.'

'Let's see if we can find some then.'

Gan climbed the ladder and slid the hatch aside. He flinched when water dashed into his face, half ducking back. Squinting, he straightened and surveyed what he could see of the deck. Climbing from the hatch he reached back to pull Ren up beside him, both glad of each other's support.

The deck still tossed and tilted but at nothing like the sharp angles of the night barely past. Splintered timbers tangled with ropes lay at a crazy slant towards the bows. A bare leg protruded from under the broken fore mast but Ren and Gan knew that if the shipman or woman lived, they would have been pulled clear by now. Most of the crew were in the rigging of the main and third masts, jumping to the first officer's shouted orders. Ren nudged Gan, nodding towards Olam halfway across a sail's spar. Riff was on deck working opposite a shipwoman, winding in thick dripping rope from over the stern.

The deck canted again and gripping Ren's arm, Gan crossed to the galley hatch. Ren pulled against Gan's hold and caught the outer rail. He peered through the gusting drizzle out over the water. The gentle waves through which he'd watched the dolphins curve and dive were transformed – the white foamed crests reached halfway up the ship's side with a sullen threat. Far enough distant to seem a toy, he saw another ship, a square of red canvas just visible from its fore mast. But stare as he might, Ren saw no sign of a third ship.

Gan had been watching one of Kasmi's officers signalling with the system of flags which had greatly intrigued him early in their journey although he had yet to learn their meanings. He too turned slowly, scanning the ominous swell of the sea in every direction.

'Where is Eternal Star?' he murmured.

They looked at each other, Ren's euphoric relief that the storm had ceased gone in the realisation that perhaps Eternal Star was lost. A flurry of wings brought Piper beside them. Her expression was solemn.

'Kasmi is distraught,' she told the two men. 'His youngest brother was apprentice shipmaster on Eternal Star.'

'What happened?' asked Ren.

Feathers fluttered when the gijan shrugged. 'It was too dark to see anything at all. The noise of the wind and the sea too loud to hear. But Culinth knew when Eternal Star hit a reef. She cried out and Kasmi knew.' She shivered, mantling her wings about herself. 'We think the crew could not live long in the water.'

Ren peered more closely in the early light. Piper seemed very young, the dark eyes shocked by the recent events. He put an arm across her shoulders.

'Willow and Leaf are all right?' he asked.

Piper leaned against him for a moment. 'We were all bumped about in that little house.' She extended an arm between her wings and displayed bruises darkening the dappled skin from the back of her wrist to her elbow.

Gan bent to examine the arm. 'Pallin will have something to soothe that. Are your siblings bruised too?'

Piper managed a weak smile. 'Yes, but Navan's got a cut head and his eye is swollen shut. He fell against a corner of the chart table.'

'Right. We'll find Pallin and see what help we can be to anyone who has taken hurt.'

'Pallin is with that strange man – the cook.' Piper shivered again. 'They cut off a man's arm.' She pointed towards the hatch to which they'd been heading.

Ren caught her hands giving them a little shake. 'Go back to your siblings,' he began but he saw Taseen emerging shakily from the hatch behind the gijan.

He touched the mage's mind and Taseen responded. 'I know Ren. Let the gijan come to me. I'll keep them busy. You help where you're needed more.'

Piper was already turning towards the old man who held his hand out to her.

'I know you don't like to be close cramped,' he said aloud. 'But it is too cold and unsteady for me up here. Come below and we'll leave the hatch and door open for your comfort. I believe I've remembered some riddles to which you'll never guess the answers.'

Ren watched Taseen retreat below followed by Piper. Leaf and Willow landed at the hatch as Piper's head disappeared.

'They use mind speech between themselves – it's obvious,' Ren said to Gan. 'But they have so far refused to touch our minds.'

'Except for the Dragons,' Gan corrected.

Ren frowned. 'Hmm. And I'm sure their minds are in fact very powerful, judging by the shielding with which they've protected themselves.'

As Ren seemed likely to stand clinging to the rail lost in abstract thought, Gan pulled ungently at his arm. 'Let's see what we can do.'

They found Pallin and the ship's cook in one of the long cabins used by the crew. A boy stood holding a lantern which gave them some precious light. The man on the bunk died as Gan and Ren drew close, and Pallin swore long and hard. The cook was silent for once, drawing a rough blanket over the man's body. The boy with the lantern stepped back, the light revealing a mangled arm tossed onto a heap of blood soaked cloths. Pallin's knees cracked as he straightened. He saw Gan and Ren then and shook his head.

'Couldn't stop the bleeding,' he said, even before he took the arm right off.'

He stumbled into Ren when the ship tilted again. He looked back at the cook gathering up various kitchen implements.

'He'd make a damn good man to have around in a fight.'

Ren stared at the cleaver the cook was wiping clean of blood and then back at Pallin in disbelief.

'He did his best. He knew all the bits of that poor lad's arm – muscles, blood tubes. He tried getting them back together before he took the arm off.'

Gan nodded. As Captain of the Lady Emla's Guards he'd seen fighting in the Sapphrean ganger wars as well as more recently in the Domain of Asat. Ren had never been among men screaming with pain from unspeakable injuries from which they took too long to die. The cook suddenly gabbled something in the direction of the boy. The lad thrust the lantern into Gan's hand and shot down the cabin to the ladder.

The cook put the severed arm under the blanket covering the corpse and got to his feet. He said something, in a muted tone barely recognisable from one whose usual method of communicating was by scream and bellow. Then he shrugged and followed the boy up to the deck, Pallin at his heels. Gan raised the lantern and extinguished the flame. He motioned Ren ahead of him to the ladder.

The sky had brightened to a dull pewter, low clouds still hurtling over the ship. They found men and women working on the fallen mast, freeing ropes and clearing rolled sail cloth. A still figure lay against a raised hatch, wrapped in a blanket, only the bare feet visible. Other crew members squatted nearby. Ren and Gan went across to help the two men who were bandaging their injured colleagues. One man looked up with a smile of gratitude as Gan reached into the basket of remedies and took out a roll of clean linen.

There were a couple of broken bones, many sprained wrists and ankles, bruises and contusions and a few minor cuts and gashes. The worst was a woman who had several long splinters embedded in her back: she had been close to the mast as it split. She was shocked, her skin waxen and cold. Her lips were bloody where she had bitten them against the pain. Gan beckoned one of the other men over, spreading his hands in the universal gesture of helplessness as he looked at the woman's back. The man nodded and gave a shout across the deck.

The cook appeared, instantly dropping to his knees beside the woman. He touched the area where three thick splinters protruded with a gentle finger and sat back on his heels when the woman went rigid. The boy who'd held the lantern in the cabin below stood nearby and the cook gave him a quiet order. Within moments the boy returned from his errand holding two flasks out to the cook.

Gently, he raised the woman's head, pouring liquid from one flask into her mouth. He recapped the flask and sat, his hand rhythmically stroking her face and brow. Slowly, her eyes closed and the cook reached for the second flask. He poured a little liquid over her back and bent to extract the first splinter. The ship rolled and shuddered and the cook bellowed. A crewman leaped to his side, bracing himself against the injured woman to keep her as still as possible. Gan also knelt, lending his strength to the crewman's in an attempt to keep her immobile. Gan swallowed when the first splinter emerged.

It was long: what damage had it done inside her body? He wished suddenly that Tika was here; he had a feeling this poor woman was going to need more help than the cook could provide. He was peripherally aware that Ren had joined them when he saw a pair of hands gently close around the woman's head. At least Ren could keep her asleep while the splinters were removed. The cook's fingers moved with an astonishing sensitivity as he located places where splinters were embedded that had snapped off below the flesh.

Red blood covered the woman's back, the cook's hands, Gan's trousers – and Gan was reminded of Tika again, only she had been covered in the lavender blood of the gijan. Sitting on the wet swaying deck in the middle of the great sea, Gan prayed to the stars that Tika and Farn had found shelter from the storm and were safe.

Chapter Eighteen

The Dragons waited through the day until at last Seela mind spoke the gijan. Her eyes whirred mauve and silver as she heard how the storm had caught the ships still among the infamous reefs. Tika and the others watched the great purple Dragon, making no attempt to hear her communication with the gijan but sensing Seela's agitation. Eventually the tenseness of Seela's body relaxed and she settled more naturally on their small refuge.

'The storm makes it difficult to focus,' she told them. Her prismed eyes flashed again. 'They lost one of their ships on the reef – the one called Eternal Star.'

'The one with the brown wings,' said Farn.

'All the crew were lost. There are many on the remaining ships who were hurt a little and one ship is damaged. Leaf said they are going south east to try to get out of the storm's reach but once they are in quieter waters they will have to make repairs before they can continue.'

'What of the injured?' Tika asked. 'Gan? Taseen?'

'They are unharmed. Leaf was upset about a man having his arm cut off. She said he died. There is a woman – Leaf thinks there are pieces of wood inside her but the child is confused and upset. She wants to return to us.'

Tika glanced at Maressa. The air mage was already trying to locate the ships through the mind signatures of those she knew on board Spiral Star. She sat cross legged against Brin's chest, her eyes unfocused for some time.

'The weather is disturbed and distorted over a large area,' she told them finally. She frowned. 'Culinth is blocked to me – I don't understand why. Ren said they are all shaken but unhurt.'

'Should we go back and try to get Ren and the others off the ship?' Tika queried.

Maressa shook her head. 'Ren said Culinth thinks the storm may well swing back and hit them from another quarter. It would be too great a risk.' She looked at Seela. 'Are the gijan coming to us?'

Seela rattled her great wings against her back. 'They are. They would not listen to me. They were very afraid on the ship – felt trapped as badly as before their wings erupted.' She turned her head to stare to the west. 'It is morning where the ships are: the gijan will not reach here until darkness covers us again.'

Farn and Storm both shifted in alarm.

'What if the weather turns bad again?' asked Storm. 'Will they be able to find us in the dark if the rain comes?'

'I'll watch for them,' Maressa offered, settling more comfortable against Brin.

Khosa abandoned Tika's lap and squirmed between Maressa and Brin for better warmth and protection from the wind. She slitted her eyes at Tika who had to smile. The Kephi truly detested and loathed being wet and yet she hadn't complained once through that dreadful night despite being nearly drowned. Storm must have picked up Tika's sympathetic thought.

'The water is quiet enough for me to find fish,' he suggested.

Concern again emanated from Seela.

'Be very careful then,' she said. 'Hunger will not bother us yet so there is no need for you to fish.'

'But a little warm food would do us some good,' Sket pointed out.

Seela considered his words. 'You are right. I forget that humans need to feed so often.'

'They only have such tiny stomachs,' Brin agreed.

Farn ambled down the small beach with Sket to collect the fish Storm brought while Seela breathed fire onto the pile of pebbles they'd used to warm themselves earlier.

'What do you make of the Bound Ones that Leaf told us of?' Tika asked, watching Sket clean the first fish.

'They are not in my memories.' Brin turned his head enquiringly towards Seela.

She sneezed, smoke wisping from her nostrils. 'There is no memory of them in my mind either, nor do I know of the Ancient Elders.'

'Did Leaf tell us exactly what Taseen said? And is there a reason the gijan will not mind speak any except you?'

'Indeed she told you what Taseen said correctly,' Khosa confirmed. 'But these gijan are untrained and will remain so unless there is even one single Elder left to instruct them.'

Tika frowned, digging a hole in the sand with a shard of flint. 'You said Namolos wanted them brought to him – does he know how they must be taught?'

Khosa was silent for so long Tika craned around Brin's chest to see if perhaps the Kephi slept only to meet turquoise eyes. Khosa's mind tone was quiet, almost uncertain.

'I know only what I have been told when Namolos walked my dreams.'

'Only what he chooses you to know then?'

'Yes.' Khosa's repy was the faintest thread of thought.

Tika tried to follow her own line of reasoning. 'And Namolos has not spoken to you or walked in your dreams?' she asked Seela and Brin.

'We know only what Grek has told us of him,' Seela confirmed. 'But Star Singer spoke warmly of him and I don't believe he would lie.'

'He told us he was damaged. Perhaps he is now unable to judge Namolos accurately.'

'No Tika,' said Brin, 'he spoke of Namolos as he knew him long ago, when my father was but an egg. He said he has had little contact with Namolos or any other since then. He spoke truly but whether Namolos could have changed is another matter.'

'He feels right,' Khosa murmured. 'As Bark felt right.'

Tika stared into the Kephi's eyes considering her words. She had felt Bark was a good soul but – he had been fearfully damaged for many years when she had briefly known him. Could Namolos be a damaged mind? Brin had followed her thought.

'From all we were told, Bark was known for his gentleness Tika. Although he was so injured, it had not changed his gentleness.'

She nodded slowly and the matter was dropped as Storm, Farn and Sket returned triumphantly with fish.

Night drew on, few stars visible through the layers of racing cloud and Seela lifted into the air, flying to meet the oncoming gijan. Maressa, Sket and Tika stayed near the heated stones, the three Dragons curving behind them to break the force of the cold gusting wind.

'She has them,' Brin announced at last. 'They are nearly exhausted.'

Sket began to mix some of his herbs in their dwindling supply of fresh water and put the small pot to heat. It seemed an age before Seela landed again, the three gijan shivering on her back. Maressa and Tika wrapped them in warmed but faintly damp blankets while Sket held a bowl for each to take a drink. They lay on the ground, tight to Seela's side and were asleep at once.

'Are they all right?' Sket asked, tucking a blanket closer round Willow's feet.

'It was too far for them to fly, especially against a crosswind.' Seela's head lowered to examine each sleeping gijan in turn. 'They are also upset by the loss of the ship.' Her tone grew thoughtful. 'What one sees, all see. Piper saw a man lose his arm yet Leaf and Willow have the same picture in their minds although they did not see it with their own eyes. No,' she refuted Tika's comment before it was made. 'Piper did not pass the image on, they *saw* it somehow.'

'Their minds are that closely linked?' Maressa was doubtful.

'They are litter mates,' said Seela.

'But Farn hatched with a brother and three sisters at the same time,' Tika objected.

'These three grew together in their birth mother's belly. They came forth within heartbeats of each other. Their minds are closer linked than I had guessed.'

'Like Tika and me?' asked Farn.

'I suspect very nearly so,' Seela agreed.

They tried to get what sleep they could through their second night on the islet and Tika woke to find Maressa gazing skywards.

'That storm's not coming back?' Tika scrambled to her knees in alarm.

'No. But I cannot reach Culinth. Ren and Olam are asleep – it is only about halfway through the night where they are and they are too weary for me to disturb them. But why is Culinth not responding?'

'Maybe she is too busy watching the weather,' Tika suggested.

Maressa shook her head. 'They are just outside the limit of the storm system – it rotated back towards the reef. The ships are quite far south now.'

'What will we do?' Farn asked with interest.

Tika shrugged. 'Are there islands we could rest on to the south?'

Maressa shook her head.

'I suppose we should go on to Wendla then. As long as we can reach Ren's mind we can let them know what we're doing.'

'I have felt the mind scanning this area already this morning,' said Brin.

'I can shield you from that until you find somewhere safe to land on Wendla.'

Tika looked at Khosa who stared fixedly at a point between Storm and Farn.

'Grek?' she enquired.

'Were you expecting someone else?' The unbodied entity sounded quite arch.

'Don't be ridiculous,' Khosa snapped.

'A small jest Khosa dear,' replied Grek. 'I will stay with you until you are settled on Wendla – I think I could probably locate this other Ship of the stars – Star Flower. It might be sensible to be close to her – if she is still sane.'

Tika exchanged a glance with Maressa and rolled her eyes. 'Do you know who it is who searches this area so busily and so regularly?' she asked.

'I sensed it a short while ago and I traced it back to a specific region. It will not be hard to find exactly who it is.' Grek sounded smug.

'There is a place a little larger than this, slightly north,' Maressa said. 'I think it will be close enough to decide where we should make for on the island of Wendla.'

'Should we wait for the ships to reach us?' asked Sket.

Tika watched the gijan beginning to stir under their blankets, chewing her lip.

'Let's see what Maressa and Grek can discover of Wendla first. We can't wait here for the others – we'll need fresh water by tomorrow, so staying on a small lump of rock like this isn't an option.'

Seela carried the tired gijan through the rest of the day. Grek stayed with the Dragons, alert for the seeking mind from Wendla. The rain water Sket had tried to collect was tainted and brackish and did little to quench their thirst. The islet Maressa and Brin led them to was higher, more rock than sand, with weathered cones rising up several man lengths. Piper found places among the higher rocks where rain had collected and found it far fresher than the little they had left.

Brin told them, after flying high ahead for some leagues, that Wendla had been visible. He wondered if it really was an island. It appeared much as the coast of Malesh had done – an endless line of cliffs rising from the sea. The setting sun at last broke through the clouds, sending light dazzling across the water. Grek informed them that the questing mind had passed over them yet again.

'I suggest you continue to shield,' he said. 'I will do a little investigating in Wendla.'

The gijan had revived but were subdued by thoughts of the ships now far behind them. They ate the fish Storm caught for them then lay against Seela, quickly falling asleep. Seela peered down at her strange brood.

'Their bodies are tired still but their minds are busy.'

'I asked last night why it is that they only communicate with you. Leaf let me into her thoughts only briefly in the City of the Domes.' Tika stifled a yawn.

Seela turned from her inspection of the gijan. 'They ask me things. Sometimes things you say or do confuses them – they do not understand. It is mostly a matter of them asking me questions rather than learning anything of them.' Her eyes whirred in the twilight. 'I have opened my mind to them as an example of my trust but they keep their minds tightly closed to me.'

Grek announced his return just after dawn. 'Namolos's information is out of date,' he said. 'The Captain of the Ship, Star Flower, has done what I did in Sapphrea.'

Only Khosa knew precisely what he meant and she sat up straight, a piece of fish forgotten under a paw. She waited until Grek deigned to continue.

'Sefri joined her mind with a member of her son's bloodline several generations past, with their knowledge and consent.'

The unbodied entity became pensive. 'My consciousness

travelled within the bloodline; Sefri seems able to transfer from one adult to another of the next generation.'

'Did you do the same thing?' Maressa asked in a faint voice.

'No. I joined with a child in its mother's belly when I first came here. I transferred my mind through succeeding members of that one family. I had to live through countless infancies until that particular host began to fail and I began again with a new foetus. They were unaware of my presence'

Tika clenched her hands on her knees. She spoke very calmly.

'Which family did you choose Grek? Who was your last host?'

The sky lightened while the four Dragons and three humans waited for Grek's answer.

'The family was of the old Valsheban people, which then became Hargon's line. I was within his mother and then – then I was part of his daughter.'

Tika gasped. 'What did you do to her Grek? Where is Mena now?'

'She is alive and in Ren's land.' More than that Grek refused to say.

Khosa crossed the patch of sand to butt her head on Tika's arm. 'Mena is well. Namolos told me.' Khosa dug a claw into Tika's leg, forcing her to look directly at the Kephi. 'Namolos said her eyes are like yours.'

Farn poked his head over Tika's shoulder, close to Khosa's. 'This Namolos – he is sure the child is well?'

'He's sure.'

'Then it must be so, my Tika,' said Farn confidently. 'We'll probably meet her somewhere on these adventures. Another girl!'

Tika met Sket's grin and reluctantly smiled herself. She stroked Khosa's head lightly. 'We must believe Mena is safe then.' She tried to convince herself as she spoke.

Khosa did not reply; Mena was well, but perhaps not as safe as Tika would like to hope. Brin rattled his wings.

'If we fly now, I would estimate we reach the coast of this land before dark.'

Maressa nodded agreement. 'We can find somewhere safe while there is light to see.'

Sket stood up. 'We could rest through the night and take stock tomorrow morning,' he said.

'Grek?' Tika asked.

'He's gone,' Leaf told her. The gijan were already perched on Seela's back, their packs clasped before them.

As Brin predicted, they approached Wendla as the sun sank into the sea stretching away behind them. This coastal region was thickly wooded with small clusters of buildings sparsely scattered through it. Brin and Maressa shielded them from both eyes and minds as the group flew lower. Trees filled valleys and climbed hills until, the land rising again, they saw an open plateau ahead. They were following Seela to land when Grek spoke, an amused note in his mind voice.

'So you didn't need my help to find Star Flower then!'

Seela stumbled, off balanced by Grek's words. Grek laughed outright.

'You were shielding but so were they.'

By then all four Dragons stood on the grass-covered ground, prismed eyes whirring as they stared around them.

'Release your shielding,' Grek suggested, and Maressa obeyed.

The air shimmered slightly, then shivered again.

'Their shields are gone too,' Grek murmured.

What had seemed a simple plateau, empty except for grass, a few shrubs and a handful of taller trees, looked very different. Sket was at Tika's shoulder, his sword loose in its scabbard. The gijan slid from Seela's back, trilling at the feel of the cool grass tickling their ankles.

'Wait children,' Seela ordered but Leaf unfurled her wings.

'There is no danger here Seela,' she called over her shoulder.

Maressa moved beside Tika and Sket, staring at the long low building set against grey rock. Smoke rose lazily from one of several chimneys. Every direction they looked plants grew – some twining up a verandah fronting the building, others in pots large and small set all around the plateau. Far more trees edged the area than they'd been aware of with the shielding in place. Flowers of every colour bloomed amid leaves of so many different greens their eyes were dazzled after three days of grey sky and sea. They stood gaping helplessly until Khosa's demands to be freed from her sack roused them. Tika stooped to let Khosa loose.

'Visitors!' A husky voice called from behind the vine covered verandah.

A moment later a woman walked into view. She was of moderate height, mid brown hair hung over her shoulder in a braid and her face was a smooth-skinned oval. She came a few more paces towards them and bowed low.

'Welcome to Green Shade. I rarely have unexpected guests.' She spoke the Common Tongue with no trace of an accent.

Tika moved forward, Sket and Farn flanking her. Hand on her sword hilt she returned the woman's bow.

'We did not mean to intrude; we believed this was an empty piece of land where we might rest.'

A small orange shape darted through the grass, disappearing into the flower-smothered verandah. The woman turned to watch Khosa then back to the Dragons.

'We had no idea such creatures were real, let alone that they still live in this world,' she said quietly.

The four Dragons reared erect, their formal greetings ringing in the woman's mind. She took an involuntary step back as Brin and Seela towered over her. When the Dragons lowered themselves, Seela introduced the gijan. Leaf, Piper and Willow stepped forward and bowed, their wings fanning out on the ground behind them. The woman stared, as helplessly as Tika and her friends had stared at the transformed plateau. She gathered herself with a visible effort.

'My name is Sefri. Please accept the hospitality of Green Shade.'

'We would prefer to stay out here,' Willow announced.

'By all means. You have only to call and someone will come to bring you to us or to fetch food or drink for you.'

Sefri hesitated then instead of leading her visitors towards the door through which she had appeared, she walked to where the flowers seemed even more profuse. The vines climbed thick wooden poles set wide apart, but tendrils draped the edge of the roof and hung down like a living curtain. The husky voice rang out again and Tika realised it hadn't been Sefri who'd called to them before.

'Sefri! They have spoken with Singer! We thought him lost! Sefri, they come from the darling boy!'

Sefri turned a look of astonishment on Tika then hurried to hold back some of the greenery. She looped the ends gently over a curved hook set in a post and moved to repeat her action on the other side. Storm moaned softly as the Ship was revealed.

They all saw at once that this Ship was hurt far worse than Singer might be. Its colour was dulled; dark grey mottled with almost black patches where Singer had glowed a soft grey blue.

'This little creature told me she's spoken with Singer.' The voice was full of delight.

Tika swallowed hard and bowed again. 'Star Singer spoke of you Star Flower and so did Namolos.'

There was a gasp from both the Ship and her Captain.

'Namolos did not know if you still survived,' Tika continued. 'And Kertiss believes you are no more.'

The Ship hissed but before she could say anything, Sefri laid her hands and her forehead against Star Flower's side.

'Do not upset yourself dearest. Stay calm and listen to what our visitors have to tell.'

Sefri moved away again. 'Sit with my precious Flower and I will have food prepared and brought to you.'

She looked doubtfully at the Dragons and Brin assured her that they would find their own food.

'Are there any farms close by – my Kindred would not take food from farms,' Tika added hastily.

Sefri gave her first smile. 'No one lives within leagues of Green Shade. I have a few goats and hens but there are wild cattle on the hills beyond.'

Sefri looked back at her ship: the Dragons and Maressa had settled themselves in a semicircle and the almost hoarse voice of Star Flower was asking questions. The gijan were investigating the garden, calling to each other from different trees.

'Come.' Sefri slipped her arm through Tika's. 'Let me show you the house while I ask for food and rooms to be readied for you.'

Green silvered eyes regarded Sefri steadily. 'Sket goes everywhere with me if Farn doesn't,' she said.

Sefri nodded. 'I think Farn is special to you, as Star Flower is to me.'

'As Mazan was to Singer,' Sket added.

Sefri's eyes widened. 'You have truly met him!' She drew Tika from the section of building which sheltered her Ship.

Sket and Tika saw the rooms opened one into the next, right through to a large kitchen. An elderly woman sat in a rocking chair beside a large stove.

'We have guests Ammi – three hungry people.'

The woman smiled. 'I'll have something to fill them shortly Captain.' She hauled herself out of the chair, giving Sket a sharp look. 'A bowl of tea might not be unwelcome I'd guess.'

Seeing Sket's expression, Sefri laughed. 'Let's sit out of Ammi's way for a while then.'

From where Tika sat she could see through the length of the house to the bulk of the Ship and the Dragons reclining close by. Sket sat down beside her.

'What do you think Lady?' he whispered.

Tika raised a brow. 'I don't know yet.'

She smiled as Sefri joined them, three bowls in one hand and a large steaming jug in the other. Sefri poured the tea for them, glancing at Tika.

'I think you understand why my house is built so?'

Tika met Sefri's grey eyes: grey she noted, but a warm grey, quite unlike the pale grey of Kertiss and his sister.

'Star Flower is fearful if you are out of sight?'

When Sefri nodded Tika relaxed a little more. 'Farn is my soul bond. He suffered a great hurt.'

'That scar running down his neck?' Sefri interrupted.

'Yes. He was barely hatched – less than half a year old. It frightened him badly and his mind was – fragile – for a time. We,' she indicated Sket, 'give him herbs if he gets upset or agitated.'

'We did,' Sket corrected. 'But Gremara helped him somehow and we've not needed the herbs since then.'

Both Sket and Tika stared when Sefri's tea bowl was set down by an unsteady hand.

'Gremara?' she asked.

'Gremara was the silver Dragon of Talvo Circle in Vagrantia,' Tika began.

'No,' Sefri whispered, 'Gremara was Namolos's daughter.'

Now it was Tika and Sket's turn to stare in surprise. Sefri picked up her bowl, cupping it in both hands.

'We have much we must talk of my dears. You must understand at once though that Star Flower can be of little or no help to you and I cannot leave her anymore. I used to be able to travel away but I can no longer risk that. We have shut down as many functions as possible, diverting all energy to her brain.' Sefri's lips trembled and her eyes were luminous with tears.

'If you know of Singer and his Captain, Mazan, you will know of the link between Flower and me. What you call soul bond with Farn is much the same, I would guess, already.' Sefri's voice was the lowest breath. 'Flower is dying. I cannot leave her – not now, not for any reason.'

They called Maressa and the gijan and sat in the kitchen, lamp lit now that night had fallen, and Ammi served them a most welcome supper. For once, Tika accepted the offer of a bed, knowing Farn was directly below her window, still talking to the poor hurt Ship with the other Dragons. Piper slept on Storm's back, Willow and Leaf on Seela and Khosa was curled by Brin's chest. Tika hugged Farn goodnight, trying not to imagine how Sefri must feel facing the loss of Star Flower.

Maressa already slept in the room they were to share. Sket took pillows and blankets, laid his naked sword close to hand and settled across the outer threshold. He sniffed. Tika sniffed.

'Sket?'

'Yes Lady?'

'It's come back – that smell.'

'Mint,' said Sket in annoyance.

Chapter Nineteen

Tika woke to find Khosa sprawled on her chest. The Kephi's whiskers bristled forward as she matched Tika's yawn.

'The female, Ammi, uses mind speech,' Khosa told her. 'There are two or three families close by who work for Sefri. Or rather, they choose to live near her and the Ship.'

Turquoise eyes stared unblinking into Tika's. 'They were here when the Ship crashed – at least, their ancestors were.'

'What a busy creature you are.' Tika scratched behind Khosa's ears causing the Kephi to croon with delight.

'They use power differently again from those in Malesh – more like we do. Ammi says the Captain was strong once she'd recovered from the crash; her son less so. But since Star Flower began to decline, so too has Sefri's use of power.'

'What of Sefri's son?' Maressa asked from the bed across the room.

'He took one of Ammi's many times great grandmothers to wife. When she had birthed some children he went with some of the men to explore Wendla. None of them returned.'

'Killed?' Tika asked.

'Ammi says it is believed the party was lost in an accident of some kind.'

Khosa slid down from Tika's bed and gave her whiskers a brisk wash. 'Sket's gone for some tea.' She sniffed. 'I don't know how you can drink so much of the stuff.'

By the time Maressa and Tika joined Sket, the sun was well risen. Tika went on outside to greet the Dragons and the gijan. She knew at once that Seela was disturbed; also that the purple Dragon was not ready to discuss her concern with anyone. Brin and Storm had just left to seek the cattle Sefri had spoken of last night. Tika draped an arm round Farn's neck and wandered along the edge of the garden. She knew Sefri was inside the Ship but only silence came from that direction.

She paused, seeing the gijan swooping towards her, and lifted her egg pendant outside her shirt. Tika frowned: it was very warm against her skin – not quite hot but too warm for comfort. Then she was smothered with feathers as the gijan enfolded her in their wings. Willow and Piper darted away, their green and yellow under feathers flashing when they dipped among the trees. Leaf held her hand, strolling on beside Farn.

'Can't you help her?'

Tika stopped in her tracks, looking down into Leaf's dark eyes. The gijan's head tilted, one side then the other.

'I had wondered that too, my Tika.' Farn sat back on his haunches, one wing half curved round both her and Leaf. His faceted eyes whirred pearl and sapphire as he regarded her solemnly.

Tika drew a deep breath. 'You don't know what you suggest. I have helped both of you but don't you realise Star Flower is not Dragon or gijan – or even human as far as I know? I wouldn't begin to know what to do.'

Leaf cuddled close to her. 'You would know, once you began. And Flower is very near her end. Sefri will not survive alone.'

Again Tika imagined far too clearly how she would feel should Farn die. Stars forbid – she would not recover, she knew.

'Maressa cannot help me,' she tried to argue, already aware she was weakening. 'Ren knows more of healing than she does.'

Leaf's tiny three fingered hands reached towards Tika's pendant but did not touch it.

'We will all help you. This Ship and Sefri are needed.'

Tika looked sharply at Leaf but gained no insight into what the gijan might mean.

'You would help Mim, or Ashta, wouldn't you?' Farn whispered in her mind.

She glared at him. 'Well of course I would, but Star Flower – what am I to try to mend? I can do nothing for the outer shell, and I don't even know where her brain is or if I could reach it.'

Leaf hopped on one high-arched foot. 'You could talk to Sefri and then you'd know better what to do.'

Tika tried to glare at the gijan too but succumbed to the dark eyes and sudden smile. The three turned back towards the house, Tika thinking furiously.

'Grek's gone to find that troublesome spy.' Leaf swung their linked hands.

Even as Tika remembered Grek admitting to being within the child Mena's body and mind, Leaf tightened her hand.

'Grek didn't hurt her,' she said. 'He is trustworthy.'

Tika didn't reply. Why were the gijan still so secretive? They seemed to know many things which could well prove useful for Tika and her companions to know, but they gave only occasional hints. They slowed, nearing the reclining Seela.

'I will speak with both Sefri and Star Flower and then the three of us will decide if anything can be done.'

She hugged Farn briefly and stepped close to Seela, leaning against her great neck.

'Will you give your strength again if I ask, dear friend?'

Seela's long face lowered to stare at Tika. 'You have no need to ask such a question, small one.'

Brin returned with Storm and after a brief argument, Storm took Farn off to show him where the cattle were to be found.

Maressa and Sket spent the morning in the kitchen with Ammi. The woman showed them a cupboard, well stocked with countless herbs, potions and roots. She freely offered replacements for Sket's much diminished supplies and explained the uses of many herbs, unfamiliar to both him and Maressa. Near midday, she brewed yet another pot of tea.

'Will the Halfling need food before she works?' she asked.

Sket stared at the woman.

'Halfling?' asked Maressa.

Ammi smiled. 'It is long indeed since Halflings were seen by humans but it was foretold that they would emerge from their hidden strongholds when the Time of Change began.' She shrugged. 'Everyone knows they look much like humans but for their eyes.'

Sket thought back over the woman's words. 'What did you mean – before she works?'

Ammi looked surprised. 'She is here to heal Star Flower isn't she?'

Maressa and Sket were on their feet before Ammi had finished speaking, rushing to the far end of the building. Tika had stepped up into the Ship without allowing her apprehension to get the better of her.

'Sefri?' she called softly.

'To your left, Tika. I am here, with Flower.'

Tika turned left along a curved passage which rose slightly. She found herself at what was obviously the front of the Ship, seeing through sloping windows the Dragons and the gardens beyond. Below the windows were tilted surfaces covered with coloured buttons, much like those she had seen in Kertiss's underground chambers. Sefri sat in a strangely shaped padded chair, her hand against the Ship's wall. Tika felt a calmness fill her.

She walked across the small room and touched Sefri's arm. The woman's head was cupped in the top of the chair and she looked dreadful. Her eyes were ringed in dark shadows, a line of pain furrowed down between her brows and her mouth was a thin tight line. Tika offered Sefri what help she could, explaining how she had healed Farn. She wasn't sure if the Ship was listening but Sefri certainly was. Her eyes opened and she sat up, leaning forward, intent on Tika's every word.

'I would be grateful if you would try.' The husky voice was the barest breath of sound and Tika looked helplessly round the room. She shook her head.

'Sefri, I have to see what I'm working on. Where is she in reality?'

Sefri waved Tika to the second chair and tapped several buttons on the top of the desk. She paused, tapped again and sat back. The tilted top lifted up and the lower part split in two, each piece sliding silently out of sight.

'You can get no closer. She is in a sealed environment: to break it would be her death anyway.'

Tika slipped from the chair to her knees, her hands flat against the transparent surface of the large box. Within floated a brain linked by wires and lights – to what, Tika couldn't begin to guess. But the colours were faded, the lights intermittently flashing and she somehow knew that Star Flower truly had little time left. She turned suddenly, catching Sefri's hands in hers.

'I cannot promise this will work, but whatever I do, you must not interfere. Stay in contact with her if you can and send her your strength. If you permit, one of the Dragons will aid you, while the others help me?'

Even as she spoke she sent an urgent thought to Brin as Sefri nodded. Sefri gasped and Tika knew she felt the surge of power from Brin's mind. She saw Maressa and Sket enter as she turned back to the Ship's brain. She steadied herself, breathing calmly, the memory of Iska teaching her the centring exercises flitting through her head. Again she laid her palms flat to the surface of the box. One more breath and she slid through the very fabric of the container.

Briefly she panicked, dragged in and down by the proximity of death itself. She felt Seela's love bolstering her and then Farn's mind joined hers and she began to work. Tika was unaware of when Sket knelt to support her, or when Maressa's hands covered her own as they began to slip. She tipped forward, her brow resting against the box. Slowly she felt Sefri's link with Star Flower and paused to strengthen that section of the brain. One organ and so much more complex than she would have thought possible!

She found pathways and circuits withered and misshapen and painstakingly she tended each one. Deep within her, Tika knew she had nearly exhausted herself. That was when voices began to sing to her, softly at first but growing in volume in proportion to her weariness. Tika didn't hear her own gasping breaths: they were lost below the tempest of song which raged through her. She saw for one heartbeat, the brain glowing, its circuits radiantly coloured, before music and darkness overwhelmed her.

And thus she didn't hear Star Flower's cries of gratitude, didn't see Sefri's pouring tears. Tika knew nothing, crushed against Sket's chest as he stumbled from the Ship with his precious burden. Ammi had set up a bed below the front of the Ship at Maressa's request and she stood waiting and watching with several members of her family. All of them sensed the great drawing of power but had been surprised to find power emanating from all four of the Dragons. Willow and Piper lay along Storm's back as if asleep, but only Seela suspected their minds were somehow linked with Tika.

Leaf leaned against Farn, her eyes closed until she turned quickly, making the humans jump. Farn trumpeted his call, head stretched high. Then he pushed forward beneath the roof. Great tears rolled down his long beautiful face as Sket staggered out of the Ship, Tika in his arms. Sket lifted Tika up so the silver blue Dragon could examine her properly before he placed her on the bed. Ammi moved to pull blankets across the small body then gasped, her hand against Tika's cheek.

'Fetch hot flasks – the Halfling freezes!'

A young man hurried to do her bidding. Ammi stared closer, watching Sket cautiously lifting a gold chain to jiggle a pendant away from Tika's chest. The shirt was charred, burnt through where the pendant had lain. Then Leaf was there, opening Tika's shirt as Tika not so long ago had opened hers. Sket unstoppered a small leather pot and held it out to the gijan. With extraordinary tenderness she smoothed the salve over the badly burnt skin.

She looked up suddenly when Farn's head lowered close over his soul bond. She dabbed a spot of salve on his nose, gave a trill of laughter and stood up, her wings fanned in glorious display. Willow and Piper squeezed between the people and the Dragons, calling aloud in their own rippling language. They too unfurled their wings, pink, green and yellow feathers quivering as the strong fragrance of mint saturated the air.

Tika had spent a full day, one noon to the next, in repairing what she could of Star Flower's brain. She spent the following two days deeply asleep, watched over by all the household of Green Shade. Sket was hugely relieved to find Farn's tears had not presaged a collapse of the young Dragon's nerves. He had refused to leave until Tika woke but he had not fretted and fussed as he had on other occasions. Sket thanked the stars for whatever Gremara had done to Farn.

Ammi, her family and neighbours took turns sitting with Sket or Maressa: Sket insisted that either he or the air mage must be there when Tika awoke. The gijan continued their games in the garden, flying now and then to peer beneath the verandah where Tika lay. Sket had been worried by Tika's coldness: her flesh felt like ice for half a day following her work on Star Flower.

Ammi was more concerned by the fact that they could not get Tika to swallow any liquid. As Tika's body slowly warmed, so her skin dried and began to flake, her lips to crack. Ammi fetched large pots of a milky ointment which they smoothed over Tika; turning her often to prevent sores on her back or heels. In spite of his worry, Sket took comfort from Farn's calm confidence. Sefri had come to offer her help but Ammi shooed her away.

'Go and talk with Star Flower. It will be a comfort to us to hear you saying your silly old poems to each other again. Off with you!'

Sket managed a tired smile. 'What poems do they say Ammi?' he asked.

'Always about gardens and growing things.' Ammi sat back on her low stool by Tika's head, automatically putting the back of her hand lightly on Tika's brow.

'Gardens?' Sket was mystified. He'd never heard any stories or songs or poems about gardens.

Ammi gave him an assessing look. 'Why don't you just sit back on those pillows and I'll tell you the tale.'

Unsuspecting, Sket settled more comfortably, half propped on pillows, half against Storm's shoulder.

'Well then,' Ammi began. 'You know the Captain and her son travelled between the stars? She had done so long before this Ship was made and the Captain collected poems of gardens from many of the worlds she visited. She has told us this tale so many times you understand. Well, the Captains were chosen very carefully for each of these Ships and the Captains learnt what their Ships were most interested in.'

'Like Star Singer,' Maressa suggested. 'He said his Captain brought him music.'

Ammi nodded. 'Just so. Star Flower had chosen her own name of course, because she loved the colours of flowers, their so many different shapes.'

'Their scent?' Sket asked through a yawn.

'Alas no. Star Flower cannot smell anything. Anyway, Sefri brought her poems and they spent the time on their long journeys going through all the poems they'd found and making a garden of their own in their imagination. The first thing Sefri did when she started to recover from the crash was to arrange this garden. Of course, it has changed many times over all the years, but it has brought great joy to them both.'

Ammi paused, watching Sket struggle to keep his eyes open. Maressa smiled and nodded to Ammi to go on.

'Sefri decided this place would be called Green Shade because it is a term used in a poem which she and Star Flower agree is one of their very favourite poems. Well thank goodness for that – I thought he'd never drop off!'

Maressa dropped a blanket over Sket's sleeping form and moved closer to Ammi. Farn reclined beside the bed, his chin resting near Tika's shoulder.

'Sket is our dearest friend,' he spoke softly in Ammi's mind. 'There is nothing he would not do to help or protect us.'

The woman touched Farn's cheek with a finger. 'Forgive me. I understand how this man feels for you and the Halfling: it is how I feel for my Captain and her Ship. But he will be of no use to anyone without some sleep.'

Farn alerted everyone in the late afternoon two days later that Tika was waking. When her eyes finally opened, she was discomposed to discover a large audience staring at her.

'It's all right,' Sket muttered, holding her hand. 'Farn told them and they all wanted to make sure you're well.'

Tika struggled to a more upright position, wincing at the pain from her chest and the tightness of her skin. She grabbed the covers as they slid down and, after a peek underneath, she groaned.

'Why do you always leave me with no clothes?' she hissed.

Ammi tutted. 'You can't wear much for a few days: your skin won't bear it. We couldn't get you to drink.'

Tika realised she had a raging thirst and drank gratefully from a bowl Ammi held for her. It was a fruit drink, laced with something that bore a strong resemblance to old Lorak's restorative, and thickened with honey. The effort of sitting up and taking a drink made Tika feel she would prefer to go back to sleep but she struggled to stay awake to deal with everyone's greetings and good wishes. The gijan were draped across Seela's back, watching her carefully with their dark eyes: the last thing she noticed before dozing off again.

It was dark beyond the verandah when she woke next. Maressa offered her another drink and held the bowl for her.

'Ammi has a bath ready if you like – she says it will help your skin.'

Tika grimaced. 'With an audience?'

Maressa chuckled. 'Everyone's gone to bed.'

'We're still here,' Farn objected.

Tika stroked his cheek as his face swung close to hers. Leaf came from the shadows to stand by the bed.

'I'll help you,' she held out her hand.

Tika sighed. 'I don't know how far I'll walk,' she warned.

Farn huffed in annoyance, reaching for her himself. He had never lifted her this way before and Tika bit her dry lips as the sheet dragged and wrinkled against her skin. Holding her between his upper arms and chest, Farn shuffled carefully down the length of the building. Ammi showed no surprise to see a Dragon carry the Halfling into her kitchen. There was a large wooden tub filled with warm water to which she directed Farn to bring Tika. Gently she took his burden from him.

'Now you go on outside. Watching a lady at her bath is not seemly.'

Farn's eyes whirr. 'She's not a lady, she's my Tika!' he began, his eyes flashing faster when Maressa and Tika both started to laugh. He backed out of the room, unsure of the reason for their amusement. Tika reached a hand out to him.

'Thank you Farn, I won't be long.'

Mollified, Farn huffed for a while, settling outside the kitchen. By the time she had been soaked, patted dry and covered in Ammi's ointment again, Tika felt refreshed although still weary to her very bones.

Three days later she tired easily but was able at least to walk slowly round the garden, wearing a loose robe that belonged to one of Ammi's granddaughters. Her skin had plumped out again due to Ammi's insistence on drinking a great deal each day. The burn between her breasts remained sore and angry looking: Ammi treated it with a poultice when Tika was lying down and with a thick layer of a salve when she was up. Tika carried the egg pendant in a pocket of the robe for now. She made no attempt to speak with Star Flower, waiting instead for the Ship to want to talk to her.

That request came, through Sefri, six days after Tika had attempted the healing. Sefri walked from the kitchen with Tika, leaving her at the Ship's door.

'Are you not coming in?' Tika was surprised.

Sefri smiled. 'Flower wishes to speak with you alone.'

'But are you not connected to her mind?'

'If we choose – then yes. But she wants to meet you privately – she'll tell me if she needs me.'

Tika considered: she knew exactly where Farn was – hunting with Storm. But his mind was not listening to hers at this moment. Very well, she would take Sefri's word that Flower was waiting for her alone.

'I am glad you've come.' Flower's husky voice was soft but much stronger than the last time Tika had heard it. The brain was no longer in view, panels back in place across the front of its container.

'Sit down Tika, and put your hand on my wall.'

Tika did as she was asked, wary when her hand touched the Ship. The instant the physical connection was made she heard Flower directly in her mind and she relaxed: there was no pain now, no dark extinction dragging at her.

'How much did I manage to mend?' she asked bluntly. 'There was a lot I didn't understand – I had to do only what I dared.'

'You have repaired a great deal more than I could have hoped for,' Flower told her. 'Communication circuits are stronger than they've been since we reached Kel-Harat. I have yet to try but I suspect, and hope, that I will reach my brothers and sisters in orbit once more. The last thing you did was to link the regenerative and diagnostic synapses.' She laughed, aware of Tika's incomprehension.

'I had lost the connection with the system years ago, which is what led to my more rapid decline. With the connection restored I can repair damage myself to a considerable extent again.'

Tika tried to understand but Flower continued: 'I can never thank you enough or repay you for what you've done for me and for my Captain. But I can perhaps help in some way with your strange journey.'

'I have no idea myself why I'm here in Wendla. I had never heard of Wendla, or Malesh, or of Survivors until recently.' Tika realised she sounded peevish.

'Your Dragon Kindred have told me much while you have been resting.' Flower's tone became deeply apologetic. 'You brought yourself to the very gateway of death for me – that is something I will long ponder on.'

After a brief pause which Tika was unsure how to fill, the Ship spoke again.

'Seela and the gijan Leaf spoke of Bound Ones and of Ancient Elders. I'm afraid I know nothing of them – they must have gone from Kel-Harat before we landed. Leaf said there were four Bound Ones, yet someone in Malesh believes they have discovered one of them where they were not in fact imprisoned.'

Tika tried to think: Leaf had told her that Taseen said one Bound One was beneath the desert, another further north, the third perhaps in Drogoya and the fourth under the sea between Malesh and Wendla. She suddenly remembered Taseen's colleague Vorna. He'd said she had discovered a Bound One located on or near her estates in Malesh. How could that be?

'Do you know of volcanoes?' Flower interrupted Tika's train of thought.

'Maressa's people live in volcanoes,' she replied.

'In extinct volcanoes,' Flower corrected. 'Before we landed here we ran many checks on this world. We found evidence of volcanic activity in the far distant past but only five active volcanoes remained. Touch the third green button in front of you.'

Tika leaned forward and tentatively touched the button. A dark square the size of her hand began to lighten in the desk top.

'These are images of volcanoes on another world. Watch.'

The screen cleared to show a range of mountains – it was as if Tika was on Farn's back, high in the air. The view closed to focus on one mountain. Tika bent closer. The mountain seemed to swell and tremble. The top exploded, boulders, dust and smoke roaring up into the sky. Then she saw red rocks, a river of redness pouring down from the topless mountain. She swallowed.

'That was only a small one,' Flower apologised. 'But you get the idea?'

'Yes I think so.'

'Well, of the five active volcanoes on Kel-Harat, three are in the seas. Leaf told me it is believed the Bound One in the sea between Malesh and Wendla is stirring. I can tell you that if indeed a Bound One was imprisoned there, somehow he has travelled the fault line, back into the land of Malesh. The instability of the area of which the mages speak is simply the volcano waking once more.'

Chapter Twenty

Tika's strength returned more quickly over the next days and she heard about the immediate country around Green Shade. Although she would have said they had flown a considerable distance inland from the coast, she discovered the sea in fact poked long fingers through the forests. Ammi informed her of small communities along these inlets, the nearest some four leagues from Green Shade. The people of this area regarded themselves as true Wendlans and deliberately kept apart from the more heavily populated regions to the south and east. Khosa spent her days inside the Ship and her evenings as close to the kitchen stove as she could manage. Tika asked Maressa where the ships carrying their companions were now and was told vaguely that they approached the Wendlan coast.

Seela, Brin and Storm disappeared one morning leaving Farn swooping after the gijan in an odd game they had devised which seemed to amuse them all greatly. Maressa finally remembered the parcel Salma had given her in Harbour City and took Tika up to the room they shared. Tika unwrapped the parcel with an odd feeling. She glanced at Maressa.

'I don't think I've ever had a parcel to unwrap before,' she said.

She could only stare at its contents. A dark green jacket was folded on the top. It had silver blue Dragon faces exquisitely embroidered on both ends of the collar. As she held it up she saw the Dragon face was worked in miniature along the bottom edge of the jacket.

'It's beautiful,' Maressa murmured, moving closer to examine the workmanship. 'Salma asked me how big you were and the colour of your eyes and hair, but she didn't show me her work.'

Next was a pair of trousers of the same dark green with the Dragon face motif stitched down the side seams. Tika put the jacket aside, standing with the trousers held against her in stunned delight.

'There's more.' Maressa was poking in the parcel.

'More?' Tika sounded quite faint.

She found three shirts of a thin fabric unknown to her, one a deep pink, the second palest green and the third a vivid yellow. Tika touched each garment, speechless at the surprise. Maressa moved to the window and drew the curtains across, shutting out the noon sunlight.

'Put them on – you can surprise everyone at the meal. Oh those gijan would be peeking in the window otherwise,' she explained when Tika raised a brow at the closed curtains. 'Here,' she rummaged in her pack and pulled out a small leather pouch with two straps attached. 'Put the pendant in there and tie it round your waist until the burn's healed.'

Tika pulled on the new trousers: they fitted perfectly.

'Which shirt?' she asked helplessly.

A flurry of heavy wings in the garden meant the Dragons were back as Maressa pointed to the pink shirt.

'It was Leaf who asked Salma to make something for you. You should wear Leaf's colour first.'

Maressa helped Tika on with the jacket, overriding her protests that it was far too warm. 'Leaf will appreciate it and you can always take it off once she's admired you.'

Tika laughed, twirling in front of the air mage. Maressa stared at her for a moment: when had the child turned into such a lovely young woman – surely new clothes couldn't make such a difference?

Sefri called from the garden. 'Tika, Maressa! There is food ready! Come down and eat!'

Maressa led the way, turning where the stairs ended beside the kitchen door, a huge smile on her face. Tika smiled back walking past her and then she froze. Gan's hands met easily round her waist and he lifted her off her feet. Over his shoulder she saw Sket holding Khosa, beaming across the room at her. Then she was submerged in a tide of greetings and laughter from Navan, Ren, Olam and Riff. Even Pallin managed a grin, which made him scarcely recognisable. An old man with wild white eyebrows sat in Ammi's rocking chair, watching the reunion with a smile. Leaf hovered over him but she looked up as Tika came closer.

She shrieked with glee bringing Willow and Piper crowding in and they examined every piece of Salma's gift of new clothes. It was a long afternoon and evening. Tika heard of the slow course of the remaining two ships, Spiral Star and Star Flame, as they fought against contrary winds and unexpected currents to make their way to the north west coast of Wendla.

Maressa had communicated with both Ren and Taseen as Culinth continued to block against the air mage's mind. Taseen argued fiercely with Kasmi over their course, finally insisting that Culinth's opinion be ignored as he, Mage Councillor Taseen, had hired Kasmi's ships and thus ordered their course. Kasmi was doubly distressed by the death of his brother on Eternal Star and by Culinth's attitude. He had no idea why Culinth suddenly and adamantly demanded they return to the pirate islands, abandoning all idea of reaching Wendla. She withdrew her cooperation as Sister of the Wind and stayed solitary and silent.

When the two ships approached the mouth of the inlet, men came in boats to board both ships. Olam had been fascinated as the Wendlans guided them inland.

'They ordered us to steer directly towards the more northern cliffs and when it seemed we must surely strike into them, they swung the ship sharply round.'

'They told us there is a very narrow deep channel up the inlet, allowing ships as large as ours to travel so many leagues inland,' Navan added.

'Kasmi was most interested,' Olam grinned. 'He's anchored now to attend to some serious repairs but I think he's got ideas for a new pirate haven here.'

Tika was up at dawn next morning, glad to know the companions were united again. She thought to make herself some tea and sit with Farn for a while but found Taseen still ensconced in the rocking chair.

'I spoke with the Ship while you slept,' he said. 'Like me, she has little need of sleep.'

'Taseen, why are we here? Did Flower explain about the volcano under the sea which you thought was a Bound One waking?'

'She did, and it makes too much sense for me to dispute it unfortunately. We are here because I think we must find out what the Wendlan government is up to. I dare not contemplate a war with Wendla when everyone's attention must be concentrated on tightening the fraying restraints on the Bound Ones.'

Tika handed him a bowl of tea and sat on the floor beside a snoring Khosa. 'Ammi and her people showed little surprise at my eyes, or at the gijan, or the Dragons. What does she mean by the term Halfling?'

Taseen held his beard out of the way of his tea and sipped. 'I haven't heard of Halflings in all my long life. Ren tells me the silvering of the eyes is a normal development of those with mage powers in Drogoya. But it is not normal among my people or Maressa's. She told me there are only now cases of such silvering since the advent of a strange illness?'

Tika's thoughts flew to Elyssa: where was she now, and was she safe?

'The Dragons say there is no change that they can perceive in my mind since my eyes changed, Taseen, so why have they done so?'

Taseen shook his head helplessly, his beard dabbling through the tea bowl. Tika picked at a thread on her old trousers; Salma's gift would be kept for special occasions only.

'Grek has been gone,' she counted on her fingers, 'why, he's been gone eleven days now.'

'Leaf told me. She is convinced he is trustworthy, Tika. I thought yesterday that all three gijan seem calmer here, steadier – had you noticed?'

'Not really,' she smiled at the old man. 'What is your advice Taseen? Will you meet the leaders of Wendla and convince them to join your people against the Bound Ones rather than wage war on you?'

'Tika I am too old to travel far overland: you and your friends will have to go to the Wendlan capital and argue for us. And child, the Bound Ones are not just a problem for my people alone, but for all this world Star Flower calls Kel-Harat.'

Tika groaned and Khosa unwound from the tight ball she had been curled in. The Kephi yawned, doing a tail end up, front end down stretch. She blinked at Tika.

'You should speak with Sefri and find out all you can about the way the Wendlans rule their land. I would advise waiting for

Grek's report but there is much Sefri, Ammi and Star Flower will be able to tell you.' She whisked her tail aloft and stalked out of the kitchen. Taseen chuckled.

'I had never thought that cats could use mind speech, but the arrogance of that particular cat somehow does not surprise me at all.'

Tika stood up as Navan came downstairs. He gave her a hesitant smile.

'I hoped you might be up. Would it be possible for me to speak to the Ship? I had an idea in the night that she might have maps of Wendla or even one of those pipes Kertiss had – with pictures inside.'

'Sefri was with Star Flower just before you came down Tika,' said Taseen.

'Right. I warn you Navan, Flower is not like Singer. Her outer structure is much damaged but her mind is less excitable.'

'Storm told us what you did,' Navan remarked as he followed Tika through the long building. He paused at the Ship's circular door.

Khosa was crouched just inside, tail tidily wrapped round her feet. 'They expect you.' She sounded smug.

Tika shook her head. 'Eavesdropping again when people think you're asleep?' she asked, stepping over the Kephi.

Farn, just waking beyond the verandah, huffed. 'She is very nosy,' he began.

Tika turned back to the door to look at her soul bond. 'You did promise you'd try to be more tactful, dear one.'

Farn's eyes flashed but he didn't argue. Tika stepped out of the Ship again to give him a brief hug.

'I *am* trying,' he whispered to her mind.

Tika laughed and rejoined Navan. He was clearly nervous at entering the Ship but followed her without comment. Sefri was in her chair, one hand against the Ship's wall. She turned to smile at Tika. Tika smiled back.

'Star Flower,' she said aloud. 'This is my friend Navan. He would like to ask you about this land of Wendla.'

'Welcome Navan.' The husky voice was warm. 'Please sit down. I will help however I may – I have much to repay Tika.'

Tika patted the back of the second chair. 'I'll leave you to your questions,' she said.

Sefri walked out of the Ship with her. 'I spoke with Taseen,' she said. 'When you go, as I believe you must, he and I and Flower will go through all the data we have concerning the first orbital surveys.' She laughed at Tika's blank expression. 'Come and have some breakfast. Seriously though my dear, you must act quite soon, to stop whoever has plans to attack Malesh from here.'

Over the next days, the companions studied the maps Navan made from records retrieved from the Ship together with more recent information from Ammi's people. Ammi volunteered two of her grandchildren to act as guides through the northern wilderness and to continue with the companions to the Imperial City of Bracca. Taseen spent a full day planning a document Tika would carry to the Emperor. The following day was spent writing it out again on high quality parchment suitably embellished with many flourishes and various seals. When he'd finished, it looked convincingly official and it decreed that Tika and her friends travelled under the auspices of the Grand Harbour Master of Malesh.

Sefri also produced an impressive scroll, claiming Tika represented the Survivor Captain and was under her protection.

'I have no idea whether my words will be given serious consideration or respect,' Sefri admitted. 'It is over one hundred years since I left Green Shade and the last Imperial Envoy to visit here was nearly as long ago. Letters and reports stopped arriving soon after Emperor Lian took the Crystal Throne, and he was great grandfather to the present Emperor. They may think Star Flower and I are dead, or of no consequence if we are still alive.'

'But you were held in esteem before?' asked Gan.

Sefri nodded. 'The bio Ships, such as Star Flower, were used for remote surveys and often as first contacts. Our orders were to observe new worlds. We would be dismissed from the service if it was discovered that we had interfered in any world's development.' She shrugged. 'Our crash landing here did not go unnoticed and Imperial troops came quickly. Until Flower's decline, we were often asked for our opinions and judgements on many matters both large and small. Several Emperors received me at the Imperial Palace and some made the journey to Green

Shade as I became unwilling to leave Flower.'

'Grek has not returned.' Maressa was thoughtful. 'I wondered if perhaps we should confront this seeking mind.'

Frowns greeted her suggestion. Sefri had shown them what she called a simple and basic machine which shielded Green Shade from any mental prying. Since Flower's more rapid collapse during the last year, Sefri had set the shielding to activate the instant any probe was detected.

'Brin and I will support you.' Tika made up her mind. 'This evening then, we will join with you while you either confront, or trace back, this overly curious person.'

'Could anything have happened to Grek?' Olam asked.

Seela's eyes whirred lilac and violet. 'He can be taken apart,' she said. 'Gremara showed me how it can be done. Whether many others would know how to do so, I can't say.'

Taseen reached a hand to touch the purple Dragon's shoulder where she reclined near the verandah. 'I know how to disperse the essence of a soul,' he said quietly, 'but it is not taught any longer in our academies.'

'As far as you know,' said Gan.

Taseen shot him a hard look but then slowly nodded. 'You may well be right,' he conceded. 'What is taught now, particularly in Vorna's department, is open to debate.'

'We are decided then?' Tika stood up. 'Maressa will try to discover who searches across the sea even as far as Malesh. Whether Grek returns or not, I say we should travel to Bracca the day after tomorrow.'

Heads nodded around the group.

'We begin by going along one of the rivers.' Navan spread out a map he'd made with the help of Ammi's grandson Jaran and Star Flower. His finger traced a winding course south eastwards. 'Jaran says we can use the rivers nearly to the forest's edge when they become unnavigable. That will take four days at the quickest.'

'That's the route I used to take,' Sefri agreed. 'Then you have two days walking through farm land until you reach a market place. Canals start there which lead to Bracca itself.'

'Canals?' Sket put aside his oiled sword and picked up Tika's.

'Artificial rivers,' Sefri explained. 'Dug out long before I came here.'

'Men would spend their days digging trenches for rivers?' Pallin asked, his tone one of complete disbelief.

'The Emperor Zorus used slave labour: the canal system was completed in a very few years apparently.' Sefri glanced round, aware of the sudden stillness. She found her gaze held by emerald eyes framed in silver.

'I was a slave.' Tika spoke softly.

Ammi muffled a gasp behind her hand. 'A Halfling? Taken as a slave?'

'My mother was taken as a slave,' Tika corrected. 'I was born a slave.'

Fleetingly her eyes met Navan's. Ammi was pale as she turned to go back through the long room to the kitchen.

'Of course I knew there was some slavery in the north of the continent. I'm sorry Tika but I didn't know you had been so treated.'

Tika shrugged. 'I am no longer a slave but I have no sympathy with those who believe they can own another body and soul. I will fly with Farn for a while, but I'll be back before that mind comes poking around.'

No one spoke until Farn had lifted from the grass, the gijan shrieking in pursuit. Storm's head twisted over Olam's shoulder so he could stare into Sefri's face.

'Are there slaves in this land now?' he asked. 'I had never heard of such a thing until Tika told her story to my Flight.'

'No,' Sefri replied. 'Slavery as such was prohibited in the time of Omak, fourteen Emperors back. I felt the servants were treated not much better than slaves, although they were free men, when I visited the Palace.'

Sket sheathed Tika's sword with a sharp click. 'Let's hope my Lady doesn't think the same when we get there.'

Olam and Riff both grinned but Gan and Navan frowned. Twilight was near when Tika slid from Farn's back, her cheeks flushed and her eyes sparkling. The companions were all gathered near the Ship. Sefri sat in Flower's doorway.

'We have deactivated the shield, Tika,' came Flower's husky voice, 'but we are not skilled in mental communication – we cannot be of much help.'

Maressa sat on the grass, her back against Brin's huge chest. Tika and Ren sat nearby, their minds lightly linked to hers. They sat thus for some time as the first stars glimmered in the green sky but no one moved. It was Seela who began to relay what Maressa saw when the air mage stiffened, her eyes open but unfocused.

There was not a simple blur of light in Maressa's mind as was usually experienced if mind met mind when far speaking. Maressa, and the others through Seela, saw a young woman. She sat cross legged on a gleaming wooden floor, staring straight towards Maressa.

'Who are you? Why do you spy on us?'

Somehow Maressa's voice seemed to thunder in their minds. The woman flinched.

'I was not seeking you stranger. I seek a mind in Malesh.'

'Who?' hissed Taseen.

'Who?' repeated Maressa.

'His name is Taseen. I have been told he can help us stop one named Vorna. Who are you and where are you? You feel close.'

Maressa did not hesitate. 'My name is Maressa. I am in a place called Green Shade.'

They all saw the woman's eyes widen in shock.

'Mage Taseen is with me, as are others.' Maressa deliberately let her gaze sweep over the four Dragons, the three gijan, Ren and Tika and Taseen himself.

'Green Shade,' the woman whispered. 'May I tell my Master what I have seen, and ask him to speak with you?'

'Who is her Master,' Taseen asked urgently.

'Say your Master's name stranger.' Maressa's mind tone had not diminished.

'Master Jakri, son of Oniko and grandson of Jael, of House Jade.'

Taseen clutched his beard, thinking furiously. 'Yes!' His hand trembled as he pointed at Maressa. 'I remember House Jade. She speaks true so far as it goes.'

'Let your Master speak with me when the moon rises. I would know your name also – I have given you mine.'

'I am the least of Master Jakri's apprentices – Hiramo is my name.'

Maressa cut the link between her mind and the Wendlan

woman abruptly and let out a long breath. Tika studied Taseen.

'Who is Master Jakri and House Jade?'

But the old mage was lost in thought: it was Ammi who answered.

'Wendla has always been divided into Houses – everyone in the land owes allegiance to one particular House.' She sniffed. 'We in the northern forests belong to no House and never will.'

Sefri pulled her lower lip between her finger and thumb. 'I'm sure I stayed in House Jade – but it was so long ago.'

Ammi nodded. 'House Jade has always stood for the middle way. Even in the oldest tales of intrigue and fighting between Houses, House Jade was trusted by all to listen to every argument and judge fairly.' She frowned. 'House Jade bred many powerful mages but even when mages have come under suspicion of any wrong doing, House Jade stayed true. I'm sure there is a tale of a mage from House Jade having his powers stripped from him by the Jade Master for transgressing mage laws.'

There was time to eat before moon rise. The mood was subdued as they anticipated Maressa's meeting with the mind of a Wendlan Master Mage. They moved from the kitchen to gather near Star Flower as the thinnest shard of moon cleared the horizon. Again Maressa sat against Brin's crimson chest and linked minds with Ren and Tika. Through the air mage's mind they saw a man, cross-legged on a wooden floor as the woman had been earlier. He spoke first, eyes as blue as Farn's staring directly at Maressa.

'I am Jakri. Hiramo gave your name as Maressa.' There was the faintest hint of a smile about his mouth. 'I do not believe you are of Malesh?'

This time Maressa kept her mind tone at a normal level. 'I am of Vagrantia, far north of the great desert. But for now I am of Green Shade.'

The man inclined his head. 'You told Hiramo that the great mage Taseen is with you. Can he stop the one called Vorna?' Jakri answered his own question. 'I suspect he cannot if he is in this land at this time. I am able to offer mages from several Houses if he requires it.'

Maressa looked to the old man. 'Speak directly to him through me,' she said.

Taseen fluffed his beard then concentrated on the man within Maressa's mind.

'You suspect correctly Master Jakri. I have not regained enough power since the last battle to thwart Vorna let alone a single one of the Children.'

Jakri gazed down at his loosely clasped hands. 'Hiramo said you are accompanied by Dragons? How long would it take them to bring you to Bracca?'

Tika glanced at Brin. 'Two or three days,' he replied promptly.

'Then could they do so? I will visit the Emperor tomorrow and arrange an audience for you as soon as you reach us.'

'Have we guarantees the Dragons are safe from attack in your land and your city?' Tika asked.

The man in their minds showed no reaction to Tika's green silvered eyes. 'My life is forfeit should any attempt to harm the Dragons or you,' he said simply.

'We will let you know our decision by dawn.' Maressa broke contact and Ammi appeared with trays of tea.

'So much for our plans,' Gan remarked, smiling thanks for Ammi's refreshments.

Tika held a tea bowl under her chin, letting the fragrant steam dampen her face. 'I think you'll have to stay here Maressa,' she said. 'Clearly Taseen's opinions will be needed and if he doesn't travel with us you are best to link us to him.' She sat back against Farn. 'Gan will come with me. Ren and Navan.' She grinned at Sket. 'Is there any way I'd be able to stop you coming?'

Gan stretched his long legs out carefully. 'Will you mind staying here?' he asked Olam.

'If no one objects, I'd like to go back down to the river and help with the repairs.'

Riff nodded vigorous agreement while Pallin scowled. The Survivor Captain exchanged glances with Ammi and cleared her throat. 'Perhaps Pallin could remain here at Green Shade?' she suggested. 'Several young ones among the families here long to learn the use of swords.'

Olam kept his expression straight although his eyes gleamed in the lamp light.

'There is no better man than Pallin to teach weapons drill,' he nodded solemnly.

Pallin didn't know whether to appear annoyed or pleased so he settled for his usual scowl. 'I'll see what I can do,' he grunted.

Tika stood up and put her empty bowl on the tray. 'Tomorrow then, we leave for Bracca.'

Chapter Twenty-One

Jakri blinked, his mind restored fully to his body once more. He got to his feet and went out through the open screen wall onto the balcony. Dark green leaves shone against the pale walls of the lamp-lit courtyard and great heavy-headed flowers were scattered like pillows among the foliage. The whisper of slippers on polished wood turned him back into the room.

A woman wearing a simple long gown of pale gold entered, carrying a tray. Jakri hurried to take the tray from her hands, scolding gently.

'Since when do you play servant to your son, Oniko?'

Her face, so similar to his and just as young, smiled. 'Don't pretend it is unusual for me to bring tea to you.'

Jakri put the tray on a low table near the balcony. Oniko waited patiently while her son sipped his tea.

'The Maleshan witch is close to raising a Bound One. Oniko, I have never killed, but I believe Kasheen is right in this – she must not be allowed one more step along the path she is making.'

'You would imperil your essence, committing such an act?'

'Oniko, you haven't felt this woman – this Vorna. That so few of our mages survived the cataclysm of the last battle is a loss to be bitterly regretted now. The few left were still in first training and the shock damaged the longevity mechanisms within them.' He bit his lip, rose and stepped onto the balcony. 'Why do I always tell you what you know far better than I?' He grinned ruefully.

'It is the teacher in you my son. But Jakri, Maleshan mages did survive – there must be some who could stop this Vorna now were they made aware of her intent.'

Jakri leaned back on the railing and folded his arms. 'So very few survived.' He paused. 'Taseen is in Wendla, at Green Shade.'

His mother's beautiful oval face flushed. She leaned forward.

'Here? He should surely be in Malesh, dealing with the witch woman.'

Oniko joined her son on the balcony.

'His powers are minimal. In all this time he has not recovered.' Jakri frowned. 'He is with a strange party. A man and woman with eyes such as I have never seen, a woman strong at far speaking, and more I'd guess. There are Dragons with them.'

Oniko's flushed cheeks paled. 'Dragons have not been seen in Wendla for millennia!'

Jakri smiled. 'There are four here now, and I asked the far speaking mage, Maressa, to send them here.'

Oniko stared down into the gardens. 'I agreed with Kasheen that perhaps another trade dispute, even a small war, might distract Vorna from her plans.'

'You have doubts now?'

Oniko looked up at Jakri, a frown marring the smooth gold skin of her brow. 'I fear we may have to fight much harder – against the Grand Harbour Master's naval and military forces, against Vorna and, spirits save us, the Bound Ones as well.'

A chime sounded from beyond the inner door and Oniko moved along the balcony to study the garden as Jakri stepped inside the room.

'Come,' he called.

The door was opened by an Imperial Blossom, a warrior whose height was accentuated by the tall purple plume of his rank attached to his black lacquered helmet. The warrior saluted.

'His Imperial Greatness requests your presence Master Jakri.'

Jakri nodded and simply followed the man from the room. He made no comment to Oniko – he'd watched the Imperial Blossom's eyes flick round the room but he thought Oniko was unseen at the dark corner of the balcony. Down the stairs, through the lower reception rooms, across the courtyard garden and the old doorman scurried to pull open the door to the outer world.

An escort of six warriors waited at attention in the shadowed street. Jakri took position in the middle of the squad, the Imperial Blossom at its head, and they marched off past the walls of neighbouring Houses. This was the highest level of occupation in the city of Bracca: only elite Houses could live this close to the Emperor in his palace above them.

The next level down was where wealthy merchants, the most skilled artisans, and richest men of business lived in a broad swathe of luxurious buildings circling the hill. All too soon in Jakri's view, trying to sort out his thoughts as he was, they passed the last noble House and marched across a hundred paces of open ground towards the towering blank perimeter walls of the palace. Their small party halted at the great bronze doors and from high above a challenge was called. The Imperial Blossom barked back his name and a password, and one half of the doors swung open enough to allow them entry.

Inside, four of the escort strode off to the right while the Imperial Blossom led Jakri and two warriors to the left. Jakri knew his way through the labyrinthine passages perfectly well but protocol demanded he be escorted every visit. It took as long to wind their way past guards at every intersection, up tiers of the palace to the Emperor's chambers, as it had to walk from Jakri's House to the palace's outer gates.

An elderly man in a grey robe, a purple quill embroidered on the left shoulder, awaited them at the top of a final flight of stairs. The Imperial Blossom saluted and departed with his two warriors. Jakri nodded at the man in the grey robe.

'Greetings Jalan.'

'Greetings Master Jakri. His Imperial Greatness awaits you.'

Jakri followed him, marvelling as always that he and Jalan had begun first lessons together: were in fact the same age. If he had not shown mage talent, he would now look as grey and old as Jalan. Not for the first time, Jakri wondered if Jalan harboured resentments over such obvious signs of their differences in status. They arrived in front of the round silver-covered moon door, two Imperial Blossoms barring their way. The Blossoms moved one pace to each side and pushed the two halves of the door inward. Jalan also moved aside.

'The Mighty One will see you alone.'

Jakri left his sandals by the door, walked forward and heard the doors click shut behind him. Eyes on the floor, he waited until a rustle of silk ahead told him the Emperor Kasheen was in the room. Jakri bowed, his upper body parallel to the floor.

'Come and sit down Jakri. We are informal here.'

Jakri straightened warily: informal became formal without a lot of warning in Kasheen's presence.

'Tell me then – what news of the witch?'

Jakri advanced towards the plain wooden chair where the Emperor Kasheen sat. He was the same age as Jakri and Jalan but looked younger than poor Jalan because his head was quite bald rather than covered in sparse grey hair. He wore a loose sleeveless blue robe over the usual green gown and his favourite blue and silver earrings swung from his ears. The large gold and diamond ring of state flashed as he waved Jakri to a lower chair to his right. Jakri drew a careful breath.

'Her plans advance Imperial One. She has tried to tempt other Council Mages to work with her but she failed to win one of the strongest. I believe, and my colleagues concur, that she is perilously close to unbinding one, if not two of the Children: Sekira and Valesh.'

Long, manicured fingers tapped on the arm of Kasheen's chair. 'Valesh was relatively pleasant but if Sekira is loosed – spirits save us! Is it really possible Jakri? I find the whole idea bizarre in the extreme that creatures of ancient myth should not only exist but be a threat to us now.'

'Great One, the histories record facts, not myths, so yes, these monstrous Children existed, were bound in darkness at enormous cost to the mages of the time. And now they may be freed once more.'

'Because of one stupid meddlesome woman.' Kasheen scowled.

'Far from stupid Ineffable One. Would that she was, then her dream of freeing the Children would remain only a dream.'

'You say a Maleshan Councillor refused to help her. Of the seven, how many will definitely oppose this fool?'

'Imperial Glory,' Jakri chose his words with caution, 'the edict of your grandfather, Lian of revered memory, ordered that far seeing be severely restricted. It is only in these last weeks that we have sought out Wendlan minds – by your command.'

Kasheen continued to scowl and Jakri wisely remained silent and expressionless. Kasheen's fingers tapped on his chair again.

'Our fleets are ready to begin an attack on the outer islands under Maleshan control. The new ships can carry a large warrior force. My feeling, and that of my advisors, is that time is limited – the witch is too close to succeeding.' He began to rise, indicating the audience was ended, but Jakri slid from his chair to his knees.

'Serenity,' he used that honorific in sincerest hope, 'one of the Council Mages is here in Wendla now. It is Taseen, he who survived the last battle.'

Kasheen sank back onto his chair, eyes boring into Jakri.

'I do not know how he reached our shores undetected. His mage powers are mostly lost, but he is here, with at least three other mages. And none of them are Maleshan. He is in the company also of four Dragons and rests now at Green Shade. Mighty One, I asked that some of these people come here, to your palace, to speak with you personally. I trust I did as you might have wished.'

In the ensuing silence Jakri held himself motionless.

'Dragons you say?' Kasheen stared across the room at the great hearth, empty now in the warmth of early summer. Above the fireplace was a Dragon face, viewed full on: a long, exquisitely beautiful face painted a silver blue which shimmered in the light of many lamps. Feathered wings flanked the face, bright scarlet tipped with gold. Jakri, following the Emperor's gaze, gave an involuntary gasp of surprise.

'But,' he began, and bit his lip hard.

Kasheen swung to face Jakri. 'But?' he asked softly.

'I have seen that depiction so many times, Great One.' Jakri found himself stammering like the youngest student. 'The face – it is identical to one of the Dragons I far saw at Green Shade.'

Kasheen stood up, walking towards the hearth. 'Tell me of this,' he said. 'Or better yet, show me mind to mind.'

Jakri swallowed. It was death to attempt mind touch with any members of the Imperial House Crystal but Kasheen had not voiced a request. He forced himself to relax, sitting back on his heels and breathing slowly. His mind quested towards his Emperor and received a shock. Children of the Imperial House were never publicly tested for mage talent although it was widely believed to occur: many in the generations of House Crystal had been revealed as powerful mages. It therefore followed that the testing was carried out by House mages, and any talents were nurtured within the House rather than through the Colleges. Jakri had often wondered whether this was wise or not. Within the Colleges students of all Houses mixed together, some making lifelong friendships, others the opposite.

If House Crystal trained its children isolated from all others, one assumed their loyalty was never divided but always given to their own Imperial House. He had wondered occasionally if Kasheen was mage gifted: now, touching the Emperor's mind he realised he was, and powerfully so. Jakri simply opened his thoughts, offering Kasheen the true memory of his recent contact with Maressa at Green Shade. He recognised that Kasheen was absorbing the memory rather than merely observing, and as Maressa had broken contact so Jakri withdrew swiftly from the Emperor's mind.

'This will be considered more thoroughly.' Kasheen indicated that Jakri should rise. 'Notify me the instant these – visitors – approach the city. You will instruct them to come to the Family Garden. You will attend me there. I will hold back the fleet until we have spoken with them.'

He gave a brief nod and Jakri bowed deeply, backing away until he felt the door behind him. Grasping the handle, he pulled open one side of the moon door and left the Emperor's presence. The Blossoms stood impassively while Jakri pushed his feet into his sandals and began to walk down the stairs. Jalan waited at the first landing and walked ahead in silence until they neared the base of the palace buildings.

'Go safely Master Jakri,' said Jalan, as an Imperial Blossom approached and saluted.

It wasn't the same Blossom who had brought him to the palace, Jakri noted, but this one was just as silently efficient in escorting the Master Mage back to House Jade. His mother awaited him in the third reception room. He recounted Kasheen's words and nodded at her exclamation of surprise.

'I too was astonished that he would suggest the Family Garden as the meeting place. There are many other Gardens within the palace which would be as private.'

'No Jakri. The Family Garden is the most sacred place to House Crystal as are our own Family Gardens. I have never heard of any other than House members being invited within any, yet he asks that you attend.'

'I'm not even sure where it is.' Jakri looked as uneasy as he felt. 'The central part of the palace has always been warded – will the Crystal Mages drop the warding for the strangers to enter? I sense the girl with silver eyes will suspect a trap, or duplicity on our part.'

'Go to your bed my son. The hour is too late for serious thought. Dawn is not far off.'

Jakri scrubbed his hand over his face. 'As usual you're right.' He turned towards the stairs. 'I would see Hiramo, J'Bak and Shek at first bell.'

Oniko smiled. 'I will have messages sent.'

Jakri slept as soon as he lay on his mat, all thoughts expunged from his mind as he'd been taught in one of the earliest lessons in Mage College. He woke before dawn and padded quietly to his shower room. He dressed in his usual pale blue gown and after rolling away his sleeping mat, he sat on his balcony. He kept his mind open, orientated to the north west and Green Shade. The first pale pink fingers of approaching day were just noticeable when he sensed Maressa's mind approaching his.

'Five of us will travel to your city Jakri. We expect to be there in two to three days. Is this agreeable?'

'It is Mistress. The Emperor Kasheen welcomes the opportunity to speak with you. He suggests you go to the Family Garden within the palace.'

'Where is this place – is it easy to locate? You will have to guide us in detail as we draw near.' Maressa paused, aware of hesitation in Jakri's mind. 'Is there a problem you should warn us of?' Her tone was wary now.

Jakri took a decision and was honest with the woman. 'The Family Garden is the most secret and sacred place within the palace. House Crystal have never allowed non members to enter, yet I am also to be present. The area is heavily warded at all times – inquisitive students often make the mistake of trying to pry but always they are detected, identified and reprimanded.'

Jakri sat awaiting Maressa's response. She sounded thoughtful rather than worried or annoyed. 'I believe that could be dealt with Master Jakri.' He saw hazel eyes blazing with determination. 'You understand my meaning?'

'I do. And I repeat – my life is willing forfeit should any harm be attempted upon you.'

'The one called Hiramo is near you,' Maressa observed. 'We will contact either of you to keep you informed of our progress towards your city.'

She vanished from Jakri's mind. He sat a while longer, watching the dark clouds fleeing before another clear bright dawn. A chime sounded beyond the inner door and he turned. A maid bowed then straightened smiling.

'Your breakfast is ready Master and your apprentices are in the book room.'

Jakri rose gracefully to his feet. 'Ask them to join me in the dining room – they are usually hungry.'

The maid smiled again as she bowed and left his rooms. He met his mother in the upper hall.

'Just to tell you my son. I will be far travelling this day. Meshka has instructions to let none disturb me.'

Jakri raised his dark brows. 'Perhaps we should discuss your travelling later.'

Oniko laughed. 'Perhaps,' she agreed amiably.

'Guard yourself well Oniko.'

She nodded and returned to her own apartments.

Jakri went downstairs to the dining room behind the second reception room. Three people rose from the floor cushions and bowed respectfully.

'Be seated and eat.' Jakri sat at the end of the long low table while two young maids glided in with parcels of napkins. Jakri and his apprentices unwrapped the parcels to find hot rolls filled with vegetables and cheese. Pots of tea and jugs of water were brought and dishes of chopped fresh fruits.

'Mistress Oniko said you wished us to attend you early Master.' Shek was the eldest of the three, born on one of the farming estates of House Jade to the south west of the city.

'And I appreciate your coming in time for breakfast,' Jakri agreed with the young man quite straight faced.

J'Bak choked on a slice of peach and blushed behind his napkin. He was Shek's cousin, a few years younger but from the same country estate. Hiramo kept her expression as bland as the

Master's.

'The food from your kitchens is renowned throughout the Colleges, Master. Any opportunity to sample its delights is never to be avoided.'

Jakri laughed and poured himself some tea. He watched Hiramo over the rim of the bowl. She was fair: her skin paler and more delicate than the golden olive of most Wendlans. Her hair too was light brown rather than the usual sooty black. Hiramo's mother had been born in Bracca to the minor House Jasper, but her father had been a tribesman from the forests of the north east. The area around Green Shade, Jakri realised suddenly. The Emperor Omak had ceded a great deal of land – useless in his opinion – to the Survivor Captain and her son in just that region.

'If you have all finished sampling?' he enquired.

He left his cushion and slid open a door into the next room – the book room where he received students and dealt with daily business. He waited until the three were seated and motionless then looked into each pair of eyes in turn.

'I will show you a meeting of minds first,' he said. 'I want no comments yet.'

He showed them Hiramo's meeting with Maressa and his own later contact. Again he studied each face before him.

'Now I will show you what should not be shown.'

As Jakri had anticipated, a hiss of indrawn breath escaped J'Bak when the apprentice realised that the man Jakri's memory showed them was the Emperor Kasheen himself.

Jakri closed his mind to his apprentices and allowed them time to consider the implications of what he'd revealed. Before he could begin speaking, there was a soft scratch at the door. He frowned. 'Come.'

The door slid open and the senior door servant entered, bowing deeply. 'An Imperial Blossom requests a moment of your precious time, Master.'

Jakri got up and followed the man to the courtyard entrance. An Imperial Blossom saluted as Jakri appeared. He offered a small black lacquered box. Jakri accepted it and looked up into the Blossom's face.

'His Imperial Graciousness says this is his authority.'

He saluted again, swung smartly about and left House Jade.

Jakri studied the box carefully. He walked into the empty dining room, the table now cleared and polished. He pressed a tiny button on one side of the box and the lid sprang open. Inside, nestled on black cloth, was a gold bracelet set with a blue stone, a green, and between them was a diamond of great value. Plumes were finely etched along the gold – the insignia of Imperial House Crystal.

Jakri slid the bracelet over his hand and felt it shrink as he did so, so that instead of sliding loosely, it fitted snug to his wrist. Jakri focused his concentration on the bracelet and found no spells or wardings set within it. There was something about the diamond but Jakri suspected that it was only a natural imbuement of a stone which represented House Crystal. Letting the sleeve of his gown cover the bracelet, Jakri returned to the book room.

His apprentices sat exactly as he'd left them; all deep in their own contemplation of the images their Master had shown them. Hiramo at least had been better prepared, having made the initial contact with Maressa, but J'Bak was clearly struggling to understand. Jakri resumed his cushion, tapping a fingernail twice on the table top between him and the apprentices. Their heads lifted and their eyes fixed on the Master.

'Comments,' he suggested.

He wasn't surprised that J'Bak spoke first this morning: usually the shyest, least confident of the three, he was badly shaken.

'The Family Garden of House Crystal,' he blurted. 'For any not a member of a House to set foot in another's Family Garden is punishable by instant execution. I have never heard of such a thing Master. If you were married to a daughter of House Crystal, it would be permissible, and for her to enter the Family Garden of House Jade. Can even the Emperor put aside such tradition? Master, I tremble for your safety.'

'I cannot see that the Emperor could issue such a command – and it was a command, not an invitation,' Shek pointed out. 'He could not command your presence and then your death Master. You are the head of House Jade, as much respected as head of this great House as for your mage talent.'

Jakri turned to Hiramo.

'I agree with Shek, Master. There is no sense in ordering your presence followed immediately by your death unless ...' she paused.

Jakri waited.

'Unless he feels that your presence would lull any suspicions of the visitors?'

Jakri nodded approvingly. 'My thought exactly. I have also received a gift from Kasheen.'

He pulled his sleeve back, extending his arm across the table. 'I feel nothing of mage craft within it, except perhaps for the diamond.'

Shek moved to kneel by the table, peering closely at the bracelet firmly sealed on Jakri's wrist. Silence thickened in the book room as Shek mentally probed the bracelet. He was highly accomplished in the study of artefacts and Jakri had total confidence in his expertise. At last Shek sat back.

'There is nothing Master. The diamond is imbued with clarity of thought.' He shrugged. 'Perhaps the Emperor wants you to see behind all words spoken at this meeting. I admit I feared it would contain a death command. You will not be able to remove it,' he added. 'There is no trigger alert to warn the Emperor if you tried to take it off, but I see no way to expand it again.'

'The Emperor?' asked Jakri.

Shek nodded. 'He would be the only one to remove it I'd think.'

'You are absolutely sure the Emperor cannot – eavesdrop shall we say – through this bracelet?'

The apprentice shook his head firmly. 'May my life be forfeit Master. I find the article harmless.'

Jakri drew his arm back and smiled. 'I hoped you'd come to that conclusion I have to confess.'

Tension in the room relaxed; even the rigidity of J'Bak's spine softened a little.

'You heard Mistress Maressa say that she would contact either you or me, Hiramo. I wondered how she knew that you were approaching the House earlier – any ideas?'

Hiramo was as gifted in far speaking and seeing as Maressa herself, but her methods in doing so were subtly different. Now she considered Jakri's question before she replied.

'We use House sigils and various other means to identify any we mind speak. I believe Mistress Maressa uses a far more specific means of identification. But we have been restricted by Imperial edict, not to far travel beyond Wendla. Mistress Maressa is accustomed to much greater distances I believe.'

Chapter Twenty-Two

Maressa had not revealed the gijan to the mage Jakri, thinking that they would be remaining at Green Shade. She tried arguing with them when it became clear they had no intention of letting Tika travel anywhere without them. Ammi had been aghast to find Tika had only two pairs of much worn and much mended trousers and three similarly shabby shirts apart from Salma's gift of clothes. Daughters-in-law were summoned and commanded to rectify the matter. Tika never saw her old clothes again.

Olam and Riff had departed with one of Ammi's sons to rejoin Kasmi and the ships. In spite of Pallin's mutters and scowls, no one doubted how pleased he secretly was to be confronted with over a dozen small boys and nearly as many small girls all hoping to learn arms skills. Maressa was content to stay with Taseen. Although botanical sciences had not figured greatly with her before, Sefri's enthusiasm together with Ammi's immense knowledge of the medicinal properties of plants had awakened her interest.

The Ship fascinated Taseen and a boy was assigned to help the old man inside the Ship where he sat in the Captain's chair and listened to Star Flower recount her travels. Tika viewed the imminent parting calmly. She had confidence in Maressa's ability to keep track of them although she rather wondered where Grek had got to.

'Have you no idea where he is?' she asked Khosa while she packed her bag.

Khosa was sprawled on the window sill watching the gijan chasing butterflies. She yawned.

'I'd prefer him to be with us but I don't know where he is. I'm surprised he's been gone so long.'

'Could someone have taken him apart, like Seela described?' Tika repressed a shiver at the thought.

'I think we'd know – somehow Namolos would learn of it and

manage to let us know in turn.'

Farewells were brief and by midmorning the Dragons and their riders were well away from Green Shade. They flew high and fast, the forest an endless green below them. From this height they caught only occasional glimpses of water where the numerous rivers widened into lakes before narrowing under the trees again. A few less wooded hilltops poked above the forest and they decided to settle on one for the night. Ammi had told them a few ritual words to use should any tribesmen accost them in the forest but none appeared.

The hill they chose for their first night's rest was close to the southern edge of the forest: as they flew, they could see patches of fields in the fading daylight ahead. The gijan had no trouble keeping pace with the Dragons but were tiring by the time they decided to make camp, and were quickly asleep on Seela's back. Farn and Storm were still energetic enough to go with Brin in the hope of finding food although they were far from hungry having fed well at Green Shade.

'Do we really trust Master Jakri?' asked Gan when they sat round their small fire.

'He offered his life as forfeit.' Tika poked a twig in the embers. 'I think probably we can. His Emperor I'm not so sure about.'

Khosa sat up suddenly on Ren's knees, staring intently just beyond Seela.

'Grek?' Tika asked.

'Greetings.' The unbodied entity sounded tired, if such a sensation was possible for him to experience. 'I have been to Namolos. Then I tried to visit Star Singer but even I could not penetrate the shielding Kertiss now has in place around the Domes. I spent three days attempting to do so before I succeeded. What I learned sent me to Harbour City. I spoke with Taseen's friends Sheoma and Tavri, and with the Grand Harbour Master himself. He was a touch surprised.'

All the travellers were listening closely to Grek's mind voice and Tika noticed the gijan too were awake on Seela's back.

'I couldn't determine whether it is by Orla's command or if the men who follow Hadjay have taken the decision themselves, but several thousand of the outer desert tribesmen ride south towards Malesh.'

'All those little villages!' Tika murmured in horror.

'I did what I could, Tika. I warned Zeminth as I went to Harbour City.'

'Have you managed to discover anything of the city of Bracca?' Ren asked.

There was a silence as though Grek was offended but he answered before Ren could say anything else.

'They have powerful mages there. They have been restricted for too long in how they use or try to extend their powers and such stagnation is never good, as we've all seen in Sapphrea.'

'What of this Family Garden where we are to meet the Emperor?' asked Gan.

'All Houses have a Family Garden where the ashes of their ancestors are interred and all important rituals take place. For instance, if a daughter of one House marries a son of another House, the marriage rites take place outside the man's Family Garden. Members of both Houses are present at the ritual but then the man takes his new wife inside the Garden to present her to his forebears. House members may take offerings of great value to lay before a particular ancestor so there could be enormous wealth just lying around within such a Garden. It is a place closely guarded by House troops obviously.'

'So why are we to meet in the so secret Garden of the Emperor?' Tika leaned back against Farn and tried not to yawn.

'I haven't been able to discover that. But I have been within the Crystal Family Garden.' Grek sounded quite smug.

'Without detection?' Navan was full of admiration.

'Indeed. I was surprised, to be honest. The Emperor is very powerful, more so than even his own House mages give credit for. He is very clever too – somewhat like Chevra in maintaining a merely average outward persona. And when one considers how long he has kept up this pretence of being far less clever than he is, one has to admire such constancy.'

'But you got in without even him knowing?' Tika brought the unbodied entity back to Navan's point.

'The wards and shields are set only against Wendlan mage craft. I will go ahead of you again to ensure the Emperor has not thought to change the wardings but I don't think it will occur to him.'

'I expect us to reach this palace by the middle of the day after next,' Brin remarked. 'Is there somewhere you could suggest we would rest tomorrow night?'

Grek was silent for a while. 'There are several large public gardens close to the city. But I think you may find yourself still among farms and large villages by nightfall tomorrow.'

'I can shield us,' Brin offered, 'as I did for Maressa and me in the lands near Seboth's town.'

'No. You need all your strength for the journey itself and for whatever you might be called on to do at the meeting with the Emperor. I will stay with you then and shield you at all times until you are within the palace grounds at least. Then I will simply observe, unless my intervention is required.'

The friends rolled silently into their blankets, trying not to think of what situation might need Grek's intervention and what form such action might take.

Tika woke early as she usually did, Farn snoring softly at her back. She sent out the lightest thought:

'Grek?'

'Yes Tika?'

'Do you rest or sleep?'

She thought he wouldn't answer.

'In my present state I have no need of sleep – as I have no need of food or drink. At times I suspend my thought processes and I suppose you could call that a period of rest.'

'Do you find it irksome – the state you are now in?'

'I can travel where I wish, faster than any solid body could. I can infiltrate through air, rock, walls. But yes, I suppose I enjoyed the physicality of living within a finite space and again yes, I miss it more than I had thought possible.'

'Is Mena safe?'

Again, Grek was silent. Then his voice was the faintest breath in Tika's mind. 'She was well and safe when I parted from her.' Another pause stretched between them. 'I bitterly regret what I forced her to do at the end. Tika, try to understand: Cho Petak was a wonderful man in the eyes of the boy that I was when I met him. All the years which have passed since our punishment, I held him in my mind as the marvellous teacher I had first known.

When at last he called me to Drogoya, I had no idea of how he had changed, the destruction he had unleashed on that poor land and its people. I was desperate to reach my beloved master again, but I was part of the young girl Mena. It didn't occur to me to unbody, to leave her. Instead I forced her to overwhelm the Dragon's mind and thus get us to Drogoya.'

'The Dragon? You mean Kadi?' Tika lay still, frozen with horror at the idea of the great midnight blue Dragon Kadi being coerced into making such an arduous flight. But she had somehow got back hadn't she? Kija had flown to the Stronghold when word reached the golden Dragon of her clan sister's injuries.

Grek had followed Tika's thought. 'Kadi was healed. By Gremara and the Observer Chakar.' He did not tell her that both Kadi and Kija had now flown again to Drogoya, into enormous peril.

'Why are the desert tribes marching on Malesh now?'

'I'm not sure if it is Kertiss and Orla's madness – they are both quite insane as I'm sure you guessed. Or it may be the being imprisoned beneath that desert has loosened its bonds sufficiently to influence not only Kertiss and Orla but tribesmen such as Hadjay.'

Tika heard Sket cough as he started to build up the fire to make the tea without which his day couldn't begin.

'Thank you for speaking to me Grek. I will try to understand why you caused Kadi to suffer.' She got up, folding her blanket to replace in her pack.

'I doubt you can ever understand,' Grek replied, 'but I appreciate your offer to try. Perhaps you may even reach a point where you might forgive me.'

Gan called her to come and eat something and Tika knew Grek would not speak to her so intimately again for a while. The gijan suddenly trilled and giggled. Khosa marched past them, bristling with indignation, and sat firmly on Ren's knee.

'What's the matter?' he asked with genuine sympathy.

'They think it fun to follow me when I hunt. They don't try their nonsense on Brin of course, but four squeakers have just been allowed to avoid being my breakfast thanks to their efforts.'

Ren immediately offered her some cold meat from his own

breakfast. She sniffed it carefully and then accepted it. Ren looked up to find Tika grinning at him. Keeping a straight face, he winked back at her.

The rim of the sun was barely touching the horizon when the Dragons and gijan took wing once more. It had been agreed that Ren would inform Maressa of their approach to the city and she in turn would contact Jakri or Hiramo. Shielded as the travellers were, no Wendlan mage should be able to know their precise location until absolutely necessary.

During the second day they flew over farm lands of all types: flooded meadows with green shoots sticking up above the water, open fields where large animals grazed, more fields with many kinds of crops. They saw the lines of canals which Sefri had described. There was much traffic on these waterways – ships called barges heavily laden with goods, travelled to and from the great agricultural estates of the Houses and the city of Bracca.

The riders saw all this through the slightly distorting shimmer of the shield Grek held around them. By midday, when Seela called a halt, there were many more buildings and thus more people. They settled in an open field in which were a considerable number of the grazing animals. These promptly fled to the furthest part of the field. Although they could see nothing, clearly they sensed unwelcome and perhaps predatory intruders.

Seela insisted the gijan stay even closer as they flew on. When the sun sank towards evening, Leaf rode behind Tika, and Willow and Piper behind Ren on Seela's broad back. The field to which Brin led them for the night was a rough empty pasture. Grek refused to drop the shielding for Ren to mind speak Maressa, saying instead that he would contact her. She was to warn Jakri or Hiramo that the Dragons would be at the Emperor's Family Garden on the morrow, exactly at noon. She was not to say anything more. Grek had decided that they should overfly Bracca and approach the palace from the south rather than the north. Just in case, he explained rather ominously.

At dawn Gan checked their appearance. He had spread his blue cloak on a compliant Brin overnight to get the worst creases out of it. Tika refused to wear Salma's gift: she stayed with the pale blue shirt and darker blue trousers provided by Ammi. Sket had checked her sword and his own as always and her egg pendant hung beneath her shirt once more. The burn on her chest had scabbed and was still uncomfortable but she preferred to have it against her skin than in the pouch at her waist. Sket and Navan also wore blue shirts and black trousers provided by Ammi. The sun had risen by the time Gan pronounced himself satisfied with their appearance and they began the last leagues of their journey.

Jakri left his apprentices in the book room of House Jade when he made his way, unaccompanied, to the palace. He wasn't sure if he would be admitted – he had not had time to apply for audience with the Emperor and he had not been summoned. He'd heard tales of casual visitors being left to wait in a room unfortunately like a prison cell beside the main gate for a whole day before being told to go away. So it was with some apprehension that he was invited inside and found himself in that very same waiting room.

But before his apprehension could grow into panic an Imperial Blossom appeared at the door and saluted him.

'If you will follow, Master Jakri, the Imperial Splendour awaits you.'

Jakri wore a pale green gown with a darker green sleeveless over robe, heavily embroidered with the sigils of House Jade. The Blossom led him into parts of the palace he had never before entered, staying on the ground floor all the way. Jakri was too preoccupied to keep track of the twists and turns of the route the Imperial Blossom led him. They passed many doors, all of which were firmly closed, and crossed many courtyard gardens. Some of these were filled with all white plants, others with all yellow; some had only green foliage and still others no plants at all only rocks and flowing water.

They turned yet another corner and Jakri saw more Imperial Blossoms ahead. A silver faced moon door was guarded by no less than ten Blossoms. They towered over Jakri, their black lacquered armour and tall purple plumes accentuating the sense of their bulk and height. The Blossom who escorted Jakri saluted and one of the guarding officers returned the salute. Then they all stood in silent stillness for long enough that Jakri's palms began to grow damp again.

A bell rang softly, two notes, and the Imperial Blossoms stiffened even further if that was possible. Jakri bowed in anticipation of the arrival of the Emperor although from which direction he might appear he couldn't guess.

'Greetings, Master of House Jade. Arise and accompany me.'

Jakri straightened and managed to keep his face impassive. He had fully expected the Emperor to come with an entourage of at least a dozen House Crystal mages, but only his wife stood a pace behind him. Kasheen glanced at the moon door and nine Blossoms moved with precision to one side while the other two opened the double doors. Jakri lowered his gaze. The Empress Sariko was rarely seen by visitors to the palace and never in public. Although she was veiled, Jakri hoped to avoid any offence by keeping his eyes well away from her.

Kasheen strode through the door followed by the Empress then by Master Jakri. A blank wall blocked their advance, and also deterred anyone outside seeing further into the Garden. Kasheen turned left and then, after a few paces, right. Jakri felt fresh air blowing against his face but continued to stare at the blocks of white alabaster on which he stood.

'Jakri, for the time you are within this Garden, I am Kasheen and my wife, Sariko. All are equally insignificant in the presence of my ancestors.'

Jakri forced himself to lift his head until he met his Emperor's dark eyes. Kasheen gave the slightest smile.

'It is close to noon. I have ordered the wards be set aside.'

Jakri instinctively looked up. Walls rose all around, all white, and all windowless to the very topmost part of the palace. The sky was a dazzling circle of blue far above.

'I know nothing more Great One.' Jakri looked at the Emperor. 'The mage in Green Shade said they would be here at noon.'

'No ceremony here I have told you.'

Jakri almost jumped as someone laughed close to his shoulder. He glanced round involuntarily and realised he was staring at the Empress who had removed her veil. She was fairer than Hiramo – her hair pale gold and her eyes grey blue. She laughed again.

'Greetings Jakri. I have long wished to meet you.'

Before Jakri could begin to compose an adequate response, a deep bass call echoed down to them. All three turned their faces up to the sky as two enormous silhouettes spiralled slowly down, two smaller shapes drifting behind them. Jakri looked quickly round the House Crystal Garden, seeing with relief that the centre was a fairly large open space bordered with low flowering shrubs.

Four Dragons reared erect, dark purple, silver grey, silver blue and crimson, their voices loud in the minds of Jakri, Kasheen and the Empress Sariko. The Dragons remained upright, wings outstretched and Tika emerged from behind Farn, Khosa in her arms. Sket stood at one shoulder, Gan's tall thin figure to her other side. Ren and Navan moved from behind Seela towards their hosts. Tika did not bow but walked steadily forward to within fifteen paces of the three strangers, her friends flanking her.

'I am Tika, soul bond to Farn, daughter of Kija of the Dragon Kindred,' she said clearly, her emerald eyes surrounded by silver scaling fixed steadily on Jakri. She proceeded to formally introduce the others, including Khosa. She paused and as she did so the three gijan rose behind the Dragons, swooping over their heads to land beside Tika.

'Leaf, Willow and Piper are gijan who travel with me.' She ended her introductions inwardly chuckling at the stupefied expressions on the faces before her.

Jakri cleared his suddenly parched throat. He had had no idea just how big a Dragon could be. And what, in the name of the spirits, were gijan? He bowed deeply with genuine respect.

'I am Jakri of House Jade. I would introduce the Crystal Emperor Kasheen and ...' he faltered. He had never spoken to the Empress, had only seen her a handful of times at great state occasions: how did he present her?

Kasheen came to Jakri's rescue. He bowed, giving Jakri another shock – since when did the Emperor bow to anyone? He took the Empress's hand.

'My wife the Empress Sariko.'

She tried to maintain her poise but Piper trilled softly, tilting her head one side then the other, and her Imperial Gloriousness laughed like a child.

'You are so beautiful – all of you.' She glanced up at her husband. 'Tell me Kasheen, did you know there was such wonder in the world?'

Half a heart beat and then the Emperor smiled. 'Sariko speaks only the truth,' he agreed.

He took several steps forward and held a hand out to Tika. Unsure of the customs of this land, she held her hand towards Kasheen. He gripped her palm firmly for a moment before repeating the gesture to all the men. The Dragons had lowered themselves and now Brin and Seela reclined, ever watchful. Storm and Farn paced closer to the humans. Farn's eyes whirred faster, the facets pearl and sapphire as he lowered his head to Sariko.

'A girl!' he said in delight.

Sket muffled a snort and Tika was furious to find herself blushing. She jabbed a sharp elbow into Farn's chest.

'I apologise if my soul bond gives offence – he is not yet a year old and has much to learn of manners.'

Sariko tentatively held her hand towards Farn's face and he leaned into it.

'I did not mean to be rude. I never do.' His mind tone was so abject Sariko had to bite her lip.

'It was not taken as rudeness – but it is long since I was a girl.'

Kasheen indicated white stone benches set among a cluster of small flowering trees.

'If you would ask two of the guards to bring refreshments Jakri?' the Emperor suggested.

Jakri went back to the moon door and repeated the request to the Blossom who had escorted him through the palace. By the time he'd returned to the Garden he sensed the visitors were relaxing. He looked at the purple and crimson Dragons and when soft lilac prismed eyes turned to him he knew they were alert for anything, no matter how relaxed the humans might be.

The sound of booted feet heralded the arrival of two Imperial Blossoms incongruously carrying large trays. As sworn members of House Crystal, they were permitted entry to the Family Garden of course. Jakri turned in time to see the Blossoms freeze at sight of the Dragons. He held his breath but Kasheen rose to his feet.

'Set the trays here, and speak no word of my guests beyond this Garden.'

The Blossoms obeyed, their faces impassive. Gan also rose, causing another brief stillness. He was as tall as the tops of the plumes on the Blossoms' helmets and had the unmistakeable demeanour of a military man of high rank. The Blossoms studied him for a moment before saluting Kasheen and departing the Garden.

'You have many such impressive officers?' Gan enquired, reseating himself.

'Two hundred within the palace and twelve hundred warriors under their command.' Kasheen suddenly grinned at Sket who had gaped at the numbers mentioned.

Jakri offered tea bowls and sat on another bench.

'We believe you plan to attack Malesh,' Tika said abruptly.

Kasheen ran a finger round the edge of the priceless porcelain tea bowl in his hand. He met Tika's silvered eyes squarely.

'We hoped it would distract the witch woman from her attempts to unbind the monstrous Child,' he agreed honestly.

'Well it hasn't. There is another Bound One in danger of gaining his freedom. He is beneath the deserts north of Malesh.'

Kasheen sat very still and Sariko, who had been chatting happily with the gijan turned to listen to Tika.

'Already several thousand of the desert tribes descend on Malesh.'

'So the Grand Harbour Master faces war from the north and from us in the east,' said Kasheen. He got up, pacing towards Brin. He turned and paced back, lines crinkling his forehead as he considered.

'I do not wish war with Malesh. Our action in seizing those two merchant ships was truly intended as a distraction, to give my mages time to stop the Maleshan witch's foolish schemes.' He paced restlessly again. 'If the Grand Harbour Master consents, I will return his merchant ships to him, goods intact, crews unharmed. Well – most of them are unharmed – there was a bit of a fight you understand. And I will send my fleet with troops, to aid him against the desert men. We dare not waste time bickering when the witch is so near succeeding.'

Chapter Twenty-Three

'Summon first rank officer Lytzee,' Kasheen ordered Jakri, who went again to the moon door.

In his absence Kasheen surveyed his unusual guests.

'I commanded that food be readied for you in the lesser Chamber of Audience.' He waved towards the blank walls of the palace. 'I have also commanded that this section of the palace be cleared of all staff: only Imperial Blossoms are in this area.'

'Imperial Blossoms?' Navan sounded mystified.

'Imperial Blossoms are my elite troops,' Kasheen explained. 'Warriors are those who aspire to rise to the rank of Blossoms. There are no warriors within this part of the palace now, only Blossoms.'

Jakri returned, the Blossom who had escorted him here earlier at his side. The Blossom saluted, keeping his eyes only on his Emperor.

'My guests and I go to the lesser Chamber of Audience. There will be complete privacy.'

First rank officer Lytzee saluted and risked a quick glance at the two adult Dragons.

'Are the ways of your palace large enough for my Kindred to move through?' Tika moved to slip her arm across Farn's shoulders.

Kasheen nodded. 'There should be no difficulty for them.'

Jakri sensed a slight increase in tension from the girl again.

'I hope there is no difficulty – it would be unfortunate if the Dragons grew annoyed.'

Kasheen laughed at the clear threat although Imperial Blossom Lytzee looked worried. The Blossom went ahead, followed by the Emperor and Empress. Khosa planted herself in front of Kasheen.

'You may carry me.'

Kasheen stared down into turquoise eyes, swallowed and

stooped to lift Khosa. She held his gaze unblinkingly in the unnerving manner of cats.

'You too?' he murmured aloud.

'Oh yes. Most living creatures have mind powers to some degree. It is most odd that humans have never noticed.' She settled herself more comfortably in the crook of his arm. 'Well – show us the way,' she said. 'I believe you mentioned food?'

They had arrived at the short passage leading to the moon door.

'Why do you hide the doorway?' Willow demanded.

'It is a spirit door,' said the Emperor. 'Spirits only travel in straight lines so any trying to enter the moon door would find a wall in front of them. They would turn back at once.'

'And how long have you believed such utter nonsense?' snapped a voice in their heads.

Kasheen stopped abruptly. Seela had just squeezed into the narrower passage and Kasheen stared back in her direction.

'Don't worry. It was Grek speaking,' Khosa kindly informed the Emperor of Wendla.

Tika moved past Jakri, Sket close beside her. She gave Kasheen an innocent smile.

'I forgot to introduce our other friend and companion – Grek. He is unbodied. What you call a spirit I think.'

Imperial Blossom Lytzee was opening the moon door as she spoke and she was fairly sure his plume shivered more noticeably at her words. Kasheen's face was pale as he searched in vain for Grek. Sariko and Jakri seemed more interested than alarmed.

'Don't worry.' Grek's voice filled their minds, including the Blossoms standing rigidly to attention along the corridor. 'As Lady Tika has just told you, I am a friend of this company. I noticed a few faded wraiths in your Garden – I disapprove that you hold them here rather than letting them free to expand.'

Kasheen opened and closed his mouth but Khosa urged him to move on.

'You can discuss that while we're eating, dear Emperor.'

Wordlessly, Kasheen followed the Blossom between a spaced rank of other such officers. Tika and Sket waited for the Dragons to clear the moon door. Neither Seela nor Brin had trouble with the width but had to crouch to pass beneath the door. The gijan walked daintily beside Seela, occasionally commenting to each other in their own tongue. As Brin's tail slithered through the door, Tika patted his great shoulder. He lowered his head for a moment, eyes whirring with excitement: adult though he was, he loved new adventures as much as Farn.

Storm had caught up with Navan and seemed intrigued by the Imperial Blossoms they walked past. Farn caused some delay by insisting on waiting until Tika and Sket had caught up with him. Gan watched a Blossom's eyes widen when Storm paused to peer more closely into his face. Gan rested his hand lightly on Storm's neck, remembering how the sea Dragon had snarled at Kertiss in the Dome. Storm would be quickest to anger he'd concluded then and had resolved to stay close to him during this visit to Bracca.

The corridors were of white stone: floors, walls and ceiling, lit from a source Tika couldn't see. It wasn't long before double doors swung open and they found themselves in a large vaulted chamber. Natural light poured in through windows set high along one wall. A long table was set in the middle of the room, almost insignificant in the otherwise empty space. There was a dais at the furthest end, on which three enormous chairs stood, carved and set with glittering crystals.

Each chair was overhung by a canopy and both Brin and Seela began to huff, advancing on the dais with some speed. Kasheen whirled, saw what was happening and unceremoniously dumped Khosa on a surprised Blossom.

'It is carving only, great ones,' he called as he hurried towards them.

Jakri, fully recovered from his earlier nervousness, was enjoying himself hugely now and found it took a considerable effort to hide his smile at hearing the Emperor Kasheen using the term "great one". Kasheen climbed onto the dais, Seela following him. She reared up to examine the likeness of a Dragon's head which formed the canopy over the central chair.

'It is a carving,' Kasheen repeated. 'Done with mage craft.'

The others had gathered near the dais now and saw the Dragon's head was made of crystal. The light refracting through the interstices of melded crystals gave it at one moment a clarity, at the next a milky opacity. The eyes were two fist sized sapphires, cleverly cut so they seemed to blink and move. The jaws were slightly open and crystal fangs protruded, dagger sharp. Seela finally eased herself down the steps of the dais and reclined some paces away.

'Why should you have a likeness of one of my Kindred in your hall?' she asked, her gaze still fixed on the Dragon's head.

'It is said that in the Time Before, Dragons ruled this land of Wendla.' The Empress Sariko walked across to Seela, standing fearlessly before her.

Seela lowered her face to study the human female. 'I have no memories of this land,' she said, her mind tone flat.

'Even so, Lady Seela, our histories say that Dragons bred with Wendlans and their sons became Dragon Lords who ruled for millennia.'

Kasheen was watching his wife and Seela but Jakri saw the looks of surprise exchanged between the other members of the party.

'But there is a new Dragon Lord.' Farn sounded pleased to be helpful. 'In the north. He is our friend.'

Regardless of imperial protocol, Jakri sat down. What more surprises would he witness this day? The man with the chestnut brown eyes surrounded by silver sat down next to him and gave him a sympathetic smile.

'Believe me Master Jakri, I know how you feel.'

'I suggest we all sit down.' Gan held a chair for Tika and Navan copied his example for the Empress.

The gijan swooped on the dozens of plates and dishes spread along the table, helped themselves to a bizarre mixture of foods and retreated to perch on Brin's back. Two Imperial Blossoms still stood at attention, awaiting orders. Before Kasheen could dismiss them, Gan suggested politely that they should stay.

'I would be interested to hear how your armsmen are ordered.'

If Kasheen was startled by the request it was only a minor shock after all the previous ones.

'Sit, sit,' he waved the Blossoms to chairs at the table.

With some hesitation they removed their plumed helmets, putting them on the floor behind their chairs and thus revealing shaven skulls. Gan smiled encouragingly.

'The Emperor called you a first rank officer I believe,' he asked the one he thought was called Lytzee. 'What is the rank above you?'

'Me.' Kasheen gave a rueful grin, shaking his head. 'I have to admit that the little you have said knocks most of my beliefs and ideas flat to the ground. Please help yourselves to food.' He turned to Tika who sat between Sket and Gan. 'Is your friend Grek here?' he asked.

'Yes,' Grek replied.

'Oh.' Kasheen couldn't help looking hopefully around the Chamber.

'If it helps, I will stay at the end of the table.' It sounded as though Grek's patience was becoming strained.

'What did you mean – about faded wraiths?'

'Spirits should not be held to one place. They either grow melancholy and fade or they become irritable and try to cause trouble. Stars above, you know of the Bound Ones?'

Kasheen nodded.

'Do you think they'll be in friendly, kindly moods if they are freed?'

'But what else could have been done with them except bind them to a place?'

It was Seela not Grek who answered him. 'They should have been taken to pieces, every particle of them scattered beyond any reuniting. But the mages of the time did not know how to accomplish this disintegration of souls.'

'Does anyone now?' Jakri asked aloud.

Khosa hooked a piece of cold fowl from the table to Sariko's knee where she had ensconced herself. 'We do.'

'You do?' Jakri repeated in awe.

'We have always believed we must keep our ancestors closely guarded in our Family Gardens so that their spirits will protect the House and guide House members.' Kasheen frowned, trying to grasp Grek's contrary view.

'If you were imprisoned, would you spend eternity protecting and helping your gaolers?' Grek asked with asperity.

'The spirits of our ancestors maintain the harmonious balance of our lives. They protect us, we venerate them.'

'I think I am beginning to understand something,' Tika interrupted. She met Ren's eyes and he nodded. She sat back in her chair. 'Someone said to me that there was stagnation in my lands of Sapphrea which could only be a bad thing. All the people I have met since I soul bonded with Farn, talk of harmony or balance.'

She lifted her hands above the table, holding them level. She dipped one hand lower than the other. 'I have understood imbalance to be bad, but I wonder if that's true after all.'

Everyone was listening closely. Tika looked helplessly across the table at Ren.

'I also was taught that balance was the most important thing but I have realised it means that nothing changes – all must stay the same.'

Silvered eyes met silvered eyes.

'Slaves must be forever slaves, emperors forever emperors.'

Kasheen stared from Ren to Tika and back. 'But that is how life, society, survives surely?'

Tika smiled. 'I am considered the leader of this group of friends.'

Kasheen nodded: that had been plain from the first glimpse he'd had of her in Jakri's memory.

She shrugged. 'I am slave born.'

She realised as she said those words that she was at last free. Those four words no longer weighed her down: they were a fact of her past, would always affect the way she acted or reacted in certain situations, but they were no more now than four simple words.

'I have changed,' she continued. 'The gijan changed. My dear friend Mim has changed.'

Again she glanced at Ren. He was smiling broadly.

'And change means altering the balance,' he said. 'Perhaps for the worst, but it could also be for the better. It could mean progress from the stagnation our world has lived in for the past millennia at least. I have come to think that to maintain an unchanging balance may be highly unwise.'

Gan listened to Ren's words and Kasheen's arguments against drastic change, but he was thinking of the girl beside him. He was poorly gifted in the power the Asatarians had believed until recently was unique to them. That was why he had chosen a life in arms, becoming Captain of Lady Emla's Guards and thus the fighting leader of the Asatarians. But he was still able to sense more than most ungifted humans. He had recognised the importance of Tika's words: I am slave born. He felt her pleasure and pride in the relinquishing of the resentment which she had used as an armour against the world.

Kasheen and Jakri had listened closely to the exchange between Ren and Tika, both aware of undertones which they did not understand. Kasheen looked down the table at his Blossoms.

'I have suggested sending warriors to support Malesh instead of attacking it Lytzee. Opinion.'

Both Blossoms stood up.

'We only exist to obey, Mightiness,' said the one named Lytzee.

'No, no, no.' Kasheen's fist on the table top set two dishes chiming against each other.

The companions noticed, as the Blossoms stood rigidly to attention, that the plume insignia was etched on Lytzee's lacquered chest plate: presumably this was the identifying mark of his superior rank.

'Lady Tika has told of thousands of desert men advancing into Malesh.' Kasheen hesitated only briefly then fixed Lytzee with the Imperial gaze. 'The old tales of Bound Ones are true unfortunately, and two at least are close to becoming freed. I do not wish that piece of information spread throughout Wendla, you understand. I repeat – your opinion?'

Lytzee's eyes had narrowed when Emperor Kasheen spoke of the Bound Ones, but he replied instantly.

'Mighty One, we are yours to command. My opinion is irrelevant but I think to aid Malesh would be wisest at this time. It would surely be to everyone's benefit if their mages together with ours could concentrate solely on containing such as the Bound Ones.'

He bowed his head as he finished speaking.

'Jakri?' Kasheen turned to the Master of House Jade.

'I'm sure all the Houses would concur, Greatness. When one considers the numbers of mages alone lost in the battle which bound the Four, it would be best to have every mage attending to the same matter.'

'Taseen was one of those mages in the last battle,' Ren interposed quietly. 'He has survived but his power has not.

Kasheen digested that remark. 'Second rank officer – your name?'

Lytzee's companion clasped his hand across his chest in salute. 'Chimchoo, Gracious Lord.'

'Send runners to all the Houses. They are to attend the palace with only two senior mages each at the fifth bell.'

Chimchoo reached for his helmet, saluted again and marched from the Chamber. Jakri thanked the spirits that the year hadn't reached the hot season when most Houses would have departed the swelter of the city for their estates.

'Forgive me,' Kasheen inclined his head to Tika. 'I trust it will be convenient for you remain for the meeting of Houses?'

'When is – the fifth bell did you call it?' Ren asked.

'Dusk,' Kasheen replied. 'Will you stay this night in the palace?'

Tika checked Brin and Seela's thoughts on the matter and nodded. 'The Dragons would prefer to rest outside these walls – can we return to your Garden to sleep, or is there another courtyard rather than the place you hold so sacred?'

Kasheen glanced at Jakri who shrugged. 'If Your Greatness intends the Heads of the Houses and their mages to meet these guests, there will be no need for secrecy.'

The Empress clapped her hands. 'My private garden is close by – a passage beyond the dais takes you to it. You would be most welcome to use it. And there are bathing and resting chambers adjoining.'

'Perhaps you could let me see the place?' Gan stood, taller than the Imperial Blossoms.

'I'll show you.' Sariko seemed delighted that the rigid etiquette of daily life was quite ignored by these people.

Gan waited for Kasheen's nod of assent and then he followed the tiny figure of the Empress towards the dais.

'I have ten warships ready to sail and another ten being readied. Each carries one hundred warriors, five Imperial Blossoms and three mages.' The Emperor caught a slight movement from the still standing Lytzee.

'Speak,' he commanded.

'Imperial Wonder, where will we sail for? Harbour City is many leagues from the desert land. I think the captains might be asked to find somewhere to land the warriors on the eastern coast of Malesh.'

Kasheen nodded. 'Tell the archivist to send maps to me – he may give them to a Blossom outside.'

Navan coughed politely. 'The Survivor Captain Sefri has maps, sir Emperor. Maps of considerable detail of all this world.'

'Does she indeed? I didn't know that.'

'Well you've never paid a visit to her have you?' Tika raised a brow at the Emperor. To her surprise he looked somewhat abashed.

'I believed she was no more. Although we had heard no word from her, I did send a message when I first ascended the Crystal Throne, but I had no reply.'

'Her Ship has been close to death,' said Ren quietly. 'Captain Sefri dared not leave her since your grandfather's time I think.'

Gan returned with the Empress. 'The Lady's garden will suit,' he told Tika.

She nodded, pushing her chair back from the table. 'I should tell you Kasheen, that there are two ships in the river close by Green Shade. Three left Harbour City but one was lost on reefs in a storm.'

Kasheen was interested. 'Ships of the Maleshan coastal defenders?'

'Erm, not exactly. The mage Taseen hired them – they are from the pirate islands, under the command of Shipmaster Kasmi. One of the ships was badly damaged and is being repaired now.'

'I will send one of my fast patrols to see how we may facilitate the repairs. Also, it would be most helpful to have a Shipmaster's opinion of Maleshan coastal waters.'

'Taseen told us that ships of Malesh do not venture far up either east or west coasts. He said there were unpredictable weather and sea conditions which made such sailing dangerous.'

Kasheen nodded at Ren's comment. 'Do all Maleshan ships carry a mage with them?'

Ren shook his head. 'Unless a Wind Sister is a mage?' He gave Tika a questioning look.

'Maressa said Culinth could ride the air and foresee weather systems but she didn't think she could manipulate them in any degree. If she could, she would surely have saved Kasmi's ship wouldn't she?' Tika was on her feet, moving towards Farn. 'Did you know there are other Survivor Captains, other Ships, Kasheen?' she asked casually.

She was watching both the Emperor and Master Jakri and saw astonishment on both faces.

'I did not,' Kasheen replied. 'I am sure Captain Sefri never mentioned the fact to any of my forebears. There are others then?'

'Two others that we know of, possibly several more. One is in the city in the desert. The Ship is trustworthy but the Captain is not.'

Gan was opening a large door behind the dais, the gijan following on his heels.

'I will tell you when the Houses have gathered,' Kasheen called.

Sariko fluttered behind Sket. 'And I will make sure you have all you need for your comfort.'

Lytzee had answered a scratch at the further door and now approached the table with several rolls of parchment.

'May I stay and see these maps, sir Emperor,' asked Navan.

'A good idea – Navan isn't it? Sit here and see what you make of them.'

Storm settled back again along the wall: if Navan was staying here, then so was he.

Jakri bowed as Ren made to pass him. 'I would be grateful for the opportunity to speak with you Master Ren, if you would allow?'

The Wendlan and the Drogoyan followed Brin from the lesser Chamber of Audience, being careful not to step on his tail. They emerged into a courtyard that had an immediately different atmosphere to the Family Garden. That had a stultifying sense of stillness and death: even the plants there had seemed to be struggling. Here, everything was alive and cheerful, reaching up the many stories of the palace to the open sky with an eagerness and vitality utterly lacking in the Family Garden. Windows and doors opened onto this courtyard, although no windows punctuated the walls soaring upwards.

The gijan were delighted to find tiny birds, brilliantly coloured, calling and darting among the trees and shrubs. They were fascinated by clouds of butterflies which drifted over a small pool. While Ren and Jakri made themselves comfortable on cushions beneath a small tree heavily laden with dark pink blooms, Sariko was bowing to Tika.

'If there is anything you need, ring the chime as I showed you inside and I will return.'

'Stay for a while if you will Sariko.' Tika sat on the grey-flagged stone and Farn settled behind her.

'You did not seem as surprised as the Emperor to learn of the reality of the Bound Ones.'

Sariko pulled a cushion closer and knelt on it, sitting back on her heels. She offered Tika a rueful smile.

'I was brought up on stories of the Elder Races and the binding of the Four. I was born to House Garnet. Like House Jade, my birth House places great importance on discovering how the past influences the present and the future.'

Just before the fifth bell sounded, the Houses, both major and minor, arrived outside the lesser chamber of audience. Tika had learnt a great deal from Empress Sariko. Likewise, Gan had joined Ren and had exchanged much information with Master Jakri. They returned to the audience chamber and found Navan still poring over maps spread across the table. Imperial Blossoms were lighting lamps set all around the walls and light seemed to emanate from the whole of the vaulted ceiling.

Kasheen joined them from a small door set to the side of the dais, resplendent in an ivory gown, hundreds of diamonds stitched into spiral swirls down front and back panels. He wore a chain round his neck, heavy gold links separated by jewels the size of plums – ruby, emerald, turquoise, citrine, amethyst, sapphire – jewels such as Tika had never imagined. She was amazed too at how quickly the Empress had changed into an equally glittering robe, garnets among the diamonds and a veil hiding her face.

The three gijan were yawning. Leaf scooped Khosa into her arms and joined her brother on Seela's back. The purple Dragon reclined to the left of the dais, Brin to the right with Piper lying along his neck. The five companions and the Empress stood between the adult Dragons, Farn and Storm reclining before them.

Kasheen gave them a broad grin and turned towards the great doors. He nodded to the Blossom who swung the doors open then marched back to stand at the Emperor's shoulder.

'Grek?' Tika's query was the merest wisp of thought.

'I am here.'

She drew a steadying breath as brilliantly robed figures escorted by plain-gowned people she guessed to be mages began to enter. Strange, but she felt a relief knowing the unbodied entity was with them when she had abhorred the very thought of him such a short while ago.

Kasheen glanced behind him with a frown as the first of the Houses and mages approached then the grin returned even as Brin rumbled softly.

'Grek has hidden us.' The crimson Dragon sounded amused.

Farn's eyes whirred with glee. 'Won't they have a surprise!'

Sket grunted and Tika felt a bubble of mirth rising within her. She watched as the gorgeously attired Heads of Houses bowed low to the Emperor, each one flanked by two mages. She noticed there were a few women present: most were mages but she saw three were clearly Heads of Houses.

When all had entered and the doors were closed again, Kasheen directed them to seat themselves around the table where the maps still lay. Kasheen remained on his feet.

'We have much to discuss my friends, but I would have you know there are other guests in my palace this night.'

He extended his arm towards the dais and Tika had time to wonder if Kasheen and Grek had concocted this piece of melodrama between them. Grek released the shielding and those around the table sat in stunned shock at what was thus revealed.

Chapter Twenty-Four

Kasheen introduced the companions and explained as much as he knew of the situation in Malesh. After the Wendlans had heard in their own minds the voices of the Dragons and then Gan's calm recapitulation of the facts, they had questions to ask. If Tika and Ren had been exhausted by the questions of Storm's Flight back on the Sapphrean coast, they were nearly beaten to their knees by the Wendlans interrogation. Almost at once House Chrysoprase demanded writing materials, endorsed by House Carnelian. Seela half rose, prismed lavender eyes darkening to violet.

'Is it permitted that these mages speak beyond the walls to their fellows outside?' she demanded.

'What do they say?' Ren asked, looking round the table and noting which faces had flushed or paled.

'They describe this place, they send images of us.'

'And we – or I at least – urge our fellows to begin checking spell books, medical supplies, deciding which of us should travel to Malesh,' one mage retorted aloud.

Tika studied the stones gleaming on the gown of the woman beside the mage: one of the three female Heads of Houses. The woman caught Tika's eye and smiled.

'I am Miako, Head of House Carnelian. We are renowned as medical practitioners.'

'It might be wiser to refrain from mind speech to those outside for now.' Ren was calm and polite but there was a suggestion of inflexibility in his voice.

An elderly man in robes as scarlet as Brin's scales and with an enormous ruby glowing at his throat, inclined his head.

'Our Dragon guests at least can obviously hear any mind speech from us, therefore as Master Ren suggests, we should desist.'

There were nods around the table and serious debate began. They talked long into the night, discussing Wendla's assistance to

Malesh in regard to both the sudden incursion of the desert tribes and the insane schemes of Vorna the witch woman. Farn and Storm followed the example of the gijan and were sound asleep before Imperial Blossoms brought refreshments to the gathering.

At some point, Tika realised Sariko had removed her veil and was talking animatedly with another woman. There was a familiarity about the second woman and when Jakri leaned across to say something, Tika saw the resemblance. Jakri observed Tika's attention and introduced her.

'Oniko, my mother, and Head of House when I am otherwise engaged.'

Tika was surprised: Oniko looked the same age as Jakri. Then she remembered that apparently mages aged differently from untalented people. Jakri named the two young men with his mother as J'Bak and Shek, his apprentices.

Sket leaned close. 'Is this arguing going on until daybreak? For stars' sake, you are as tired as Farn – leave them to it and get some sleep.'

Sket's words encouraged an eye watering yawn and Tika managed a smile. She looked across the table and saw Gan was watching her. He tilted his head towards the dais and she climbed to her feet, Ren and Sket following suit. Sariko reached for Tika's hand.

'My maid is within hearing of the chime should you need anything. I will stay here a while longer.'

Tika struggled with another yawn. 'You are more open to change than is the Emperor, I suspect.'

Sariko laughed. 'Oh most definitely. As a Head of House as Oniko is, I would have much freedom, much influence, but as the wife of the Emperor I have none. I welcome anything that might change that!'

Farn opened one eye, the facets a soft blue. He rippled his wings and back muscles and followed Tika from the chamber. Storm slept on and Seela and Brin continued to listen to the words and thoughts of the Wendlans. Khosa trotted behind Sket and reached the Empress's courtyard just as Farn settled around Tika. Khosa sat regarding them for a moment, both already nearly asleep. She flicked a glance up at Sket.

'Open one of the doors inside for me. Grek watches in the

chamber but I would – explore – this palace.'

Sket grinned in the fading starshine. 'At your command majesty.'

Khosa ignored the sarcasm, recognising the affection in Sket's voice. He opened the required doors and returned to sit leaning against a tree trunk close to Tika and Farn. Ren snored gently a few paces away.

The second bell had rung, signifying mid morning before Gan, Navan and the three Dragons rejoined them, the gijan now wide awake and hungry. Navan and Gan went inside to try to catch up with some sleep as Sariko emerged accompanied by three Blossoms carrying food and drink. Tika regarded the Empress with admiration: she had changed her robe again and, despite having less sleep than Tika, Sariko's face shone with wellbeing.

'Jakri remains with some of the mages,' she told them. 'The Heads of Houses have left to consult their families and begin preparations. Oniko is still here – she requests audience with you.'

Tika pushed her fingers through her tangled hair and wondered just how Sariko managed to look so perfect.

'We don't give audiences Sariko – if Oniko wants to talk to us, ask her to come out here.'

The Blossoms withdrew and a few moments later Oniko appeared. She began to bow but Tika shook her head and smiled.

'We are not used to all this bowing all the time.'

Sket handed Jakri's mother a bowl of tea and Oniko folded herself gracefully onto a cushion.

'I far travel,' Oniko began without preamble. 'I think you sensed Jakri's apprentice Hiramo's mind seeking westwards of late.'

Brin rumbled. 'She was not present in the hall,' he remarked.

'No. She remains in House Jade,' Oniko agreed. 'But I used Hiramo to conceal my mind. Once she reached her limit in travelling, I went on.'

'To Malesh?' asked Ren.

Oniko nodded. 'I tried to trace the witch woman but I could only snatch glimpses of her. She was not aware of me, but she has a system of constantly changing defences which is quite unique. Travelling so far is taxing in the extreme so I never had enough time to properly locate or observe her.'

'And if you had?' Tika swirled the tea in her bowl, watching Oniko from beneath her lashes.

Oniko paused. She bowed her head. 'I would have tried to destroy her.'

Sariko gasped. 'You would imperil your spirit?'

Oniko gave a wry smile – she had used the same words to her son barely three days ago and pretended to be shocked that he had reached such a decision.

'If the witch woman frees a Child, my spirit will be sorely endangered anyway. The cost would be worthy.'

'Sariko told us more of the Bound Ones yesterday than I had heard from Taseen.' Ren reached for the tea pot.

Tika looked at Seela. 'Sariko said at least one of the monstrous Children used Dragon blood to somehow change or enhance her power.'

Seela's eyes blazed in anger. 'Tell me of this.' Her tone in their minds was fraught with suppressed rage.

Sariko quickly repeated one of the many tales she had learnt as a child. Tika watched carefully, hoping Seela would stay in control of her temper. To her relief, the anger shifted to a deep confusion as Seela listened closely to the Empress, to her words and to the feelings beneath the words.

'You will tell me more.' Seela stared down her long nose at the tiny Empress. 'I would know every tale you can recall.'

Sariko obediently sat in front of the purple Dragon and related every story she could dredge from her memory.

'House Jade also teaches its children the ancient stories but I'm not sure if many others do,' Oniko said softly to Tika. 'The Dragons of the Time Before were much fiercer I think, wilder too. They had great physical and mental powers but less wisdom.'

Tika studied Oniko carefully, her smooth gold skinned oval face, the gleaming black hair piled in intricate coils on top of her head and held in place with long carved jade pins.

'The stories say the Dragons thirsted for blood, although once the Dragon Lord half-breeds had risen to power, they reduced the attacks by Dragons upon humans who had displeased them.' Oniko watched Willow suddenly fly high above them, spreading his wings to drift lazily down in the midst of a host of butterflies.

'These you call gijan are unknown to me but clearly it must be their feathered wings that are depicted beside the Dragon faces in our emblems.'

She pulled a thin gold chain free of her gown, holding it for Tika's inspection. It was a flat oblong of palest green jade, a Dragon's face etched on it, flanked by feathered wings. Tika regarded the stone denoting Oniko's position as Head of House Jade. Oniko lifted it, a questioning expression on her face.

'This is the token of my House,' she began.

'I know. I mean I guessed it was so. I was given this. It is of great importance but I don't yet know what that importance is.'

Tika freed her pendant, holding its gold chain so that it swung from her hand. In the still shadowed courtyard the rich red gold of the pendant's backing shone as if alight, and a tiny pulse within the amber filled front flared in time with her heart beat. Oniko did not touch it but leaned close to stare as it dangled between Tika's fingers.

'I have never seen such a thing,' she said sitting back again. 'Our people know much of stones and of certain metals, but this is new to me. House Amber has a large collection of amber in which insects were trapped at the time the amber flowed from a tree, but nothing like this. It almost seems there is something alive within it.'

A bell rang in a distant part of the palace and the midday sun blazed down into the Empress's courtyard within its deep well. Gan and Navan emerged from the inner rooms blinking at the brightness. Oniko turned to speak to them and Farn rested his head over Tika's shoulder. He kept his mind voice tightly focused for his soul bond only.

'Seela becomes angry more quickly of late.'

Alarmed though she was by Farn's comment, Tika kept her eyes on Piper, dangling her legs from a branch some distance across the garden.

'Could it be that she is tired, or wishes she had stayed home in the Sun Mountains?'

'No.' Farn was definite. 'Storm gets cross much faster too – it's something to do with this land we think.'

'We?'

'I spoke of it to Brin. He doesn't seem disturbed and neither am I.' There was a note of pride in Farn's tone.

Tika turned against his chest to hug him. 'But Brin thinks something is affecting both Storm and Seela?' she asked.

'Mmm. Do you remember when we first met Storm's Flight? Brin and Khosa both said that the sea Dragons were wilder than our Kindred.'

'You're right. And Storm was very angry in Singer's Dome.' Tika glanced round the courtyard. 'Where is Khosa?' she asked aloud.

'She went off exploring,' Sket replied, resheathing his sword and reaching for Tika's.

'Can she get back here all right?'

Sket shrugged. 'She'll surely mind speak someone if she wants a door opened.'

Tika's green silvered eyes unfocused as she searched for Khosa's mind signature.

'Where are you?' she demanded when she had located the Kephi.

'Busy,' came the curt reply.

Tika sighed and released the contact. She had sensed some agitation from Khosa's mind but she didn't doubt Khosa would call for assistance should she need it.

In fact, Khosa was crouched on top of a high cupboard washing a torn ear. She had been greatly displeased to find a large number of cats – as her kind seemed to be called here and in Malesh. As befitted cats who dwelt in an Emperor's palace, they gave themselves disgustingly superior airs. One, a slender short haired female with slanted blue eyes and a kink in her tail, had screeched appallingly at Khosa's approach.

Her wails reached a pitch that hurt Khosa's head and so she had slapped her smartly as she would one of her children. She was astonished to find herself bowled over and attacked, not just by the noisy female but by two males who had appeared from nowhere. Khosa wasted no breath in screaming back at these three ill mannered brutes: she set to work with claws and teeth.

One of the males fled first, howling from a deep scratch from the corner of an eye down across his nose. The second male had ripped Khosa's ear before she got both her back feet under his chest and raked down the length of his body. When he fled, the female backed away. Khosa's orange fur stood on end, her tail thrashing furiously and the other female decided discretion might be the wiser course for now.

Khosa had also left the area at speed, looking for somewhere to attend to her ear and take stock of her next move. Now she froze as she heard the sound of claws in wood: another Imperial cat was climbing her cupboard refuge. She backed away, her fur fluffing around her and her eyes narrowed to slits. A mottled face cautiously peered over the edge of the cupboard and then the rest of the cat appeared.

It was a male, rather elderly and rather tatty. He surveyed Khosa for a moment and then advanced, belly low, until he could touch her face gently with his own. Khosa kept still, her fur still puffed to make her seem twice her actual size. The male began to croon gently and his rough tongue started to work on the torn ear.

'I am Khosa,' she murmured to his mind.

The male paused and stared into her turquoise eyes.

'I am Akomi.' He blinked his own tawny gold eyes. 'Few of the cat folk talk now.'

He continued to clean Khosa's ear. 'I am the only one in the palace to mind speak. When I try to touch the minds of others, they sense it only as an irritation. Then they attack me so I keep my own company.'

'You must be lonely.' Khosa shifted slightly as the edges of her ear rubbed uncomfortably.

'I pass my days watching and listening, both the humans and the cats. And I wait to die.'

Khosa glared at him. 'Wait to die – pah! You will travel with me now Akomi. I am Queen of a great estate in my homeland and so I command you. But first, show me where the humans are in this place who speak of secret things.'

Akomi peered at the ripped ear to see if it had stopped bleeding and then stepped back from Khosa.

'I think I have an idea of what you mean. I'll take you there if you wish.'

Khosa butted her face gently against the older cat. 'Let's go then. And thank you for your kindness.'

Akomi led the way: a long slithering jump from the cupboard and a hurried run down a corridor. They passed maids and menservants and reached a broad stairway guarded at the foot by two Imperial Blossoms. Akomi slowed to a nonchalant saunter and marched up the middle of the stairs.

'No one pays us any attention,' he murmured in Khosa's mind.

'I found that a tremendously useful fact in my dealings with humans in Gaharn,' Khosa agreed.

Akomi turned left at the top of the stairs and trotted more speedily down a long passageway. He turned right onto another, much narrower staircase which ended in another corridor. Tall windows on their right striped the floor with patches of light and shade as the two cats padded soundlessly along the stone floor. They passed several closed doors on their right until Akomi halted outside one.

'They call the human who lives here a mage,' Akomi explained. 'He is the oldest of all mages in the palace, perhaps even in all the land. Kasheen told him he would not expect him to continue as chief advisor to the Crystal Throne when he became Emperor. From what I've worked out, Kasheen never liked him and used his great age as an excuse to have him put aside. Of course, the mage has hated Kasheen ever since.'

Khosa noted that Akomi's mind tone had brightened enormously since his first words to her on top of the cupboard. And from what he'd just told her, he had followed the human intrigues within the palace closely, even though there was no other cat with whom he could share his gossip and amusement. Akomi crouched, his tail round his front paws. In the shadow he was scarcely visible.

'You can hear them quite easily – perhaps not their words but their thoughts are loud enough.'

Khosa squeezed between the wall and Akomi's side and crouched comfortably. Akomi sniffed her ear and licked it a couple of times then both settled and opened their minds.

The patches of sunlight and shadow moved position and a bell rang from the floor below and still Khosa and Akomi sat listening.

'Close your eyes,' Akomi warned, pressing Khosa tighter to the wall.

The door flew open and a grey-robed figure hurried out, his sandals flapping against the floor as he went quickly back along the passage in the direction of the stairs. A querulous voice barked a command and other feet approached. Then the door was firmly closed again. Khosa eased away from Akomi, did a tail end up, front end down stretch and blinked.

'Can you get us to the Empress's garden now? Preferably without meeting that insolent female again?'

'Certainly. Do you have friends there?'

'Aah.' Khosa paused. 'I haven't had a chance to explain much have I? Well, I'll tell you what I can on the way.'

By the time Akomi had led them, in and out of chambers, along outside window ledges and then down a dark, seemingly abandoned corridor, his whiskers were quivering with excitement. He took them into a brighter part of the palace and dashed between ranks of Imperial Blossoms to arrive, a touch breathless, outside a large iron studded door. He turned to Khosa.

'These are the Empress's day rooms.'

'Tika?' Khosa sent the thought through the door. 'I would like you to meet a friend I have found.'

In a very few moments the door opened and Khosa slid through Tika's feet, Akomi close behind. Tika shut the door and turned to stare at Khosa's new friend.

'His name is Akomi and he is the only cat in this place who can use mind speech – if you can believe that's possible.'

Tika regarded the new cat. His fur was splotched with black and brown and flecks of white, but the eyes that stared solemnly back at her shone like old gold coins. Tika knelt, reaching a hand to him.

'Welcome Akomi.'

She looked at Khosa to try and ascertain what else she was expected to say and saw Khosa's ragged ear.

'What happened to you? Oh Khosa, that must hurt – come here.'

She scooped Khosa into her arms, exclaiming over the wound even as she began to heal it. Khosa began her throaty croon and Akomi crept nearer, watching as the tears closed and Khosa's ear grew whole again. A little bald but whole.

'Thank you,' Khosa murmured. She looked up into Tika's face when she had slid off the girl's lap. 'Twice today I've had to offer thanks.'

Tika grinned. 'Then we should mark this day as most unusual, shouldn't we?'

Khosa's tail whisked upwards and she stalked towards the courtyard in dignified silence. Tika reached for Akomi, lifting him gently.

'I thank you for coming to Khosa's aid,' she began and felt the old cat tense in her arms. She rubbed her cheek against the top of his head. 'This is Farn, my soul bond.'

Farn had managed to squeeze halfway into the room, his long neck extended to reach Tika.

'You were healing, my Tika – are you well?' His eyes whirred grey and cobalt with concern.

'I'm fine, dear one. Khosa was hurt; she had half her ear ripped off.'

Farn winced at the idea then focused on the creature in Tika's arms.

'This is Akomi, Farn. He cared for Khosa and brought her back to us safely. He is the only cat here who has mind speech so Khosa – and I – invite him to join our company.'

Tika was allowing Akomi to hear her conversation with the silver blue Dragon and she hoped Farn realised she was asking him for kindness to this very different Kephi. Farn's long beautiful face lowered to nearly touch Akomi.

'Welcome Akomi. It must be very boring to have no one to talk to.'

Tika sent a pulse of gratitude to him, and then one of caution. Akomi, leaning back against her chest, was slowly stretching a predominantly brown paw towards the tip of Farn's nose. Farn stayed quite still as Akomi's paw, claws retracted, rested upon the soft blue hide.

'I have only heard the humans talk of the Dragon folk. I am so glad I have lived to see one such.'

Farn's eyes flashed with relief and he gently drew away. 'Then come outside and meet three more,' he said cheerfully.

He began to reverse out of the room and Tika stood up, still holding Akomi. She scratched her fingers behind the old cat's ears and he half closed his eyes in pleasure.

'There are three gijan – other winged folk, Akomi. None of them will harm you,' she told him as she followed Farn into the sunlight.

They found Leaf crooning over Khosa, the Empress Sariko standing half enfolded in the black and dusky pink feathered wings as they examined Khosa's ear. Piper and Willow swooped from the trees to enclose Tika, trilling to each other as they regarded Akomi. Curved talons touched him lightly then Piper caught the old cat from Tika's arms and carried him across to Seela. Tika sent a pleading thought to the Dragons:

'Don't let those gijan frighten him – he is not young and has been very solitary.'

Willow looked over his shoulder at Tika, small pointed teeth showing in his smile.

'We will be gentle Tika.'

Tika frowned. She had sent that thought focused only to the Dragons – how had the gijan overheard? She watched Willow take Akomi ceremoniously around the courtyard introducing him to everyone. Mistress Oniko came to stand beside her.

'We had no idea other creatures had mind powers.'

Tika laughed. 'The same mistake was made in my land,' she admitted. A thought occurred to her. 'Do you have Merigs here?'

'Merigs?' Oniko frowned but when Tika sent her a mental picture of the birds she referred to, Oniko's frown cleared.

'Oh yes, they are common birds. We call them crows.'

Tika concentrated hard for some time, Oniko watching her with puzzled interest. A harsh croak echoed from high overhead and Oniko followed Tika's upward gaze. A Merig drifted down between the blank walls and landed prudently on the highest point of a thinly branched tree. He shuffled dusty black feathers into a semblance of tidiness and clattered his horny beak.

'Someone summoned a messenger?'

The Empress and Mistress Oniko gaped at the hoarse voice in their minds. Tika moved towards the tree, squinting up at the bird silhouetted above her.

'I have spoken with many of your kind in my land far across the great sea. In that land they are known as Merigs.'

The beak was clattered again. 'We are crows in this land. You say my cousins across the water carried messages for you?'

'They did, and very bravely too on several occasions.'

The crow stretched to make himself taller.

'Do you know of a place northwest of here, called Green Shade?'

'Of course. I have been there myself several times. I came from my egg not far from that place.'

'How long would a message take to reach there?'

'If you wish me to take it all the way personally, perhaps four or five days. If you ask me to relay it through my brethren, the message would be there by tomorrow's dawn.'

Tika put her hand on her sword hilt and bowed, her other hand over her heart.

'Would you relay a message then, to say Tika and her companyions are all well and hope to be in Green Shade again in the next few days. The message goes to Maressa, air mage of Vagrantia who abides there.'

The crow repeated the brief message and launched himself into the air. Tika turned, shaking her head at the stunned faces of Sariko and Oniko. Before either could speak, an Imperial Blossom entered from the outer door.

'His Mighty Gloriousness requests your presence in the lesser chamber of audience.'

Chapter Twenty-Five

Seela and Brin said they would stay outside: they would listen, through Ren, to whatever was said in the audience chamber. The gijan too preferred to remain in the courtyard. As Gan led the others along the passage followed by Storm and Farn, Grek spoke to Tika.

'I have been to Namolos,' he told her quickly. 'Time is of the essence. She who Vorna seeks to free is fully awake. I stopped in Harbour City to urge Chevra to warn his mages to prepare for catastrophe.'

They had entered the chamber by now and found a few Heads of Houses and several more House mages still with the Emperor. Kasheen broke off his conversation with one of the Heads of House.

'House Amethyst,' he waved at the man to whom he'd been speaking. 'Asaji. He has promised a mage for each of my ships to give added protection.'

This was said with some satisfaction although its significance escaped the companions. Gan nodded nevertheless to encourage Kasheen to further revelations. When none were forthcoming, Tika folded her arms.

'I have been informed that we have little time left,' she told the Emperor. 'The one you call witch woman is far closer to achieving her goal than we had thought.'

The Head of House Amethyst frowned. 'We will do all we can from here Mistress Tika, I can promise you we will spare nothing. This cannot be allowed to happen.'

He bowed hurriedly and turned, his ornately embroidered lavender robes swirling around him and strode from the hall. The Emperor stared at Tika.

'You have been informed?' he enquired.

'She has indeed,' snapped Grek.

Kasheen stiffened then sat down, forcing himself to seem more relaxed than he was. 'I should have guessed.'

'I went as close to the woman's estates beyond Harbour City as I dared.' Grek spoke in all minds and people still in the chamber turned puzzled faces to each other.

'The very air is disrupted for some distance around. Behaviour is changing amongst both humans and animals in the vicinity. I had hoped for help from Namolos but he is already engaging with Cho Petak.' Grek hesitated. 'Cho Petak is now unbodied and he knows all about undoing the threads of a soul.'

There were murmurs among those mages still present and Kasheen felt it necessary to explain exactly what Grek was. Gasps of shock replaced the murmurs but Tika spoke over the increasing noise.

'Can your ships sail today Kasheen? And your mages – have they found any ancient spells that might have relevance to our predicament?'

A mage in a plain dark blue gown nodded. 'We have found some which may be of use. We are transcribing them now and it has been agreed that all our knowledge will be shared.'

Kasheen agreed. 'I have decreed that the palace is open to all for now – this chamber is freely available to mages of all Houses and the archives and laboratories are also at their disposal.'

Tika repressed a shudder at the memory of Orla's laboratory but she trusted such places here could not perpetrate such evil experimentation.

'The first ten ships will sail on this evening's tide,' Kasheen continued, 'and the second fleet will follow within days. The captains have said that by stripping the ships to the barest essentials they can carry fifty more warriors each, plus two more Blossoms and perhaps two extra mages. That means the first fleet will have one and a half thousand warriors, seventy Blossoms and fifty mages. The second fleet will carry the same. I have already called in ships from some of the seafaring Houses for conversion to transports for more warriors.'

Ren did some calculations in his head and imagined how incredibly close-packed men would be in those ships. Tika took a step forward and saluted Kasheen formally.

'I and my companions will go at once to Green Shade and from there back to Malesh. I will try to urge the Grand Harbour

Master to intensify his efforts – in the north with his armsmen but his mages should concentrate on the Bound One within Malesh.'

A mage in the lemon yellow gown of House Citrine interposed. 'Excuse me Mistress Tika, but from what you've told us there could be a similar problem rising in the desert. The Grand Harbour Master would be most unwise to send men unaided by any mage craft into such possible danger.'

Tika bit her lip: of course the man was correct. She gave a curt nod. 'I take your point and will so inform the Grand Harbour Master.'

'I would ask that Master Jakri accompanies us,' said Ren unexpectedly. 'He will surely be more adept at keeping contact with the Wendlan mages than either ourselves or the Maleshans.'

Kasheen thought rapidly. He glanced at the Heads of Houses still in attendance and noted their nods of agreement.

'Very well. Summon Master Jakri at once,' he called to an Imperial Blossom.

'The Maleshan mage Taseen will remain at Green Shade,' Ren went on. 'He is too frail to travel far or fast but his wisdom may still count for a considerable amount.'

Again Kasheen considered Ren's words.

'I will send someone to keep him company.' He saw Tika's scowl. 'No – I mean someone to keep him company – nothing more. Perhaps Mistress Oniko would agree.'

Tika had to admit there was some sense, and kindness, in Kasheen's proposal.

'He would appreciate that I'm sure.' She saluted Kasheen again. 'Perhaps we may meet in happier days Emperor.' She turned on her heel and left the chamber.

'Navan!' Kasheen called, holding out a bundle of parchments. 'Copies of the maps we looked at – they may be of use.'

'Thank you, sir Emperor. I think they probably will.'

'Good luck Navan.'

Navan met the Emperor's dark eyes with some surprise. 'And good luck to you and your people sir. May the stars guide your paths and guard your hearts.'

Navan saluted and hurried after the others. He found them gathering their few belongings and making their farewells to the Empress. Ren was talking rapidly to Mistress Oniko whose face was alight with excitement.

'I will go to House Jade at once and ask Hiramo to come to Green Shade with me,' she was saying as Navan drew level with them.

An Imperial Blossom loomed behind them. 'Mistress Oniko, the Mighty One offers you passage to Green Shade on a patrol boat. It would reduce your travel time by half he suggests. I am to escort you to House Jade to collect anything you might need and then to the boat.'

Oniko began to bow to Ren but he caught her shoulders and kissed her cheek. 'Look after the old man when you get there,' he told her.

Navan smiled at her and she hurried to Tika and Gan to say goodbye.

The Empress pressed a ring into Tika's hand. It was set with diamonds and garnets and had the Imperial plumes engraved on the gold mounting.

'A small token,' she said, folding Tika's fingers over the ring. 'Any Wendlan will give aid should you require it if you show this ring. Sell it in Malesh if you need coin.' She laughed and produced a dark brown bag. Tika started to smile in return.

'Thank you,' she said. 'Akomi will surely travel comfortably in this. And thank you for your hospitality.'

'I do hope we meet again my dear, in calmer times.'

Jakri arrived panting for breath. He wore dark green trousers and shirt instead of a robe, and carried a shoulder pack.

'I feared I would delay you,' he gasped.

Tika was already on Farn's back with Khosa in her sack. Ren had persuaded a rather dubious Akomi into his own sack and cradled him in his arm upon Seela. He held out his free hand to Jakri.

'You're with us,' he grinned.

Jakri suddenly realised the enormity of what he was doing and swallowed hard. But he caught Ren's hand and found himself astride the purple scaled back. The Imperial Blossom stepped forward hesitantly.

'The Great One commanded me to travel with you,' he said to Gan.

Gan stared into the rather pale face. 'Chimchoo isn't it? I think Brin can take you as well.'

'Of course I can,' Brin retorted. 'You and Sket are mere feathers on my back: another will make no difference.'

Navan was already on Storm and the gijan enfolded the Empress Sariko in their wings.

'I wish I was coming with you,' she cried when the gijan lifted into the air.

Brin rose first of the Dragons, Sket and Gan waving down to the Empress, the Imperial Blossom behind Sket rigidly upright with eyes firmly closed. Seela was next, then Storm and Farn, rising to the open sky far above the Empress's courtyard garden. When Farn cleared the surrounding palace walls, Tika looked back, focusing her vision. The Empress still waved, her cheeks shining with tears, and then Farn was wheeling to the north and the courtyard vanished from view.

Sket felt the Imperial Blossom behind him slowly relax as Brin set a fast but steady pace which ate up the leagues from Bracca. The gijan snatched occasional rests on Brin or Seela while Akomi risked a cautious peek from his sack. They passed over all the farmlands, settling well after dark at the southernmost edge of the great forest.

Having lived all his life within the imperial palace, Akomi was nervous of the space in which he now found himself. He went hunting with Khosa but reluctantly, and returned to their camp with obvious relief to curl up and sleep on Tika's lap. Khosa sat beside her. Tika stroked the old cat gently.

'Will he be all right Khosa? I think he may be old for adventuring – like Taseen.'

'He will manage; I will make sure of it.' Khosa climbed onto Tika's knees as well and curled round Akomi.

The Imperial Blossom found it unsettling that no one seemed to use titles or rank in conversation: Tika had already scolded him half a dozen times for calling her "Mistress". Chimchoo appeared least alarmed by Sket who had now involved him in a complicated discussion of weaponry. Storm and Farn slept, leaning against each other.

'There will be great trouble in Malesh,' Seela suddenly spoke in their minds.

'There will indeed,' Ren agreed, reaching to stroke her face above him. 'It might be wiser if you stayed at a distance my dear, while we see what must be done.'

Seela rattled her wings. 'I will be with you,' she snapped, moving her head out of Ren's reach. 'But I have a bad feeling whenever I think of Malesh.'

'I can't say I feel good about it either.' Grek was present in their minds.

Tika eased the surprising weight of Akomi and Khosa from her thighs. 'What did you mean Grek, when you said Namolos was engaged with Cho Petak?'

'I could speak with him only briefly: he could not spare me much time. He lies in a room, guarded by his students and followers but he far travels nearly all the time.' A note of awed admiration tinged Grek's tone. 'He far travels distances beyond belief and in ways I do not begin to comprehend.'

The company were on their way again well before first light and by the time the sun set they landed in front of the house at Green Shade. Maressa came running to meet them and exclaimed at the sight of the Imperial Blossom Chimchoo. Tika managed to choke back a laugh when Pallin marched from the side of the house followed by a squad of variously sized children, but Farn's tact was an erratic matter.

'Would you like me to inspect your armsmen, Pallin?' he asked, eyes whirring with glee.

Pallin spun round, clearly unaware that his trainee armsmen were behind him. He gave them a ferocious scowl.

'Why aren't you abed? Fighters take rest when they can to be fit for whatever the morrow might bring,' he roared.

The children fled precipitously as Sefri hurried towards the companions.

'A crow brought a message but you're back sooner than I'd expected,' she exclaimed when she had extricated herself from the gijan's embraces.

Maressa shook her head slightly at Tika – so, she had not passed on Grek's reports to Sefri as yet. Tika returned Sefri's hug.

'We must rest and tomorrow the Dragons must hunt and sleep. We will tell you our news then.'

'Welcome,' called a hoarse voice and the Imperial Blossom

Chimchoo paused in mid salute to Sefri.

She smiled up at him. 'It is many long years since we have seen an Imperial Blossom in Green Shade,' she said. 'But I think Star Flower wishes to welcome you all before you sleep.'

They gathered beneath the verandah next morning near the Ship, Star Flower. Tika was alarmed by the way Taseen's fragility had increased in the few days since she had seen him and was glad that Mistress Oniko was on her way to keep the ancient mage company. Jakri was fascinated to meet one who had somehow survived the final battle of the Elder Races. Pallin took over from Sket in putting the Imperial Blossom more at ease with involved talk on the subject of military tactics. By midday the general mood was sombre, Sefri, Taseen and Star Flower having been brought up to date on the situation in Malesh.

Sefri offered a small piece of comfort.

'Star Flower has reinstated some of her transmitter networks and has communicated with some of the Ships in orbit.'

Blank faces met this news.

'I do not pretend to understand your talk of Bound Ones and the havoc you fear they might wreak, but if absolutely necessary the Ships in orbit have weapons of great power.'

Blank faces brightened into hopeful smiles but Sefri raised her hands.

'The power of our technological weapons is indescribable. I would only recommend their use as a last desperate resort.' She sighed. 'They can be targeted very specifically but in a close battle situation, they would probably destroy as many of your men as your enemy's.'

Taseen shook his head. 'It may come to that Captain Sefri. If an armsman has an infected hand, the only way to save his life may be to remove the whole arm.'

'Like Jal.' Farn's mind tone still reflected the horror he'd felt when he realised Jal had only one arm.

Sket rubbed Farn's chest. 'Jal would be dead now Farn, but he lives and no doubt he's a great help to young Mim in the Stronghold.'

It was obvious that Farn was not reassured but he made no further comment.

'We will stay here one more full day,' Tika announced. 'The

Dragons have three more people to carry and so they must feed well and be rested before I will let them face the risk of flying across the sea.' She glanced at Chimchoo. 'Do you know how long a patrol boat will take to get to the inlet below?'

He shook his head.

'We will probably have left by the time Mistress Oniko gets here then.'

She knelt by Taseen's chair. 'She brings one of Jakri's apprentices.'

'Hiramo,' Taseen agreed. 'He has told me of her. She may even be able to far speak you in Malesh.'

Jakri cleared his throat. 'My mother Oniko is the one to do that.'

Tika remembered Oniko's words in the Empress's garden. 'We should definitely be able to stay in contact then. Maressa and Brin will be able to meet either of their minds halfway I'd guess.'

Pallin stood to attention, his scowl a thin disguise for discomfort.

'Lady Tika, Olam and Riff are still with Kasmi. The Emperor sent help with the repairs on Spiral Star. I know Olam will want to stay with the star-damned floating boxes.'

He stopped and Tika helped him out.

'Your place must be with Olam of course.'

Pallin sighed in relief. 'Seboth would skin me if I let anything happen to the boy.'

Tika considered the boy – Olam. He was at least thirty cycles old: boy indeed! But perhaps to one of Pallin's advanced age, Olam was still a mere boy.

'To be honest Pallin, I have been worried by the numbers of us the Dragons would have to carry, so three less is a help really.'

By the time Tika and her companions, who now included a Wendlan Mage who was also the Head of a major House, left Green Shade, Grek had reported a rapid deterioration in western Malesh and intense fighting in the northern farming communities. Then he departed for destinations unrevealed and the Dragons increased their speed of flight across the sea.

In Harbour City, Chevra had ordered his wife and two

daughters to return to the Xantip palace. He sent a full squad of armsmen to ensure that Eorlas understood his order was not to be ignored. He had evicted several disgruntled courtesans from his apartments and closeted himself at all hours with his cousin and spymaster Harrip. Piles of ancient tomes and several maps purloined from the archives were now scattered around his study.

Councillor Vorna had not remained long in the palace; had dismissed out of hand the talk of a war with Wendla as trivial and of no concern to her. She had taken Bajal with her this time, since when Fental had secluded himself in his rooms. That left Sheoma, Tavri and Lessna – three out of his seven Mage Councillors. Chevra still had doubts as to Lessna's loyalties but could not exclude her from discussions without alerting Vorna to his suspicions – if Lessna was in fact allied to her. Harrip had found no evidence either way, but inclined to the worst, citing Tavri's wariness of Lessna.

This afternoon low clouds rolled in from the sea, blanketing Harbour City in a humid dampness unnoticed by Chevra and Harrip as they finalised the movement of three thousand armsmen towards Vorna's estates.

'You would do better to be totally honest with your College of Mages.' Grek was suddenly inside their heads.

Chevra was still unsettled by the comings and goings of the unbodied entity: Harrip longed to recruit him into his spy network.

'Why can you do nothing?' Chevra sounded peevish.

'I cannot.' The admission was made quietly but added enormously to the two Maleshans' worry. 'I was never what you would call a trained mage. Vorna would be aware of my presence at once. I have warned you, she has a system of defensive wardings the like of which I've never come across before. After much thought, and debate with Taseen, we conclude it will take several mages to dismantle her wardings before getting near her. And once the wardings are gone, Vorna herself is probably the single most powerful mage in this land at least.'

Chevra digested this information, his skin growing cold in spite of the humidity. He glanced at Harrip.

'Summon the College Administrators if you will. They must work harder now than they've probably done for years.'

'I went only briefly to the north,' Grek told Chevra when Harrip had gone to pass on the message to a servant. 'The farmers are surprisingly well organised. The raids they have endured for so many years have led them to take ingenious steps to defend themselves. But the numbers of fighters still pouring south from the desert give the villagers no respite.'

Chevra leaned back in his chair. 'I know. My wife used to complain that the patrols were too infrequent and that I was wrong to reduce the garrisons. We had problems in the Tooman province which necessitated the use of more armsmen than I'd expected to put the insurgents down.'

'Your wife and children,' Grek changed the subject abruptly.

Chevra looked surprised. 'I have ordered them to return to the palace,' he said.

'Send them to Wendla.'

'Wendla?' Chevra sat up straight. 'Why should they be sent away?'

'They must not be risked here as hostages.'

Chevra gaped but Grek continued inexorably.

'The boy must be kept clear at the very least, but it would be best if your girls too are in safe keeping.'

Chevra's thoughts whirled: one daughter was older than Merkas and distressingly like her mother in temperament in his view. The other daughter was barely past her fifth birthday. He had set eyes on neither of them since Eorlas had left the palace three years ago. She would have got Merkas away too if Harrip hadn't had her watched so closely.

In the great scheme of things, Chevra had no illusions that he was an outstanding ruler. He had kept things running in Malesh, curbed the exigencies of outlying provinces such as the Tooman uprising, and made sure that no one merchant became too much more successful or powerful than any other.

'Will you help me explain to the Administrators?' Chevra asked in a humble way such as none of his Councillors would have recognised.

Grek considered the request. 'I will,' he agreed finally. 'I have already assessed your two Administrators and their minds are both strong and sharp. It will not take long to convince them of the peril facing Malesh.'

It was as Grek predicted: Dersu and Fenelon listened without interruption while first Chevra outlined the situation and then Grek filled in many of the gaps with frightening clarity.

The older of the Administrators, Dersu, sniffed. 'We have had our suspicions for a very long while, Grand Harbour Master. Taseen sent warning two years ago of things worsening and we always heed Taseen's words.' He mopped his forehead: corpulent as he was, the speed with which he'd been rushed from the College through the palace looked to have exhausted him.

Fenelon paced restlessly. 'Many of us have been worried by Vorna's ambitions for much longer than you might think,' she said. 'My predecessors left reports of their suspicions and we have tried to monitor her activities. As our invisible friend has said, Vorna has built a myriad of defences.'

'Can you break them?' Chevra interrupted.

'Some of them yes, quite easily,' Dersu replied. 'But we are fairly sure that once such warding is broken, another is activated.'

'And whatever is activated may well be aggressive rather than defensive,' Fenelon put in. 'The entire region around Vorna's estates – a circle between one and two leagues across – is virtually impenetrable to any of us now. And believe me, I have people working constantly on this. It isn't a massive shielding – the air is somehow wrong, the very particles are misshapen and so far seeing is impossible.' She bit her lip, glancing at Dersu.

He sighed. 'Four mages of the third rank have been unconscious for over twenty days since trying to penetrate Vorna's estates.'

Chevra was deeply shaken. Mages of the third rank were extremely strong – for four of them to be incapacitated to such a degree boded ill indeed for any direct attempt on Vorna.'

'The Wendlans know of her. They call her the witch woman.' Grek sounded pensive.

Fenelon followed his line of thought. 'Witches and wizards were more common in the Time Before.' She frowned. 'Most of them were solitary, individualistic. That was why the College of Mages was founded if the histories are accurate: to bring those individuals with powers into a community where they were encouraged to develop and use those powers for a common purpose.'

Dersu began to nod. 'But it took a long age to gather in all the talented ones. There are many records of solitary wizards causing untold damage to further their own personal desires – wealth, control of an area, control of a section of the population.'

'What happened to them?' Chevra was curious although he had a good idea what Dersu's answer would be.

Dersu mopped his forehead again. 'If they refused all overtures from the College they were either stripped of their powers or destroyed.'

Chevra leaned forward eagerly, his hopes rising. 'You can strip a mage of his powers? I didn't know that.'

Fenelon gave a harsh laugh. 'It isn't something we talk about too often but yes, it can be done. And it is done today if a student is unbalanced or wayward in his use of power.' She gave Chevra a lop-sided smile. 'We would never stand a chance of doing such a thing with Vorna.'

Chapter Twenty-Six

Bajal sat in a shadowed corner of Vorna's library and workroom in an annex of the main building. Vorna's estates lay some twenty four leagues north west of Harbour City and two leagues from the west coast of Malesh. Bajal's hands gripped the arms of his chair, the knuckles white. He stared unblinkingly across the large cluttered room at Vorna. The Mage Councillor half lay upon a couch, her eyes closed, a smile flickering across her face. Bajal felt sick but dared not move. A headache had begun to niggle behind his eyes as he and Vorna approached the estate boundary six days ago and had grown steadily with every heartbeat since.

Now, his eyes burned, his throat felt too tight to allow air into his lungs and he knew his head would explode if he moved it too quickly. The very air felt too thin; smelt as though it was somehow burnt, its acrid taint scratching and stinging his skin. He had lost track of time: whether he'd been sitting here for the morning or for several days he had no idea.

Vorna had quite forgotten that Bajal was even in the same room. The Bound One, Valesh, was awake and talking to her. As Vorna had expected, poor Valesh was only saddened by her long imprisonment, not angry, crazed, or vengeful as Taseen and those other fools had predicted. There had been no one left to help Vorna finish her training after the final battle a millennium past and so she had sought a way of her own. No senior mages survived with any power left to speak of – Taseen's case was not unique though he was the most senior to have survived.

Vorna had searched the unscathed library in Xantip palace and had learned much that she should have remained ignorant of. With no one senior to guide her, she put her own already skewed interpretation on most of her readings. The title the Wendlans gave her – witch woman – was in fact far more accurate than any might have guessed. Vorna had no feeling for any such abstract ideas as community, society, or morality: what she wanted, she went for and got. She had never formed close ties with any other person; regarded the awed respect given her by her students and apprentices through the millennia as only her due.

And she was so close now, she was within reach of gaining control of the phenomenal powers of a Bound One. It never occurred to her that in fact the opposite was true of course. Vorna spent longer and longer in mental communication with Valesh. Valesh had lain Bound and silenced deep beneath the sea since the last battle, until she had found a way here. She had been Bound after her brother Qwah was trapped in the desert. The human mages had been strong enough to bind her but they were weary from their long struggle and several tiny errors had crept into the spells they cast.

Valesh had been Bound and cast into dreamless, endless sleep – or so the mages believed. But her sleep was not dreamless nor was it eternal. Her dreaming mind had soon found Vorna and immediately she had recognised the human female's power, and also her weaknesses. Chief among the latter was Vorna's overweening sense of her personal superiority.

Valesh struggled hard to rein back her fury: that she should need this pathetic human's aid enraged her every time she thought of it. She knew her brother Qwah would never have found such patience as she had needed to exercise over these years. She was so close to freedom! She was desperately tempted to force the issue right now but Vorna still had not discovered how to untangle the spell which would keep Valesh tied to this one place. She was sure her mind was nearly loosed enough to lift her essence up through the layers of ensorcelled rock and earth, but until Vorna could undo the placement spells, she would still be trapped in this little part of the world.

Valesh had grown cunning during her imprisonment but cajole as she might she had been unable to persuade Vorna to approach other mages, seek other minds in her quest to free her. Valesh had suggested that others might have access to forgotten knowledge of which Vorna knew nothing. Vorna had been offended by the very idea and Valesh had to waste a great deal of time soothing the woman's ruffled self esteem.

No other mages came to Vorna's estates through the years

except her favoured apprentices. Valesh had been both amused and annoyed at the dreadful lack of talent these apprentices had. She recognised Bajal now, he was in the room with Vorna, but his mind was collapsing, folding in upon itself. And it had been a weak mind to begin with.

Since the time she was Bound, Valesh had no communication from her siblings. She did not even know if they had been destroyed completely or were Bound as she and Qwah had been. When she first stirred she found herself within a fissure of the world's crust far beneath the sea between Malesh and Wendla. The mages must have believed it would be impossible to escape such a place. Vorna smiled on her couch in the library as Valesh's amusement swept through her mind. The heat of the magma had obliterated some of the spells cast to keep her deep below and so she had risen, moving with the molten rock as it seeped through the fault line to end in cooling basalt under Vorna's estates. Valesh continued to murmur her seductive blandishments to Mage Councillor Vorna with a tiny fraction of her mind. By far the larger part of her essence swelled and writhed, flexing incessantly at the holding spells and snarling for release.

The Tower rising above the sprawling College of Mages in Harbour City had four floors and a deep basement. For many years now only the top floor had been in frequent use: for annual Conclave of the highest mages and at midsummer for the induction of students to the ninth and lowest rank of mage. The floor below the Chamber of Conclave was a library, filled with parchments and books, journals and letters, accessed only by mages who had achieved fifth rank status or higher.

Once a mage had been raised to the fifth rank he or she usually paid ostentatious visits to the Tower archive. However, only half a dozen such visits were made at most: the apparent confusion and the quantities of dust put off even the most assiduous mage. Vorna had managed to search only a small section of the Tower archive while Taseen lay unconscious after the final battle. She didn't expect to find anything of worth and was distracted by many other things at that period. She had found herself the only mage left in the College with real ambition to do more to make her desires become reality.

A few old men and women remained – mages of third and second rank who had chosen specialist study and teaching rather than playing active parts in the ruling of Malesh. The damage sustained by all of them meant that although technically they lived, in fact they were mere ciphers. Taseen surprised everyone by recovering sufficiently to be transported back to Harbour City and his apartments within the College. His mind regained its astuteness and he became a much appreciated lecturer and tutor while freely admitting he could teach theory only. He always admitted to his classes that he could no longer exercise any power: a confession which was always received in appalled silence. These ninth rank mages were too newly come to their talent and the thought of losing those gifts was beyond their comprehension.

Taseen was often to be found in the Tower archive in the years after the final battle, but once he had secretly transferred many volumes from the Tower to his own apartments, dust gathered ever more thickly on shelves, desks and window sills. In her careless belief in her own invincible strength, Vorna had failed to see that certain volumes had threads of warding along their spines: she, as most others, merely noticed a gap where a book appeared to be missing. Since Taseen's discreet "borrowing", the gaps on the shelves were exactly what they seemed.

Through the years Taseen's fears had grown and he tested students and young mages to no avail until at last Sheoma and Tavri presented themselves at his tutorials. Aware that time was running out, he forced them to learn, to read, to be on constant guard against Vorna. Tavri now stood in the centre of the Chamber of Conclave. He had been speaking steadily for the better part of the morning to a packed and silent audience – every mage at present within the College, from ninth to first rank. He finally bowed and stood waiting for questions.

Sheoma sat across the Chamber from Tavri and had been scanning face after face as he spoke. Now, as she had anticipated, most of the highest ranking mages bent close to each other, speaking softly before Zerran got to his feet. In the silence before he spoke, the sound of young laughter drifted up from four floors below: students with unexpected free time in which to chatter and remember how young they were.

'We are grateful that you see fit to inform us now Mage Tavri,' Zerran began. 'Many of us have had our suspicions if not fears of Vorna's duplicity. We have discussed the matter among ourselves.' He indicated the row where sat the first and second rank mages. 'It might have been wiser if Taseen had confided his own fears much sooner.'

Having delivered his reprimand his expression relaxed. 'I personally can confirm many of Tavri's words. I tried to locate Vorna during the night, thinking it might be possible whilst she slept.' He grimaced. 'She is beyond the need for sleep now I believe. There is increasing distortion around the whole of her estate. I could find no chink through which I might enter.'

Glances were exchanged among many mages: Zerran was first rank, one of the most powerful mind manipulators in the history of the College. If he couldn't penetrate whatever surrounded Vorna, it was certain no one else could.

'You omitted part of your story Tavri. You told us that Taseen is now in Wendla and that message birds will shortly arrive offering the help of both Wendlan Mages and armsmen. But there have been visitors to this city of whom you have not told us I think.'

Tavri stood up again. 'You know of visitors?' he asked.

Zerran nodded. 'They were so heavily shielded that I could not identify them, which is why I ask you to do so now in this Conclave.'

Tavri gave a weary smile. 'Eight humans, two of whom had silver eyes, one man from another world, three great Dragons, one sea Dragon, three newly-fledged gijan and a cat.'

Nothing disturbed the silence this time until Zerran managed to find his voice again.

'Gijan?' he whispered. 'Surely we may have hope now.'

Tavri shook his head. 'Newly-fledged I told you, and without Elders to teach them. One of the humans, the girl with silver eyes, used healing powers to extract their wings. The gijan have been kept as slaves in the desert city for years.'

Zerran sank back onto his chair, his face as white as his hair. 'The Dragons then; surely they must have an idea of what to do? Their kind have race memories if I recall the text books correctly.'

Again Tavri shook his head. 'One of them grew angry just because she has no memories of this land or of the gijan, or the battles in which her kind fought and suffered. The gijan have said that they remember gatherings north of the desert where their people met with the Dragon kind.'

Sheoma interrupted suddenly. 'Mages,' she called. 'Those of whom Tavri speaks are nearly here. The air mage from the north, Maressa, tells me they will land in the rear court garden of the temple of the Elder Races near the north gate.'

She met Tavri's eyes, nodded and hurried from the Chamber: the Grand Harbour Master should be present at this meeting. Two hundred or so mages in the Chamber were also on their feet. Zerran raised his hands and his voice.

'We shall make our way to the temple.' He glared at a few of the younger mages. 'And with dignity please.'

The companions were approaching the coast of Malesh, the endless buildings of Harbour City cluttering the entire shoreline of the long curving bay. They flew high enough to see the waters beyond the western promontory of Harbour City. They were all aware of a shimmering patch of unmoving fog further to the north west which indicated the whereabouts of both Vorna and the Bound One.

Maressa far spoke Sheoma then passed the message among the friends.

'Most of the Maleshan mages will be waiting for us as well as the Grand Harbour Master,' she warned them.

'Poor Taza, inundated with yet more uninvited guests,' Ren said with sympathy.

Grek was still absent, a fact which bothered Tika now that she had seen the miasmic air which concealed a Bound One. She had no idea what this creature might actually look like: was it unbodied and therefore invisible like Grek, or was that foggy cloud hiding some strangely disfigured monstrous shape? Somehow she never thought of the Bound Ones as resembling humans although they were supposedly of human blood. There had been no discussion among them on their rapid journey from Wendla regarding what they must face.

Farn was still calm although he was quieter, less likely to tease. Storm was contented with Navan on his back and the sea beneath them. But Tika noted his eyes whirred restlessly, white and grey lights sparking in them more than usual. Brin was his usual self, but Seela was withdrawn, almost silent although she appeared to mind speak the gijan who continued to sleep on her broad back whenever they landed to rest.

Tika also worried about the wisdom in bringing Akomi: he was weary from the travelling and the strangeness of everything after his restricted life in the imperial palace seemed to be overwhelming him. Tika pushed all such thoughts from her mind as Brin, still shielding them, began to lose height, seeking Sheoma's mind signature in the chaotic jumble of streets and houses that made up Harbour City.

The lower they flew, the larger the city seemed, until they could see only buildings in any direction. But at last green fields appeared ahead of them. They knew they were approaching the temple of the Elder Races which was not far from the northern gate through which they'd entered the city before. Peering down past Farn's shoulder, Tika saw the streets were empty of the usual pushing crowds, were instead lined with brown uniformed armsmen. She saw that the section where the temple stood was ringed with men who blocked the passage of furious citizens.

They glided over the temple's domed roof to the garden behind and Brin released the shielding. The companions stared down into a sea of upturned faces. Tika glanced across at Jakri sitting between Ren and Maressa on Seela, and he offered her a nervous smile. Then they were landing – carefully, because the space was more restricted than they'd hoped. Mages pressed back, out of the way, but still found themselves alarmingly close to the four Dragons. The gijan fluttered down to stand hand in hand beside Farn, their heads tilting from side to side as they searched the faces around them. Leaf trilled and dashed between the Grand Harbour Master and Zerran to enfold the priest Taza.

The Maleshans didn't know whom to stare at first: the amazing Dragons, the feathered gijan, or the young woman who stared at them with emerald eyes surrounded by silver. Farn huffed into the sudden quiet.

'Well, we're here, and you're here. What happens next?'

Tika smothered a laugh and moved towards the Grand Harbour Master, hand on her sword hilt and Sket at her shoulder.

Chevra and Harrip were the only two she could see wearing trousers and shirts rather than long robes so she had assumed they weren't mages. Harrip bowed and introduced Chevra and Zerran. The mages were quickly losing their nervousness, pressing closer to hear what the visitors might say. Zerran, more aware than the others of considerable tension among the new arrivals, smiled at Tika.

'Tavri told us your company consisted of four Dragons – whose magnificence we now see.' He bowed to Seela and Brin. 'Three gijan – who are more beautiful than I had imagined they might be.' Piper giggled and half extended her wings, revealing the pale green under feathers.

'Tavri also said there were eight humans and a man from another world.' Zerran looked up at Gan's tall thin figure, still smiling.

Gan saluted, returning the smile. 'I have come to believe that is true sir, although I was born in Gaharn, far to the north.'

Zerran nodded, turning next to Ren who cradled Akomi in his arms. 'Tavri mentioned a cat,' he said.

Khosa wriggled free of Maressa's hold and stalked forward. 'Two cats,' she corrected coldly.

Zerran hid his surprise at being mind spoken by a cat and apologised for his mistake.

'If I am correct, you are from Wendla?' he enquired of Jakri.

'He is Jakri, a Mage and the Master of House Jade,' Ren explained. 'And he bears the authority of Emperor Kasheen.'

Jakri extended his arm, revealing the gold jewelled band around his wrist, the imperial insignia clear to see. He handed a wad of folded parchment to Chevra.

'The Emperor Kasheen confirms in writing that ten ships with fifteen hundred warriors are on their way to assist you in the north. Fifty Mages accompany the ships, and while one Mage must remain with each ship, forty are at your disposal.'

Chevra was plainly taken aback by the numbers Jakri mentioned: Emperor Kasheen was concerned indeed by the situation in Malesh. Chevra wondered fleetingly if he could have responded so quickly and so generously had Malesh and Wendla's positions been reversed. Before he could reply, the young woman with the strange green eyes spoke.

'If you have discovered anything to help us get close to the Bound One please tell us. There is little time left.' All saw a shudder ripple through her small frame. 'I have to be much nearer to the actual essence of the creature in order to have a chance of destroying it.'

None of those listening missed her use of the word "I" rather than "we". Many if not most studied her with a new respect – so young she seemed, yet apparently she would be the one to take on the imprisoned Child. Zerran asked most of the mages to leave the confined temple garden, the few who remained being those who had made the study of events before the last battle and earlier their life's work: to the previous amusement of most of their colleagues. Zerran sat in one of the seats cut into the wall nearby and without invitation, Tika joined him.

'You probably know as much as we do,' he said quietly.

'The great Dragon Seela has told me how a soul is unmade,' Tika replied in just as quiet a tone. 'But I have to be close, close enough to see with my eyes, not just through my mind.'

Zerran felt her mind probe his and stayed calmly relaxed. She must have been reassured by what she found for she gave a quick nod. She lowered her voice even further.

'I have decided that I will try to go straight to Vorna's estates: not that I think there is still a woman called Vorna anymore. She will have changed, or been changed – I can tell that just from the lightest touch of the cloud there.'

Zerran waited patiently, understanding that this young woman was choosing to tell him what she could discuss with no other now. He could tell she was working hard to maintain an attitude of casual calmness while she kept a discreet eye on the young silver blue Dragon. He had begun to follow her to where Zerran sat but had been intercepted by an armsman and the young man with silvered eyes.

'Farn is my soul bond but I cannot – *cannot* – allow him to join me. The crimson Dragon Brin will try to keep both Farn and Storm asleep for as long as he dares. Seela will take me into the heart of that cloud which hides Valesh.'

Zerran glanced at her. 'You use her name so openly?' he asked.

Tika shrugged. 'It matters not, now. She is awake, aware.

When she was strongly Bound, mentioning her name tugged at her consciousness, brought her through some of the layers of spells. Zerran, I go tonight to be at the location for sunrise. She is of darkness – her strength will be slightly less in daylight.'

Zerran flinched inwardly at the thought that mere daylight would have much effect on a monstrous Child. The young woman stared into his face, the green eyes magnified by tears.

'I have discussed this only with Seela and Brin as I said.' She gave him a shaky smile. 'I doubt I'd get away without Sket's company.'

Zerran recognised the armsman in the picture in his mind as the one nearest the silver blue Dragon.

'Sket appointed himself my personal guard – it seems a lifetime ago but it is less than a year in fact. Please Zerran, keep the gijan safe here – lock them inside the temple if you must. They must survive and go to Namolos's island far to the west.'

Zerran had to ask. 'Why do you tell me these things?'

Again the strangely beautiful eyes framed in black lashes met his. 'It is likely Seela and I will not return, or if we do we may be changed as Vorna must be. If we do return and you have any doubts as to how damaged or altered we might be, you will destroy both of us.'

In spite of long years of cultivating an impassive exterior, Zerran could not hide his shock at Tika's words.

'Quickly,' she forestalled any protest he could make. 'Open your mind to me and I will show you how to untie the threads of a soul.'

Thoughts whirled in Zerran's head but then images appeared, stark and clear. He drew a deep breath as Tika broke contact with his mind.

'You must show those of your colleagues in whom you have complete faith how this is done. It will be the only way to defeat Valesh if I fail, but again you must understand you must be close to the Bound One. The ones you choose to cast this power must be guarded by others, the strongest mages you have.'

Zerran reached for her hand, appalled at the smallness, the fragility of the bones of that hand, but before he could find any words, Ren approached, Akomi trotting at his heels. His chestnut silvered eyes narrowed briefly then he smiled.

'Taza's dear wife and daughter have food prepared – as always,' he said lightly. 'And Salma has more new clothes for the gijan.'

Tika gave Zerran's hand a squeeze and got to her feet.

'I have to thank her for the ones she made me. Excuse me please Zerran – no doubt we will speak again in the next few days.'

Zerran's heart, an organ that rarely troubled him the way it seemed to lesser mortals, twisted with pain. Would he ever speak to this girl woman again? As Tika vanished among the fluttering wings of the gijan, Zerran too rose from the seat.

'I must get back to the College, young man, but I hope to return before twilight if I may?'

'Of course,' Ren agreed. 'We will be here until a decision is made regarding what course of action we must take.'

Zerran nodded, his heart twisting again: the decision has been made, he thought with deep anguish.

Chapter Twenty-Seven

Zerran came back to the temple as he'd said he would with about thirty mages. For the first time that Taza could remember, the temple gates were closed and barred, guarded by a detachment of Harbour City armsmen. Zerran had told his chosen mages what the young woman planned to do: he had also warned Chevra.

They joined the companions to eat a meal in the lower common room and Ren asked after the scholar Hariko. Zerran frowned.

'He has not been seen since you were last in the city.'

He checked around his mages but all shook their heads – they knew nothing more of him.

Taza again offered the companions the use of the upper apartments which Tika quickly accepted. Tired from their journey over so many leagues of sea, everyone seemed ready for sleep. The gijan refused to stay in the apartment though, insisting on joining the Dragons in the garden. Maressa and Tika watched from the window.

'Seela is very unsettled.' Maressa sounded worried.

The purple Dragon had refused to let the gijan on her back but they persisted until, amazingly, she swung upon them with a snarl. Much confused and chastened, Willow and Leaf retreated to Brin while Piper nestled along Storm's back.

'I expect she is tired,' Tika replied. 'Don't forget she's nearly as old as Fenj.'

Maressa fought against a yawn then moved to the door. 'I'm for bed – are you coming?'

'In a moment.'

The room seemed empty now; just Tika by the window and Sket, as always, cleaning his weapons. Khosa and Akomi had retired with Gan and the heaviness of sleep weighed the air in the apartment. Tika stretched.

'I'll sleep with Farn,' she began but Sket was already on his feet waiting to go with her. She met his eyes and he smiled sadly. Oh stars, he knew! Tika swallowed and went swiftly down the stairs.

She paused by the arched doorway into the main part of the temple. Zerran's mages murmured together, passing papers and books between them. They grew silent when they saw the small figure in the door. Zerran stayed where he was, cross-legged on a heap of pillows, but he lifted a hand towards her.

'Gods and goddesses save you,' he said softly.

But she had gone. She curled against Farn's chest listening to the steady thump of his heart. She wept bitterly, her hand on the egg pendant at her breast. Should she leave the pendant with Farn? Would it help him if –? No, she finally decided, it must stay with her.

In the darkest part of the night, Brin sent a thought trickling into her mind.

'They sleep deeply dearest one, if you insist on this plan.'

Tika stood up, staring at Farn's beautiful face resting back between his wings. In the starlight the scar down his neck showed dark between the glimmer of his scales. She turned away, already aching at the idea of leaving him, and moved to embrace Brin. Wordlessly he sent love and concern pouring into her mind and she stepped across to Seela. As she pulled herself onto Seela's back, Sket climbed silently behind her.

'Thank you,' she whispered aloud.

His wiry arm held her firmly round the waist. He said nothing, just sat like a rock, as Seela lifted into the night sky, circling once before flying north west towards Vorna's estates and a meeting with one of the Bound Ones.

All three were deep in their own thoughts for half the flight. It was Seela who spoke first.

'There must be no room for regrets, small one. I know it is easier for me to say that and to believe it: I have had a long life and you are still new to the world. But regret will stifle you my dear, and make you falter when you should move without hesitation.'

'I know, but it is so hard.'

Seela felt Tika's mind struggling to push thoughts of Farn back behind a thick wall.

'Don't do that,' she chided gently. 'Your love for him should be your shield, your support, not hidden away and denied.'

Tika considered Seela's suggestion while the leagues vanished beneath the Dragon's huge wings.

'You're right,' she agreed at last. 'Together we are strong, so even the thought of him encourages me a little more.'

Sket, listening in his own mind to the conversation, tightened his arm round Tika's waist.

'You shouldn't have come Sket.' She spoke aloud, the wind of their flight blowing her words back to him.

Sket snorted in irritation. 'And what should I do?' he retorted. 'My place is with you, no matter what we face.'

Seela's laugh rang in their minds.

'Of course he should be here, silly child. You could have no one better beside you now.'

Sket's mouth opened in astonishment at Seela's compliment but he didn't reply for she was slowing the beat of her wings, flying lower with each stroke. The sky behind them was less dark as the sun began to reach up to the eastern horizon. Ahead, the sky was still littered with paling stars but there was a blemish, a rising dome of grey nothingness towards which they flew. Seela landed perhaps four hundred paces from the ball of cloud, Tika and Sket sliding from her back. Sket shivered. The air seemed to ripple and twist, like it had in the heat of the desert.

As the pre-dawn light strengthened, they saw buildings within the distorted air. Seela lowered her head towards Tika and Sket but before she could say anything the ground on which they stood shuddered and heaved. The purple Dragon extended her wings, hooking their talons into the protesting earth while Tika and Sket were thrown flat. The ground stilled again and Sket helped Tika back to her feet.

'Was that the creature?' he asked.

Tika nodded. 'She is so close to freedom.

She threw her arms round Seela's neck, hugging as much as she could reach.

'You are sure of this?' she asked.

Seela nuzzled against Tika's head. 'I will go now and you will know when to make the attempt on this foulness. Succeed for me, small one, and for us all.'

Tika forced herself to release the purple Dragon and lifted her chin.

'May the stars guide your path and guard your heart Seela of Sun Mountain. And know that I love you.'

Seela's eyes whirred, violet and lavender facets shot with gold and then she lifted from the ground. She climbed rapidly until she was higher than the dome of twisted air. Tika tore her gaze from the great Dragon and concentrated on the buildings flickering within the murk. She found the smaller building, set slightly apart from the large house in the centre. That was where the twisted power emanated. She began to run towards that place, Sket at her side. Tika stared only at the building but as they neared the intangible wall of fog, Sket glanced up.

Seela hovered directly above the spot on which Tika concentrated. Seela's scream of rage and pride rocked Sket back on his heels for a moment but Tika neither paused nor looked up. The ground underfoot began to buckle again and Tika grabbed Sket's arm, trying to keep her footing on the shifting earth. Sket caught a last glimpse of the newly risen sun firing Seela's scales to a blaze of purple light when she closed her wings, diving into the cloud, fire spewing from her open jaws.

Then Sket was inside the fog, pulled in Tika's wake. The ground writhed beneath them and sound battered Sket nearly senseless: inhuman sounds from somewhere below him and shrieking bellows from a great Dragon. He tried to breathe but the air tasted poisonous and there didn't seem to be enough to fill his lungs anyway. Tika pulled his arm and he peered at her, disorientated. She sat down cross-legged, one hand pulling her pendant free of her shirt, the other drawing her sword and laying it across her knees.

Sket, gasping, fell beside her, sweat streaming down his face as the ground heaved yet again. He dug the fingers of one hand into the soil, the other hooking into Tika's belt. He blinked, trying to see what it was that Tika focused on as he felt her back stiffen against his hand. Seela was on top of the smaller building, her wings thrashing the disrupted air, fire still pouring directly down. A rumble began far underground and, as Sket stared, the main building slid sideways, disintegrating as it fell.

A wind sprang up from nowhere, gusting from all directions,

hot and foetid. Sket covered his nose and mouth with a hand, glancing at Tika. She remained rigid, her eyes open but unseeing. He shuffled closer to her, trying to protect her as things began to fly through the air – branches, fence posts, a whirlwind of straw, roof tiles – all hurtling madly around them. Crouched over Tika, he felt power thrumming through her whole body. Her right hand clenched on her sword hilt and light flashed along its blade. Sket's ears rang with the continuous noise and he hunched lower. He gasped in terror when he saw Tika's left hand clasped around the egg pendant.

The oval glowed a deep amber, so brilliant it shone through her skin to reveal the darker lines of her bones. Should he leave her? Should he pull her hand free? He couldn't think, for the noise increased now to a rapid drumming which rose through the earth into his very body. He looked frantically towards the smaller building and felt Tika convulse within the shelter of his arm. A line of blackness streaked up from the burning building, impaling Seela and rising through her body up towards the sky. The Dragon screamed, a cry of mingled pain and triumph, and then her body exploded into a thousand glittering fragments.

Pain roared through Sket. A tiny part of his mind still functioned clearly enough for him to realise he was experiencing some of Tika's agony because he held her so tightly against himself. He stared down at her. Her face was a rictus of torment, her eyes still open, staring at something awful beyond imagining. Her knuckles were white where she gripped her sword but the blade itself slipped from her left knee, its tip sinking into the ground. Sket turned his eyes away when brilliant light flared and danced along the metal and Tika's body arched backwards in agony.

Sket's head was spinning, he could scarcely breathe and dawn seemed to have changed its mind: darkness increased about them. The ground contorted more viciously than ever and Sket, Tika clutched in his arms, was tossed about as easily as the chaff flew at winnowing. He was aware of things hitting his back, his head, then of sliding downwards, endlessly down. Finally a roar grew loud enough to burst his eardrums and the entire world seemed to explode about him.

In Harbour City the first earthquake struck at dawn. Brin had to rouse Storm and Farn from the deep sleep he'd induced in them and perhaps fortunately, both young Dragons were at first sluggish and slow to awareness. The gijan woke together, instantly alert. Brin flinched at the sharp stab of fury they sent to his mind. Willow and Piper streaked skywards before Brin could recover and were swiftly gone from sight. Leaf stood in front of him, dark eyes blazing at him.

'Our lives are hers,' she hissed aloud as the companions hurried from the temple.

Gan realised at once that Tika was not here. When he saw that Seela was missing as well he was filled with the chill of foreboding. Maressa was nearest Farn as the ground trembled again. Farn's head turned, checking around the garden.

'Where is my Tika?' he called. 'Does she still sleep inside?' His eyes began to whirr faster and he rattled his wings in increasing agitation. 'I cannot feel her mind! Where is my Tika?'

The paving under their feet buckled and stone flags snapped in half. Zerran emerged from the temple, supporting himself against the wall. He began to speak but the three Dragons suddenly bellowed in grief and outrage. Brin and Farn reared erect, the death song of the great Dragons pouring from them. Storm also rose erect but he did not know the songs of the great Dragons so stood in silent sympathy. Huge tears rolled down all three faces and Maressa slumped against Gan. Ren swayed towards Jakri whose mind had also received Seela's call as she died. Gan met Zerran's eyes over Maressa's head. Zerran could only nod and manage a tremulous smile before he turned back into the temple.

When the Dragons lowered themselves they found the humans had grabbed their packs and were ready to go. Farn was more distressed than Gan had seen him since the creatures of the Void had attacked them on the Sapphrean coast. He looked in vain for Sket before he guessed Sket had gone with Tika. The realisation gave him a crumb of comfort to hold on to as he joined Jakri and Maressa on Brin's back. Ren, with Khosa in her sack, climbed cautiously on a trembling Farn while Navan took Akomi with him on Storm.

Leaf shot skyward and Ren clutched wildly at the edge of

Farn's wing as he followed. It was plain that Farn was oblivious to all except his desperate need to locate his soul bond. Even high above the city, the low rumbling roar reached them. The riders looked down and saw the buildings moving, swaying, collapsing in dust-shrouded heaps. Gan watched as the perimeter wall of the city slumped inwards. He was guiltily grateful that he could not hear the cries of people no doubt crushed in the devastation. Lifting his gaze ahead, he was surprised to see the gijan Leaf some way in front, her wings beating in powerful strokes.

Nearing midday, they were all in a state of shock. The earth still shook and split open; great fissures opening beneath them as though the ground had grown jaws with which to swallow trees, livestock, people, and closing them again with a jarring snap. Leaf slowed and began to descend and the riders saw Willow and Piper below on a seemingly steady piece of pastureland. The Dragons landed, even Brin breathing hard from the speed of their flight. Farn stumbled, almost tipping Ren over his shoulder, and Maressa ran towards Tika's soul bond.

Ren slid from Farn's back, immediately loosening Khosa's carry sack while Farn collapsed to the ground. His eyes whirred more slowly but their colour was alarmingly faint. Ren caught Farn's long face between his hands, forcing his mind into the young Dragon.

'Farn, she may be all right. Did you feel her death? Farn!' he shouted aloud, tightening his hands and shaking Farn's head. 'Answer me, light damn you! Did you feel her death as we all felt Seela's?'

Jakri had joined them, his hand lightly against Farn's brow. Whether he did anything or not Ren wasn't sure, but a spark kindled briefly in a prismed eye.

'No,' Farn whispered. 'I didn't feel that, but I can feel nothing from her – nothing at all.'

'Farn.' Ren was determined to bully Farn out of this pit of despair into which he was sinking too quickly. 'Farn, remember Sapphrea? When Tika collapsed after we fought those red eyed creatures? She shielded herself – even against you, while she recovered her strength.'

Ren was unaware that everyone stood watching him as he

waited for Farn to respond.

'What you say is true,' Farn agreed at last. 'But if she has collapsed somewhere here, then we have to find her.' He pushed himself up a little, staring in the direction of what had been the estates of Mage Councillor Vorna.

They all followed the direction of his gaze. A line of blackened grass delineated the exact position of the outer edge of Valesh's disruptive field. Beyond was a vista of grey, black and brown rubble. What had once been buildings were low humps of burnt stone and in the centre of this still smouldering circle was a crater. Ren was about to speak but Jakri cut in first.

'Farn, you cannot find Mistress Tika's mind signature, but it would appear that your friend Sket is with her. Can you perhaps find his mind?'

Ren could have kicked himself for not thinking of such an obvious plan and waited for Farn's answer. Brin had moved closer and he too was clearly extending his senses over the large area of devastated earth before them.

'Yes,' Farn murmured. 'Sket is there somewhere, within that hole.'

The gijan were already airborne, skimming low before vanishing below the level of the ground. Navan had stepped onto the ruined earth and bent to pick up a large chunk of soil. It felt warm and he tossed it across to Gan. The solid looking block crumbled when it hit Gan's palm and he frowned. He walked onto the burnt ground a little further than Navan. The soil crunched, losing its firmness and becoming fine dust which drifted slowly up behind him. He stared across the league to the crater where the gijan had disappeared.

'This is too dangerous to walk on,' he said thoughtfully. He took another step forward and his foot sank calf deep. Navan grabbed for Gan's arm as Emla's Captain pulled himself free. He moved back, onto the undamaged land and turned to the companions. Farn slept and Jakri nodded when Gan raised a questioning brow. Yes, Farn would be a risk on this terrain if he lost control. Gan studied Storm and Brin.

'Can you see where the gijan have got to?' he asked. 'Whatever you do, don't land anywhere on the burnt land.'

Maressa was sitting down, sorting through the packs for her

medical supplies and remedies. She desperately missed Sket's presence – he was the one who was always ready in such emergencies. Now it seemed highly probable that he would be the one in need of help.

Tika had no idea where she was. She seemed to be travelling rapidly down dark tunnels but somehow she could see. Not that there was much to take note of: jagged black rock, with other tunnels at intervals. She found the tunnel she travelled widening into a large chamber, but it was as featureless as the tunnel. She was aware that it was her mind travelling here: she didn't have an inkling of where her body was. Perhaps she was dead. The thought didn't bother her until she remembered Farn and pain lanced through her.

'That's right, think of him,' a voice told her.

She spun round but there was only the empty black cavern. But she had recognised the voice.

'Seela? Is it you? Where are we?'

'This is one of the places Between and I cannot stay here long. And you should not be here at all.'

'Are you –?' Tika found she couldn't finish her question.

'Dead?' Seela's laugh chimed in Tika's mind. 'My body is dead of course, small one. I am permitted to stay here only a short while.' Seela sounded vague. 'Time is of no consequence in the places Between.'

'Did we destroy Valesh?'

'Mostly. A few fragments survived but even should they reunite, they will offer no threat.'

'What is this place Between? How do I get back to my body Seela – I can feel no life thread?'

For a panicky moment Tika thought Seela had gone, then she heard her voice again but more distantly.

'You must follow Sket's mind. He is nearest. I can help you no more dear one. Places Between are many. All strange. All different. This is one of the lesser ones, the place Between life and death.'

'Seela!' Tika's mind shrieked the Dragon's name into the empty silence. There was no reply.

Tika turned slowly: the cavern had many tunnel openings in its walls, but which one had she come from – they all looked identical. Her essence, or spirit, or mind, moved to the nearest. Was she a ghost, or unbodied forever, like Grek she wondered wildly? She went quickly into a tunnel, following the main path and ignoring the many side openings. She saw light ahead and hurried faster.

Tika stared. There was something transparent, like glass but not, sealing her away from the scene on the other side. Lord Hargon sat propped against a boulder, talking to someone. Dear stars above, he was talking to Mist! Tika pressed against the "glass". Hargon was ill, his face a skull covered with tightly-stretched skin. As she watched, he lifted a thin hand to Mist's face and Tika could see how much effort the movement cost him. The strange window through which she stared became dark, dark as the walls around her.

She turned and with rising fear began to search other tunnels. Tika had no sense of time passing – Seela had said time was of no consequence here and so Tika couldn't guess if she had been wandering one day or a full ten day. But she did have a sense of weariness. She stopped, trying to calm herself as Iska had taught her. Was her increasing tiredness a warning that somewhere her body weakened? This place was like a puzzle and she must simply try to solve it.

Panic became more difficult to suppress as tunnel after tunnel led her to dead ends or to other windows through which she saw scenes she couldn't begin to understand. Tika slammed to a halt and sniffed. How could she smell with only her mind? But she could see, hear and speak – could she touch? She tried to lean against the wall but had no feeling of the rock against her arm. Concentrate, concentrate, she ordered herself. These were irrelevancies. She sniffed again. She could smell mint, very faintly but very definitely.

Tika tried to follow the tenuous trail of fragrance, several times losing it as she turned too soon into the wrong opening. It grew stronger; she was sure it wasn't false imagining.

'Hurry!'

Who was that – Seela again? Tika dared not stop to question, hurrying on after the strengthening scent. Although bodiless, she felt as if she was stumbling now, exhaustion sapping her determination. She turned yet again and saw a faint grey light at the further end of the tunnel. It took an eternity to reach it and she was terrified it would be sealed against her like all the others. Just before she reached the end, she paused, peering into the dimness. The passage had led her to a tiny space enclosed in grey black rock. Light seeped weakly down from a gap well above Tika's head.

Dust motes sifted in the line of light and covered the two bodies sprawled on the floor. Sket lay on his side, his left arm flung across Tika. His hand looked wrong: coated in dust as it was, she could still see it was bloodied. She saw her own body lying at an awkward angle, her head twisted to one side and her right arm outstretched, still gripping her sword. No dust settled on the blade which nonetheless looked blackened as though by intense heat.

Something blocked the light briefly as it moved across the gap high overhead. Tika looked back at her body and forced herself forward, fearing that her passage would yet again be barred. But it wasn't. Without pausing for thought, she slid her mind back into her body which shuddered violently. She was aware again of her heartbeat: slow, perhaps too slow, but she was alive. And she hurt.

From the agonising pain between her breasts, she guessed her pendant had burnt her again. Her left hand throbbed somewhere between Sket's chest and sharp stones. Everything ached and her eyes were so encrusted with dust that she couldn't force them open. She held herself still, praying she might hear Sket's breathing but instead she heard rock sliding and grating as it fell somewhere nearby. Dear stars, after all this were they to be buried completely?

Tika struggled to unglue her eyes and stiffened in shock as a hand touched her face. She felt a cheek laid against hers and then a strong arm slid under her shoulders, another under her knees. She was lifted against a naked chest and the dust caking her face split as she smiled. A high ululating cry reverberated through her cheek and she managed to croak out the name.

'Leaf.'

'My life is yours,' the gijan whispered and launched herself up from the depths of the crater.

Chapter Twenty-Eight

It took two full days for the gijan to locate Sket and Tika. When Leaf and Willow landed among the companions carrying their precious burdens there was a flurry of activity. Neither Brin nor Storm had been able to fly far down into the crater where once Vorna's library had stood. Brin tried to explain about the strangely swirling air currents and the equally worrying changes of temperature. Gan tried to comfort the huge crimson Dragon – he had never heard Brin admit so openly that any flying conditions frightened him. Jakri and Ren had discussed Farn's state as soon as Jakri made him sleep soon after their arrival. They agreed that keeping him unaware was best for now: his life signs were not good, which they all feared was mirroring Tika's condition. All three mages checked him regularly as they waited for the gijan to return.

None of the gijan were communicative: they made their displeasure with Brin extremely clear. They repeatedly circled within the crater, working from the top downwards, checking and double checking. Leaf thawed enough on the second day to confess that the air and the rock inside the crater was still in a state of such flux that she and her siblings were confused time and again by conflicting reactions to their mind probing.

Khosa curled with Akomi against Farn's chest, both cats disturbed and distressed. Driven nearly mad by inactivity and a feeling of useless frustration, Gan and Navan searched the outer area for anything to make a fire. As Maressa pointed out to Ren, they had enough fuel gathered now for a beacon, let alone a small cook fire. Navan discovered a water supply which he then found was contaminated. Storm and Brin quartered the area until they uncovered a clean spring about half a league away. Gan found some wooden pails, battered but usable after a few repairs, and they all felt happier knowing plenty of water would thus be available when Tika and Sket were found.

The sun was setting for the third time amid lurid red clouds when the gijan cries rang out. Everyone was on their feet, staring at three feathered creatures flying slowly towards them. Leaf landed first, her high arched feet stepping daintily across the dry grass, Tika held easily in her arms. She laid Tika gently in front of Farn, leaned over to kiss her lips, then stepped away. Willow repeated his sister's movements, placing Sket carefully beside Tika. Jakri gave both a cursory inspection and then snapped orders. Neither Ren nor Maressa were strongly gifted in healing and both were mightily relieved to find that Jakri apparently was.

Maressa and Navan fetched warm water to wash the filth and dust from Sket and Tika's faces. Sket remained unconscious but Tika's eyes opened as soon as her eyelashes were unclogged. She looked up into the anxious faces above her and opened her mouth. Jakri placed his middle finger between her brows and her eyes closed instantly. Gan frowned. Jakri glanced up at him.

'She has severe burns Master Gan; the pain will be bad at first while I clean them'

Gan bit his lip. Jakri had cut away Tika's torn shirt to better get at the burn on her chest and breaths caught as they all saw just how bad the injury was. Jakri bent close, shaking his head.

'I will clean this then I will have to try to use power to at least begin the mending.' He looked up at the others apologetically. 'I am trained in the use of healing herbs and in practical treatments but I am not an expert in using power to heal.'

Ren grunted. 'Maressa and I are next to useless.'

Navan had pulled Tika's sleeve free and turned her left hand palm up. Jakri's golden face paled. The hand was burned to the bone. He swallowed hard and stood up.

'Clean her of this dust and I'll check Sket properly.'

Ren and Navan bent to their task, Brin and Storm peering worriedly over their shoulders. Willow was helping Maressa get Sket's clothes off and begin to clean him. Jakri found a large bump on the side of Sket's head which he frowned over, then Maressa gasped. She had lifted Sket's left arm to pull off his shirt and the water she had then sluiced over his arm revealed his damaged hand. The two fingers furthest from his thumb were completely mangled, the smallest finger nearly detached in fact.

'They must be cut off,' Willow said calmly.

Jakri stared up into the gijan's dark eyes.

'If you can heal then help me now,' he said softly.

Willow stared impassively back. He tilted his head one side then the other.

'We will,' he agreed. 'They must both be cleaned before we start, but these,' he pointed to Sket's hand, 'must be cut off.'

Jakri nodded. Tiny pieces of bone stuck out from Sket's fingers and he could see no way of repairing such damage.

'I can do that.' He sounded more confident. 'That is the type of treatment I am practised in.'

Willow moved to stare down at Tika and up at Farn. 'Wake the young Dragon,' he said to Jakri. 'His strength will help her.' The gijan met Khosa's slitted turquoise eyes and he smiled. 'Don't worry, he will be calm.'

Jakri rose to touch Farn's brow. He waited a moment then turned away to scrub his hands in the water Gan had ready for him. He instructed Ren to fetch his pack and search out a packet of instruments which Ren then set out on a clean cloth near Sket. Ren repressed a shiver seeing the slender blades of obsidian set in smooth jade shafts. Jakri checked the level of Sket's unconsciousness and set to work, Gan and Ren passing him whatever he requested. Queasy though Ren felt, he found himself admiring Jakri's skill. The Wendlan removed the fingers, scoured the injuries for bone chips and neatly stitched a flap of skin over each knuckle. He sat back with a groan, surprised to find how dark the sky had grown.

'I can bind it if you wish,' Ren offered, and set to work.

Maressa and Navan stood one each side of Farn. Maressa sensed the young Dragon's distressed feelings had been muffled somehow: there had been no near hysterical outburst when he'd woken to find Tika returned to him which is what they had all feared might happen. He had simply lowered his face to hers and studied her burns intently, his eyes whirring sapphire and pearl. But there had been no panic.

The three gijan stood around Tika, Leaf and Piper facing each other across her prone figure, Willow at her feet. They extended their huge wings, raising a black feathered wall around them, Farn at Tika's head. They joined hands, Leaf and Piper placing their free hands on Farn's shoulders, and bowed their heads.

Maressa, Navan and the two cats crouching forgotten by Farn's chest, watched.

A faint glow surrounded the burn between Tika's small breasts. Flesh began to move, to ripple, and slowly the hole was covered with fragile new skin. Leaf had left Tika's chain around her neck but had moved the pendant so that it rested on the ground beside her head. Maressa and Navan both felt the gijan relax momentarily and then Piper stooped, moving Tika's upturned hand off her stomach to lie on the grass. Again the tension hummed between the gijan and the exposed bones of Tika's hand were concealed beneath a flimsy layer of new flesh.

The gijan sighed, furling their wings. Leaf looked over her shoulder to where Jakri was attending to Sket's skull.

'Master Mage,' she called. 'We can do no more for her hand. You will know better how to finish this mending now.'

Jakri got creakily to his feet and hobbled on numbed legs to Tika's side. He bent to lift Tika's hand, peering closely in the failing light.

'It will need dressings daily, many salves for encouraging suppleness, and a system of exercises. But she must not attempt to use this hand for anything other than the exercises I will show her for some time to come.'

The gijan all nodded agreement, casually turning away to hop onto Brin's back. His eyes flashed in alarm: he had felt the sting of disapproval from the gijan but now they acted as if nothing had annoyed them. Storm crept closer to Farn, his grey scaled face touching Farn's neck. Farn turned to him then back to watch Tika. Jakri was ordering that his two patients be wrapped warmly and for either tea or a thin broth to be readied: he would rouse both invalids sufficiently to allow them to swallow a good amount of fluid before letting them settle for the night.

Maressa sat between Sket and Tika. She would watch through this night while the others rested. Jakri soon rolled in his blankets and slept. Ren and Gan sat quietly by the fire, the sound of Navan's cloth working Tika's sword blade the only sound.

'I have given no thought these last days for what the people of Harbour City may be suffering,' Gan murmured.

Ren refilled his tea bowl from the pot perched above the embers. 'Maressa has far spoken Sheoma,' he said, speaking as softly as Gan. 'The temples of the Elder Races throughout the city withstood the earth movements.'

Navan paused in his rhythmic working on the blade. Ren shrugged.

'Sheoma says none of them understand why that should be. And the Xantip palace is unharmed. She says Zerran estimates half the population is dead or missing and nearly every building is unsafe if not in ruins. Many people are living in the public gardens, afraid to stay near the remaining buildings. The priests of the temples of the Elder Races are providing food as they can for all who are in need. Sheoma said the people are shocked at present, too dazed to help themselves. She also says that the Wendlan mages on the Emperor's ships report the earth shook in the north, although nowhere near as badly as here. It did not stop yet more warriors pouring from the desert. There is terrible fighting throughout the northern farmlands.'

Ren fell silent and Gan wondered just what they were supposed to do now. Khosa butted her head against his bent knee and he obligingly stretched out his long legs to offer her his lap.

'Tika and Sket will not be able to travel for many days,' she said in their minds. 'Grek will surely return and advise us what our plans must be.'

Akomi crept onto Gan's lap beside Khosa and Gan absently scratched the old cat's ears.

'I've noticed the gijan have grown taller,' Navan remarked. 'But even so, I am surprised at the strength they must have. Leaf carried Tika as easily as you or I would carry Khosa or Akomi.'

Gan sighed. 'The longer we go on, the more confused I seem to become,' he confessed. 'It sounds as though Harbour City itself is in chaos: where might we find supplies I wonder?'

'Brin says the region here appears virtually lifeless.' Navan set Tika's sword aside and began to work on Sket's. 'He has seen very few humans and he said their minds feel empty.'

Ren got to his feet, filling a tea bowl to take over to Maressa. 'I am concerned by Grek's absence,' he said.

He returned from checking the two injured ones and sat back down.

'Grek was afraid,' Khosa mind spoke them. 'He feared he would be unmade if he ventured too near the power vortex Valesh was creating.'

'And would he?' asked Ren.

'Of course. While being unbodied has many advantages, it is also an extremely vulnerable condition in a situation dealing with a large body of wild energy – which is what Valesh had become.'

'Can we be sure that Tika's mind has suffered no – contamination?' Gan asked.

Khosa yawned and gave the sleeping Akomi's head a brisk wash before she answered. 'I cannot be sure, but I suspect those gijan can. They would not have healed her had they any doubts.'

'But they adore her,' Navan interposed. 'They all told her that their lives were hers when they woke after their wings came.'

Khosa yawned again. 'If they suspected Tika had been manipulated by Valesh's warped intelligence, they would all have died, Tika with them.'

She buried her nose under Akomi's chin and left the three men to silently ponder her words.

Jakri was tending his patients and Maressa was fast asleep when Gan woke in the early morning. He stirred the embers of the fire and set a pot of water to boil. Then he crossed to where Jakri knelt beside Sket. Seeing Tika's eyes were open he squatted next to her. 'How do you feel?'

'As if Farn has sat on me all night.'

Farn rumbled above her and Tika struggled to free her right hand from the cocoon of blankets. 'I'm teasing dear one,' she assured him, letting his face rest against her palm. She tried to push herself up and Gan helped prop her shoulders on Farn's chest.

'Sket's been sick and Jakri says he's feverish. I can't help him – there is nothing left in me at the moment. Jakri won't even let me try.'

Jakri glared over Sket's chest. 'Just regain some strength and you can help, but if you try now you'll fail and hurt yourself badly into the bargain. Fever I can deal with and it isn't unusual for a patient to be sick after a bump on the head such as Sket has suffered.'

He glanced up at the sky and Gan followed his gaze. The wind had been light, blowing off the western sea two or three leagues away, but it had swung round during the dawn. The sky looked dirty, a brownish red. Gan rose to his full height, his head very nearly level with Brin who reclined close by.

'It is dust,' Brin told him. 'I flew to seek meat for Farn. At the moment, it is high but I think soon it will fill all the air.'

Gan tried to imagine the vast sprawl of Harbour City cluttered with fallen buildings and its people choking in the pall of dust of which this must be the furthest fringe. He glanced down at Tika and Sket: Tika's eyes were closed again.

'Brin, did you see any buildings close enough to us here where we might shelter? We have no awnings with us as we had in the desert – there seemed no reason to pack them. Tika and Sket can't lie unprotected if the wind brings that dust storm this far.'

Brin drew his massive hind legs beneath him. 'I will search now,' he said.

Storm leapt into the air behind the crimson Dragon and Gan watched them fly for a moment. The line of dark cloud seemed nearer, but he hoped it was just his imagination. The two Dragons came back much sooner than Gan had dared hope. Brin gave him a mental picture of what Gan guessed had been a storage barn. The ground around it was broken and uneven: clearly it had been hit by the earthquakes. Several buildings nearby were virtually unrecognisable as such, piles of stone and what had been a sort of mud brick.

After consulting Jakri, it was arranged that Farn would carry Tika and Jakri; Gan would hold Sket secure between himself and Maressa on Brin while Storm carried Navan and Ren. Akomi had yowled in surprised horror when Willow scooped him into his arms and took off in pursuit of Storm. Piper followed his example with Khosa. Khosa was able to maintain a calmer manner but she missed the security of her carry sack when being conveyed through the sky.

Gan saw that they were less than half a league from the sea as Brin landed as smoothly as he could for fear of jarring the still unconscious Sket. Navan and Ren reached to lift Sket from Gan's arms and Gan had a quick look at where they found themselves. He was pleased to see that the earthquake had tilted the barn into a piece of rising ground behind it. He tested the stability of the remaining uprights and was relieved that the space within was large enough for all of them, Dragons included. He found Navan behind him, Sket limp against his chest, and nodded, indicating they should move deeper into the partially collapsed structure.

The gijan followed them, chattering in their strange liquid tongue, and set Khosa and Akomi on the floor. Akomi fled into the darkest corner, terrified he might be subjected to another flight in such a rough and ready fashion. Khosa paused long enough to wash her face, proof that she was perfectly calm, before strolling after Akomi. To Gan's astonishment, the gijan then set to work clearing fallen timbers from the back corner where the building had come to rest against solid earth.

Since Tika had freed their wings, the gijan had led a carefree existence, never helping find or prepare food or firewood, merely eating whatever was provided and keeping their own company far more than associating with the companions, even Tika. After doing what they could for Tika's burns, they had gone to sleep on Brin's back. If they grieved for Seela, none of the companions had seen any sign of it. Yet they had flown tirelessly from Harbour City and for the two days of searching the crater. What sort of creatures were they, Gan wondered. In the City of the Domes they had been cowed, subservient, frightened of their own shadows, but since their wings had emerged, they were apart, almost arrogant. But now at least they were working efficiently to clear a good sized space where Tika and Sket could lie sheltered and safe.

Brin insisted that Farn fly with him and Storm to find meat both for themselves and to bring back to the barn for the companions. They could be grounded for days, he told Farn, if the dust continued to fill the air. Once he'd seen Sket settled, Navan hurried off to gather broken timbers for firewood and to Gan's continuing surprise, Piper and Willow went to help him. Jakri used his mage powers to locate water: a well had vanished under what he guessed had been the main farmhouse but he tracked the underground water until he found it near enough the surface to dig down to. Gan had followed with two of the pails he'd found days before.

When they had carried the water back to their shelter, they saw that the gijan had uncovered a stone trough knocked on its side near the ruined house. Their strength was demonstrated again by the ease with which they moved the trough inside the barn. Maressa scrubbed the inner surface before the gijan tipped the trough upright, then they made several trips back and forth for water with which to fill it. The sky was darkening rapidly and the leading edge of rusty cloud swept high overhead. The Dragons returned with only five hoppers between them, animals Jakri called rabbits. Brin reported, with some embarrassment, that they had found a small group of cattle running in confusion, obviously escaped from farms that no longer existed. Gan rubbed Brin's thick neck.

'You must feed where you can old friend. Did you see any people?'

'None at all.'

Tika had woken and was surveying her left hand, wrapped completely in its bandages. 'What happened?' she asked generally.

Ren sat next to her. 'I think you must have been holding the pendant,' he said.

Maressa had removed the chain and its pendant from Tika's neck during last night, putting them in the leather pouch she had used at Green Shade, and which now lay within reach of Tika's right hand. Maressa had also slipped a shirt over Tika's upper body, covering the wad of dressings on her burnt chest. Tika stared down at her front and sighed.

'It does seem to happen a bit too often now,' she said. 'Perhaps it had better stay in the pouch for now at least.'

Ren returned her smile then they both looked towards the opening of the barn, beyond the Dragons. At first it seemed like rain but the rustling sound was not that of rain. It was soil, gathered up by the wind and carried the twenty six leagues from Harbour City, increased by what it collected nearer at hand, and now falling on these farmlands. Although barely mid afternoon, it darkened and cooled in the barn, enough for the companions to need to light a small fire already. Ren was able to make glow stones from a few suitable pebbles he'd picked up outside which helped raise their spirits.

Jakri thought that Sket was surfacing from his concussion. He asked if Maressa or Ren had any willow bark in their supplies: Sket would have an appalling headache. Maressa searched her pack, knowing Ammi had given them a goodly supply of willow bark along with so many other herbs.

'It isn't here.' She frowned. 'Maybe Sket took it.'

She reached for his back pack, the standard issue pack used by all Emla's personal Guards with its distinctive blue badge depicting a stylised flower. She tipped the pack up and out fell rolled shirts, a pair of trousers, many paper and cloth packets of various herbs, two pots of salves and other oddments. Navan was the first to notice Maressa's stillness. The others turned to see what she was staring at. Gently she lifted the purple scales. They glittered in the light of the fire and Ren's stones. Five perfect scales, each the size of Maressa's hand. She knelt, not knowing what to say, while her tears made the scales sparkle even brighter.

In the Grand Harbour Master's apartments Chevra paced restlessly. He had only to look from one of the many windows in this room to see the extent of the devastation of his City. Administrator Fenelon had occupied the upper chamber in the College tower and from there she organised mages into units to struggle with as many of the City's problems as they could. Chevra's armsmen were still digging through rubble, in the vain hope of finding trapped survivors. Mage healers had set up emergency infirmaries at key points throughout the City.

Administrator Zerran divided his time between the tower and the temple of the Elder Races nearest the northern gate of the City. A dozen mages remained there, helping Taza and the other priests as they tried to cope with citizens dazed by their experience of earthquake on such a massive scale. Seven third and second rank mages had died in the temple and six in the tower, caught in the terrible backlash of power as they tried to restrict Valesh's energy to a specific area. In the tower, Fenelon assigned three of the strongest far speakers – mages of the third and second ranks – to maintain constant contact with the Wendlan ship Mages now anchored off the north eastern coast. The forty Wendlan Mages, whom Emperor Kasheen had offered Chevra, had changed their plan. They had intended to put ashore near Harbour City to assist the Maleshan mages against Valesh. That battle had been decided before the Wendlan ships reached the Maleshan coast. Most of Kasheen's Mages therefore continued north with the ships, only ten of their number, escorted by two Imperial Blossoms, going to the Xantip palace to offer their assistance to Chevra's mages.

Zerran was closeted now with Sheoma, Tavri and Fenelon, receiving the latest communication from the north west – where Vorna's estates had once been.

'Are they absolutely positive Tika has emerged mentally untouched?' Zerran asked yet again.

He remembered the child woman fixing him with those strangely altered eyes and insisting that she must be destroyed should there be any hint of suspicion that Valesh might have infected her mind. Fenelon knew of that conversation. She had been amazed by the way Zerran's usual impassive composure had been shaken by Tika's words when he repeated them to Fenelon.

Now Sheoma went over Maressa's last message.

'Maressa said that the – erm, cat – told them the gijan would have killed Tika if there was any doubt.' Sheoma still found it difficult to accept that other creatures – even cats – had mental powers apparently matching humans. 'The cat said the gijan would have died with her. Maressa also said that no one has yet spoken of the purple Dragon who died.'

Zerran bowed his head. 'She didn't merely die Sheoma. She was sacrificed herself.'

Chapter Twenty-Nine

In the desert City of the Domes, the Ship, Star Singer, hummed the counter point harmony of a Repsian folk song. Kertiss and Orla had not spoken to him in all the days since the party of travellers had left the great valley. They had not even walked through his chamber: Kertiss had sealed the door leading to his and Orla's quarters and Singer had no idea if they were still shut within or were using other access tunnels which he knew had been installed. He wept when the visitors left, fearing for their safety in the light of Kertiss's anger at their precipitate departure.

When the very tall man had held Tika's hand against his outer skin, Singer received a strange pulse of jumbled information. It was several days later before he'd bothered to try untangling that information. Even Singer's sophisticatedly enhanced mental networks found the task intriguingly difficult. He continued to allow his music to fill the chamber around him, just in case Kertiss should appear, but it was music from his memory cubes, not him singing in real time.

He realised, with growing excitement, that this tiny pulse of information contained a very great deal. Singer calculated and transposed, ran diagnostics on certain of his systems and then did it all again. There was a thread of song interwoven among various formulae which niggled at him. Eventually he found it distracting him to the extent that he applied all his concentration upon it.

It was a simple melody which seemed to invite harmonies and descants being embroidered around it. He finally began to sing the tune in the pure strong voice for which he had been famed, using different systems to add various harmonies. As the music filled both himself and his chamber, he found he liked it: it was joyous, a wordless song of triumphant affection, the like of which he had never heard in his long existence.

When it reached its natural end, Singer was silent for a while,

then he sang it all over again. It cheered him enormously and as
he worked on during the next days at defining the information
Tika's mind had passed to his, he sang it regularly to himself and
his mood remained more cheerful than for a millennium. Singer
became excited as well as cheerful when he finally understood
what the information, untangled and redefined, actually
contained. He worked constantly then, running test after test
through all his systems, reactivating those he had shut down as
soon as he'd landed and sworn to Kertiss were irretrievably
closed.

A day came, or night – Singer had no idea of the passage of
planetary time confined below ground and below the great Dome
as he was – when the soft hiss of the entry ramp opening made
him fall totally silent. It was the ramp which could be activated
from either down here or from within the Dome. Singer waited,
external heat sensors checking the whole space of his chamber,
but nothing registered. Time had little meaning to Singer so he
just waited.   At last he decided there had perhaps been a
malfunction in the operating system, or someone above had
brushed the activating slab by accident. Singer set an automatic
alarm around the perimeter of his chamber and returned to work
on his internal systems.

He thought of Mazan, his beloved first Captain, whenever he
felt his excitement growing too overwhelming. Finally, he closed
all the reopened and renewed synapses and sent a questing pulse
up to the shielding above him. The shielding was the first thing
Kertiss and Orla had rigged when they arrived here. He could
have shrieked with glee but he managed to remain silent. He had
found gaps in that shielding! Kertiss had never bothered to check
it once he'd set it up – why bother when Star Singer was mortally
damaged and verging on madness?

Trying to stay calm, Singer sang a nonsense song Mazan had
taught him, about a tiny stumblebug who believed he'd grow up
to be a joolar. He reached the end and was about to repeat it
when someone spoke his name.

'Singer? Singer! Are you well little brother?'

Star Singer's memory cubes spun as he struggled to find the
name: Flower! Star Flower! 'Is it really you Flower?' Singer
called, suddenly afraid this was another of Kertiss's traps.

'It is I – Star Flower,' came the reply, the husky voice unmistakeable now. 'Singer, I was so hurt when we landed and I nearly died but a native child has healed me – a female named Tika.'

Words were jumbling in Singer's frantic excitement. 'Tika was here – she was here! She's done something to me too. Where are you Flower, where have you been all this time? I am in a desert three quarters of the way south on the largest continent.'

'I know, Tika told us. We are in Wendla, a large island south east from you. There are battles near your desert – is Kertiss involved in causing these troubles?'

A chime sounded subliminally and Singer could only call briefly before he broke contact.

'Someone comes. I will speak with you again dear Flower!'

Singer strove desperately to maintain his control. His voice trembled slightly as he began to sing the nonsense rhyme again. His visual scanners searched the chamber and he saw a shadow advancing from the ramp entry. The sound of his own voice calmed him and he began the second stanza as the shadow grew longer, closer, darker. But then he had to stop singing as he saw the figure entering his chamber.

A female, as tall as the man who had carried Tika from here. She stood facing Singer. From high arched, four toed and taloned feet the slenderest of ankles were just visible beneath the long white sleeveless robe. A scarf of sky blue material was tied at her waist. A face of exquisite beauty, scaled in delicate gold, tilted to one side as she stared at the Ship, her wings furled behind her shoulders.

'Thank you for singing to us for so much of our captivity. You made it more bearable.'

Her voice was a joy to one who loved music as did Singer. He realised now that she was the statue in the Dome, to which Kertiss had affixed the ramp mechanism.

'Who are you, beautiful lady?' he finally managed to murmur.

'I am named Flute. I am a gijan Elder.' She bowed, her great black feathered wings flaring, the pinions sweeping the floor behind her. She straightened, dark blue under feathers briefly visible as she furled her wings once more. 'We must go, great

Singer. Sadly vengeance is a failing rather than a virtue but it is necessary that some retribution be made for the sufferings our children have endured. How may I open the floor so that you too may fly free again?'

Singer was about to protest that he could no longer fly, then he thought of the alterations he had made to his own synapses and the physical systems within his circuitries.

'The panel against the back wall, Lady Flute. If you place your hand against it and press, it opens the floor and sets the lift in motion.'

The tall beautiful creature stepped to the place Singer spoke of and pressed the slightly offset stone. The roof of the chamber hissed smoothly open and the piece of floor on which Singer rested began to rise. The gijan Elder walked back towards the ramp and was waiting as Singer's lift settled into place. He scanned the vast expanse of the Dome, automatically calculating and assessing: two hundred and twenty gijan Elders stood in a group, silently watching him. As one, they bowed to him, their wings rustling against the floor.

'How were you made into statues?' he whispered.

Flute tilted her head again. 'Valesh,' she said the name with distaste. 'She and her brother Qwah imprisoned us thus. For us to be freed means Valesh is destroyed and Qwah damaged. We hope we will meet you again Singer, for we owe you much, not least our sanity.'

'Wait.' Singer spoke urgently. 'Put your hand against me Lady Flute, that you may know my heart.'

Flute's head again tilted to the side but after a moment she walked forward and laid her palm flat against the Ship's side. Her dark eyes widened and she stood quite motionless. With a sigh she took her hand away and stepped back.

'You showed me yourself,' Singer whispered. 'I have never felt someone like you, except perhaps the human female Tika.'

'I am a high magician of my people,' Flute told him. 'You too revealed yourself. We recognised the one you name Tika when she visited you here. We were just reaching towards our release and we knew who she was. But we must go Singer; we must fly far through this night to escape the desert.'

Flute bowed, as did the massed Elders behind her.

'Fare well, Elder friend.'

'Where do you go?' Singer called as the gijan turned their backs to him to head towards the arched entrance.

Flute paused. 'First we find the children held in this place, then we go to different parts of this land. I will find the female Tika. She will help us to destroy Qwah completely.'

She bowed once more and hurried after the other Elders. Singer watched until Flute vanished at the far side of the Dome. He pondered for a while, trying to imagine a conversation with Mazan. He almost thought he heard her wonderful chuckle, and his decision was made. He checked his instruments and the status of his power units. Kertiss had never bothered to verify Singer's statement that the Ship had no power supply left. Surprisingly, Singer found he was quite calm.

He was under no illusion: he may well destroy himself within the space of this day. But he would at least die under the sky – he might even see the stars again. He powered the ducts which forced the cushion of air beneath his great bulk and began to move, turning slowly to face the opposite end of the Dome. Star Singer moved steadily until he reached the ramp that sloped first downwards, then up: up to the outside world.

He paused as his scanners showed him another dome above him, a dome of darkest blue velvet upon which jewelled stars were flung in glorious abandon. His sound receptors picked up screams in the immediate area, cries, and the clash of low technology weapons. Somehow Singer suspected the Elders would not be gentle in retrieving their lost descendants.

Singer steadied himself, increased the amount of air beneath him and engaged the power network. The thrum of energy quivered through the entire Ship and Singer ran the automatic checking sequences that had not operated for a thousand years. He concentrated fiercely: he *would* succeed. Mazan had taught him too well for him to let her down and fail now. He hovered above the Dome in which he had existed for all this time one moment longer and then set a course south west. At last, Star Singer flew once more.

Jakri said it was two days and Ren argued it was three since they'd been secluded within the half-fallen barn. The darkness at night was only a little darker than that during the day.

'Nothing living could last outside in that, could they?' Navan commented to Gan when they stood near the entrance. He held his hand out but pulled it quickly back, wincing as he did so. They studied the scratches on the back of his hand, inflicted in that brief instant by the dirt particles and worse that drove through the air.

The gijan were unsettled. They disliked the noise the wind made moaning and whistling through any gaps it could find. They disliked the permanent gloom and the dust that seeped and sifted into their feathers. Farn was fully restored, oblivious to the fact that the Mage Jakri had kept his full awareness suppressed for most of the six days since Tika and Sket left him behind in Harbour City. He reclined now as close to his soul bond as he could manage, supervising Jakri and Maressa when they changed the dressings on Tika's burns. Sket lay close by and Farn kept a careful eye on the armsman too.

Gan noted that Farn grew more distressed over Sket's missing fingers than he had over anything else. Jakri said that Sket was definitely on the mend, although Sket complained that his eyes "were funny". Jakri assured him this symptom would pass and added tartly that he hoped Sket's grumbling would pass too. By the third day (or the fourth if Ren was correct rather than Jakri), the amount of dust falling seemed noticeably reduced.

Khosa joined Gan and Maressa as they tried to peer through the pall of still choking air. Akomi had taken up residence on Tika's lap, and slept much of the time. When he woke, Tika and Farn encouraged him to tell of his life within the imperial palace. Tika gradually realised why Khosa had insisted Akomi join them: she tried to imagine living among crowds of people yet be totally unable to communicate with any of them, and shuddered at the thought.

'Could Grek travel through this?' Maressa wondered.

Khosa stretched and turned her back on the weather. 'I would have thought so,' she said, twitching the insidious dust from her ears. 'But perhaps not. I admit I expected him back by now, so maybe he cannot move through such foul air. Tika's getting up.'

She trotted deeper into the barn and sat primly beside Akomi as they watched Jakri and Navan help Tika to her feet. Storm,

Willow perched on his back, watched too. Tika's face paled and Farn's eyes began to whirr faster in alarm.

'It's all right Farn. She is only weak – that's why we must get her up and moving for a while.' Jakri soothed Farn while steadying Tika's swaying body.

'This is ridiculous,' Tika complained. 'I'm not hurt so why can't I even stand up?'

Jakri met her green silvered eyes but said nothing.

'Sorry. Do you think I will find any power comes back?' she asked quietly.

'Try a few steps Mistress Tika,' Jakri encouraged. 'Yes. I hope you regain your mental strength but it is tied to your physical wellbeing too you know. You can still use mind speech, so I have every hope you will recover fully. It will take time though and patience is needed.'

Supported by Jakri and Navan, Tika got as far as Brin. Perspiration beaded her face and she was trembling. Brin lowered his face to her level.

'I am so sorry Brin,' she said aloud.

The broad crimson brow pressed against hers, tears the size of her fist rolling slowly down his long face.

'It was Seela's decision.' His mind tone was sad but firm. 'We will sing of her courage in our histories.'

Tika put her good hand against his wet face and closed her eyes for a moment. When she opened them, she found Leaf leaning down to her from Brin's back. She smiled at the gijan.

'Farn told me you found us and you carried us to safety. How can I thank you Leaf?'

Leaf's dark eyes regarded Tika steadily. 'Our lives are yours,' was all she said. She gave the tiniest nod and turned back to Willow and the important task of cleaning their feathers of this appalling dust.

Tika watched them for a while then turned to totter between Jakri and Navan towards Storm. She spoke to the sea Dragon and to Willow, draped along his neck, then struggled back towards Sket. He sat propped against the wall, his face as pale as her own and his heavily bandaged left hand cradled across his chest.

'Let me sit here for a while,' Tika begged Jakri. She caught Sket's eye. 'If there's a chance of some tea, we'd both really appreciate it.'

Jakri gently lowered Tika alongside Sket even as Navan went to the fire to make their tea. To Tika's relief, Sket's familiar grin had appeared when she looked at him next.

'Never seem to make enough tea do they my lady?'

She stretched to reach his right hand with hers. 'We make a matching pair,' she said. 'Does your hand hurt?'

Sket's grin stayed in place. 'Armsmen expect to get bits chopped off. A couple of fingers is nothing.' He saw her sceptical expression and squeezed her hand. 'Really, I swear by the stars it is of no importance. It might have made a bit of difference if it had been my sword hand, but this won't bother me, I promise my lady.'

By the time Tika lay down in her blankets again she was exhausted. She fell instantly asleep and slept half the day away. She woke to find everyone else rolled in their blankets except for Navan, who sat quietly beside her.

'Would you like a drink?' he asked softly.

'Yes please.' Tika tried to push herself up when Navan went to the low burning fire to pour her some tea. She bit her lip as she moved awkwardly, twisting the burn on her chest and causing a jolt of fiery agony.

Navan handed her the bowl, sliding his arm under her shoulders to raise her a little higher.

'Navan, I haven't told anyone what happened yet. Can I tell you?'

Navan's arm tightened briefly. 'I don't expect I'll understand,' he warned her.

She spoke softly, recounting all she could remember.

'Did you actually see Valesh?' Navan asked when she paused to sip her cooling tea. He felt a shiver ripple through her.

'Yes. She was a huge shape, constantly changing, but not quite solid. If she had reached a more solid state, I doubt she could have been defeated. I understand now why Taseen said they were called monstrous. She was like something from your worst nightmare multiplied a thousand times over. Because her shape shifted from one aspect to another, it was difficult to keep track of the threads of her being. Seela gave me time to do that.'

'How did those scales get inside Sket's pack? It was fastened tight when the gijan brought you back to us.'

Tika shook her head. 'I have no idea. I think he was unconscious from the time Seela died.'

'As were you,' Navan began, but Tika shook her head again.

'I was dragged out of my body by Valesh's death pangs. At least, I think that's what must have happened. Perhaps Taseen might know. My body was with Sket, but my mind went to a very strange place.'

She twisted to look closely into Navan's face. 'Did Mayla ever speak of places Between?'

Navan frowned. 'I was taken from the women's quarters at seven and I spoke only rarely to her after that. I don't remember such a phrase.'

Tika sighed. 'It was a grey place, something like the Domain of the Delvers in form: tunnels leading all ways. Seela spoke to me there. She said there are many such places but that particular one was the place Between life and death which is why she was able to be there for a very brief time.'

Navan listened in silence.

'She said I must hurry from that place, but I couldn't feel the thread that links me to my body. That's what makes me think I was pulled there by Valesh. Seela then told me to follow Sket's mind but I couldn't find him. I know now that he was unconscious, so his mind was lost to me anyway.'

Navan pushed a pack under Tika's shoulders and went to fetch more tea for her.

'I went down so many tunnels Navan, and all so strange.'

She rested the tea bowl on her lap and reached for his hand. 'All of them ended in a sort of sealed window. Many were dark and I could see nothing. But one showed me Hargon.'

Navan gave an exclamation of shock. 'Hargon?' he echoed.

Tika nodded. 'He looked very sick. He was sitting near the sea Dragons' caves and he was speaking to Mist. Then the window grew dark and I saw no more.'

She sat silent for a few moments before continuing. 'I could tell that I had been too long from my body, that in fact my body would die soon if I couldn't get back and then I wouldn't be able to get back at all. I think I started to panic, rushing down every tunnel I saw. Then I smelt mint, like Ren, Sket and I did at the coast – do you remember? It seemed as good a chance as any so I tried to follow the smell and it led me to Sket. I remember hurting and knowing I was in my body, although I wasn't sure if Sket was alive. Then Leaf was there.'

Tika seemed to relax once she had told Navan all she could of that time and she soon drifted back to sleep. Navan tucked the blankets around her and sat watching through the remainder of the night. He found much of what she had told him beyond his ability to comprehend but he recognised three things clearly. One was how terrified she had been, both when she was trying to unmake Valesh and when she found herself in the place Between. The second was that despite her fear, her courage had carried her through. The third thing was what an incredibly powerful mind was contained within this small person.

Next morning the sky had cleared enough for them to venture out. They came back coated with a layer of fine reddish brown dust but the wind no longer hurled granules of grit with the almost lethal intent it had previously. Gan fetched more water, pouring it from pail to pail through a cloth to remove the dirt, but Jakri told him not to bother. The Wendlan Mage placed his hand in the water, murmured a few words and smiled.

'It is pure now,' he said. 'A very basic spell.'

He was surprised that neither Ren nor Maressa had known of such a thing and repeated the words to them. They were as thrilled as children when they discovered it really was that simple to ensure safe drinking water. They were all concerned about their rapidly dwindling supplies. Storm ventured outside cautiously, studying the sky still streaked with angry colours. It was some time before Farn wondered where his friend had gone. Navan and Maressa hurried out just in time to see Storm flying towards them. He gave them four stout fish with an air of modest pride. His offering was received with delight, especially from Khosa and Akomi.

That evening, sitting round their comforting fire and with three of Ren's glow stones cheering them further, Gan offered his opinion that they would be able to travel the next day.

'Yes, but where?' asked Maressa. 'Olam's still in Wendla. We don't know where Grek is. Should we go to Harbour City to help the people there? Or try to find Namolos?'

They sat in silence considering the choices Maressa offered them. Eventually Tika realised they were all staring at her.

'Why must I be the one to choose?' she asked irritably. She sighed. 'To be honest, I know where we should go but I'm not keen on the idea.'

Farn leaned over her shoulder to press his cheek against hers in sympathy.

'We have to go back to the desert. Valesh's brother is much damaged, nowhere near as strong as she was. But he is still powerful enough to cause plenty of difficulty. He must be unmade too.'

Next morning they gathered their belongings and prepared to leave their haven. Jakri had decreed their travelling was to be gentle, no long flights to weary his patients. Although they protested that they were well enough, both Sket and Tika were still far from fit. Sket was bothered by a continuing dull headache which annoyed him more than the tingling in his hand, while Tika would not admit just how badly her burns still hurt.

They were all outside when Brin reared erect, staring to the north east. All they could see was a dark shape flying towards them at considerable speed. Suddenly the gijan wailed and threw themselves flat on the ground, clouds of dust rising around them, their wings half extended.

There was no mistaking what she was as she landed gracefully in front of them. Her scales sparkled even in this diffuse sunlight and her great wings gleamed black over her shoulders. The blue sash at her waist contrasted with the dark blue of her under feathers. She bowed, her wings spreading on the ground behind her.

'I am the Elder, Flute. I seek the one named Tika.'

Chapter Thirty

Orla was revelling in her new situation. She had summoned the leaders of the desert warriors – armsmen were not needed in such a secure place as the City of the Domes but there were always men and women to be found who relished a life in arms. The desert fighter Hadjay had reported back to her on the treacherous deaths of his brothers and their failure to kill the strange visitors. He had been incandescent with rage and sorrow: so easy to manipulate. Hadjay, by Orla's command, sent for the nearest tribal leaders. Usually, any such dealings were conducted through the intermediaries of the Keepers but this time, resplendent in uniform, Orla herself had met them in the Dome of Assembly.

The warriors had knelt before her, their foreheads touching the floor. She gave them a slightly slanted version of events and was thrilled to see how quickly these fierce warriors went from abject awe to bloodthirsty eagerness. She produced maps of such detail they murmured in astonishment and nodded when she indicated the route they should take to Harbour City. Orla knew nothing of Harbour City, seeing it only on the several occasions the Ship over-flew the planet prior to Kertiss deciding where they would land.

Even on magnified scans it had seemed a small place of modest primitive buildings – except for the great fortress on its eastern promontory. The desert men could tell Orla nothing of the land of Malesh. They raided only a few leagues below their desert for the sheer sport of it; they had no ambitions towards conquest and governance. But Orla did. She had had plenty of years to experiment in her laboratories beneath the greatest of the three Domes and had been content to do so until the last twenty years or so.

She had begun to dream in her brief periods of sleep. To begin with she had disregarded them, but when they persisted she found herself thinking of them while she worked. Orla didn't discuss them with Kertiss: they rarely spoke to each other. She didn't know what he thought of her and didn't care. He was the older of the two of them, and male, and even in the enlightened times in which they'd been born her stupid parents had lavished their love, praise and, more importantly, the very best education they could buy on him.

She had worked through computers at home and at the inadequate school to which she was sent, stealing Kertiss's access codes to keep up with all he studied. She had turned her back on her parents the day she achieved the highest marks in her graduation classes and was immediately offered her pick of research jobs. Kertiss got a low percentage of marks in his graduation examinations and still their parents threw a party to celebrate their wonder boy's achievement.

She lost track of him for years and then found, somewhat to her horror, that they were on the same training programme for captaincies of the new bio Ships. After some thought, it seemed sensible to choose to do a joint captaincy – she knew she would be able to manipulate him even if he did believe he was the senior officer. But they had been rejected by the board. Kertiss had shrugged it off but Orla couldn't believe she had failed to get something on which she had set her heart.

They'd been crossing the middle concourse of the bio Ship docks when sirens sounded their warnings. She had grabbed Kertiss, pulling him against the tide of panicking workers and tugged him towards the nearest Ship. They'd swung round a corner straight into Captain Mazan. Orla didn't hesitate. She hit the woman in the stomach, kneed her face as she doubled over and shoved her into the path of a rushing crowd of workers. Orla hauled Kertiss with her and jumped into Star Singer's door.
The Ship was young, far too highly strung and emotional, but he had got them to Kel-Harat – a whole world she would make her own. And now she felt the time had finally arrived to fulfil this ambition.

The tribal leaders had gone to gather their warriors throughout the eastern desert and Orla promised supplies and invincibility. She had quietly manufactured several small psionic disrupters modelled on her personal one, carried by all the crews of bio

Ships. Now she wondered about some of the other weapons still on board Star Singer. Days passed when Orla was preoccupied with reports diligently sent back to her from the first wave of invading warriors. She had been working to replicate the small hand communicators as well, which had lain, long forgotten, on a shelf in one of her laboratories. It had proved an impossible task and Orla cursed the brain back on their home world who had so cunningly made it precisely so that it could not be duplicated. Their damned righteous policy of non interference.

Orla knew the desert men were moving south, band after band, as those from further in the great desert followed the call to arms as they received it. It occurred to Orla that she hadn't seen Kertiss for many days. She went briskly through to his section of the underground complex and couldn't find him. She frowned, then her brow cleared. He may be in a regeneration tank. She palmed the door panel and went quietly into the room. Lights flashed and flickered in a steady rhythmic pattern monitoring the status of Kertiss's body.

Orla walked round the tank slowly, watching the indicators. She turned to the control panel and studied it for a while. Then she smiled. She reached out and with one finger flicked a switch upwards. She depressed two buttons on the lower panel and moved back to the tank. Orla patted the lid.

'Sleep long and deep, brother dear.'

She closed the door behind her and turned left to return to her quarters. She hesitated and swung back, striding down the corridor towards the Ship's holding chamber. She was several paces into the chamber when she stopped in her tracks. Her gaze went at once to the roof: it was closed, so presumably the Ship was in the Dome. An equipment malfunction? Surely none of the Keepers knew how to activate the lift, even if they might know of the upper access point?

Her soft-soled native shoes made little noise as Orla walked up the ramp. She stared. The Ship was not there. Slowly, Orla looked round the Dome, hairs prickling on the back of her neck. Empty plinths lined the circular walls, but there was no sign of a single statue. Who could have moved the huge figures without triggering any of the alarms Kertiss had put in place? Orla's stunned mind began to click into action. It would have taken a lot of man power, a lot of time, to carry the great statues from the Dome. And the Ship – had he been towed out somehow? And when had this happened? Damn stupid Kertiss and his inefficiency! She ignored the inconvenient thought that maybe she should have checked his work herself.

She heard the sound of running feet, the slap of leather sandals against the stone floor, and she looked towards the Dome's main entrance. Momentarily she wondered if she should stay, but her hand rested on the butt of her personal psionic disrupter which she had taken to wearing constantly over the last days. Three figures appeared opposite Orla, three Keepers, who continued to run towards her. She waited until they arrived, breathless, to bow before her.

'Monsters, Lady Survivor,' one of the Keepers gasped, careful even in his distraught state to keep his eyes lowered.

'Monsters?' Orla allowed amusement to colour her tone.

All three Keepers nodded vigorously. Another glanced nervously at the empty plinth beside Orla.

'The statues – they were alive. They have killed many in the Ring Complex, Lady Survivor.'

'The statues were alive,' Orla repeated, her disbelief plain to hear. 'Even should that be true, why would they kill anyone?'

The third Keeper, who had remained bent over in an attempt to regain some breath, straightened. 'They seemed to be hunting the gijan Lady.'

'Gijan?' Orla remembered some experiments she had run on the strange little animals. They all died extremely quickly, so she had abandoned them. But why would anyone want the gijan? She didn't believe for one moment that the statues had come alive – such superstitious nonsense these primitives believed!

'Never mind,' she said to the three Keepers. 'Go and see if any are still here – gijan I mean. Any you find, bring them to me.'

She lifted a hand in dismissal and the Keepers bowed again before turning to trudge back across the vast Dome. Orla waited until they disappeared and moved to the ramp to return below. She would consider this. It was evident to her that someone had planned and executed the theft of the Ship and the statues, arranging some sort of disturbance in the Ring Complex to distract any attention from what was happening in the Dome.

Something caught her eye as she began to descend the ramp. She retraced her steps and bent to pick up the object half hidden behind the plinth. It was a feather, sooty black and as long as her arm. She drew it between her fingers and smiled. Very clever. Whoever had stolen the Ship and the statues was indeed thorough in their planning, executing and laying of false clues. But they would be no match for her. Carrying the feather, she went swiftly down the ramp, closing it behind her. Without a glance at the space the Ship had occupied for so long, she went through the corridors to one of her laboratories and put the feather on the work surface. Orla switched on the power to various units and then sat at the work surface, giving the feather a close visual examination.

It looked like a normal feather but from what bird? The largest birds she had worked on here on Kel-Harat were the huge carrion birds of the desert. Some of the water birds in the valley had large wings but, as far as she could recall, none were black. She dropped a tiny spot of a solution onto a section of the feather and waited. The colour was natural: there was no reaction such as would indicate the use of a dye. Orla cut two small sections and placed them inside the units. She nodded to herself and placed the feather in a drawer. She would go through to the Dome of Knowledge and frighten the students while the units analysed and quantified the sections.

When the Lady Survivor appeared in the Dome of Knowledge the students working there froze in their places. The Survivors appeared once a year when students gathered in the Dome of Assembly, and they were regarded with terrified awe. To have one of them suddenly in their midst was frightening and shocking. Who knew what happened to some of the students who were called to work in the Survivors secret quarters under the Great Dome? A few returned to the Ring Complex, mindless and docile. Most were never seen again.

Hezwa glanced up as the usual low murmur ceased all through the Dome. Her eyes met Orla's and her spine felt filled with ice. She refused to show her fear, rising from her chair beside a student and moving across the floor of the Dome to bow to the Lady Survivor.

'Lady, this is an unexpected honour. How may I serve?'

Orla merely glanced at the Keeper of Lore. She had no idea of her name; she rarely bothered with such trivialities.

'I would like to see any texts concerning the statues in the Great Dome,' she replied calmly.

Hezwa bowed again and called across to a senior student to fetch several volumes she named for him. He hurried to do her bidding and she turned back to find Orla studying her more closely.

'I heard there was a disturbance in the Ring Complex last night.' Orla watched Hezwa's reaction as clinically as she would observe one of her laboratory specimens.

Hezwa struggled, and succeeded, in maintaining a calm relaxed composure. 'Indeed there was Lady. I heard that some drunken tribesmen ran amok. There were several deaths I understand, including Keepers. No students were involved; the tribesmen were unable to penetrate the Ring as far as their dormitories.'

'And you witnessed this – drunken brawl?'

'No Lady. I was visiting a friend in the city. I returned here at dawn and it was only then that I heard what had happened.'

Orla strolled to one of the desks and stared absently over a student's shoulder. Hezwa could see the boy trembling even from where she stood. Orla wandered back.

'I would see the bodies of the dead,' she announced. 'Tell one of your students to escort me to where they are.'

The students within hearing lost even more colour. Hezwa bowed.

'I will take you Lady. The dead are in the mortuary, the wounded in the infirmary.'

'Wounded?' Orla asked sharply. Hezwa spread her hands. 'I heard there were two still living Lady, but that there was little hope of their recovering.'

'You will take me to the infirmary at once.'

Hezwa nodded, exchanged a quick glance with another Keeper who had prudently stayed half hidden by a book stack, and led the Lady Survivor down to the tunnel leading beneath the Sanctuary. Orla was mildly intrigued: she hadn't been this far from the Great Dome in centuries she realised, not since this system had been excavated in fact. The two women, one native to Kel-Harat and in her fifties, the other from a planet galaxies distant and, thanks to regeneration treatment allied with genetic modification, near the end of her second millennium, were of similar height and build, and now they matched strides along the passages.

Hezwa had seen some examples of Survivor technology and had a healthy respect for their system of spying throughout the Sanctuary. But she was also fully aware that neither Orla nor Kertiss had the slightest talent for, or belief in, the mental powers known to exist in this world. Her father had told her there was once a tradition of men and women strong in such gifts, and held in high regard by the Valley people and the surrounding nomadic tribes. Since a time before the appearance of the strange Ship and the two Survivors, such talents were hidden though, and taught secretly within families. Hezwa had been born to such a family and she had recognised instantly that, of the party of visitors shown round the Domes a while back, three of them at least were also strong in mental powers.

They reached a junction where three other tunnels met in a circular space and Hezwa chose the one on the right. The floor rose and they emerged into a corridor busy with younger students moving to different classes who paused, staring at the woman with Keeper Hezwa. One whispered to another and word quickly spread that a Survivor was within the Ring Complex. Hezwa strode on, ignoring the way the whispers swept around them and students pressed away from her and her companion. She was glad to leave the students behind as they reached a quieter section where the infirmary was situated. Hezwa led Orla up a wide flight of stairs and into an airy sick room. Many tall narrow windows opened onto the Sanctuary and the three Domes in its centre.

Three of the twelve beds were occupied by apparently sleeping patients but a healer rose from a table and came towards the visitors. Hezwa touched his mind, warning him to remain as calm and impassive as he could. He bowed to Orla.

'I wish to see those injured in last night's troubles,' she said coldly.

He bowed again and led her away from the large room to a smaller one along the landing. The door opened as they approached and two young men came out, carrying a stretcher with a shrouded figure upon it. They passed Orla without a glance and she followed the healer and Hezwa into the room. Several healers were bent over a body on a high bed. The scene resembled a butcher's stall rather than a place of healing. As Orla drew near, a man shook his head and stepped away.

'No good,' he said. 'He's gone.'

He saw Orla standing at the foot of the bed and could only stare. Hezwa introduced Shiro, the most senior healer in the City, to the Lady Survivor. Shiro didn't look at Hezwa, simply waited for the Survivor to speak.

'I would see what injuries your patient received,' she said.

Shiro gestured to a young woman to remove the sheet that had been drawn up over the body. Orla flinched inwardly although outwardly she was like stone. A very young man lay naked on the bed. Four lines ran down from his shoulders to his groin. Orla could see his lungs through the smashed ribs, coils of intestines on his thighs. Her mind went back to the gijan: four digits on hands and feet, with talons for nails. But gijan were scarcely as tall as her waist – they could not have inflicted this damage. She lifted her gaze from the corpse to Shiro's face.

'What did this?' she asked. 'I have yet to see weapons cause injuries like this.'

Shiro regarded her steadily. 'I didn't see the attack. All those who did claim to witness it, describe giant humans with wings, like to the statues within the Dome of the Singer.' He did not add that many had also seen a great shape rising from the courtyard partly enclosed by the Domes, rising and then moving silently to the south east, blotting out stars as it passed.

Orla's mind raced: how could the statues have done such a thing – were they mechanical, from some long lost technological past of this world? She gave Shiro a brusque nod and turned on her heel. Hezwa hastened to escort the Lady Survivor back beneath the Sanctuary. Waiting nervously near the entrance to the Dome of Knowledge stood the student Hezwa had directed to fetch the books Orla required. Hezwa took them from his arms and continued walking to the restricted area which ended at the Survivors' quarters. The student fled, grateful not to have been expected to attend the Lady Survivor any further.

Hezwa had never been this far into the Survivors' territory and when they turned a corner to see a solid door blocking the way, she slowed to a halt. She had no more desire than her students to go further, the glowing lights on a panel beside the door made her very afraid. Her people, the Vintavoy, who had lived within the Valley since before the desert was made, had seen the Survivors use their little flashing boxes and their oddly shaped machines to wreak havoc on human bodies. They had no understanding of what they were or how they functioned, only in what they could do. Hezwa held out the pile of books and Orla, taken by surprise, automatically accepted them. Hezwa bowed and turned away, striding back round the corner before Orla could order her to stay.

Orla was well aware of the fear she inspired in the natives and rather enjoyed the sensation. She smiled as she palmed the side panel and the door swung silently open. Orla spent most of the day studying the books Hezwa had given her and had to admit to a faint sense of unease. The books told the history of the final battle of the Elder Races and the description of the gijan Elders undoubtedly matched the statues that had stood in the Great Dome.

But she could not comprehend such a thing as a statue suddenly coming to life. She understood the practice of cryogenics, but that was accomplished only with the use of complicated technology: these statues had been free standing, nothing connecting them to any form of life support systems. She picked at some food left ready for her by one of the students who had become vacant-minded menials and worked for her and Kertiss as domestic droids would have done at home.

She lay down, her thoughts circling round and round, and as she had expected, and hoped, she dreamed. To begin with, her sleeping body trembled: he was so angry! The man she dreamed of was the most handsome creature, male or female, that she had ever seen. His skin was darker than her own and his eyes usually shone with loving kindness when he gazed at her. But he saw the thoughts in her mind, of the Elder statues, and how she was trying to understand the meaning of their disappearance. The loss of the Ship was insignificant – he had never seemed to appreciate exactly of what importance the Ship might be. His rage tore at her mind and she sobbed in her sleep. When his fury became more controlled he spoke less harshly to Orla, suggesting what she might do. In her relief and gratitude she promised to follow his every wish.

During the next days Hadjay returned, reporting a setback in the invasion of Malesh. He told Orla of the very ground shivering just beyond the desert – in places, strong enough to cause buildings to fall. He'd heard the earthquakes had been far worse further south. But he also told of strange fighters coming from the direction of the coast who had inflicted considerable losses on his men. Their skins were golden, not as dark as that of the desert men, and they fought together in such a way as Hadjay had no experience of. They were led by giants, he reported, who wore black shiny armour and tall purple plumes in their helmets. Orla suggested they were armsmen from Harbour City but Hadjay doubted this: they did not resemble Maleshan people any more than they were like the Qwah.

'Can you defeat these new armsmen?' Orla asked bluntly when Hadjay fell silent.

His eyes were fierce. 'We will die to the last man, Lady, but I think they will beat us. More and more of them come from the east. As well as the leaders in black armour there are men among them in plain dress, without weapons or armour. They are always protected by the ones with plumed helmets. I think they are wise men who give commands to the warriors.'

Orla, who had never given any importance to mental powers, was inclined to agree with Hadjay's reasoning, although she felt a tiny pang of unease at the back of her mind.

'The desert men can continue south or withdraw,' she decided. 'I have a mind to travel north.'

Hadjay's eyes widened in surprise.

'You will pick your best men – at least twenty five of them – and in two days I will go with you. Northwards.'

She hadn't really known what she would say until the words were spoken. Having made her announcement she would follow it through. While Hadjay arranged horses, supplies and men, Orla chose the weapons she would take, putting them into an old survey pack while keeping her personal disruptor at her belt. She recorded her intentions in one of the units in her bedchamber, then summoned the empty-headed menial staff. Clearly and simply she ordered them to continue maintaining the Survivors' quarters, feeding the specimens in her laboratory and collecting food as usual from the main entrance near the junction with the Dome of Knowledge.

She emerged above ground in the great expanse of the Sanctuary as the moon rose, carrying two packs. Hadjay would have taken them but she insisted they remain with her. Accordingly, he strapped them behind the saddle of the horse a tribesman held ready for her. In a double column with Orla and Hadjay at its head, the riders moved out of the Sanctuary, through the Ring Complex and past each circle gate of the City.

Orla glanced back once, a sudden nervousness making her hands tighten in her horse's mane. She had never been this far outside the Domes since her arrival here and she looked up at the rounded shapes still visible in the light of the half moon. Resolutely she faced forward again and imagined the man in her dreams applauded her courage.

Chapter Thirty-One

Tika was irritated that she was still unsteady on her feet but Navan moved up beside her, his arm and shoulder unobtrusively supporting her as she moved towards the gijan Elder. Sket was at her left side, nearly as wobbly as she was but refusing to abandon his post as her personal Guard. Tika didn't dare risk bowing – she suspected she would end up flat on her face – so she merely inclined her head and hoped she wasn't offending the Elder.

'I am Tika, soul bond of Farn.' Her voice at least sounded strong enough and Farn's chin rested comfortingly on the top of her head.

Gan approached from beyond Navan and they saw the Elder stood eye to eye with him, if she wasn't fractionally taller. But Flute had eyes only for Tika at the moment. She stared down at the small human. But was she entirely human? What did those silvered eyes mean? Clearly she was weak, physically and more so mentally, and Flute was unsurprised. To take on one of the monstrous Children and destroy her was more than the Elder Races had been able to achieve.

'I would know of your trial with Valesh.' Flute paused. 'Shall we sit more comfortably? I see you are not recovered.'

Knowing how the three young gijan never sat on the ground, Tika wondered if Flute intended to remain standing, towering over them all even more. Flute read her thoughts and, with a smile, sat gracefully on the ground, both her enormous wings swept to one side. Everyone followed Flute's example and it was as Ren and Maressa sat close to Sket that Flute saw the three gijan still flat on their faces. She stared at them, then at Tika.

'Who are these gijan children?' she asked, her voice taking on a low melodic tone. 'Rise and answer me.'

Leaf was on her feet first, followed by Piper and lastly Willow. Their expressions reminded Tika of the cowed little faces of the slaves she had first met in the City of the Domes.

'I brought them from the Domes,' Tika said before Flute could say more. 'They said they were litter mates, so instead of bringing one as I'd planned, I brought all three.'

Flute stared at Tika again, then back at the gijan. 'They have their wings,' she said.

Tika shrugged, wincing at the pull of her healing burn. 'I was shown what I should do to release their wings but I'm afraid I didn't know the songs that should be sung at such a time.'

'Your names children?'

One by one the three stepped one pace forward, bowed and gave Flute their names. Her eyes narrowed then she nodded, looking back at Tika.

'They gave you their lives?' she asked.

Tika remembered how each gijan when they'd recovered from the agony of having their wings released, had given her their names followed by the words "my life is yours".

'They did,' she agreed. 'And they have redeemed that vow – they found Sket and me trapped inside the rock. And you,' she continued more boldly than she felt. 'I was told there were no Elders in this world.'

Flute leaned forward, resting her elbows on her knees. 'Two hundred and twenty one of us were suspended in time.' Her head, covered with dark curls which tangled down her spine, tilted one side then the other, a glint of amusement lighting her eyes.

Tika frowned: Flute was teasing her – what did she mean? 'The Dome,' she exclaimed. 'The statues in the Dome!'

She was filled with both horror and sorrow at the idea of this magnificently beautiful creature being somehow frozen in motionless silence since the final battle a thousand years past. Flute studied her clasped hands.

'We searched for the young gijan when you released us from Valesh's spell.'

Tika put two and two together and guessed that the Elders must have been freed when Valesh was unmade. Flute glanced up briefly, her eyes blazing.

'We killed those humans who tried to stop us.' She dropped her gaze again. 'The children have been taken to safety. Also, the Ship, Star Singer. He too is free.'

Ren stiffened. In what context was the Elder using the word

"free"?

'Singer was not destroyed?' he asked urgently.

Flute looked at him for the first time and was startled to see his eyes were silvered like Tika's.

'Destroyed? Of course not. He flew as we did. He said he was going south east to the island of Wendla.'

Tika and Maressa both found they were in tears, to Flute's consternation.

'Was that wrong of him? Why do you weep?'

'No, no.' Tika wiped inelegantly at her face with her sleeve. 'He said he couldn't fly anymore. He must be trying to reach Star Flower.'

'There is another Ship?'

'There are several I think.'

Khosa stalked towards the Elder Flute carrying a mouse in her teeth. She offered it to the Elder and sat primly while Akomi hurried to join her. To the companions' surprise, Flute reached a talon to stroke between Khosa's ears, then did the same to Akomi.

'It is long indeed since I have even seen one of your kind, little sister.' Flute spoke simultaneously aloud and in their minds. 'I have missed the company of your folk.'

Khosa arched her back beneath Flute's hand and rubbed against her knees. Akomi was shyer until Flute encouraged him to press closer. Now it was Flute's turn to weep. She held both cats in her arms for a moment, her face buried in orange and mottled brown furry backs.

'A bowl of tea would be welcome,' Sket said loudly.

Gan laughed and began to unpack one of their bags while Navan bent to rekindle their fire. Tika and Sket, followed by Farn, made their way across to the Elder. She looked up as they approached. It was a touch disconcerting to discover they were barely taller than Flute even sitting on the ground as she was. Flute looked over Tika's shoulder and saw the young gijan perched on Brin's back.

'They must begin their training quickly,' she said. 'I have summoned one of my litter mates. He was one of our best tutors of the young. I think those three may have difficulties.'

Tika nodded. 'We have let them do more or less as they please I'm afraid, but when we have scolded them they have just flown away. Seela,' Tika faltered. 'Seela was the only one of us who had any real influence over them.'

'Seela?'

Sket's arm was round Tika's waist and it was Farn who sent the Elder a mental picture of the huge purple Dragon Seela who had died to give Tika the time to unmake Valesh. The Elder hooked both Tika and Sket closer, aware through Farn of the grief that still filled all this company.

'We had planned to travel on, when you came.' Tika managed to control her tears yet again.

'Perhaps you would consider staying here until Rainbow can reach us? I think there is much we must talk of before I can advise you – if my advice would be of any help.'

'Oh it would.' Tika felt the reassurance from this ancient Elder that she was used to feeling in Fenj's company, and she was so very tired of carrying all the responsibility of this strange journey.

Sket nodded his approval and Flute suddenly grinned at him.

'I have yet to taste tea again – I have drunk water only since I left the Domes, and it is a thousand years since my last bowl.'

Sket was appalled: he couldn't survive without frequent doses of the stuff. Flute's laughter rang out across the ruined farmyard and heads turned to see what caused the Elder's amusement. She got to her feet, Khosa and Akomi marching in front of her. She leaned forward to touch her brow to Farn's and his eyes whirred: clearly she said something to his mind. Flute took Sket's left arm near the elbow and Tika's right hand and walked them slowly back to the barn. She paused to speak to both Brin and Storm but paid no attention to the young gijan pretending, Tika was fairly sure, to be asleep on Brin's back.

They talked all day; at least, the companions did while Flute listened with close attention. Akomi seemed to find comfort in the presence of the Elder and tried his best to keep her lap to himself. Jakri spoke of how his Emperor and Wendlan Mages had been aware of the machinations of the Maleshan witch Vorna long before anyone other than Taseen had suspicions of her here. Ren described Drogoya, and how Cho Petak was bringing ruin to his land. Maressa told of life in Vagrantia and the strange illness that had struck her people as well as those of Ren's Drogoya.

Gan explained what he had pieced together of his people's arrival in the lands near Spine Mountains.

Tika had the most to tell, from the time of her running away from Hargon's slavery to the present time. It was mid afternoon before the Elder had heard of all their trials and tribulations and she suggested a rest: Tika and Sket were almost asleep where they sat. Navan was worrying about finding food. They had intended to move on today precisely because their supplies were so low. Storm rattled his wings.

'I can fetch fish again for you,' he suggested eagerly.

'I'll come too, but I'll wait on the shore!' Navan got to his feet and went to climb on Storm's back.

'We must find somewhere we can reprovision, Lady Flute,' Gan said when Navan and Storm had departed.

She nodded. 'I understand. It will be best to go north, towards the desert again. There was less damage from the earthquakes that way.'

Gan stooped to pull a blanket over Tika's shoulders. He moved closer to the Elder.

'If you want Lady Tika to fight the Bound One in the desert, there is no way I will permit her to do any such thing while she is so very weak.'

Farn's eyes suddenly flashed. 'I will not allow it either,' he said firmly.

Elder Flute didn't answer; instead she rose swiftly and stood at the open side of the barn. Gan could see a dark shape flying fast from the north, directly for them.

'Rainbow,' was all Flute said.

The Elder landed beside Flute and they embraced, the newcomer's dark violet under-feathers briefly visible when he folded them against his back. When he moved into the barn it was immediately apparently that he had listened as he flew, through his litter mate's mind, to the companions' stories. He walked straight to Brin, raising a hand to the crimson Dragon's face.

'We feared all of your Kindred were lost, brother. How glad I am to see those fears were unfounded.'

Rainbow went from Brin to Maressa, stooping over her to greet her gently. He clasped Gan's shoulder.

'We have a thousand years of information to catch up on

Captain Gan, and many new people to learn of.'

He had words of greeting for Ren and Jakri and then stood staring down at Tika and Sket. Even though they were both asleep, the Elder bowed deeply, his wings flaring out over the floor behind him. He straightened, his hand reaching to Farn's scarred neck. Farn's eyes whirred pearl and sapphire as Rainbow spoke to his mind. Finally Rainbow turned again to Brin and said something in the trilling language of the gijan. He waited a moment and repeated himself, his tone now cold and sharp.

The young gijan, with obvious reluctance, slid from Brin's back and stood before Rainbow. Both Jakri and Ren noticed their glances in Tika's direction and moved to sit discreetly blocking Tika from their view.

'We will use the common tongue', said Rainbow, his voice much milder. 'It is too rude to use a language others do not comprehend.'

Leaf raised her chin to stare up at the Elder – her head barely reached much above his waist. Rainbow held her stare.

'These good friends busy themselves preparing food and drink,' Rainbow continued. 'It would seem you have no part to play in such work.' His head tilted to one side as his words were met with stubborn silence. He sighed. 'It is late in the day but I command you to fly. Circle above this place and let me judge your abilities.'

The three gijan children hurried to the barn's open side, clearly relieved, but they were brought to a halt by Rainbow's next words.

'I have commanded you to fly. And you will fly until I command you to land once more.'

There was a brief silence during which Flute settled by the fire, her wings swept to one side. Gan was pouring tea into bowls for Flute and Rainbow. He smiled broadly as they took the bowls and inhaled the fragrant steam blissfully. He suspected Sket at least would lose his sanity should he have to forego his precious tea for a ten day and yet these Elders had survived a thousand years since their last taste of the stuff. He waited while they savoured their drinks.

'Will the gijan not land somewhere out of sight?' he asked, refilling their bowls. 'I know my recruits would creep off somewhere, to avoid such an order.'

Rainbow smiled, small pointed teeth briefly revealed. 'I have spelled the air. They can only fly within its limits.'

Gan digested Rainbow's comment. Jakri chuckled and Maressa nodded. She would never have thought to manipulate air to form a cage but she could see how it might be done. Khosa approached, carrying another mouse corpse to Rainbow. No one had noticed what Flute had done with her gift but they now watched Rainbow take the mouse from Khosa, tilt his head back and swallow the mouse with scarcely a gulp. Ren closed his own mouth with a snap that jarred his teeth. Khosa sat facing Rainbow and mind spoke the company.

'You have not yet been told of Namolos.'

Gan bit his lip. Tika hadn't mentioned either Grek or Namolos: was it this arrogant Kephi queen's place to do so? But Khosa was already explaining that Namolos was another Survivor, living on an island in the western sea. Namolos had somehow altered himself, or his mind at least, and was now one of the strongest users of power Khosa had heard of.

'How far is the distance that you could mind speak each other?' she asked Rainbow.

He shrugged. 'Flute called me from here when I was on the eastern desert coast. There was no difficulty in our reaching each other.'

'That is further than I could ever manage,' Maressa admitted. 'I can contact a mage in Harbour City – that is perhaps twenty, thirty leagues? But I cannot far speak much more than that. A Wendlan Mage – Jakri's mother Oniko – speaks from Wendla to Harbour City and that is the furthest of any I've known.'

Navan and Storm came back with fish and were introduced to Rainbow. The Elder spoke for some time to the sea Dragon, questioning him about the strange healing worked on Mist by the silver Dragon of Talvo. By the time the fish was baking, Tika and Sket had roused again. Rainbow and Flute then watched closely while Jakri and Maressa changed the dressings on their injuries. Farn as always became disturbed when Sket's hand was uncovered revealing the loss of his fingers. Even Tika wasn't sure why such injuries distressed her soul bond to the extent they did.

Flute lifted Tika's wrist and studied the palm of the hand. Rainbow put a talon against the curled in fingers, gently trying to pull them straight. Jakri watched.

'I was unsure whether to bind them flat,' he confessed. 'The burn was to the bone.'

When the Elders stared at him in some surprise, he raised a shoulder in a half shrug. 'The gijan children healed her this much, but they said they could do no more.'

There was a flurry of tension between the two Elders before Rainbow replied.

'They should not have even attempted healing. I understand why they did of course, but with no training they could have caused even worse damage.'

He settled cross-legged at Tika's side, cradling the back of her hand in his own.

'Will you trust me, little Lady Tika?' Black eyes stared into green and Tika nodded, not trusting herself to speak.

'They have merely covered the bones with skin,' he explained gently. 'There is no flesh, no muscle. I can mend that.'

Tika nodded again. Rainbow smiled and Tika's eyes closed immediately. The Elder cupped his free hand over her burnt palm and bowed his head. The companions felt power building around the Elder and Tika and sat, scarcely daring to breathe. Time ceased to exist as Rainbow sat, his body relaxed, his head bowed, beside Tika. At last his head came up and his eyes opened. Tika opened her eyes at the same instant, looking first at Rainbow in awed recognition, then down at her hand. She exclaimed and held it out for her friends to see.

It had a sheen of soreness about it but the skin was plumped out and her fingers straightened and flexed with a certain stiffness but clearly without causing her pain. Rainbow gave Sket a sad smile.

'I cannot remake what is lost.'

Sket grinned. 'I keep telling everyone, especially my Lady, two fingers more or less is no bother to me.'

'Erm, Elder Rainbow,' Maressa began. 'It is dark outside.'

Rainbow nodded. 'But only just. A little longer will not hurt.'

Tika gave Ren a questioning glance and he murmured an explanation.

'There is another burn.' Rainbow pointed at Tika's chest.

'It is well healed,' Jakri told him.

'I would still see it.'

Jakri unbuttoned Tika's shirt and loosened the bandage he'd wrapped right round her chest. Again the Elder bent forward, cupping his hand over the still-angry burn. When he removed his hand there was an oval scar which looked as though it was from a long-healed wound.

'Thank you,' was all Tika could say.

'Food's ready,' Navan reminded them, and while they sat around the fire, Rainbow went to the entrance of the barn.

Moments later the gijan children stood before him and this time all three bowed deeply. Rainbow indicated the fire and the dishes of food with a casual flick of his hand and Leaf led her litter mates to stand beside Navan. He kept his expression blank as he heaped three bowls with the baked fish and a few mashed grains and handed them up to the gijan. They took their food, bowed to Navan and retreated to eat on Brin's back. A change from the way they usually grabbed what the wanted when they pleased – the same thought was in all the companions' minds.

'I would ask what caused your burns, Lady Tika,' Flute asked.

Tika reached beneath her blankets and withdrew her leather pouch.

'It has happened several times before, when I've been healing, but never this badly,' she said. She untied the top of the pouch and lifted the pendant out, letting it swing from its gold chain, winking in the firelight. Flute laughed and took the chain from Tika's hand holding the pendant in her fingers.

'These things are still in the world!' Her eyes sparkled like the gold chain. 'How came you by this?'

Tika explained about the cave where the Dragons kept their treasures and Flute handed the pendant back to her.

'Clearly it still has power, especially when attuned to the bearer as it plainly must be with you. But one alone will not defeat the other Children.'

'But Tika did,' Navan corrected quietly.

Flute shot a sharp glance at him and nodded. 'That is true,' she agreed. 'They come from the Time Before. We found two or three of them and we knew they were once articles of power but we never divined their use or construction to any degree.'

Tika slipped the chain over her head, letting the pendant lie outside her shirt. She kept her mind tightly screened, keeping her memory of the hidden cave in the Domain of Asat firmly locked away from any other prying mind. There was something about Flute's casual handling of the pendant, her almost dismissive comments, that sounded a faint warning to Tika. Ren filled the ensuing pause with questions about the Elders' knowledge of Drogoya and the rest of the evening passed listening to Flute speak of her travels as a very young gijan in the land called Drogoya.

When everyone settled to sleep, Tika lay awake. She trusted Rainbow she thought: he had disclosed much of his nature when he had linked his mind to hers as he used their combined knowledge to heal her hand. That had intrigued her. She had always tried to heal by herself, she had never thought of using another's awareness of their own body to assist her. She had drawn basic stamina from the great Dragons during healing but that was all.

Flute seemed a different matter. Mostly it was her reaction to the pendant that bothered Tika. Khosa crept beneath the blanker, her whiskers tickling Tika's chin.

'You welcomed the Elders more warmly than I have ever seen,' Tika murmured to Khosa's mind.

'I felt I recognised them,' Khosa replied as carefully. 'But now I am inclined to a little caution.'

'Where is Grek?' asked Tika.

'I fear something has befallen him,' Khosa answered, curling into a compact ball. 'He has been gone too long now.' She yawned, a gust of fishy breath making Tika wrinkle her nose.

'Where should we go now Khosa? North again, or to find Namolos?'

'North. Until we hear from either Grek or Namolos himself we should stay in this land.'

Khosa was snoring in ladylike harmony with Farn long before Tika managed to sleep but she had slept during the day and woke feeling better than she had since Seela's death.

'Khosa,' she spoke to the Kephi's mind only, as people began to stir. 'Khosa,' she repeated, prodding a finger into the centre of the orange ball of fur. Turquoise eyes glared at her. 'What do you know of the places Between?'

Khosa's fur stood on end. 'What do *you* know of them?' she hissed in alarm.

Tika hurriedly outlined her experience after the unmaking of Valesh, keeping a watchful eye on the still-sleeping Elders. Khosa began to stalk up and down Tika's outstretched legs.

'Nolli might know,' she said eventually. 'All I know is they are places to be avoided.' She calmed enough to crouch, staring up into Tika's face. 'I have only heard whispers, and what I heard made me disinclined to hear more.'

'Where did you hear the whispers?' Tika was insistent.

Khosa slitted her eyes and thrashed her tail. 'In Lady Emla's House of course. No one ever took notice of a Kephi asleep on a windowsill.'

Tika gurgled a laugh and climbed from her blankets. She lifted Khosa in her arms, burying her face against the warm fur. 'We will discuss this further my friend.'

Khosa wriggled to get free and stalked to the opening of the barn. Akomi lifted his head and trotted after her. Flute left soon after they'd eaten a frugal breakfast, giving no explanation for her departure. Rainbow merely told them that they would no doubt see her again once they had journeyed far enough north.

Once again the company packed their things and climbed on the Dragons. Farn was glad to carry Sket and Khosa as well as Tika: he regarded Sket as close to Dragon Kin as a human could be. Storm took Navan and Ren with Akomi tucked deep in his carry sack while Brin carried Gan, Maressa and Jakri. Rainbow lifted into the air first, followed by the young gijan flying close behind him.

When Farn rose into the air, he spiralled higher and turned to look westwards. From this height, near the horizon, they could see the black hole scarring the grey landscape. Farn roared out a trumpeting cry and Tika blinked away yet more tears as they paid their last respects to Seela.

Chapter Thirty-Two

Flying over an eerily empty and twisted land, there was little conversation during the morning. When they stopped at midday, near a stream, Tika wandered restlessly. Gan called that tea was made and she joined the others.

'We go to Harbour City,' she said, accepting a bowl from Ren.

'We go north,' Rainbow contradicted.

Absolute silence brooded over the group. Tika smiled at Rainbow, her eyes chips of green ice.

'I said we travel to Harbour City,' she repeated quietly. She shrugged. 'Where you choose to go is your decision of course.'

Rainbow's head tilted to one side, his face impassive. 'The gijan children follow you,' he said. 'Therefore I go where you go.'

Tika glanced over at the gijan perched on Brin's back. They sat perfectly still, obsidian eyes fixed on her. She smiled at Rainbow again and got to her feet. Subdued talk began behind her. She walked round Brin, his huge body blocking her from the sight of the others. The gijan swivelled on Brin's back and slid down to stand facing her.

Tika studied them: Leaf was the same height as she was now and the male, Willow, was a couple of fingers taller. Tika sighed and held her hands out to Leaf. Leaf took them, her head tilting side to side in query. Tika swung their linked hands then released them, moving closer to put her palms against Leaf's face. She stared straight into Leaf's eyes.

'Your life is your own,' she said softly and kissed Leaf's brow and lips.

She repeated her actions with Piper and lastly with Willow and smiled at the three. Their feathers rustled as they extended their wings, enclosing her in a cloud of dusky pink, pale green and brilliant yellow. She thought it was Leaf's hand that rested on her pendant but it was Piper who spoke.

'You saved our lives. You brought forth our wings and we gave you our lives.'

'You have given our lives back to us,' added Willow. 'You have not given them to an Elder as you should.'

Before Tika could voice her concern, Piper trilled a laugh.

'If you relinquish our lives, we are glad to have them for ourselves,' Leaf whispered. 'The Elders frighten us. We don't know why.'

Now Tika was worried and as she pushed herself a little free of the enfolding wings, she saw Brin's long beautiful face lowering to stare down with equal concern in his prismed eyes.

'We have found that no-one can enter our minds, not even them, if we block our thoughts,' explained Willow. 'We think it is a strength gijan learnt in the City of the Domes.'

'If you truly return our lives to our own keeping, we would like to find somewhere to grow, to know ourselves,' Piper murmured.

Nolli. The name was in Tika's mind even as Brin sent the same name to her.

'North,' she said. 'To Gaharn and Lady Emla and Nolli, a Wise One. They will love you and help you learn of yourselves.'

A fleeting memory of Iska touched Tika and she knew she was right to tell these children to go to the Golden Lady. The gijan wings closed round her again and they whispered in their own tongue words she did not understand. But she did understand the love that poured over her from their minds. They loosened their hold, Piper leaning close once more to touch the pendant Tika wore.

'We gave you our lives. Call us, and we will come if ever you have need.'

Tika caught each triangular face in her hands and kissed the gijan one more time before breaking away from them, her thoughts in turmoil. She knew she would be unable to hide her disturbed feelings from the others, Rainbow in particular, so she summoned Farn and was in the air with him before anyone had time to realise what she was about.

There was consternation from the Elder but Ren merely shrugged. 'Tika grieves for Seela.'

Jakri caught his eye and nodded. 'Grief takes its own time,' he agreed. 'And Mistress Tika's grief is mixed with guilt.'

Rainbow regarded the Wendlan Mage. 'Why would the Lady want to go to Harbour City?' he asked.

'We have friends there.' Sket's tone was flat. 'People who were kind to us. The City has taken terrible damage so Maressa tells us.'

'Kind?' Rainbow was puzzled.

Sket snorted and Maressa answered the Elder in his stead. 'Kindness is important to us,' she explained. 'Life to humans would be unbearable if no one offered kindness.'

Farn landed again and Tika came to claim another bowl of tea. Khosa left Gan for Tika's lap but made no comment. They were soon ready to travel on, Khosa and Akomi changing places for some reason unclear to Tika or Ren. Instead of continuing north-north-east, they angled south east, seeing villages and towns crushed below them, some smouldering still, others lifeless heaps of rubble.

They agreed to spend the night some five leagues outside the perimeter of Harbour City: they had all fallen silent at the endless stretch of devastation which was all that remained of the closely-packed and thriving City. Maressa would mind speak Sheoma and ask where they should land in the morning. Tika felt Akomi move in his carry sack against her chest.

'We'll be stopping soon,' she soothed him.

'I'm used to this now,' he retorted. 'In fact I quite like it. Do you know how old Khosa is?'

Tika blinked. The question took her by surprise. She stared along Farn's neck while she thought.

'No,' she replied at last. 'But she has children and grand-children.'

The odd sound in her mind was, she realised, Akomi chuckling.

'She doesn't,' he said with some glee. 'And she is far older than I am.'

'Did you hear that?' she asked Farn.

'Yes. And nothing would surprise me at all about that Kephi.'

Gan and Brin chose a field to settle in for the night, half of it raised a man length above the other half in a great step of raw earth. Gan, Sket and Navan went scavenging for food while the

Dragons hunted for meat. Ren had pointed out that the food supply was probably a major problem within Harbour City. Remembering the kindness and generosity of the priests of the temple of the Elder Races, they had no wish to impose their appetites on people sorely pressed for food.

Everyone settled for sleep, Tika alone staying by the fire. She looked up at the sky but the dust layer, although thinner, still obscured the stars. She moved to her blankets against Farn's chest and saw three pairs of gijan eyes staring at her from Brin's back.

'May the stars guide your paths and guard your hearts.'

The message pulsed from her in a heartbeat and she settled to sleep. When they woke at first light, the young gijan were gone and Rainbow's anger was terrifying to behold.

'You must tell me where you have sent them.' He towered over Tika, his voice ringing almost painfully in Tika's ears.

Sket was beside her, his sword half drawn from its scabbard. He glared up at Rainbow, half again as tall as himself.

'You will speak with respect if you address my Lady,' he snapped.

For a moment Gan thought Rainbow would attack Sket and he eased the throwing knife strapped to his forearm down to the palm of his hand, ready for action. Tika seemed quite relaxed. Her brows quirked in amusement at Rainbow's temper.

'Elder Rainbow,' her tone was brisk. 'I gave the children back their lives, to live as they choose. Where they are is their concern: I have no idea of their plans.'

She was lying – Gan knew it, but he prayed Rainbow was really as ignorant of reading human expressions as he appeared to be. Rainbow clenched his taloned hands but kept them at his sides.

'If you did not want their lives, they should have been given to me.'

Tika's eyes blazed with a fury to match the Elder's.

'No one owns another.' Her words hissed low. 'You, me, no-one has the right to possess any life other than their own. The children are free to go where they wish and I pray the stars bless them and keep them safe.'

The companions murmured agreement behind her and Storm

suddenly pushed between Tika and Rainbow. His eyes flashed and his lips drew back in a snarl, his fangs bared a handspan from the Elder's face.

'You offend this Flight.' Storm's voice pealed in their minds. 'You will leave before we are forced to punish your offence.'

Rainbow regarded Storm with contempt and started to raise a hand but Tika intervened.

'Get you gone for now, Elder Rainbow. It seems you have perhaps forgotten your manners in your long sleep. You do not rule this world although, by your actions now, it would appear you believe you do. Tell your Elder brothers and sisters that your help against the Bound Ones would be greatly welcomed despite your failure in the last battle. But your help will not be at the cost of our own independence.'

Brin's eyes whirred rose and scarlet, threaded with gold. Tika realised he'd slammed a shield between the Elder and the companyions and she saw that Rainbow knew of it too. His smile was chilling. He turned without another word and rose into the sky, flying north with powerful beats of his wings. Gan gave a gusty sigh of relief and Farn twined his neck with Storm's, his eyes glowing with admiration at the sea Dragon's behaviour. Sket was glowering after the disappearing Elder, muttering under his breath. Jakri arrived beside Tika with a huge smile on his face.

'Where have they gone Mistress? They certainly didn't belong with those Elders.'

Tika grinned back at him. 'Just pray they can fly fast enough and undetected, Jakri,' she told him.

The atmosphere was far lighter as they ate cold meat for breakfast before moving into Harbour City. They were to go to the Xantip palace, Maressa had told them after mind speaking Sheoma last night. They were quickly off on the short flight, a rising stench filling them with dread. It was while they were aloft that Sket, behind Tika, cleared his throat.

'What is it Sket?' Tika recognised Sket's hint that something troubled him.

'I guessed you were telling those youngsters to go off. You sent them home didn't you?' He didn't wait for an answer. 'I gave that Leaf one of Seela's scales.'

Tika twisted to look up into Sket's face. 'Why did you do that?'

'Don't know. Just felt she should have it.'

Brin was circling to land, giving no time for Tika to pursue the subject. Sheoma was waiting for them with the Administrator Zerran, Grand Harbour Master Chevra and many others unknown to the companions. They were in a high-walled garden, undamaged by earthquake or the fires which had swept through parts of the City. Dersu, head of the College of Mages who had not been present at the temple days ago, was introduced.

Looking round the many people gathered in the garden, Gan smiled at the sight of the purple plumes of two Imperial Blossoms. Jakri went at once to the group of Wendlan Mages who stood slightly apart from the Maleshans, and was greeted with delight. The two Imperial Blossoms surveyed the Dragons impassively although Gan's sharp eyes saw the faint shine of perspiration on their foreheads.

Maressa noticed, firstly, the fragrance. Roses climbed the walls, spilled over wooden frames and peeped shyly from dark green foliage. After the smell of rotting bodies it was a most welcome relief. Then she saw the priest Taza standing well back behind the dignitaries, and she hurried to embrace him. Heads turned and Taza blushed that he might be thought to be pushing himself forward among his betters.

Maressa understood at once and linking her arm firmly through his, turned her dazzling smile upon their audience. She led him through the crowd around Tika and Sket to greet Ren, before Sheoma pounced on her.

'I do hope some of them will go away soon,' Sheoma commented. 'We have much to talk of.'

Maressa's eye was caught by Administrator Zerran. He stood a little apart, watching Tika closely. While Maressa stared, she saw a look of relief cross his face and he advanced to speak to Tika. She remembered Tika sitting in the temple garden with Zerran the evening before she flew with Seela and Sket to confront Valesh. In the same moment, it dawned on the air mage that Tika must have feared that, should she survive, she might be infected by some of Valesh's malignancy.

She must have shared that fear with only the Administrator,

Maressa now realised, and he had been studying Tika so carefully in case such an evil had come to pass. Tika had still spoken only to Navan in detail of what happened at Vorna's estates, unknown as that conversation was to Maressa. She wondered now whether they had been right to leave Tika alone with her thoughts rather than encouraging her to speak freely of what had happened.

The Grand Harbour Master gestured to one of the several armsmen standing by the door into the palace and the men moved forward, gently but firmly ushering many mages from the garden. The wind gusted and bent the heavy-headed roses, even in this sheltered spot, but it also brought the taint of corruption from beyond the palace walls. The Wendlan Mages came forward to greet Tika and her friends and then sat together on one side of the large paved space, the Blossoms standing rigidly behind them.

'We can offer tea to drink, or wine, but we have little food I'm afraid,' Chevra apologised. 'We had good stocks in the warehouses but they were among the first buildings to fall.'

'We saw the extent of the damage,' Tika replied. 'So many of your people must have died surely?'

Chevra sighed. 'At the last census there were thought to be around two million citizens. Far more than half of those have perished.'

Tika blanched. She had seen the crowded streets herself, but she had never imagined two million people would live in one place. Were there two million people in the whole of Sapphrea she wondered? She pulled her attention back to listen to Chevra.

'My sea commander, Bavvis, has taken every ship capable of transporting men to the north, to rendezvous with the Emperor's ships.'

Administrator Fenelon raised her hand and spoke at Chevra's nod. 'The sea bed shook as the land did. There have been reports of flames and hot rock spouting from the waters. No ships were lost though, but there was damage to some.'

Chevra nodded again, this time to one of the Wendlan Mages. The Mage inclined his head.

'I am Tashi, Mage of House Chrysoprase.' He spoke in heavily accented common tongue. 'Word from the northernmost of our Mages, those who move with the first warriors, says that the invaders are faltering. Fewer numbers came from the desert until two days ago when desert men were seen retreating rather than advancing into Malesh.'

'That is good news surely?' suggested Gan.

Tashi looked dubious. 'We – our colleagues now at the edge of the desert – have made mind contact with people called the Vintavoy.'

Gan frowned but Tika wondered. 'Are these people in the City of the Domes?'

'They are, but they say they are people native to the Valley, not the Qwah of the desert tribes.'

'The Keepers, or at least some of them.' Tika was sure she was right.

All the companions had been aware that at times the various Keepers they'd met had been in mental communication with others – others who presumably made the decisions.

'Our Mages have spoken with one called Hezwa, a female. She says one named Orla has gone northwards with a band of warriors.'

'Orla?' Ren asked in surprise. 'She is one of the Survivors.'

Tashi spread his hands. 'Hezwa tells us she is gone. She and other Vintavoyan colleagues smashed their way into – wherever this Orla dwelt. They found no trace of one called Kertiss.'

'They broke in to the Survivors quarters?' Ren was enthralled. 'How did they do it?'

Another Wendlan in dark, rich brown shirt and trousers gave a seated bow. 'Nirian of House Carnelian,' he introduced himself. 'The Vintavoy woman said the doors were forced, every strange box – she used the word "machine" – was smashed with heavy bars of metal.'

'And the other Survivor, Kertiss – was not found?'

Nirian shook his head. He spoke the common tongue far more haltingly than Tashi but with less accent. 'Hezwa says alarms sounded – shrieks and whistles and bells. But when the boxes were broken the noises stopped. The only thing of any strangeness she said was a strong smell of mentha. I do not know its name in your tongue.'

Nirian looked helplessly at his colleagues. Tashi snapped his fingers. 'You call it mint,' he said triumphantly.

Tika and Ren could only gape at him. Gan missed their

reaction and asked only if there was any clue as to where Orla might be going. The Wendlans conferred.

'We only know that she and her warriors ride directly north,' Tashi eventually replied.

Navan began to rummage in his pack. He pulled out a tight roll of parchments and knelt on the stones, flattening out one of his maps. There were exclamations of astonishment by both Maleshans and Wendlans at the detail of the map. Navan grinned.

'The Ship, Star Flower made these maps,' he explained.

His finger descended on the southern edge of the great swathe of desert which barricaded Malesh from Sapphrea. The long line of the Valley of the Spiral Star ran west to east, nearer the coast at its eastern point than its western end. Navan moved his finger north, towards the great plains of Sapphrea. He sat back on his heels, estimating distances.

'Was it eight days or so from the coast to the Valley?' he asked Gan. 'Then six or seven through the Valley. I forget. And another ten perhaps from the City of the Domes out of the desert to Malesh.'

Chevra was on his knees beside Navan. 'It is closer – from the Valley to the northern edge of the desert. This woman Orla may already be beyond it and into the upper lands.'

Gan felt a twinge of alarm. It was a long way indeed from the desert to Gaharn; perhaps half that distance to Vagrantia. Vagrantia's volcanoes were plainly marked on the map. He studied it, weighing up Orla's options. Did she too have maps made when Star Singer orbited this world before his landing? If she had, she would surely veer east of north, for Vagrantia. He wracked his brain to remember whether there had been any mention of Vagrantia while the company was in the City of the Domes but he couldn't recall.

Tika got to her feet and paced restlessly between Farn, Storm and Brin, unaware that all eyes followed her. She faced the gathering.

'We must speak of many things,' she said finally. 'Some of you saw the gijan who travelled with us?'

Several heads nodded and Tika guessed that the Wendlan Mages at least had been in the Imperial Palace when Kasheen summoned the Heads of Houses and their Mages. Her eyes rested sadly on Taza.

'We said there were no Elders left to train our three young gijan. There are. There were two hundred and twenty-two huge statues in the greatest of the three Domes in the desert. We discovered they were Elders, suspended in time by Valesh somehow during the final battle. When she was destroyed so was her spell.' She watched Taza's face light up. 'They are scattered now I think, but two came to find me and the gijan in our company.'

Tika was aware of how closely Zerran watched her and listened to every word.

'They were male and female, Rainbow and Flute. They are both as tall as Gan and winged of course. Flute told us they had rescued all the gijan kept as menial slaves in the City and had taken them to safety. She followed us I think for our three gijan. Those three pledged their lives to me when their wings came – they should have pledged to an Elder, Flute said. She summoned Rainbow to be their teacher and his first lesson was a harsh one to instil obedience.'

Tika sat down on the stone slabs again and sighed. Brin took up the story using mind speech.

'Tika gave the gijan their lives back.' His eyes whirred, moving from face to face below him. 'They told her that they feared the two Elders, but they couldn't say why. They fled in the night to find a place of safety for themselves. Flute had already departed we know not where, but Rainbow was greatly angered.'

A picture of the tall Elder filled their minds and murmured exclamations rose.

'So what I'm saying,' Tika resumed, 'is that perhaps a thousand years trapped as statues has changed the nature of the Elders.' She held up her left hand. 'My hand was burnt to the bone, but Rainbow healed it. I felt a vast compassion in him but then he seemed not to understand the word "kindness". And Brin showed you his rage. Flute said that they killed many humans rescuing the gijan in the City. There were no armed men in that section when we were there so the Elders killed teachers, healers, maybe students. They could surely have spoken to them, asked that they give up the gijan. Flute seemed unconcerned.'

Taza's face had grown white as he listened.

'Taza?' Tika asked gently.

'The Elders were slow to join the final battle: to take life would condemn the killer to insanity – they could not kill.'

Silence followed Taza's words, broken by Ren.

'Maybe that was what changed these Elders then,' he suggested. 'I felt no sense of madness about Flute or Rainbow, not even when Rainbow grew so angry. He maintained his control. But perhaps that has altered them, for they are surely not as you describe, Taza.'

The Grand Harbour Master's cousin and closest advisor agreed. 'I would suggest we treat these Elders with respectful caution until we know what they intend.' He shrugged. 'The histories say the gijan Elders ruled this world together with the Dragons: that they had humans in their councils to whom they listened. What Lady Tika has told us of the two she has encountered together with Lord Brin's information suggests there is a violence and arrogance about them now.'

Tika saw Taza's stricken expression and was saddened that his lifetime of service might end with his beliefs as ruined as his City. There was murmuring among the Wendlan Mages and Tashi spoke again.

'The mage Dersu,' Tashi bowed in his direction, 'sent five of his mages to join ours with the front line warriors.' He paused, looking to Dersu to continue.

'We sent five mages led by Tavri, whom you met I believe?' Dersu waited for Tika's nod. 'We sent them as soon as we felt the immense power fluctuating from Valesh. We had no idea what energies the Bound Ones might generate – no way of recognising the signs of their particular powers when activated.'

He glanced round, relieved to see that his audience was following his explanations

'We have never known the precise locations of any Bound One, but we concluded that now we have felt Valesh's mind signature, we might be able to pinpoint Qwah's position in the desert.'

Tika and Gan both leaned forward eagerly. 'And have you?' Tika asked.

'Tavri reports a large area with a similar mind signature

diffused through it. It is far weaker than Valesh's but also badly fragmented.'

Tika's hopes rose. She knew that without Seela's action she would never have survived her confrontation with Valesh.

'Tavri cannot far speak well so he sends his news through a Wendlan Mage.' Dersu gestured towards Nirian.

'The latest report told us that the energy field is mostly gone from the desert.' Nirian was grave. 'A fragment here and there. One source moves northwards. We fear the Bound One has discovered a host in which to conceal his essence.'

Chapter Thirty-Three

The company were impressed by the organisation Chevra had put in motion regarding the recovery of his City. By one of the docks he had ordered a burning ground be cleared. So many had died, several generations of every family, that they had no one left to identify their bodies, to mourn them or arrange their death rites. Chevra commanded that priests representing every temple be brought to chant the prayers over the shattered corpses dug out day after day from the ruins. Anyone who could heal or nurse was encouraged to go to the infirmaries set up around the City. Squads of armsmen toiled to clear water systems and increase the supply of clean water for the survivors.

Later that day the companions went inside the palace, to the Debating Chamber where a few dishes of dried fruits and nuts were offered to them. Ren, Gan and Navan peered from the windows, watching the tiny figures below working ceaselessly to move great blocks of stone from one of the streets leading up to the palace. Maressa touched Tika's sleeve and when she turned, pointed at the floor. Chevra's long heavy table stretched from one side to the other of a mosaic circle edged in black tiles and patterned in green, blue, white and crystal. Tika stared.

Chevra and Zerran were bemused to see the two women suddenly hurling furniture around. It was the sort of thing Chevra was more accustomed to – his wife had frequently thrown things. The Wendlan Mages moved prudently out of the way when Ren hurried from the window to struggle with Chevra's massive throne. Maleshans and Wendlans looked at a breathless Tika. She beamed, waving at the floor.

'We have these in the north.'

Jakri stared at the floor. 'There is something similar in the Imperial Palace, although different colours I think.'

'Does it work?' Tika demanded of Maressa.

The air mage closed her eyes, her feet on the outer edge of the circle. She grinned.

'It does.'

'Can we use it to warn Lady Emla and Lady Thryssa?' asked Gan. 'I fear Orla is heading in their direction and they can have no idea what's been happening here.'

'Paper and ink?' Maressa looked hopefully at Harrip. 'What shall I say?'

'A basic warning,' Gan said decisively. 'A description of Orla and the Elders. We can send more details later. I really would be relieved to know Gaharn and Vagrantia are alerted to the situation they might face as soon as possible.'

'Have you scroll tubes?' Tika enquired while Maressa sat at Chevra's great table, now ignominiously wedged half in, and half out of the Debating Chamber.

The company crowded at Maressa's shoulder, watching her write her message twice on separate sheets of parchment. She rolled one and slid it into a tube Harrip offered her. While Ren rolled the second message, Maressa walked into the circle, placing the tube on the square blue slab at its centre. She retreated to stand just outside the circle and began to murmur softly. There was a soft implosion of air, a faint gulping sound, and the tube was gone.

She took the second tube from Ren and sent that one on its way through the circles. A babble of excited chatter broke out between Maleshan and Wendlans while Chevra stared at his floor, his mouth open and his complexion pasty.

'Now we wait,' Tika told him.

For some reason she felt unaccountably light hearted: there were active circles here! It made Gaharn, Sapphrea, the Stronghold, Vagrantia, seem comfortingly closer. A cold wind began to gust in from the sea as the sky darkened and Chevra himself went round shuttering the windows. Maressa found herself in the middle of a mayhem of mages, all battering her with questions she was quite unable to answer. They fell silent as the air in the chamber suddenly tingled.

There was a tiny popping noise and two figures stood in the centre of the floor. Tika gave a helpless shriek and flew into Emla's arms. There was a bustle near the partly jammed door and Farn's long neck craned over the table, his eyes whirring pearl and sapphire. Finally Emla finished mopping Tika's tears and her own and faced the room, her arm holding Tika close to her side. Gan gathered his wits and stepped forward, saluting the woman who stood as tall as he. He turned smartly.

'The Golden Lady, Emla of Gaharn City,' he announced. He glanced at Emla's companion. 'And her personal Guard, Shan.'

Tears threatened again when Emla caught sight of Sket's grinning face, but first she went to Farn. With no heed to her dignity she scrambled over the table to hug him fiercely and greet Brin and be introduced to a bashful Storm. She looked over her shoulder to Tika.

'Is Seela outside?' she asked.

Lady Emla was appalled at the wave of grief which poured into her from all directions. Shan helped her back into the chamber where she found that a man named Ren, with eyes silvered as Elyssa's had been, was the only one able to give her a coherent account of what had taken place.

The evening sped by as Emla listened to the companions relate their experiences. Harrip spoke for Chevra, his report crisp and concise befitting a man as highly intelligent as he. She listened to the Wendlan Mages, and the Maleshans, filing away every word in her phenomenal memory. She had shot one warning glance at Shan before sending her Guard off to renew her friendship with the Dragons squeezed in the passageway beyond the chamber. Emla had absolutely no intention of telling Tika that Kija and Kadi had flown to Drogoya a full season past and not a word had been heard from them.

She explained that time was necessarily short: she had told her people she would return within a set span. Lamps were lit and placed around the chamber as night wore on. It seemed only moments had passed when Emla got to her feet, calling Shan to her.

'Maressa will instruct you on using the circles,' she told Chevra and Harrip. 'Please keep us informed. I will arrange for grain to be sent to you as soon as I get back. You must tell us what else you have urgent need for and we will do what we can to ease the suffering of your people.'

'There was a circle in one of the Domes,' Navan suddenly remembered. 'If we travel north, we can send messages from there.'

Emla frowned. 'One of these Bound Ones you speak of was nearby I think? Maressa, be very careful of that circle.'

She gave Gan a quizzical look. 'Do you return to Gaharn, my Captain?'

Gan knelt before her. 'Lady, you should choose another Captain. I must stay with my friends, with my family.'

Emla's green eyes sparkled with tears again but she nodded, turning to hug Maressa in farewell. She and Shan walked to the edge of the circle and began to follow the pattern inwards, chanting softly. The air popped and they were gone. Tika climbed over the table to the Dragons and they made their way back out to Chevra's garden. Maressa made to follow but Sket stopped her.

'I'll go Lady Maressa. Leave them be a while. We all forget she's scarcely more than a child.'

Dawn was smearing the sky with grubby fingers when Zerran quietly left the Debating Chamber. Kilting his robes round his elderly knees, he sincerely hoped Chevra would have this table moved as quickly as possible. He walked along the passage, marvelling that a Dragon the size of Brin had managed to squeeze through it. Zerran paused at the door to the garden: the three Dragons seemed asleep; their heads back between their wings. Khosa and Akomi were curled together on a blanket next to Sket who sat patiently working on a sword belt. He glanced up at Zerran and nodded his head towards the further end of the garden.

Zerran walked along one of the narrow paths close to the wall, the scent of dew-laden roses almost overpowering in its richness. Tika sat on a stone bench, her back to the wall and her knees drawn up to her chin. He sat beside her in silence for a while before he sighed and leaned back more comfortably.

'You were glad to see the Lady Emla,' he said. 'She is wonderfully tall.'

Tika giggled. 'Of all the things you might say, you choose "she is wonderfully tall"!'

Zerran smiled. 'Well, she is. Has it made it harder, seeing her and knowing you could go to her through the amazing circles?'

Tika turned her head, resting her cheek on the top of her knees to regard the Administrator.

'Easier I think,' she said, surprising him. 'Knowing she is still there, knowing life goes on in her House as it has for so long.'

Zerran nodded. 'And you,' he said softly. 'You are much changed little one. Valesh did not infect you with her madness but you are changed deeper than I had thought you might be.'

'What do you know of the places Between?'

Zerran's shock was palpable. Tika continued before he could answer.

'Valesh somehow got me to such a place. Seela called it the place Between life and death.'

'Seela was there?'

'Yes but only briefly. She said she was not permitted to stay long.'

Zerran stretched his hand to rest it on Tika's tangled dark hair. 'She was dead; she should have been beyond the place Between.'

Tika told him of the tunnels, the windows which showed scenes she neither recognised nor understood. Zerran listened, asking no questions, until Tika stopped speaking.

'We have long known of the places Between. They are extremely perilous places. They are Between time, Between worlds, Between life and death as the one you were cast into. I do not understand the reason you say you smelt mint, but I understand your concern that it may be connected with the smell reported by the Vintavoy woman in the desert city.'

He thought for a while, his fingers absently working to free a knot in Tika's curls. 'The smell of mint is benign, I am positive. You say Ren and Sket have also smelt it?'

Tika's head nodded under his hand. 'Nirian said their Mages sense Qwah's presence moving north. If Orla left the Domes, I would guess she goes at Qwah's bidding, whether she is aware of that or not. But it worries me that there is no information about Kertiss. Orla was the one who would consider every possibility before she acted – Kertiss was not as clever as her, I suspect. I would much prefer to know exactly where he is.'

Tika moved, her legs dangling from the bench as she stretched her arms over her head. 'I think we must go soon. Orla is too far ahead of us.'

Zerran got to his feet, hands in the small of his back. 'I'm too old to stay up all night and then sit on a damp stone seat,' he groaned. 'I'll ask Tashi and Sheoma to far speak the Mages nearest the desert.' He looked down at Tika. 'You told us the journey through the desert from the City to Malesh was bad: can you manage that again?'

Tika stood up. 'We had to travel at the pace of their animals. The Dragons will fly much more quickly.'

They began to walk back down the path. 'Why have you no horses here?'

'I don't know. We only know of them because the desert tribesmen ride them when they raid the northern villages. The local people believed them to be monsters, years ago.'

To Zerran's relief, a team of burly armsmen were wrestling the enormous council table out of the doorway and down a corridor, no doubt to wedge itself somewhere further in the palace. Sheoma and Tashi were already in the chamber.

'Tavri says that the Wendlan Mages have split up. Ten of them and two Maleshans, with a group of two hundred and fifty warriors, are already in the desert. The other Wendlan Mages are either shielding them from the heat or doing something to the weather – he isn't entirely sure.'

Sheoma bowed to Tashi. 'The Wendlans manipulate power very differently than we do.'

Tashi returned the bow: Wendlans seemed far more formal than Maleshans. 'We have much we can learn from each other Mistress Sheoma when these naughty times are past.'

Tika blinked.

'You mean bad times,' Sheoma corrected kindly.

Chevra was mortified that he could offer no supplies for the companions' journey. His City had been famed for its wealth and prosperity, and now it was no better than the poorest village. Tika quietly asked Jakri if he'd prefer to stay with his countrymen but he declined at once.

'If it is acceptable, Mistress Tika, I would journey on with you and your friends.'

'We go into yet more danger Jakri,' she warned.

'I know. But I have come to feel much respect for your abilities and affection also.' His faintly golden skin flushed slightly at his admission but Tika smiled.

'If you come, you must accept being counted friend, equal

among us all.'

It was late afternoon when they saw the dark line of the great forest ahead of them and Brin spiralled lower, looking for somewhere to rest overnight. The small towns they had flown over had suffered some damage in the earthquakes but nothing to compare with the devastation in Harbour City. Brin found a large patch of pasture close to the first trees, and the party landed. They had seen a cluster of farm buildings about a league back, hidden now behind a low hill. Navan suggested he walk back and ask for food. Maressa produced some coins which Sheoma had insisted she take for just this sort of situation. She suggested she and Gan accompany Navan while the other four found firewood and began brewing the inevitable tea.

It was dark enough for early stars when they returned, although no stars penetrated the dust hanging in the upper air. They brought fresh bread, a large round of cheese and a string of pungent onions, which occasioned moans of delight. Navan told them the farm people said they'd felt the earthquakes only mildly: the domestic animals had panicked but there had been no damage to land or buildings.

When Tika curled against Farn's chest he rumbled softly.

'I'm glad you aren't going to walk through these trees without me my Tika.'

Tika remembered the horror of being parted from Farn for three days when they'd come south, and pressed closer to her soul bond. Farn had not yet mentioned their being apart when she had gone off with Seela. Tika wondered if he actually remembered or whether Brin and Jakri had kept him unknowing all that time.

'Will we see Zeminth's village?' he asked.

'I hope so. I hope they didn't get caught in the fighting but they may well have done.'

It took a full day of strenuous flight to cross the wedge of forest which spread right across Malesh. Navan estimated it was perhaps three hundred leagues west to east, from studying his maps. (Tika had heard Sket ask why the drawings were maps on land but charts on ships, but Navan hadn't known the reason.) The second day from the forest they saw the first burnt-out farms. Wooden roofs, their timbers charred stumps, and stone walls blackened and cracked. Maressa was by now within far speaking distance of the Wendlan mages and she told Brin to fly further to the east.

'That takes us close to Zeminth's village,' he replied. 'Shall we stop there?'

Maressa explained to Jakri as they flew, of the first village they had encountered after leaving the desert. He laughed at her description of Storm's inquisitiveness towards donkeys. The buildings were badly fire-damaged they saw as they flew lower, but then Farn trumpeted. People were working around the buildings and they stared up as Farn called again. By the time all three Dragons had landed, villagers were running towards them. Best of all, Tika saw two young boys supporting the frail figure of Zeminth.

The village had withstood several assaults on it, the companions learned, and Zenidor led them to a huge stone-lined cellar beneath the ramshackle ruins of the barn. He grinned at them.

'Big enough for all our people and our animals. We can get everyone hidden very quickly – we practise quite often. So when the raiders get here, they think the place is abandoned.'

Gan was impressed, both by the ingenuity of the scheme and the discipline needed to make sure everyone knew what to do and did it as fast as possible. The villagers were disturbed to hear of the devastation in Harbour City – there had been no tremors this far away. Tika and her companions did not tell these people a great deal of what had befallen them since they had last met, but they did warn them of the gijan Elders. Old Zeminth was much shaken by the mental picture Brin gave him of Rainbow's fierce anger.

Food was still plentiful under Zeminth's careful management and the companions enjoyed the best meal they'd had since they could remember. They were given generous supplies when they set off the next morning. Towards afternoon they were following the thin silver thread of the river leading to the long lake beside which they had camped for several days while Tika freed the gijan's wings. They saw there was now another camp, neatly laid out in regular rows of tents.

Brin guided Farn and Storm lower and the purple plumes of

Imperial Blossoms became clearer. Tavri was hurrying towards them when the Dragons landed at a little distance from the nearest tents. When the riders had dismounted, Brin lifted into the air again followed by Storm and Farn on a quest for fresh meat. After the first introductions, Tika wandered away from the large encampment, Sket trailing her as always, and Akomi winding himself round her ankles.

'It was somewhere about here, wasn't it?' Tika asked.

Sket came closer peering at the ground. He toed at a small pile of stones. As they toppled, black marks of fire showed on many of them.

'Exactly here, Lady.'

Tika sat down, gazing out over the lake. 'I was so very afraid Sket. I thought I might kill Leaf, and even when she survived the idea of having to do the same for the other two scared me witless.'

Sket hunkered down beside her and poked at the stones of their old campfire. Tika noticed the bandage round his left hand was grubby and she touched it lightly. Before she could speak, Sket glared at her.

'How many times must I tell you it doesn't matter? And it doesn't hurt no more, a bit sore is all. I can leave all this bandage off in a day or so. Jakri said so.' He forestalled any argument.

'It seems I'm scared most of the time these days.'

Sket nodded. 'I know my Lady, but it doesn't show.'

Tika's laugh rang across the water and she punched Sket's knee. Akomi sat in front of them staring from one to the other with huge golden eyes. Tika scratched behind his ears and he collapsed in blissful delight.

'Lady Emla will watch for our gijan. Farn's brother and sisters are still at her House, and Hani and her daughters. She said they follow Lorak's replacement everywhere.' Tika met Sket's gaze and they both chuckled.

'Who's taken old Lorak's place then?' he asked.

'Someone called Grib – I don't know him – do you?'

Sket's grin broadened. 'Lorak's cousin, or nephew – a relative of some sort. Very like him too.'

'Six Dragons and three gijan should keep them all busy.' Tika stood up: Gan had called from the main camp and she waved acknowledgement.

They walked slowly back, Akomi buzzing happily in the crook of Tika's arm.

'Zerran thinks the smell of mint means something helpful,' she said quietly. 'But he could tell me nothing more.'

Sket grunted. 'Then let's hope we smell it all the way home.'

Tika was still laughing when they reached Gan and it gladdened his heart to hear it. Sket joined Navan who was squatting by one of the tents talking to Wendlan warriors.

'We leave tomorrow Gan, no matter what the news. There is an urgency in finding Orla.'

Gan nodded. 'Why hasn't Grek been around?'

'Khosa thinks something's happened to him but stars know what. He can find us if he's able to, but we can't count on him suddenly reappearing any time soon.'

They ate their evening meal in company with several Wendlan Mages and Imperial Blossoms as well as with Tavri and his two colleagues. Conversation was general; Gan encouraging the Blossoms to relax enough to comment on their and their warriors reactions to the very different terrain here. It transpired that the Blossoms were much worried by the prospect of entering the desert. They had scouted a very few leagues in from the cliffs glowering behind the camp and were not happy at the thought of an eleven day march despite the considerable help offered by their own Mages.

Tika found her eye caught by one of the Wendlan Mages. He offered her a shy smile and left his place to bow before her.

'You were in the Audience Chamber with – with House Amethyst!' She was glad to remember correctly when she saw the surprise on the Mage's face.

'You have an excellent memory, Mistress,' he said. 'I am Siko, of that House. My sister is with the advance party – she says they are within the City of the Domes.'

Tika sat up straighter. 'Did they meet any desert fighters?'

The group round the fire had fallen silent to listen to Siko. 'They met some alarm in the Valley at first but when it was clear they intended no harm they were made welcome. They were guided to the City. My sister has spoken with the Vintavoy woman, Hezwa, who seems to have taken charge of the place.'

Tika mind spoke Brin who, with the two young Dragons, was dozing, replete, a small distance away. 'How long will it take us to get to the Valley, Brin?'

'Two days small one, three at most.'

A helmetless Imperial Blossom, his shaved head making him seem strangely vulnerable and diminished, now told Gan that another squad of warriors was to be deployed forward tomorrow afternoon. Although their Mages were able to shield the warriors from the worst of the heat, travel by night was deemed safest.

'How long did the first squad take on the journey?' asked Navan.

'Eight days,' Siko replied, watching Khosa washing her whiskers with great thoroughness.

Gan nodded. 'They made good time. Are they intending to go north, as we are? Your Emperor ordered his warriors to Malesh to assist in repelling the desert tribes – they have done so.'

'Three quarters of this force still here,' an Imperial Blossom waved towards the rows of tents, 'are to rejoin their ships. We sail for Harbour City to be of whatever help we can to the civilian population. His Gloriousness so commanded through far speakers two days ago.'

'About five hundred warriors will be in the City of the Domes within ten days,' another Blossom clarified.

'Ten of us will accompany them,' Siko added, 'as well as ten Imperial Blossoms.'

'I think you will find the Valley people harmless enough,' Maressa said thoughtfully. 'Hezwa made it clear I think, in one of your reports, that the people native to the Valley itself are not of the same race as the desert tribes?'

The Mages nodded.

'We know of two entrances to the Valley – it would be wise to check for all others in case the tribesmen decide to enter. There must be more than those two ways in and out.'

'We had thought of that, Mistress. We inflicted heavy losses on the tribes. Their wounded, needing a place to recover, could well be a threat to the peaceful farmers we understand occupy the Valley.' The Blossom who spoke rose as a single drum beat a rapid volley, paused and then repeated.

Sket and Navan reached for their swords but Tavri stayed their hands.

'The drum tells the warriors it is time for sleep,' he explained.

The companions discovered the drum also told the warriors to rise, long before dawn. They were grateful to be given extra water skins, filled from the lake, and bade farewell to the Emperor's men. They flew high and fast, Brin's memory sure and certain of the route although he'd only flown it once before.

Chapter Thirty-Four

It was early on the third day after leaving the Wendlans' camp that Brin, Storm and Farn drifted slowly down to the circular courtyard known as the Sanctuary. They had rested during the hottest part of the two days and had not suffered anything like as badly as during their previous experiences of the desert. Two Imperial Blossoms came from the Ring Complex with several Wendlan Mages and two Keepers, one of whom Tika recognised as the Keeper of Lore, Hezwa. She seemed to carry herself more confidently Tika thought. She realised that Hezwa and her people had probably felt as oppressed as the gijan, albeit in very different ways.

Hezwa was introducing the Keeper with her: Shiro, the highest Keeper of Healing in the Valley. The company were offered the same rooms as they had used before but all noticed the changed atmosphere at once. Students sat under the verandahs, their occasional laughter sounding across the Sanctuary, and people wandered across the open courtyard.

Tika studied the four Wendlan Mages and suspected one of the two women was Siko's sister: she had the same rather square jaw as he. Tika sat down in the shade and smiled at the woman.

'I'm sure you are Siko's sister – am I right?'

The woman returned the smile as well as a formal bow. 'You are indeed, Mistress. I am Edo, Siko's older and far wiser sister.'

Tika laughed, liking the woman immediately. Two young students brought in trays of a cold fruit drink and the company were briefly reminded of the gijan who had served them before. Gan stood near the door while they quenched their thirst.

'We would like to see the Survivors' quarters, Keeper Hezwa,' he said. 'It is of concern to us that Survivor Kertiss has not been seen.'

Hezwa frowned. 'We have been all through the complex beneath the Great Dome,' she said, unable to hide her shudder.

'We found many animals and birds in one room. We had to kill them – they had suffered in unbelievable ways and could not be healed. But of Survivor Kertiss we found no sign.'

Tika drained her mug of fruit juice and stood up. 'I saw some of those poor creatures,' she said. 'I am glad to know they suffer no longer.'

They went from the cool dark of the Ring Complex into the blazing white heat of the Sanctuary, between the Dome of Assembly and the Dome of Knowledge, to the entrance of the Great Dome. The space inside seemed even more vast with only the low plinths to mark where the statues of the Elders had stood for more than a thousand years. They walked across the Dome, dust motes dancing in the beam of light from the transparent capping.

'It feels different in here,' Ren murmured beside Tika. 'Is that because the statues are gone, or the Survivors?'

'Perhaps it is a mixture of both,' Navan spoke from behind them. 'The Elders weren't the most cheerful of beings and the Survivors were definitely unpleasant.'

They reached the opposite side of the Dome and the plinth upon which, Tika realised, Flute had stood. The ramp was open and they turned down it without pause. The chamber in which Star Singer had rested seemed surprisingly large in its emptiness but they didn't linger. Tika found herself walking more stiffly and forced herself to relax. But she kept her hand on her sword hilt and noticed that Sket and Navan did too.

The door was open, gouges in the front panels testifying to the violence with which it had been forced. There was no chattering now as they walked more slowly, peering into room after room, each of which revealed broken pieces of metal and wires scattered across the floors. They eventually reached the furthest end of the Survivors' quarters leading up to the Ring Complex and Tika stopped. Hezwa regarded her anxiously.

'That is all there is Lady.'

'No.' Tika turned back and strode along the strangely lit passage. She halted at a doorway as if reluctant to go in.

The others had followed and now clustered round Tika. She moved slowly into the room, stepping over thick ropes of metal and crunching switches and buttons underfoot. She placed one hand on the nearest box and shivered. Before, it had felt unlike stone, warm to the touch: now it was icy. She traced a line near the top of the box and drew a deep breath.

'Can someone help me move this?'

One of the Wendlan Mages was beside her nearly as quickly as Sket. Tika glared as Sket put his bandaged hand on the box and he glared back. There was room for most of them to stand around the large construct.

'This is a lid I think. Maybe we can slide it off between us. It probably opened by means of Survivor magic, like the ramp in the Dome. Push that way.' Tika, at one of the shorter sides, pointed the way she meant.

At first there was no movement. Then an Imperial Blossom gently moved Tika and took her place, Gan next to him. They heaved again and there was a loud sucking noise. The lid slid rather too rapidly towards the further end. When the men had lowered the surprisingly heavy piece to the floor, they peered within the box. It seemed three quarters full of a totally black, viscous fluid. When Shiro extended a cautious finger, Tika warned him away.

'I have no idea what it is Keeper Shiro, but I think it is definitely wiser to be safe than sorry with any of the Survivors' things.'

'Sefri might know,' Maressa suggested.

Tika met her gaze. 'She might. If anyone is in contact with Hiramo or Oniko in Wendla, they should ask. But until we know, we don't touch.'

'What are these things?' Edo had turned to examine the second box.

Ren frowned, recalling Kertiss's explanations of some of the things he seemed so proud of. 'Kertiss called it a – a regeneration tank.' His brow cleared then darkened again. 'He said he could grow new life – arms and legs. He told us that he and Orla spent time inside these "tanks" to keep themselves always healthy and young.'

His words were received in a queasy silence. Tika moved to the second box.

'Let's get this over with,' she said grimly.

Again the lid was at first reluctant to move, then there was the sucking noise and the lid slid smoothly away. The stench that arose was overpoweringly awful and there was a rush for the corridor. Tika stayed where she was, hand clapped over her nose and mouth, Sket the same at her side. The bloated, naked and disintegrating corpse stared sightlessly back at them. She caught Sket's arm and walked unsteadily to join the others still gasping in the passage. She swallowed back her nausea.

'Well, now we know where Kertiss is.'

Shiro wiped perspiration from his forehead. 'I'll get this area thoroughly cleansed Lady.'

'Not until we know what that liquid is,' Tika corrected him. 'Better to seal this room until you're sure it's safe to touch that stuff.'

They made their way quite rapidly to the junction of tunnels leading to the Ring Complex, all more than relieved to leave that gruesome discovery behind them. Hezwa led them straight up to a door which accessed the Sanctuary and everyone stood for a time, gulping clean air into their shocked bodies.

'We'll rest for a while, then we must travel on at nightfall,' Tika told Hezwa.

The Wendlan Mages and their guardian Blossoms had already vanished into the Ring Complex. Now the companions began to walk across to where the Dragons reclined, basking in heat even after two days in a desert. Tika hung back a moment.

'I wondered, Keeper Hezwa, if you know anything of the places Between?' she asked. She could almost see the Keeper's mind racing through her archives, sorting references.

'I think I've heard of them. I will search for you. I'm sure I have heard of them – a passing comment in a text perhaps. I'll look at once.'

'Thank you, I'd appreciate it. But we must leave as soon as the sun sets.'

Hezwa hurried away in the direction of the Dome of Knowledge but Shiro remained with Tika, his expression deeply concerned.

'I have only heard tales of the places Between – years ago when I was an insignificant student. They were referred to as places of darkest terror and although we all believed them to be stories told just to frighten the wits from us, there was something about them that was truly frightening.'

Tika merely nodded and mind spoke Maressa. She smiled up at Keeper Shiro.

'May we go to the Dome of Assembly? We have to check something – please come with us.'

She saw Maressa emerge from their rooms across the Sanctuary and began to walk with Shiro towards the Domes. She nearly fell over Akomi and stooped to lift him, scolding him gently. Maressa caught up with them at the arched entrance and they followed Shiro inside. The tiered seats rose around them but the great circle on the floor was what drew Maressa and Tika's attention. Shiro watched as the two women moved slowly round the black edge of the circle. Maressa closed her eyes and Shiro was startled by the sudden surge of power. She let her breath out in a gusty sigh.

'It hasn't been used for far longer than any other I've seen,' she said. 'And it is uncontaminated.'

Tika smiled with relief. 'We will go to our rooms, Keeper Shiro, but if you and Keeper Hezwa would meet us here again shortly before sunset, we will show you what your circle does.'

The companions managed to sleep through the middle of the day, dozing rather than sleeping deeply. Maressa had obtained paper and she had written to both Lady Emla and to Grand Harbour Master Chevra. She rolled the papers and tied them with thread, ready to send through the circle. When students arrived with food as the heat of the day began to cool there was little talk. No one knew how Orla might have changed, affected as it seemed likely she was by the influence of Qwah.

Tika noticed Khosa was quiet again, staying close to Ren, whereas Akomi was busily begging choice titbits from everyone's plates. When he was given something he retreated, every time, to crouch by Tika to eat his prize. It was with a certain reluctance that they put their packs outside and walked across the Sanctuary. Brin stayed where he was but Farn paced steadily behind Tika and Storm followed him.

They found Hezwa and Shiro waiting just inside the Dome of Assembly. Maressa explained the functions of the circles, as far as they were understood now at least. Tika stopped listening at that point, her thoughts veering off to follow the idea Maressa had suggested. Who had made the circles? Every one she had seen had been a work of art: beautiful patterns laid out in different coloured stones, many of those stones valuable and rare. Yet only Thryssa, and Rhaki she corrected herself, had known the circles could move people and objects across incredible distances. Maressa was shown how to use the circles by Thryssa: apparently only the High Speakers of Vagrantia had retained the information, passing it on to their successors alone.

But Tika had a strong feeling the circles predated the Vagrantian, or Valsheban civilisations. The circles still functioned. Who, or what, could build such a thing that would endure through time as they had? She brought her attention back to the Dome. Maressa had placed one of the rolled parchments on the dark green square in the centre of the circle and moved back to stand outside the black edging tiles. She spoke the words of the chant and Tika frowned.

She had heard the chant many times, but always softly murmured. Now she heard Maressa saying words she could not understand. What language was she using? Did she even know the meaning of the words she spoke? There was a soft pop and the parchment vanished. Shiro and Hezwa gasped in astonishment. Maressa placed the second parchment on the central stone and repeated the words. She sat on the first row of benches and began to explain how the messages, or people, could be directed to different circles. She gave the Keepers the words for the circles in Harbour City, Gaharn and Vagrantia, and made them repeat the words over and over.

Again, Tika realised she hadn't known each circle was called into use through a changed word within the chant. And how did Maressa know the different words? She guessed it was somehow revealed when Maressa first approached a new circle – she always stood outside it, eyes closed as though in mind contact with someone. In contact with the circle itself? But there was a soft sound, followed almost at once by another and two scrolls lay on the green square. Maressa went to fetch them, unrolling them and reading them quickly before passing them to the Keepers.

'I have shown you how to use the circle to send messages,' Maressa told them. 'One of you could send a person through but I have not shown you how to move yourselves through. That is more involved and I haven't the time to explain. We will show you when we return.'

Her eyes met Tika's and Tika knew Maressa had very serious doubts that they would in fact come back to this City hidden in the middle of the desert. Maressa scribbled a few words on the bottom of one of the parchments and gave it to Hezwa. The Keeper's trepidation was plain to see as she returned the scroll to the centre of the circle. She drew a deep breath and recited the words Maressa had used. There was a mixed expression on her face when the parchment disappeared: part delight, part apprehension. Maressa stood up.

'I asked Administrator Fenelon in Harbour City to send back to prove you reached her. It will not take long I'm sure. But we must leave. Stars bless you Keeper Hezwa, Keeper Shiro.'

They were rising above the Domes within moments of returning to Brin, and none of them looked back. It was a shorter distance to the northern edge of the desert – as Navan had judged from his map. Evening of the second day saw them landing on scrubby hills. Rough grasses grew in scattered patches but no other vegetation had managed to root in the poor soil. Behind them to the west rose ranges of the high mountains through which they'd travelled when they left the coast.

The sky was clear, the wind blowing from the east, strong enough to flatten the grass. Northwards were endless flat lands, broken only by occasional low hills. The companions set up their usual camp as dusk fell and stars began to appear.

'Is something wrong?' asked Maressa.

Heads turned towards Jakri to whom Maressa had addressed her question. He held out his arm and the gold bracelet, given him by Emperor Kasheen, glinted in the firelight.

'I've told you how it shrank to fit my wrist as soon as I put it on. It keeps loosening and tightening now, and it feels warm all the time.'

Tika stepped over Gan's long legs to squat beside the Wendlan. She examined the bracelet with her eyes, her fingers, and her mind. There was no sign of any join: it was as though made in one piece to fit Jakri's wrist. She touched her pendant. Since her burning she had worn it round her neck still, but within its leather pouch in the faint hope of some protection should it heat again. Tika shook her head.

'There is something about it but it is beyond my ability to see exactly how it has been charged.'

'Charged?' Ren sounded alarmed.

Tika shrugged. 'Something works within the metal but what it is or what it does I cannot see.'

Navan tossed a thin strip of leather across the fire to land on Jakri's lap. 'Next time it loosens, slip that beneath it.'

Tika gave him an approving grin.

'Can you sense Orla ahead of us yet?' Gan's question sobered Tika at once.

'She is closer than I expected her to be,' Maressa replied. 'She should be leagues further north, given the length of time since she left the City.'

'Why would she hang about?' Sket asked. 'Is she expecting our company?'

Brin rattled his wings. 'I have sensed a change in the air.' His mind tone was uncertain. 'It is like the way the air altered around Valesh, but not quite the same, nor so definite.'

Maressa sighed. 'There is a patch that I cannot see inside when I look north.'

'Like the cloud around Vorna's estates?'

Maressa kept her expression neutral although her heart ached at Tika's question. She knew that of them all, Tika would again bear the brunt of whatever faced them, and she also knew how afraid she was.

'Something like that,' she agreed calmly. 'Less dense.'

No one felt much like talking after that. Tika wrapped her blanket around her, Akomi draped over her shoulder, and leaned against Farn.

'I will be with you this time, my Tika.'

She opened her eyes to see Farn had angled his head down close to hers. 'Brin told me, when you and Sket were lost, that I could survive without you.' The large prismed eyes reflected dizzy patterns of stars. 'I would not wish to though. So we will stay together.'

Tika stretched to press her palm along Farn's cheek. 'We will stay together,' she repeated.

'Me too,' a sleepy voice agreed.

Farn inspected Akomi and huffed softly but said no more.

Brin called a warning before midday. Below, they saw a dark shape, motionless on the plain. The Dragons spiralled lower until they could see it was one of the desert horses. Only small patches of its white hide were visible, the rest was the dark reddish brown of drying and dried blood. They landed at a distance and Jakri, Navan and Gan approached. They walked round the carcass touching nothing, then rejoined the others. Gan stared back at the dead animal.

'Something killed it, and its rider.'

'There is a person there?' Maressa asked in horror.

Gan nodded. 'Half under the horse. The animal seems to have been turned inside out but the man was intact. Definitely dead but right way out.'

Ren swallowed, holding Khosa tight against his chest. 'Orla?' he asked.

Gan thought for a moment. 'No. I cannot imagine any weapon being able to do such a thing.'

'But why?' Maressa whispered.

Tika turned away to remount Farn. 'Why not? Valesh would have thought it fun; I see no reason not to think Qwah would have the same sense of humour.'

When they camped that night Khosa mind spoke Tika for the first time for several days.

'You must assume Grek is no more,' she said. 'I have tried and tried to reach Namolos but I cannot. I tried when we were by Vorna's estates, nearer his island I thought. But I get no response.' Khosa's mind tone was ineffably sad.

Tika propped herself on her elbow and studied the small orange cat sitting beside her.

'Who are you Khosa?' she asked.

Khosa turned her head, turquoise eyes glittering even in the darkness. 'Akomi told you I was old. Silly old cat. It is true though. I am very old. I have been Khosa through many generations.'

'Like Grek, in Hargon's bloodline?' Tika asked carefully.

'Something like that, yes.'

'Who is Khosa?'

'Khosa was once upon a time Lemora.' Khosa sounded

wistful but she turned away without saying more and picked her way daintily round the dying fire to curl against Ren.

Namolos's body lay in his bed at the top of the airy spacious house on the cliffs. Students came and went, turning the body, rubbing oils into the flaccid skin, brushing the white hair. They murmured to each other occasionally, but their eyes turned constantly to the body of their Captain. Sea birds screamed, their raucous laughter drifting through the open windows together with the scent of the flowers from the gardens below and the strong smell of brine from the sea.

Several floors below, the sea swished softly at the mouth of a shallow cave. Two hundred paces inside the cave lay the Ship, Star Dancer. A woman sat in the pilot's chair in the front of the Ship.

'Abesh, he has been gone too long.' Dancer's melodious voice was filled with anxiety.

'I know.' The woman spoke soothingly. She knew Dancer understood how worried she was but it was important to her to try to stay outwardly calm, to believe Namolos would return safely.

A qualified Captain in her own right, Abesh had gone on board Star Dancer with her two tiny daughters the morning of the uprising on their home world. Her husband had long anticipated such an event and had insisted that very morning that Abesh take the children to the dock. As always, the children had been delighted to visit Dancer and Dancer had been as happy, telling them riddles and nonsense tales when the sirens began. Namolos arrived in a breathless rush and Dancer surged from her mooring, racing into the star fields followed by dozens of other bio Ships. The girls grew while Dancer travelled through both space and time. When they reached Kel-Harat, they both showed a strong desire to involve themselves in the troubles besetting this world.

When Dancer landed here, crippled in her flight systems beyond hope of repair, she and the family hoped they had found safety and security. For two hundred years they established themselves; sharing their lives with the people on this island, teaching them and learning from them. When Namolos discovered the extent of the disease that was insidiously maturing, he had determined to do all he could to fight it. All four of his family had enhanced mental capabilities: he and Abesh had early agreed that minds were of greater importance than technology.

The girls, apprised of the situation Kel-Harat faced as predicted by their father, took their own decisions and followed them through. Dancer had spoken of the girls frequently in these last days when either Abesh or a senior disciple, Elka, of whom Dancer was especially fond, had sat with her. Attuned to her Captain as she was, Dancer knew he was weakening. She could only guess that his mind had been trapped far away in this world he had come to love so deeply.

Abesh too believed her husband's mind was trapped but she had no idea where or by whom. He had spoken less and less of the things he had discovered over the last years, except to say the "disease" was progressing far more rapidly than he had hoped. After five days, his students had become greatly alarmed by Namolos's continued mind travelling. Abesh had tried, again and again, to link with the residual thread of his consciousness in the hope she may be able to strengthen him at least. She would have preferred to be able to pull him back forcibly, or follow his mind herself to wherever it was held.

She found, to her horror, that he must have foreseen this eventuality, and had barred all outside access to his mind. Even to her. She continued to try. She sat with him during the nights while Elka was with Dancer. She spoke aloud to him. Occasionally she railed at his absenting himself from her so totally. Then she would dry her tears and talk sensibly again.

'It is nineteen days.' Dancer's voice brought Abesh out of her thoughts.

'He is receiving nutrients by line,' Abesh told the Ship wearily. 'He is massaged and exercised – you know all this Dancer. Why must you make me repeat it each day?'

Then she sighed, putting her hand against the Ship's inner wall. 'Forgive me Dancer. But we are doing all we can for him. We just have to wait for him to come back.'

'He will,' said Dancer quietly. Then more firmly: 'He will.'

Chapter Thirty-Five

While on Farn's back, Tika had studied the small book which Hezwa had given her. Hezwa had apologised that it was all she could find but if Tika wished she would search further. Tika had tucked the book in the waist of her trousers, behind her sword belt, and half forgotten it was there. At first she thought it was in another language but eventually realised it was written by hand; a hand that enjoyed flourishes and curlicues in a very tiny form.

They flew over unending and changeless plains for three days, slightly east of north, but had yet to catch up with Orla's party. They had found no sign of Orla's passage either – no more corpses and no signs of camp fires. Navan and Sket had walked some distance around the dead horse and discovered no tracks in any direction. Brin was disturbed by the bodies of the horse and human.

'In these sorts of lands, any animal that dies attracts birds – bigger than Merigs but like them to look at. They feed on dead things and they travel leagues when they scent one.' He rattled his wings, his eyes whirring in agitation. 'This animal has been dead more than a day – why are the dead-feeder birds not here?'

When the company remounted and the three Dragons lifted skyward, Brin wheeled back. He spat fire down onto the horse and continued to do so until it was a shrivelled smouldering heap. They camped for the fourth night under a clear star-filled sky, and were woken by a deluge of rain descending on them. They hadn't bothered erecting the tents the Wendlan forces had given them because Maressa, checking the sky as she always did just before they made camp, had said the weather would remain clear. The men struggled with the tents against a rising wind and constant hammering rain. Brin tried to shield them from the worst of the wind with his enormous body. Storm held Maressa and Khosa under his wing while Farn sheltered Tika and Akomi.

Jakri suddenly dashed across to Farn, his eyes wide with

surprise. 'Edo far spoke me! I have rarely been able to far speak more than a couple of leagues.'

'Well, what did she say?' Tika was rapidly finding she agreed with the cats' opinion of wet weather.

'Earth tremors. Not bad but noticeable enough to be disturbing.'

'In the City?'

'Yes, but more importantly perhaps, she reports rain.'

'Rain in the Valley is not uncommon I think.'

'But this rain was in the desert – north of the Valley.'

'In our direction you mean.' Tika shivered, peering out into what should be the light of dawn and was most definitely not.

She mind spoke Maressa, cowering against Storm several paces away. The sound of the wind and the rain battering against Farn's scales and leather wings made it hard to hear Jakri, standing as close to her as he was. Maressa listened and at once attempted to send her mind up through the downpour. Jakri dashed back to help with the tents and Tika watched Maressa, knowing the air mage was struggling to get her mind aloft.

As suddenly as it had begun, the rain stopped and the wind dropped to a gentle breeze. The company stared at each other, the tents just in place. They looked up: not a cloud to be seen in any direction, just the pearly rose of dawn. Tika looked down: she was ankle deep in glutinous mud and her clothes were beginning to steam. She looked at Brin, and had to smile. He looked magnificent in the light of dawn – each wet scale sparkling deep crimson, his wings darker yet. He caught her thought and proudly reared erect, water droplets spraying around him like diamonds.

Gan squelched away from the tents and glared. 'If that was another example of Qwah's humour, I did not find it amusing.'

Although Tika knew it was Qwah's doing, she found herself giggling helplessly.

'Brin,' she finally managed to gasp, 'see if you can find meat. We can't travel on until we've dried out a bit at least.'

They were having increasing difficulties finding anything to burn on the fires which they liked to kindle night and morning but when Brin returned later with the large carcass of a wide-horned heavily-built grazing animal, he had better news.

'About five leagues west,' he told them, 'there is a small hill and it has bushes on its far side.'

Navan swiftly cut the haunches from Brin's kill and gave them to Farn and Storm, cutting other portions for the company's supper. Gan took a length of rope and went with Brin to gather fuel for the fire on which they could cook their meat. They decided to stay where they were for the whole day when Maressa, somewhat puzzled, reported that the strangely distorted air which seemed to indicate Orla's position, was at the same distance from them as before.

'So she's made camp somewhere cosy too,' Sket grunted, chipping mud off his boot soles.

Ren laughed briefly. 'It appears Survivor Orla has kept deliberately so near and so far from us since we left the desert. And the sudden attack of bad weather today – a very minor inconvenience when you think about it. Why not lightning and thunderbolts?'

Jakri nodded. 'Anyone who can work that much weather would find lightning no problem.'

Tika rubbed her chin on the top of Akomi's head. 'You think Qwah is observing us – all the time?'

Jakri pursed his lips. 'I think in some way he is fully aware of where we are. I'm not sure that he knows it was us – you – who destroyed his sister.'

Gan frowned. 'You could be right,' he agreed. 'If he knew who we were, or Tika at least, we might have got the thunderbolts.'

Sket scowled at Gan: he'd thought exactly the same but he'd had the sense not to mention it aloud.

'Do you think Qwah might be smart enough to guess we'd travel by night?' Navan sounded thoughtful. 'The land is getting hillier – not much, but definitely not as flat as before. Could we get closer during the night and keep one of the hills between them and us? He might not suspect we'd move closer.'

There was a long silence following Navan's comments until, as always, Tika found everyone staring at her. She shrugged.

'We could try. Anything you can think of will help. All I know is that I have to be close, unfortunately very close, to be able to unmake these creatures.'

They waited until full dark before the Dragons carried them

high into the sky. Maressa was checking ahead with the very weakest tendril of her power and guiding them slightly obliquely towards Orla's position. All of them were growing nervous as the sky lightened fractionally on the eastern horizon. It was with considerable relief that Brin took them down in a faster descent than usual to land in the lee of an extremely small hill: Brin was about the same size. Nevertheless, they flattened themselves against the rough grass and Jakri, Ren and Maressa held their minds in readiness for any change or assault upon them. Tika leaned back against Farn's crouched body, her fingers rubbing Akomi's slightly furrowed brow and let her mind drift. They had estimated they were within a league of Orla and her escort of tribesmen: still not near enough Tika thought. But she let her mind float, formless as the breath of wind that scarcely moved the grasses around her.

Jakri, lying just beyond Sket, suddenly went rigid and Tika, her mind loose and unfocused, watched him distantly. She allowed a tiny part of her thought to touch his mind and flinched involuntarily. There seemed to be a maelstrom of activity going on through the net of power which, in her near trance like state, was quite clear to her. She withdrew slightly and saw the chaos flashing in his mind was not actually touching the part that was Jakri's core. He was acting almost as a mirror, reflecting what was happening around and through him.

Tika withdrew further, floating over the hill low to the ground towards Orla's camp. She felt tension tightening all around her, forcing her drifting mind to slow its progress. It was like wading through deep mud and she slowed more with each breath. Tika's mind slid sideways and she felt her way round a roughly circular barrier. By the time she was back at her starting point, she was worried. The barrier was impenetrable to her probing mind but she was unable also to judge its real size.

She let her mind drift back to her body. She was amazed to realise the sun was halfway down the western sky. Tika raised her head cautiously and saw that Jakri, Ren and Maressa all appeared to be asleep. Gan, Navan and Sket were watching her, differing degrees of concern on each face. She managed a smile, her face feeling tight. She guessed her skin was sore from the sun beating down on her for most of this day.

Ren opened his eyes a short while later and winced, putting a hand to his reddened face. Maressa woke as the earliest stars appeared but Jakri lay unmoving until night was well advanced. The Dragons were flexing cramped muscles when Tika at last sat up.

'Can we fly on, Brin?' she asked. 'If we could get even slightly ahead, it might be an advantage.'

Gan nodded. 'They may only be watching for people to follow and it does seem clear they don't expect us to move at night.'

Jakri groaned. 'There was a tremendous anger – did you feel it? But he didn't locate us.'

'Are you sure about that?' Gan asked sharply.

Jakri rubbed his forehead while Maressa mixed willow bark powder in a bowl of cold water.

'I tried to cast an illusory spell. Such spells are commonly used in Wendla, usually for entertainments at grand House celebrations. For fun you understand. I tried to sandwich us between an illusion of this turf and the real ground we lie on.' He gulped the drink Maressa pushed into his hand, grimacing at the bitter taste.

'Somewhat to my surprise, it seemed to work.'

'What about you Ren, what did you sense?'

Ren stroked Khosa's back as she perched on his knees facing him. 'I didn't realise what Jakri was doing of course. I had a feeling of suffocation – which Jakri's illusion would account for I guess. But there was an appalling malevolence.' He shook his head. 'I can't describe it other than that it was questing, casting, as though for a scent, a trace of us. He went a long way down our back trail – I hope he has done no further damage in the City.'

Tika filed away Ren's remarks and turned to Maressa.

'I felt similarly enclosed at first but Jakri's action explains that now. I tried to go high above them and to begin with I could see nothing. But as Ren said, the creature searched south. I don't know if he was just careless or if he is far less controlled, or is just plain weaker than we thought.'

The air mage clasped her drawn-up legs, her chin on her knees. 'He seemed to pour himself south and he left Orla's camp quite exposed. There are about thirty tribesmen with her. She seemed the same as when we met her, but there is something very wrong about the tribesmen.'

'Wrong?' Tika pressed.

Maressa shrugged. 'They were sitting all exactly the same, and the horses also. Like statues.'

Everyone stared at her, their minds filled with the statues in the Great Dome. Living beings made into statues by Valesh and her brother.

'I think they were held temporarily like that, so he didn't have to bother what they might be up to.'

'But Orla wasn't so held?'

Maressa thought for a moment. 'No. She was walking around, looking at the men, looking mostly to the north.'

Tika stood up, Akomi in her arms.

'Let's move on then. Even though he was searching southwards, something was blocking me from getting close enough to the core of his being. I can do nothing from a distance.'

She climbed onto Farn's back, Sket behind her. 'We will land further from them next time, Brin,' she mind spoke the crimson Dragon. 'I think we will have to approach on foot.'

Brin did not reply as he rose in front of Farn, but Tika was aware of his unease.

Orla felt more at peace, more relaxed than ever in her long life. The man who had invaded her dreams was with her all the time now. She wandered idly around the group of tribesmen, giving them as little attention as she would give to furniture. She thought of him as the Man. She could not think of a name fit for him and he had so far not told her what name he gave himself. Orla knew he was annoyed over something but as long as he was not displeased with her, she paid little attention to his mood.

One of the tribesmen got to his feet and stood rigidly to attention. Orla smiled. The man turned to face her, smiling back. The smallest fraction of the Survivor's mind told her he was a tribesman, but her body told her he was the Man. The Man's eyes were warm with affection as he reached to hold her against him. Orla's gaze settled on a rampart of higher hills some leagues to the north, and the tribesman released her, sitting cross-legged and blank-eyed on the ground again.

'My son will be born in those hills,' the Man whispered, and Orla blushed, her hand resting on her already thickened waist.

It seemed an inevitability that she should bear him a child. Thoughts of her own sterility, her vast age, were insignificant: the Man told her she would bear his son and so she was pregnant. The fact that her body was changing so rapidly did not alarm her. She was cushioned against everything by the warmth and love with which the Man surrounded her.

He roused her from sleep that night and she went meekly to one of the horses a tribesman held for her. They rode fast under a star-crowded sky, and on until the sun was halfway to noon. Two horses collapsed. Orla glanced over her shoulder and saw men sitting beside the downed beasts but then they were quickly out of sight. They halted for the rest of the day beside a tiny streamlet that appeared briefly then soaked away into the ground after only a few paces on the surface. Orla sensed the Man was concerned and ventured a cautious query.

'Wicked ones follow us my dearest beloved,' he replied. 'There is nothing for you to worry about. Concentrate your mind only on my son.'

'He will be beautiful,' Orla sighed. 'As wonderful as his father.'

'He grows well,' the Man agreed lovingly.

'He grows faster than I would have thought possible.'

There was the faintest touch of doubt in Orla's words. The Man enfolded her with affection.

'But he must, mother of my triumph. This world has need of him for its very survival!'

Orla was suffused with pride. A child of hers to be of such importance! And she knew the Man was right. By the time they had left the desert she was aware of the child, conscious within her. She had been shocked and afraid and also very sick at the waves of fury and hatred that had poured into her body and mind from the small cluster of cells multiplying so fast in her body. She had fallen deeply asleep, her body still shuddering with dry heaves. She woke immediately tense at the prospect of another day as awful as yesterday, but she felt well, comfortable and at peace. Orla asked the Man why she had been so ill and he held her and soothed her.

'The boy did not understand that you are his mother. He fretted to be released from his confinement. I have explained to him and calmed him. He knows now that he must wait a while longer to be born and held in his dear mother's arms.'

In the days since, Orla had felt well, calm and content. She wore one of the tribesmen's cloaks now, her belly was swollen to what she would have thought was full term. But she wasn't worried. She had given herself to the Man: he would look after her. He seemed much pleased with her and often now he would stroke her distended stomach and smooth his strong hands down her back. They rode on into the hills which proved steeper and higher than when observed from far across the plains.

The horses were sure-footed even though their hooves occasionally dislodged stones which flew over the edge of the trail. Orla vaguely wondered how the desert men knew their way but decided the Man had probably given them precise directions. Camping one night, deep in the crowded hills, Orla asked the Man about those who pursued them. He laughed, a warm rich sound that thrilled Orla to her bones.

'They met a line of fire my dearest. They were surely burnt to cinders. I have felt no trace of them since, so they need not be of concern to you now.'

'Oh they didn't concern me,' Orla answered. 'I know nothing could harm me when you are here.'

They rode for two more days, deeper and deeper into the hills, until Orla admitted she didn't believe she could ride much further. Her body was so grossly swollen, riding a horse was becoming impossible. The Man was a trifle displeased and Orla hastily said she would try again tomorrow.

'It is only one more day,' the Man told her. 'A place where you and my son can rest and wait for his birth.'

Orla's hand was on the great mound of her front, feeling a foot or a hand pushing restlessly up against her.

'I fear to wait much longer,' she said. 'Already he is grown so large birthing him may be difficult.'

For the first time she felt a twinge of alarm. Could she deliver herself out here in this wilderness, with no pain relief, no instruments, no one to help her?

'I will help you, beloved. My son will come forth fit and healthy. Do not worry.'

As Orla drifted into sleep, that tiny part of her mind which was struggling to maintain its existence, pointed out exactly what the Man had said. He had told her the boy would be fit and healthy: what about her? Could she really believe she could survive this ordeal, as ordeal she knew it would surely be? The next day was bad enough. The weather grew cloudy, the wind stronger and colder, and rain gusted into their faces on and off through the whole day.

Orla's discomfort was intense although two empty-eyed tribesmen helped her: one riding behind to hold her sideways on the horse, another beside them to make sure the animal moved steadily. Orla was half fainting by the time she was carried in to a low deep cave, the horses clattering and snorting behind her. A bed was made of blankets and cloaks well out of any draughts and a fire blazed cheerfully between her and the cave mouth. The tribesmen sat near the horses but Orla was beyond noticing their gaunt skeletal appearances.

She had been conscious only of her pregnancy, had been totally unaware that she had not eaten since she had left the desert, existing only on sips of water through all these days. Neither did she notice the fire burned without fuel, the flames writhing and leaping just above the rock of the cave floor. By now Orla was feverish, her mind fidgeting from thought to thought.

'What is our son's name to be?' she suddenly asked aloud.

'His name is Karlesh.' The Man's voice swelled with pride.

'I don't know that name.' Orla sounded petulant. 'I would have liked to name him.'

She didn't see the ferocious sneer that crossed her beloved's face as pain stabbed down her back and legs. She moaned and the Man seemed to be even closer to her.

'It is time,' he said the scowl replaced by a look of delighted excitement. 'He will soon be in the world.'

Orla struggled through that night, trying to find a position which would give some relief to the pains tearing through her almost constantly. The tribesmen sat unnoticing near the mouth of the cave while Orla turned and twisted. She felt agony rip through her groin and screamed. She raised herself to lean her shoulders against the rough stone wall and tried to see over the enormous lump of her belly. She put her hand down, moaning with pain, and brought it away bright with blood. She twisted herself, her breath sobbing in great gasps, to try to see what was happening.

Sweat poured from her and she bit through her lower lip. The skin was torn along her groin towards her left hip and the flesh gaped, assisted by a small hand which appeared to have black talons at the tips of its fingers. Orla felt blood, hot and thick, pumping between her legs and her brain cleared to an icy clarity. She was dying but she would not let this monster survive. Orla writhed as her skin was wrenched apart. She gathered her little remaining strength and reached down again.

She felt nothing as she grasped an arm and pulled. Then pain forced scream after scream through her bitten mouth, but she held on, tugging the child from her. For the space of three heartbeats she stared at the thing she had grown within her. Slime- and gore-covered as it was, it was laughing, its wide mouth open showing tiny sharp teeth. For three heartbeats, each slower, weaker than the last, Orla stared into its narrow slanted eyes.

With what she knew was the very last of her life, she moved her other hand round its neck, attempting to crush the life from this abomination she had contributed towards making. It laughed aloud, a high pitched cackle, and twisted one of her hands, free with no apparent effort. It sank its teeth into her other hand and she heard her own bones crunch in its jaws. Orla felt the last faint bump of her pulse and life winked out of her eyes. The fire continued to blaze, Qwah thinking his child might like to see properly for a while.

Karlesh climbed towards Orla's face, smearing his fingers across her bloody mouth. He licked his fingers and giggled, bending his head to tear a lump of flesh from her breast. He sucked the blood from the gobbet, chewing only a little of the flesh. He slithered back down to the puddles of blood pooling under Orla's hips and lapped thirstily. He belched, peering over Orla's thigh towards the men sitting motionless between him and the outside world.

'They will feed you until you are strong enough to leave this place my son.' Qwah's voice rang with pride.

The child stared at a spot halfway up the cave wall, straight into Qwah's eyes in fact.

'You are so thoughtful, father,' Karlesh replied, sucking a finger, the picture of childish perfection to the doting Qwah.

Behind his veiled eyes, Karlesh studied the threads of his father's being. What a primitive he was!

Chapter Thirty-Six

Namolos was exhausted. He had been locked in mental combat with a mind utterly alien to any he had encountered, and for far too long. He knew his wife, colleagues and students would be doing everything possible to sustain his body until his mind returned. But that body was weakening fast. It was an interesting problem. If his body died his mind paradoxically would be stronger. If his mind was thus strengthened, he knew there was a good chance of him damaging the other mind badly enough to win his own release.

Grek had told him of those called the Bound Ones. Namolos had sensed these entities, secure within their confining spells, centuries ago when first he began to travel within the very fabric of the world. He had recognised them as purely evil energy and had thereafter avoided the sites of their imprisonment. He was deeply alarmed when Grek told him what was happening in Malesh and in the desert which separated Malesh from the Sapphrean plains, but by that time he had already encountered the other mind.

He had to decide quickly, and knowing that Tika, Farn and Khosa were already placed to intervene against the Bound Ones, he chose to send his mind north. Namolos was taken completely by surprise. One moment he had been part of the air, an insignificant particle among a million others, and the next he had slammed into conflict. He had long known of the power of names. He had listened to the wise ones of the island on which he had landed with his family. At first, in spite of his serious, attentive expression, he had scoffed privately at their simplistic beliefs. But over time he saw what those simple beliefs could achieve.

Slowly, Namolos and his wife learnt, and were stunned by the immense power simplicity could produce. His daughters learnt more quickly, each showing an aptitude for different aspects of the wise ones' teachings. The concept of naming had been one of the hardest for Namolos to fully understand but when he did, he was awed by the conclusions it might lead to. Now, if he only knew the name, the true name, of this creature he was locked with, he would have more than just hope with which to fight it. That the creature did not know Namolos was a huge relief, but it seemed to have a completely different mental configuration to any Namolos had come across.

He had slid through the waters of the immense seas, listening to the tiniest polyps and to the greatest whales. He had overheard the great female Avgoor talking to the sea Dragon Storm and also to Tika. Star Dancer had first picked up the anomaly which Namolos found was a malignancy poisoning this beautiful world of Kel-Harat. While it grew extraordinarily slowly, he had yet been unable to pinpoint its exact position. The Ship had only discovered slight energy changes, but they moved, never appearing to remain in the same place long enough for Namolos to approach.

Namolos had discussed his findings with the wise ones of the island and they had evinced alarm verging on disabling fear. They refused to discuss it further with him, so he was left to increase his abilities in far travelling and search it out himself. Abesh and their daughters, analysing Namolos's findings piece by piece, had agreed that whatever this creature was, it had to be found and disabled, if not destroyed. The Ships still in harmonic orbit had been unable to trace Namolos's creature. They concluded that Star Dancer's receptors were altered in some way when she made her descent through the atmosphere, making her more susceptible to local energy fields.

Dancer ran systems diagnostics of increased subtlety and agreed with her sibling Ships. Namolos now understood that the very slowness of the creature's growth and advance had been the cause of his grave misjudgement of the situation: he had assumed there was plenty of time to deal with it. Approximately four centuries ago the activity of the malignant energy began to accelerate, taking Namolos by surprise. His daughters left the island, determined to help prevent this creature destroying the only world they had ever known. While time was insignificant to Namolos, it still seemed too long to be without his children and he had been able to contact only one of them, and that only briefly once in this past year. She had seen her sister she told him, but could no longer contact her any more than either of them could contact him.

It was many days since Namolos had felt the destruction of Valesh, the reverberations of that event shivering through his mind. It was in the aftermath that he found the entity he so feared had split itself – one part was on the great land mass east of his island which contained the lands of Sapphrea and Malesh. The other part was still in the second continent on the opposite side of the planet. Namolos felt that most of the creature – the older, more knowing part of its essence, was in the further land. That must be his target now; it had to be.

He despaired that he had no means of warning those brave children of what they must now face, particularly the child Tika whose existence he had worked so hard and patiently to bring about. The unbodied Grek had vanished. Namolos suspected he had returned to the lands of Drogoya and become assimilated or destroyed by the thing which, in this particular time, on this parti- cular world, called itself Cho Petak.

The Ships in orbit had reported other signs of an intelligent energy pattern. In turn, Namolos investigated and although also alien to anything he knew, he found it was benign and quiescent. The orbiting Ships told Dancer that the second life form had become more active of late – within the last planetary year. Namolos decided he could wait no longer and after telling Elka he was far travelling indefinitely and that no attempt must be made to recall him, he sank his consciousness into the very being of Kel-Harat.

And now twenty days had elapsed, as all his household were all too aware. Namolos held one grain of comfort: locked as they were, the other mind could focus on nothing other than trying to free itself. It would be a small price to pay, Namolos felt, if his life could neutralise this threat to his world.

Tika and her friends had very little warning of the fire which seemed to sweep from horizon to horizon. While there was only a knee-high coarse grass on which to feed, the fire reached upwards several times higher than Brin. Jakri suspected an illusion, the type of spell he had used himself only a couple of days earlier, but it was quickly apparent that the fire was real enough. It sped towards them, the outer ends curving in to encircle them.

The Dragons lifted into the air bearing the companions high to avoid the hungry grasp of the flames. As they flew over the fire, the heat was intense. They put more distance between themselves and Orla's camp, racing through the night towards the hills. They found a sheltered meadow, overlooked by steeper slopes, and settled to rest. Ren was convinced they had not been seen rising above the flames and he believed they now had an advantage. Valesh's brother would think he'd been successful and had lost his pursuers.

Jakri was inclined to agree although both Gan and Sket expressed doubts. Maressa let her mind soar into the higher atmosphere and the others waited patiently for the air mage's report. She blinked and smiled at the faces watching her expectantly.

'Ren's right. There is no sign at all of him taking any sort of care now. Orla rides towards the hills, perhaps ten leagues east of us. There is no sense of a shield or wardings, no disturbed air around her.'

Navan had collected a few small desiccated bushes and suggested making a fire. Gan scowled.

'Smoke is an obvious giveaway,' he said firmly.

'Nonsense,' Maressa overrode him. 'By the time any smoke gets above these slopes, it will have dissipated enough to be invisible.'

'One of you should keep close watch on Orla,' Gan insisted and with that Maressa had no argument.

Tika was surveying the meadow. 'This seems as good a place as any to wait,' she announced.

Sket grunted but Tika ignored him.

'I have a feeling they will rest for a few days once they feel they are safely hidden among these hills. Don't forget how far and how hard they have ridden lately. Their horses must be near exhaustion and from what we heard, this is Orla's first trip ever outside the Domes. She must surely be at the limit of her endurance.'

'What do you suggest?' Gan demanded.

'That we wait,' Tika repeated. 'If Brin could be ready to shield us at any moment?' She waited for the crimson Dragon's assent in her mind. 'The rest of us can take turns watching where Orla is heading and where she stops.'

'Then?' Gan pressed.

She smiled at Lady Emla's Captain of Guards. 'Then I will do what I must.'

Akomi butted against her leg and she scratched the old cat behind his ears. Khosa had stalked off towards the nearest slope. They were all wary of using Qwah's name and referred to him only as Valesh's brother, but they felt he was somehow less than Valesh. Tika was sure that Valesh would not have cast the fire spell without returning to check on its success or otherwise: Qwah had apparently simply assumed they could not survive his circle of flames.

They spent an idle day, Maressa and Jakri taking turns to overlook Orla's progress.

'There's something wrong with Orla,' the Wendlan remarked after his latest turn of far watching.

'What?' asked Farn. His eyes whirred rapidly, indicative of anxiety.

Storm slept quietly leaning against Brin's flank.

'I can't make it out,' Jakri apologised. 'They are travelling much more slowly. I get the feeling she has a fever.'

'Is he still with her though? Tika asked.

'Oh yes, more concentrated around her than before I'd say Mistress.'

'What is it he wants with Orla?' Tika fretted. 'She has no mental powers: she regarded them as tricks, foolish games. Both she and Kertiss ridiculed the idea of such things. So why does he need her with him?'

There was a considerable silence while they pondered why a Bound One might need the company of a Survivor, but no one came up with any solution. Farn was restless, pacing round the meadow every now and then, his gaze rarely leaving Tika.

'He wasn't like this before Lady,' Sket murmured. 'Not when we went off to that witch woman's place. And I'm clean out of the mixture Lorak gave us to keep Farn calm. I could make up something from the herbs Ammi gave us in Green Shade, but it wouldn't be the same as Lorak's and I don't know how it might affect the youngster.'

'Don't worry Sket. I think it's partly something that Brin said to him.'

Tika stood up and walked over to the silver blue Dragon, sliding her arms round his shoulders and pressing her face against the scar that wound down his long neck. Brin's face lowered towards Sket.

'I will protect him, Dragon friend. Never forget that I will protect him, even as you protect his soul bond.'

Brin's mind tone was sombre and, quite frankly, rather than comforting Sket he found himself more perturbed than ever. Jakri and Gan were asleep. Ren and Navan were investigating a small pool some short way up the western slopes, with Khosa following them with interest. Sket's hand went instinctively to his sword as Ren suddenly straightened, clutching Navan's arm, but he relaxed again when the two men bent once more to the pool. Tika and Farn wandered back, Farn appearing calmer to Sket's experienced eye. Tika turned to Sket just as he turned, frowning, to her.

'It's back again,' he said tersely and examined the ground around him. 'Can't see the star-cursed stuff anywhere, but I can smell it.'

'Zerran said it was a sign of something benign.' Tika was also poking among the tangled grass. Akomi sneezed and both Sket and Tika stared at him. He sneezed again.

'Don't tell me you can smell mint?' she mind spoke the old cat.

'I don't know what mint is, but there is a smell here, a sharp and ticklish smell.'

Tika laughed at his description, picking him up and rubbing her cheek against his whiskery face. Ren and Navan joined them. 'You'll never guess,' Ren began.

'That you smelt mint,' Tika grinned at him. She sniffed. 'It's gone again now, but we smelt it here. And so did Akomi.'

'They've stopped,' Maressa interrupted. 'Orla and the tribesmen. A cave or something I think. Everything is concentrated on a very small area.' Her eyes met Tika's and Tika smiled affectionately.

'Then now is the time we approach closer. Can you keep close watch while we travel? I don't want him to catch any hint of my mind until it's too late for him to do anything unpleasant.'

Maressa swallowed. 'Of course I can.'

She turned to stuff her blanket into her pack to hide her face from the others, especially Tika. She had a very bad feeling inside her this time, far, far worse than when they knew Tika would have to face down Valesh.

Brin led them eastwards. He flew low, hugging the hilltops, and kept their pace much slower than usual.

'There.' Maressa mind spoke them all. 'The hill to the right with a sort of step on its top.'

They peered through a persistent drizzle to the hill Maressa indicated.

'Land us on the hill behind,' Tika directed Brin.

When the Dragons set down, the companions dismounted and huddled close together. Tika wanted as little use of mind speech as possible lest Qwah pick up the faintest hint there might be danger close by.

'Well, I must take my chance now.'

Tika studied each face around her and knew just how much she had come to love every one. 'You will wait here, although I'd prefer you to move further away. I will go onto that hill, the cave is close to the top I judge, from Maressa's picture of it.

'I will take you.' Farn's voice was soft, perfectly calm, and his eyes gleamed pearl and sapphire in the grey gloom soaking them all.

Without a word, Sket climbed onto Farn's back, his expression set like stone. Akomi leaped up Sket's leg and glared balefully down at the companions as though daring them to make him move. Tika took Maressa's hands in hers.

'Stars bless you and guard your heart,' she murmured.

Maressa choked back her tears and hugged Tika's small body fiercely against her own. Tika freed herself gently and moved to Ren, to Navan, to Jakri and Khosa. Khosa's turquoise eyes burned into Tika's but she said not a word. Tika hugged Storm and then stood before Gan's towering figure. He bent down to her, pushing her unruly curls off her forehead as he'd done so very many times before. Somehow he managed a smile.

'Stars guard you, little one.'

Tika's throat ached with tears but if Gan could smile, well so could she.

'Family, Gan?'

'Always family Tika.'

She nodded, hugged him hard and lurched away towards Brin. She leaned against his broad chest for an instant and then moved quickly to mount Farn.

'Shield your minds now,' she ordered as Farn lifted away.

Tika did not look back, instead she forced all thought of those friends from her mind, centering her concentration as Iska had taught in her first lessons in the use of power. Farn landed as gently as thistledown on the oddly stepped hilltop and Tika slid from his back. Her pendant hung at her chest, free of it leather cover. She nearly jumped out of her skin as claws dug in the top of her shoulder. She bit back an exclamation; she need to focus her attention on what she must do, not yell at a mottled old cat.

Sket moved to her right side and she was distantly aware of him hooking the remaining fingers of his left hand firmly under the back of her belt. Tika's mind sank into the bare rock beneath her feet, filtering through the ancient layers until she knew she approached air once more. The grey dimness of the rock gave way to sudden firelight and Orla's corpse.

Above on the hilltop, Tika's body went rigid and Sket tensed, murmuring prayers his grandmother had taught him and which he'd not repeated for years. While Tika's mind watched, she saw the misshapen child lap at Orla's blood and then turn its head towards the cave wall opposite Tika. For one heartbeat, Tika saw the thing that was Qwah, then it disintegrated in a mass of nothingness and diminishing screams. Her attention snapped back to the thing which still squatted in Orla's gore. Tika gathered every scrap of concentration before her heart could beat again but the thing laughed, staring straight at her. She heard thunder, the hiss of lightning far overhead, then something tore within her mind and she fell.

As she fell she caught the briefest glimpse of Brin, his great wings outstretched, trying to cover the companions as lightning, thick and solid as real spears, plunged among them. Beyond the protection of those massive wings, impaled and unmoving lay

Maressa and Gan. Tika's ears were filled with the sound of Farn screaming in pain and anger. She fell, a weight at her back and the faintest smell of mint in her nose. She fell unendingly it seemed, but then she landed with a thump that completely winded her. She lay, breath whooping into her battered lungs.

She opened her eyes and found Sket wheezing beside her. Akomi was squeezed between them, every hair on his body on end. He stared into her face, whiskers bristling forward around his nose.

'Where are we?' He spoke in her mind, his tone offended, aggrieved and frightened.

Tika's breathing was coming under control and Sket was peering around them. She struggled up, wincing as her ribs protested. She stared at the jagged dark stone walls and her heart sank even further. She touched her pendant and found it was cold as any inanimate lump of stone.

'I'm afraid we're in a place Between,' she said aloud, her words sounding weak and small.

She stared at Akomi, then at Sket. She reached to touch them and felt her own legs and arms while Sket watched her warily.

'We're here completely,' she said. 'Not just our minds.'

'Is that good or bad?' Sket asked.

'I don't know.' Her voice wobbled treacherously. 'Did you – did you see anything – just as we fell?'

Sket's eyes narrowed. 'No. What do you think you saw then?'

Tika grasped at the thin excuse Sket offered. 'Nothing really – we weren't even looking in Brin's direction, were we?'

But she knew in her heart that she had seen true. Maressa, the beautiful Vagrantian air mage, pierced, pinned to the rock with a spear of flame. And Gan. But no, she mustn't, she couldn't think of that now. Somehow she got herself to her knees, then to her feet, helping Sket as much as he was helping her. She looked around. It was dark but she could see and she knew Sket and Akomi could too.

Briefly, Tika sent her mind questing outwards for Farn. Nothing. It was like a mirror – her probing mind simply rebounded on her.

'I'll try and explain,' she told Sket, lifting Akomi to her

shoulder. 'I was in a place like this after we faced Valesh. Seela explained a little.'

'Seela?' Sket touched the strap of his pack and Tika remembered he still had four of Seela's purple scales tucked in there.

Before she could describe the place Between life and death, Akomi sneezed. Sket and Tika sniffed at the same instant. The very faintest fragrance of mint. Tika felt hope surge through her and she tugged Sket along the passage in pursuit of that elusive scent. They had taken half a dozen shaky steps when laughter echoed down the tunnel. A voice neither of them recognised said something in a language they couldn't understand. The laugh rang out again and the voice spoke in the common tongue.

'Gotcha, meddlesome brat! Gotcha!'

The story continues in 'Dark Realm' …

Books in the "Circles of Light" series

Soul Bonds

Vagrants

Drogoya

Survivors

Dark Realm

Perilous Shadows

Mage Foretold

Echoes of Dreams